Killer

IN THE

Crowd

By

P N JOHNSON

Burning Chair Limited, Trading As Burning Chair Publishing
61 Bridge Street, Kington HR5 3DJ

www.burningchairpublishing.com

By P N Johnson
Edited by Simon Finnie and Peter Oxley
Cover by Burning Chair Publishing

First published by Burning Chair Publishing, 2022

ISBN: 978-1-912946-23-5

There was a split second of silence before Suzi shrieked and jumped into the air, her hands hitting the strings of her red Fender guitar.

"Hello, we're Décolleté and this is for you!" I screamed as the fans erupted. The assault on the ears of those in front of us began. Speakers pulsed, spewing airborne emotion at the speed of sound. The opening power chords screamed out. Cassie's desperate drums demanded to be heard. Rocky's bass thumped. Heads shook, hands waved, the audience jumped and cheered. The lights burst on and off like a supernova as I scanned the heaving crowd and started to sing.

Behind me were four fired up females recapturing their youth. Décolleté were alive and full of fire, just as they had been with Mum three decades ago; their fingers less nimble, their bodies less taut, but their passion still as strong. Colours changed, from deep reds and cool blues to brilliant white and everything in between, darting in and out of the smoke billowing onto the stage. But how did I get here, from drama teacher in front of a class, to a rock star in front of thousands? The fans were raising their arms, cheering and calling my mother's name, wanting me to be her, reborn, to glimpse what once was. But where was she?

Where was Betzy Blac?

1. Raven Rain

Earlier…

Raven Rain found dead in hotel horror!
The relentless downpour hit my fringe and dripped onto my cheek as I stared at the news stand, unable to tear myself away from the chilling words in front of me. The shock of the headline on the soaking wet paper made me gasp.

I had always believed Raven Rain was my father.

I could visualise the scene. I could see him lying there, eyes open—staring, empty—pills in one hand, a glass hanging from the other. Wine trickling slowly onto the booze-soaked carpet. His last lyrics frozen on his lips, the last encore missed. The woman beside him in bed, naked, almost unconscious, unable to scream. Her face was out of focus but I was sure I knew who she was, his relationship with the former model was well known.

But it didn't make sense; he had everything to live for. He'd given up drugs. He'd survived his early punk years of excess, so why would he have overdosed like this now? No, this was no accident.

I opened the damp pages and there, on page two, next to his picture was one of his former lover: my mother. I expected to see her there, beside him in happier days, but I knew this would bring everything to the surface again and link me to them both.

I was suddenly aware of a man across the road. He was watching me. He had old-fashioned glasses, an outdated haircut and a thin dark coat. I knew I'd seen him before. I was about to walk away when a voice from behind made me turn around.

"Ah, Miss Edgley? I thought I recognised you," smiled the pushy woman rushing up beside me, demanding my attention. She was typical of the parents of the girls in my class, carrying the obligatory designer handbag just to show she could. It completed a look that was worn to do one thing: shout, *I'm rich!* and overshadow my own department store clothes.

"I'm Dawn: Becca's mum? Becca Jowell? She's in your drama group, doing *West Side Story*?"

I smiled politely but behind the façade I was unimpressed.

"*Shows a lot of promise, and puts a lot of effort into drama,* you wrote on her last report," she continued.

Why did they do this? Why now, the worst time? It was raining, the street was busy, I had to get back to work, and I'd just found out the man I believed to be my dad had been murdered. She made no attempt to share her Burberry brolly with me, determined to keep her own hair immaculate and dry while mine was flattened by the demeaning downpour.

"I'd be happy to talk at the parents' evening next week?" I said. Cars drove through puddles, water splashed over the pavement hitting my shoes.

"I just wanted to say Becca would do so well as Maria, she really would, it's an ideal part for her, especially as she shows a lot of promise, as you said yourself. I'm sure Darren, my husband, would be happy to make a donation to the production, for the whole cast of course. You must know him? Darren, Darren Jowell, the footballer? He plays for..."

"Yes, yes I know," I smiled, interrupting. She waited for me to show gushing acquiescence to her social status, but none came. So she had a famous husband. Well I had a super famous mum and a dad who was all over the headlines, sadly for all the wrong reasons. *Don't upset her, Cath,* I thought to myself, smiling benignly.

"I've already cast *Maria*, but Becca is the stand-in, so you

2

never know. And she does have a good part. Now I'm sorry but I must dash; your daughter's class will be waiting for me." I smiled and turned away, knowing yet another email from a persistent parent would be winging its way to the Head, keen to question my casting. In my school, money talked and the Jowells had sacks full of it.

The watching man had gone. I took one last glance at the rack of newspapers. Yes, the woman pictured next to the shot of Raven Rain and his current muse, was Betzy Blac. My mum. Lead singer and songwriter from Décolleté.

It was a secret I'd tried to keep. Raven being my dad wasn't really known, even within the music industry. Even though Raven had denied I was his daughter, I'd always been told I was. When people knew who my mum was they treated me differently: badly. They expected me to act like she did on stage. With a mum like Betzy Blac and a dad like Raven Rain it's surprising I turned out sane and able to hold down a *proper* job at all. I learned to hold back, mind my tongue, keep below the parapet. Had my mum brought me up, maybe I'd be different.

So many pop stars' kids are confident, positive, talented. I was none of these; I was quite the opposite.

I had to get back to work, to Beckthorn School for Girls, teaching English and Drama to Becca Jowell and twenty others like her, all with desperately doting mothers minding their fresh, fragile blooms. My pupils were the privileged elite at one of those expensive boarding schools behind big walls in the Home Counties just south of London. The ones you come across hiding behind a large notice board and big gates down small roads in expensive suburbs. It was the perfect place for me to hide and so different to the small-town High School I attended.

My mum was that infamous fiery post-punk princess; although Aunt Trish, who brought me up, always said that beneath the image she was a bit like me. I'd always wanted to be her. I studied drama and English at college, but I never had the confidence to be the performer I dreamed of becoming, so I decided to teach it instead.

But what now? If Mum became headline news again, and if she and Raven were revealed as my parents, my job might not be safe. The daughter of an infamous punk princess and bad boy front man teaching the delicate daughters of the rich? It didn't fit very well at all. My mum wore her heart and her sex on her sleeve. She was everything the school I worked for wasn't. And as for Raven Rain? Where to start.

I hurried to my waiting car, water dripping onto the side of the seat as I opened the door. I dived in, slamming it shut to keep out the driving rain. My windscreen was fogged, my hands cold, my feet wet. I put my bag on a passenger seat liberally decorated with old petrol receipts and parking slips. A damp smell overpowered me. I was feeling vulnerable, the headlines going round and round in my head. I started the engine, turned on the wipers and pulled out from the car park. I had a feeling it wouldn't be long before the press came calling. It had happened before.

Stories surfaced in the papers every few years: *What really happened to Betzy Blac?* It was the classic rock and roll mystery. Big star vanishes. Murdered? Suicide? Abducted or run away? The speculation had filled pages of print and hours of airtime. Aunt Trish protected me from it in the early days, when I was only a kid, but now I was fair game. I'd stayed under the radar for years, but they'd soon find me, now that Raven was dead.

I turned on the radio. It was the top story in the news: *Police say they're treating the death of former punk frontman Raven Rain as unexplained. Music stars have been paying tribute to the singer whose band, The Scented Slugs, were regular chart toppers in the early '80s. A so far unnamed woman found at the scene is being treated in hospital under police guard.*

I switched it off. For a long time I imagined seeing Mum everywhere, although I had no idea what she would have looked like now. She could be almost any woman in the street; she was a master of make-up and persona. That vision gave me a warm reassurance, but in reality I had to come to terms with the sad fact that she was probably dead, lying in some unmarked grave. Unnoticed but never forgotten, by me or her fans. I just clung on to the hope that she was living a secret life and I could carry on with mine.

The journey back to work was painful. The downpour slowing the traffic in the already clogged, congested streets. Eventually I reached roads alongside fields and then the narrow lanes leading to work; and there they were, the imposing gates of *Beckthorn School for Girls*. Outside was a van with '*Satellite TV Services*' on its side. I hurried to my classroom just in time, smiling through a dozen "Hello Miss" welcomes from my final year drama girls, eagerly waiting for my lesson to start. The school secretary stepped into my path and stopped me like a roadblock ensuring I couldn't pass.

"Miss Edgley, don't forget the meeting tomorrow re parents' evening, Miss Miles is insistent you attend. Oh, and there's a small question over your casting in the musical."

"I bet there is. The email has landed," I muttered as I pushed past her and walked into my room, knowing I'd have to argue my case again. Talent over influence. Another staff room drama, but I was more worried about having a major drama of my own.

*

I ended the last lesson and picked up my bag, ready to go. As soon as I switched on my phone it rang. It was a withheld number.

"Is that Catherine Edgley?"

"Who's this?"

"I'm Jem Marin, a reporter with Top World News Agency; we supply the papers with stories. I've been asked to talk to you about the sad death of Raven Rain."

"Er… How did you get my number?"

"It must be a sad time. I'm sorry to be intrusive but there's a lot of sympathy out there. Have you spoken to your brother?"

"Brother?"

"Travis Brennon?"

"Who? I haven't ever spoken to Tr… Look, I don't have any comment to make, okay?" Travis Brennon, Really? My brother? Did I have a brother?

"Travis Brennon's management have just confirmed he was Raven Rain's secret son, and word has it you're Raven's daughter, so that makes you his sister."

I had no words.

"Just one last question please, Miss Edgley. Do you think your mother, Betzy Blac, Raven Rain's former lover, is still alive?" I didn't answer. "Ms Edgley, your mum was loved by millions; any thoughts or clues to what happened to her would be welcomed."

"Yes, and I'd welcome you leaving me alone." I felt myself welling up. My throat was tight, my voice strained.

"Wait, Catherine, just give me a second, please. I understand you're upset. There's a theory trending on social media that if Raven Rain was murdered, Betzy Blac was killed as well and her killer has struck again all these years later. That killer has not only murdered your mother, but has now killed your father as well. Do you think that could be true? Do you think you or Travis Brennon are also in danger?"

"Er…"

"Your aunt, Trish Black, told me she thought it possible. Do you?"

"Aunt Trish? You've spoken to my aunt? What else has she said?"

"Yes, we spoke to her. So you don't disagree with her then. It is possible? You won't rule it out? Murder."

"I… Don't know. I…"

"So you don't think it's impossible that Raven and your mother were murdered by the same killer?"

"I… I don't know. Sorry, I'm going to go."

"How well did you know the woman in the room with Raven Rain, Ms Edgley? We understand it was the model, Sacha

Tillens?"

"I don't know her," I replied, flustered.

"I understand there was a picture of your mother, Betzy Blac, on his phone. Why would that be? Their relationship ended a long time ago."

"Sorry, I have to go." I ended the call. Travis Brennon, my brother? I collected my things and left the school in a whirl. As I walked out to get into my car the satellite TV van's door opened and the driver rushed to the open gates, holding a camera.

"Miss Edgley! Over here! This way Miss Edgley. Great, got it, thank you!" He smiled and threw the camera onto the passenger seat, a job well done.

"Hey!" I shouted. But he was soon behind the wheel, revving up and driving away, leaving marks in the gravel as he sped off and disappeared down the road.

Head down in my car, I drove as fast as I could and soon reached my dull suburban street a few miles away. Whatever would Mum have thought of this very ordinary commuter box that I inhabited? It wasn't exactly rock and roll. Far from it: the essence of pedestrian normality. I nodded through the car window at Eileen, one of my friendly but uninspiring neighbours, who watched my return. She seemed fascinated. I looked ahead in the small cul-de-sac where I lived and saw why.

Outside my house were cameras and journalists. I knew this day might come, I knew people would hound me because of my mum and dad. I felt my throat tighten and my heart race as I slowed down approaching my house. Should I drive away or park down the road and come back when they'd gone? No. Why should I run away? I'd done nothing wrong. What would they ask me? Who killed Raven Rain? How should I know? The reporters already seemed to know more about my mum and Raven than I did. And Travis Brennon? A major star, described as the '*Sexiest singer in music today*' by one magazine I read. Everyone knew him, my girls at school had posters of him, he had a string of bestselling songs and thousands of screaming fans. Totally gorgeous too; but my brother? Seriously?

2. DC Dennison

The reporters turned as one when they heard me approaching. A little press pack all of my own. When I'd tried to get the local paper to cover my school's production of *West Side Story* they weren't interested; but all of a sudden, bang. These were the nationals, right outside my place. I wasn't going to be intimidated though. However unimpressive this insignificant 1970s semidetached house was, it was still my home, and right now I needed seclusion and solace. I crawled forwards, forcing them to part as I parked on the little drive leading to the front door.

"Catherine Edgley," said the first reporter as I stepped out of my car, slamming the door. She was a woman almost half my age, barely out of college.

"Sophie Eriksson from the Mail. When did you last speak to Raven Rain?" The other two edged forward, one framing me in their camera viewfinder, the other poised to record everything I said. I'd never spoken to Raven. I'd never met him. I said nothing. "Raven Rain was writing a book, do you have it?" Sophie Eriksson asked.

I shook my head.

"Josh Turner, BBC radio news," said the next in line. "The London evening paper claims in its online edition that you aren't ruling out murder."

"No, I didn't say that. What I said was that I didn't know."

"Ellie Khan, Sky News. So is it possible that Raven Rain and

Betzy Blac may have been the victims of the same determined killer? A killer who's struck again after thirty years?"

"Possibly," I replied curtly. "But I couldn't say that; I really don't know. The conspiracy theories will start feeding on this and I don't want fan the flames."

"Who would want to hurt them? We'd love to do a proper interview with you, for the fans; it's attracting massive interest. The picture of your mum and Raven being arrested naked and drunk in that fountain is Paris in 1983 is everywhere again. Is that an embarrassment to you?" asked Ellie Khan, moving closer.

"Oh really? What do you think?" I mused, remembering the shot. It was hardly Mum and Raven's brightest moment. I remained emotionless as I fixed a firm stare and pushed my way to the front door with a polite "thank you." I reached for my keys, went in and shut the press out just as my phone rang.

"Miss Edgley," it was the head's secretary. "Miss Miles is not amused, not at all. She would like to see you."

"Oh?"

"Yes: *oh* indeed. Just after you left, the police were here. Detectives. They were looking for you. Miss Miles wants to see you first thing tomorrow morning. Goodbye."

Then the house phone started ringing and at the same time I noticed a smell, the sort of smell that meant one thing: a culinary calamity. I let the call go to answerphone and saw there were twelve messages for me already. I went to put my mobile down when it started buzzing again. I threw it onto the sofa in the front room and went to the kitchen. I'd left the slow cooker on, but sadly not on slow enough; the setting was *high* and the stew I was looking forward to resembled a dried-up lunar landscape. As I scraped it into the bin, the sound of a hand delivered envelope coming through the letter box caught my attention. I ignored it and turned on the TV. The caption under the presenter read: '*Conspiracy theories flood social media over Raven Rain's death. Police say the singer's death is "unexplained".*'

There were pictures of forensics officers walking from Raven's flat, and then shots of Sacha Tillens, Raven's fiancé, leaving hospital wearing a hat and dark glasses, her hand over her face, a police officer shielding her from the cameras. Then I saw the picture of Mum flash up on the screen and heard the newsreader explain the new interest in her disappearance:

"Raven Rain's home is said to have contained numerous pictures of his former partner, singer Betzy Blac who famously walked out of the limelight after what was her band Décolleté's final concert in October 1984. Raven Rain was, according to his fiancée, the former model, Sacha Tillens, writing a book. His Manager, Chris Latham, is refusing to comment or confirm the book details, but it's believed that the singer had been in talks with a number of publishers who were vying for the rights to the work, which the singer was close to completing. It's understood that the officers seen at the musician's home in West London this afternoon were looking for that manuscript. Meanwhile the hotel room where the singer was found dead is still sealed off this evening. Hotel staff are refusing to discuss the incident. In other news…"

I switched off the TV and fell into my favourite chair, kicking off my shoes. I tucked my feet under my shins and hugged my knees in the dimming light. My head dropped. I felt very alone. I could see the shapes of the reporters outside at the end of my short, featureless front garden, its neat, dull lawn edged with gravel and a few straggling roses where it met the pavement. Opposite, Eileen—my well-meaning but irritating neighbour— was watching with interest.

I stayed still in the dim, unlit sitting room, not wanting to show any movement for fear of being filmed through the window. I ignored another knock on the door. I wanted a friend, but I didn't really have any, apart from Kate and Jane, two teachers at school; and if I did, where were they when I needed them? My old roommates from university were still in touch, but it was very much a yearly reunion and the occasional calls or emails. Every time I befriended someone they found out who my mum was and then they changed. My mum became a fascination and

I was pumped for information, information I didn't have. They assumed I'd inherited her money, but it was locked away until she was either declared dead or she turned up. I'd kept quiet about Mum in recent years, it was the easiest thing to do. No one at school knew my secret, although that would soon change.

Gazing upwards, my eyes fell on the photo frame in the corner of the bookcase. The photo it displayed now was one of Mum and me on my first day at school. It *had* housed my wedding photo, as if I needed a reminder of another hole in my life. The picture it once held of a happy bride and groom was long gone; like the couple it portrayed, it had passed into history. I kept the frame because it had been given to me by Aunt Trish. My marriage had been a short, uninspiring let down. I blamed myself, but then Steve, my ex, could do that: make me think it was all my fault.

Next to the bookcase was my graduation picture. That was where Steve and I began, after I'd thrown away Coll, the man who should have been in that photo with me. The man I stupidly betrayed. I felt tears dampen my eyes. I wiped them away, trying to hold on to the now and the today, but it wasn't easy. What had I really achieved? An average job in a posh girls' school. All my dreams of becoming a performer, being on stage like Mum, had ebbed away, lost in a rush of reality and passing years.

My phone rang again. This time I had to answer, it was Aunt Trish, or so I thought...

"Catherine? Hello, sorry to bother you. It's Linda, your aunt's friend, you know? I live next door."

"Yes, of course. Sorry, is Aunt Trish there?"

"No, I'm calling on her phone to let you know she's in hospital, love."

"What?"

"I'm with her now. Don't worry, she's okay, but they're fussing around her so I said I'd call you to let you know."

"Fussing around her? What's happened?" My mind was racing.

"She's had a heart attack, Catherine. Some reporter woke her up and started asking questions about her sister, your mum, and she found it upsetting. She came round to tell me and, well, she collapsed. I went with her in the ambulance and they say she's stable, but…"

"Stable?"

"But I heard them saying her heart is very weak."

"I'll come and visit her as soon as I can," I said. Poor Aunt Trish, this was the last thing she or I needed right now.

"Ward 6, coronary care. She'd love to see you." I wanted to see her. A coronary? It was the stress of the reporters, I was sure. She worried so much about publicity surrounding mum when I was younger. My thoughts of Aunt Trish and a hospital visit were distracted by a loud knocking on my door. I wanted to ignore it but the letterbox was opened and I had to respond.

"Ms Edgley, it's the police. Can we come in please?"

"One minute." I replied. "Linda, I have to go. Send her my love; I'll be there as soon as I can," I said, and ended the call.

Two detectives, a man and a woman, held their warrant cards up for me to inspect as I opened the door. Behind them cameras flashed and recordings were made. More pictures fuelling the rumours, feeding the news.

"Hello. I'm DC Kate Dennison and this is DC Darsh Patel. We need to talk to you." I recognised the woman; she'd been in the TV pictures. She was the officer shielding Sacha Tillens, the future Mrs Rain. She was emotionless, formal, with choppy, dyed blonde hair. She wore a smart, navy blue work suit. Black cleated loafers clung to her feet. I shut the press out behind them.

"Yes, yes of course, this way. Is there a problem?" I pointed to the settee, and the two detectives sat down; the woman directed her attention to me whilst her male colleague scanned the room intently. He was more informally dressed. A lightweight jacket gaped open revealing a plain shirt and loose tie. His thick dark hair was neat and short. The end of a tattoo poked out under the cuff of his left arm. A calm friendliness masked suspicious questions and blotting paper eyes seeking any scrap of information in my home that could help build a case.

"As you know, Ms Edgley—or can I call you Catherine?"

"Yes, of course."

"As you know, Catherine, Raven Rain—or, to give him his birth name, Nigel Carter—was found dead in what are currently thought to be suspicious circumstances; although we are awaiting toxicology and other test results. However, there's been mention of a book he was writing."

"Yes, so I gather from the news."

"This could be evidential, so it's important we retrieve it. Have you any idea who might have it?"

"No, it's the first I've heard of it. Why is it important? What's in it? Did he know what happened to my mum?"

"We're not sure, Catherine. We think it's possible it may reveal what happened to your mother, and there's always the possibility that someone may have killed him to get it."

"It says who killed her? Betzy Blac?" I gasped. I suddenly realised I had to find out, not least for Aunt Trish. I knew she'd had angina for years and she been warned her heart wasn't as strong as it should be. I was in shock. That morning I'd causally glanced at a newspaper and my world had changed, and now it was changing even more—Raven's death, the press interest, Aunt Trish, and now the police? My throat was getting drier and my mind was in overdrive.

"It's just one theory we're looking at, Catherine," replied DC Dennison.

"I really need to know what happened to her. Promise me you'll tell me if you find out she's dead," I pleaded.

"We've nothing more at the moment, Catherine. But if we have anything definite, we'll let you know," continued DC Dennison.

"Betzy Blac really was her name you know, or a shortened version of it. Elizabeth Black. I still use my married name Edgley, but probably not for much longer," I said.

"Yes, we know," said DC Patel. "At the moment she's still officially a missing person."

"Well, she's never turned up, never contacted me. I last saw her when I was seven years old. Can you imagine what that does to a child?" And still does, even though I was now an adult. This had gone on long enough: the mystery of Mum's fate was pulling me apart, and had nearly killed Aunt Trish. "Can you please look into Mum's disappearance again too?" I asked.

"We'd need more evidence to reopen the investigation, I'm afraid," said DC Patel.

"Please, I have to know what happened. And my Aunt, her sister, she really needs closure. If we can finally find out the truth about Mum then maybe something good will come out of Raven's death."

"Of course. We do understand," said DC Dennison sympathetically, a kind smile flashing across her otherwise sullen face.

"If you hear anything, from anyone, we need to know. Anyone who knew her or him, or who has any clues, they'll probably tell you more than they'd tell us," added DC Patel.

"Who in particular?" I asked.

"People she worked with, her old band members, old friends, and especially her old fans," said the female detective. Her colleague was still scanning the room. Did he really think I had the missing manuscript sitting on a shelf? I wish I had got it, I had to know what happened to my mum, and now I was even more determined to find out. Whatever it took. Wherever it took me. Even to her grave, or mine. But my determination was tempered by reality. I still had a job to do. I had girls to teach and besides: I was a simple teacher, not a detective.

"We have to ask you, Ms Edgley," said DC Patel firmly, notebook in hand. "Where were you the night before last? The night we believe Raven Rain died."

"Sorry," I said, flustered. "Where was I when Raven died? I was here, lesson planning. I'm a teacher." It hit me. They actually thought I might have killed him; murdered my own father.

A text landed on my phone. I looked down. My mouth fell open when I read it.

"Catherine your life's in danger. Trust no one. DD."

The shock was evident on my face. I didn't know a *"DD"*. Was this a hoax? A sick joke? Who'd sent this text? I was scared, and you didn't have to be a detective to realise that.

"Are you okay, Catherine? Bad news?" asked the woman officer.

"No, sorry, there's so much happening."

"Can anyone verify you were here?" asked DC Patel.

"Oh my neighbour Eileen across the road at number fourteen: she will have noticed when I came home, she seems to just watch everyone all the time. Are you interviewing Travis Brennon, the singer?" I asked as the phone rang, again.

"Feel free to answer it, Catherine," offered DC Dennison.

"No thanks, probably another reporter." I grimaced. "Travis Brennon," I reminded her.

"We know who Mr Brennon is," she replied.

"My brother, so I've just been told," I said proudly; not everyone had a brother like Travis Brennon. "So are you interviewing him as well?"

They remained silent, emotionless.

"Will you keep me informed of developments?" I asked, looking at the woman detective.

"Let's stay in touch. Thank you for your help, and please let us know if you find anything that may help. Here's my card. Oh, one more thing: would you mind giving us a DNA sample so we can rule you out from being at the crime scene?"

"Of course, is it really necessary?"

"I'm afraid it is, if we're to rule you out," replied DC Patel as he pulled a small plastic stick from a sterile pack, pushing it around my mouth before sealing it in a bag. So I was a suspect; the possible killer of Raven Rain.

"All done, thank you Miss Edgley," he said.

"Please stay in the area for now, Catherine," said DC Dennison. I nodded and showed them out as the cameras recorded the scene, some of the reporters probably disappointed I wasn't being led away in handcuffs.

As I closed the door, another message arrived from the unknown texter. My hands shook as I read the words. They were simple and stark: "*Find Raven's manuscript before they do. DD.*"

But who was DD?

3. MiSS MiLeS

I peeked through the curtains to see the reporters filming the police driving off, watched keenly by Eileen across the road. Soon they would be gone, I hoped; and, sure enough, fifteen minutes later they packed up and left. I grabbed my coat and got into my car. I had to visit Aunt Trish in hospital.

The roads were quieter now the evening traffic had died down. A slow drizzle persisted as I headed off into the night.

Her sister's disappearance all those years ago had badly affected her as well as me. She'd had the added pressure of shielding me from the speculation and stories at the time. I remember when it happened we took an unexpected holiday, flying off to the Canaries and away from the press and the papers.

I turned into the hospital carpark; there were just twenty minutes of visiting hours left. Leaving my car I ran into the drab, busy building and, rather than wait for a lift, I hurried up the stairs. The sign for Coronary Care hung across the corridor like a premonition of my own future. If Aunt Trish had a weak heart, did it run in the family?

"She's in the corner. Sorry, but you can only stay for a few minutes," said a nurse holding a clipboard. I looked at the frail old woman lying in the far bed by the curtained window, a monitor beside her and tubes in her arm.

"How is she?" I asked quietly.

"Your aunt is very weak. She should be able to go home in a few days, but it may take several months for her to recover. And

Miss Edgley," she said leaning in, demanding my attention, "she does have a weak heart. This may be a warning… she may not survive another one." I nodded and walked up to the bed.

"Hello Aunt Trish." I said, sitting in a padded chair beside her. The lights on the monitor flickered in the corner of my eye. There was an untouched cup of tea on a bedside cabinet.

"Catherine, how nice of you to come. Are there any reporters outside?"

"No, no, they've all gone, I doubt they'll bother you again. You know, tomorrow will be a different day and a different story." I smiled but I wasn't convinced, and neither was she.

"They'll be back. It never stops; the world wants to know what happened to your mum, they always will. And so do I, Catherine." I held her hand and squeezed it tightly. "I know I'm on borrowed time, Catherine. I'd so love to know what happened to her, before… before I go."

*

Back home, I ran a deep hot bath, took my Bluetooth speaker into the bathroom and put on a favourite chill-out playlist to drown out distractions. I sank up to my neck, trying to hide in the womblike warmth of the water and the descending dark.

I got out when the bath began to go cold and there was no more hot water in the tap. With my dressing gown on, I went downstairs. Peace and normality had returned to Chestnut Close. On the doormat lay an envelope and three florist's cards. I must have missed them knocking while I was in the bath. The envelope contained a handwritten note from Eileen:

"What a commotion. You must tell me all about it! A persistent and rather pushy man with glasses was asking if you lived here, I didn't tell him, but I think he knows. Didn't like him at all. Eileen."

I opened the door to find three large bunches of flowers. Tied to each of them were notes. I took them in as I walked to the kitchen to find a vase, a beer glass and jug; I only had one vase, a giveaway sign of being single. I read the messages: *"So sorry to hear about Raven. As his and your mother's former Agent, we need to talk. Please call. Kind Regards, Chris Latham."*

The next simply read: *"Sad day, your mum loved the bastard. Always. Suzi Scums xx"* It was from mum's old guitarist.

The last one took me by surprise: it was from Travis Brennon:

"Hi, I'm in London. We need to talk. Let's meet soonest. Call me. Trav B x"

There was a mobile number. Wow! Travis Brennon. Plenty of women would give a lot to get flowers from Travis Brennon, and his phone number too. Could he really be my brother? This international American superstar, related to me? Little Cath?

How sad that the only reason I was finding out about a long-lost brother was because our dad was dead. I'd somehow reconciled myself to never knowing what had become of Mum, but this was a crossroads; events had conspired to force me into action. Raven's death and poor Aunt Trish: I'd never had so many reasons to find out what had happened to Mum until now. Staring at the lingering remains of the dried-out supper still stuck to my slow cooker I opened a tin of beans. I slipped two pieces of bread into the toaster, although my appetite had dramatically diminished.

*

"Miss Miles will see you now," the school secretary gave me a curt smile and turned back to her computer screen, her instruction delivered. Her demeanour towards me had changed. She'd swiftly moved from uninterested and superior to gloating and gleeful, no doubt anticipating and enjoying my possible demise. I'd been summoned by a phone call just after 8am, insisting I was there within the hour. Just to put me on the back foot, knowing I'd have to rush and skip breakfast to ensure a timely arrival.

I walked into the Head's study and there she was, in the low-lit chamber, partly silhouetted by the cool morning light coming through the tall windows behind her. The chilly atmosphere wasn't helped by the dark wood panelled walls adorned with paintings and photographs of old glories and past people. It summed her up; she was always looking backwards, seeking answers to the present by referring to the past. The smell of freshly sprayed polish was overwhelming, mixing with the odours from an electric air freshener puffing out chemical fragrances from a wall socket by her desk.

"Sit, Miss Edgley," commanded the ageing Miss Miles. I obeyed, sinking into the worn leather seat which seemed to be offering me as little support as my boss. She was avoiding my eyes, looking at a pile of open newspapers on the solid dark desk. Head down, her tight, short grey hair looked unloved. Her ugly gnarled hands with their closely bitten nails were drumming slowly at the desk, the marks of previous drumming clearly visible on the old, stained wood.

"I don't like all this," she exclaimed loudly. "I do not like it at all." She looked up, fixing me in her snake-like stare. Her lips pursed.

"I realise it's not ideal, Miss Miles, but surely you'd agree that it's hardly my fault," I replied.

"It's not what we want to be associated with. How can you assure me it will all go away? How can you assure me this school won't be associated with your parents and their—shall we say—unsavoury activities?" Her head tilted up and sideways. Her eyes bored into mine, staring out through her decades-old glasses. She was waiting for an assurance that I clearly couldn't give.

"I can't… I can't control what the police may uncover or what the press might report. I can't stop them saying who I am and where I work, but I haven't linked any of this to the school or my job. I haven't given any formal interviews."

"The police were looking for you," she said accusingly.

"Yes, and they found me, at home. It was routine. I haven't been arrested Miss Miles, Raven Rain may have been my father but I never actually met him, and it's not certain by any means—

his name isn't even on my birth certificate. He always refused to meet me."

"Look, Catherine, I understand this situation is not of your choosing," she seemed to soften, but only momentarily, "but if it brings this school into disrepute in any manner, any manner at all, your contract will be ended. Do you understand?" I detected a growing determination to get me out of the door.

"Yes, of course, Miss Miles. Will that be all? I have a class to take." I smiled politely, but her next comment raised the stakes.

"No, it isn't all. You're clearly under a lot of stress. I think it's best if you take the rest of this term off. We've engaged cover to take your classes. We'll talk again before the autumn term begins. That's all."

"But Miss Miles. Please, I've got *West Side Story…*"

"Not anymore, Miss Edgley, it's out of your hands. It really is for your own good. Now, please leave."

"Miss Miles!" I said, raising my voice, surprising us both. "I must protest."

"And so must I, Miss Edgley, and I must also protect the integrity and reputation of this school. It simply cannot be associated with, with, people like that dead punk man and your mother."

Lost for words and desperate not to let her see the tears which were forming, I turned and walked out. I was too upset to go into the staff room; I'd probably explode, do something I regretted, like send an all-staff email telling her to sod off. I couldn't believe I was going to miss the end of year show. I'd worked so hard on that, coaching the girls, and it was all being taken away from me because my father had died. How could a stand-in teacher write the girls' reports when they didn't know them? It was hardly fair on them, or me.

"Cath! What's happened?" Two of my colleagues had spied me, head down, wiping away the just-formed tears as I made for the door.

"Kate, I've been suspended. Immediately," I blurted out.

"What?" said Jane, astounded, her textbooks and bag clutched to her chest. "It's been a shock to see your name in the newspaper reports, but he was your father?"

"We had no idea. No idea who either of your parents were," added Kate sympathetically, her face pained. "But it's no reason to take it out on you."

"What a cow Miss Miles is," said Jane.

"Careful," I replied. "If she hears that or sees you talking to me, you'll be tainted too."

"Let's get together soon, have a coffee," said Kate, her arm reaching around my shoulders.

"We're here for you Cath," said Jane.

"Thanks,' I said, as the school bell rang. "You better go, she'll be after you next." They both shook their heads and turned to go to their respective classrooms.

I walked out. *Always look for positives*, Aunt Trish had taught me, however difficult it seemed. At least I was still being paid, and it gave me time to devote to the search for the truth about Mum and Raven; but however I spun it, I was still shocked and sad. *West Side Story* would be a success, with dewy-eyed parents seeing their little girls all grown up on stage playing adults in love. I'd seen many of them emerge from the cocoon of childhood, and this was the passing-out parade. I was giving them confidence to express themselves, to face the world and to take control. However, control had been abruptly taken away from me.

Standing by my car I saw Miss Miles watching me from her study window. Maybe I'd have the last word. I pulled Travis Brennon's card from my bag. Too nervous to call, I texted him.

"Hi Travis, it's Cath Edgley, thanks for your flowers and card, I'd love to meet, where and when would suit you? Cath."

I agonised between familiar, friendly and formal. If he was my brother I should be warmer, but this was a global star and, until now, an unreachable celebrity to the likes of me. I hit send and a burst of adrenalin surged through my stomach. I got into my car and started the engine. As I released the handbrake a text landed which made me feel both sad I was going but pleased I'd be missed.

"We've just had an all-staff email saying you've been given extended leave for personal reasons. I've just told some of your girls who're in my class, they're very upset. Especially Emily and Chloe. Talk soon. Jane x"

I replied: *"Thanks Jane. Tell my girls to take the stage by storm, I'll be with them in thought x."*

As I drove out of school the June sunshine washed over the old stately home, the hub of Beckthorn, interrupted by passing grey and white clouds. I was leaving the classrooms and corridors echoing with the sound of giggling girls, the daytime's silent dormitories holding faded secrets of fevered night-time chats and revelations about relationships. I didn't know if I'd ever return.

I drove home and was drawn back to my own failed relationship. I'd met him at university, when he lured me away from my then boyfriend, Coll, who I should have stayed with. Steve had just seemed so much more exciting, and I'd unbelievably acted out one of my mum's songs: *Two Lovers in One Night!* It was so unlike me, cheating on poor Coll, and for what?

I'd always gone for the wrong guy, apart from Coll. He was good, but so understated and lacking in confidence I failed to see it. A string of flashy, trashy lovers had left me always looking for something more. Steve swept in and I just ran with it. We were on and off like cricket in the rain. My third year at university saw him cheating and coming back, saying he'd change, and I just wanted to be with him so I went along. We did split, but we met up again when I moved to Beckthorn School for Girls. He was living nearby. We fell into bed and back into love, or so I thought. It seemed obvious to get married, but it wasn't to be a happy ending. It had only lasted eighteen months. That's how long it took me to realise my shiny new husband Steve

24

was being true to form and sleeping with someone else. Turned out he'd been sleeping with her since before we married. He'd even had sex with her at our wedding reception. Apparently they found a sordid solace in an empty toilet whilst I was telling our guests how much I loved him. The wedding ring I'd put on his finger a few hours earlier was barely warmed up before those same fingers were holding someone else.

I was almost home when my phone announced the arrival of a message. I pulled into a layby and glanced down. It was from Travis Brennon. This was weird, a text from a mega star, *the* Travis Brennon; he was stunning compared to me. Whoa, did we really have the same genes? We didn't look anything like each other. I was darker skinned, with brown hair, small and petite; he was Nordic looking, statuesque, blue eyes, blonde hair. Maybe it was our different mums' DNA, not Raven's, that had determined the differences.

"Cath, thanks for getting back. Z Z's café on Wardour Street, Soho? Tomorrow?12:00? Trav."

I replied: "*Hi. Lots to discuss. Tomorrow at 12 is good. Thanks, Cath Edgley."*

I smelt the scent of excitement running through me. I'd listened to his music, seen him perform on TV, and found it difficult not to admit I fancied him. Who didn't? Who wouldn't? But I couldn't; I had to clean those thoughts up straight away, he was my brother, for God's sake.

A reply dropped. "*C U there, ZZ's, 12, Trav.*"

Would I really have someone to share this with? It just seemed too good to be true and maybe it was. Another text was still on my phone, the one from the mysterious DD, their words echoed in my head: "*Trust no one."*

4. Travis Brennon

So what do you wear to meet your long-lost brother? What do you wear to meet a pop star?

The two demands collided, giving me a sleepless night and a waking headache. Staring blankly at my wanting wardrobe, I ran my searching fingers through the row of dull work clothes and a few weekend outfits. Greys. Sober blues. Dull deep reds. I didn't go on dates or for evenings out, apart from the odd trip to the local cinema or a pizza with Kate and Jane from work, and I wasn't used to this. I decided to go in early and raid the racks at some of the central London stores. I'd be walking along Oxford Street so I'd have plenty of choice; if, of course, I could remember how to shop as a woman, not a respectable private school teacher dressing for parents' evenings and speech days.

As I left the house a florist van drew up outside. A woman checking the address smiled and handed me a bunch of flowers. There was a card:

"Come back soon Miss, we need you! Chloe and Emily, your West Side Story girls (PS Becca 'jumped up' Jowell is now playing Maria!)."

So her mum had got her way. I put the blooms, mostly freesias and alstroemeria, in water; thinking how sweet it was of the kids to do that. I closed my door and I headed off to London and my mystery meeting with Travis Brennon, global superstar and, if Aunt Trish and the press were to be believed, my secret brother.

Having parked out of town I caught a train, jumped on a

tube and walked out onto Oxford Street. I negotiated the wide pavement and the jostling crowd and was soon in my first shop and beginning to panic. Time was slipping away and I was still in my old jeans and a very unflattering top. I looked at myself in the mirror. What had I become? Was I really my mother's daughter? What was I wearing? Drab, dull and unimpressive. I was dressed not to upset the most conservative of parents at school events; and okay, so this wasn't a date, but come on, I needed to feel better about myself. I spied a flimsy, loose bright blue top and cut-off jeans. Could I? It was more laid back Betzy than uptight school ma'am. Should I? Yes. I grabbed them and already felt better, even a bit taller if that were possible; certainly more confident. Why not, there was a new me waiting in the shadows.

It was warm, early summer, and I needed to look chilled and laid back. Come on Cath, shoes, I said to myself, you're Betzy Blac's daughter for god's sake; act like it, at least once in your life! I pushed caution aside and picked up a pair of bright red Converse shoes. They'd be more at home on my girls than me, but I took them to the till. Heading to the loos I put my new outfit on and stuffed my old jeans and top into my woven shoulder bag. Confidence rising, I slapped on far more make-up than Miss Edgley the teacher would ever wear, and then I was there, the new me, heading into Soho ready to face the world, and ready to meet the famous Travis Brennon. As I walked out of the shop one of Mum's old hits was playing on the store radio. A smile overpowered me sweeping away any lingering doubts. Surely this was a good omen.

Z Z's Café is a small eatery near the top of Wardour Street. Scrubbed wood tables and a plank floor greeted me as I walked in. Two guys behind the counter looked as if they'd be more at home on a surf beach. Faded weekend pass bands from various music festivals were decaying on their wrists. The music thumped out and there, in a corner, sitting alone and clutching a large cappuccino in one hand was the most stunning guy in the place; in fact the most stunning looking man I'd seen in, well possibly, ever.

Tall, blonde, fit and clearly wealthy judging by the designer clothes adorning his body. Yup. There was only one Travis Brennon. A major celebrity, but I'd never seen him in the flesh, or even dreamed I'd ever meet him. Could he really be my brother? He looked up, sunglasses on, sensing my presence, his other hand holding his chin, helping him to hide from searching eyes.

"Travis?" I offered.

"You'd better be Cath," he replied quietly, his voice edgy.

"I am. Well, I was last time I looked in the mirror." I laughed. He ignored my attempt at humour, making me feel small and uncomfortable. "Can I get you a refill?" I smiled, trying not to show how starstruck I was.

"No thanks, I've only just got this." He seemed to relax and there was a glimpse of a brief smile on his lips. "Any more caffeine and I'll be wired. I don't like stimulants. My dad did enough of them for all of us."

"Don't. I read about it many times. Embarrassing. My mum did too," I replied.

"Legendary partying, but it didn't do them much good. So can I get you a coffee?"

"No, it's fine thanks. I'll get mine," I replied. "Back in a sec." I queued at the counter for what seemed like an age. It hadn't been the opening I was expecting. For someone who'd wanted to meet me and suggested we got together he didn't seem that keen. I was feeling self-conscious. Had I left a label on my new top or cut-offs? Oh god I hoped not.

"So," I said, finally sitting down opposite him. Knocking the table, spilling coffee. "Oh sorry!" I could feel myself going red as I mopped it up with a paper napkin.

"Don't worry, these are tense times," he said quietly. Travis Brennon took off his sunglasses and the full beauty of his face was revealed. His eyes flashed, a soft blue vision which quickened my pulse.

"Look I'm really sorry about your dad; well, mine too," I said. "Although sadly I never met him, but it wasn't for the lack of trying. It's awful, especially the press pictures of that grim hotel room."

"Thanks Cath. About that," he said looking into my eyes. "Cath, hang on, sorry—do you mind turning your phone off?"

"Okay," I replied, hesitating and surprised. "I guess there's a reason?"

"I'm being paranoid I know, but someone met me once for a little chat and was recording the whole thing, and it went online. I'm just wary."

"I wouldn't do that; but sure, yes, of course." I was a little taken aback, but did as he asked. We waited as my phone closed down and the screen went black.

"There you are. You're safe," I smiled.

"I'm sorry to have to tell you, Cath; whatever you've heard, Raven Rain wasn't your father."

"What?"

"I'm so sorry, it must be a shock, I know."

The blood drained from my face. I sat staring at Travis in disbelief. My heart was pounding.

"But how do you know?" Just yesterday I'd been told I had a new family member, now I seemed to be losing one.

"He told me himself."

"But my Mum and Aunt Trish?" I broke off – they'd always told me Raven was my dad, that's what I'd believed growing up. The media obviously thought he was too. "Are you saying they lied to me?" I demanded.

"I can't answer that, Cath. I'm just telling you what Raven told me. He was certain he wasn't your dad."

For a moment, I wished I'd had something stronger to drink than coffee.

"Well how did *he* know?" I asked, hearing a note of hostility in my voice but not caring. Who was this guy after all? A superstar, yes, but that didn't mean anything, not really. DD's warning came back to me: *Trust no one.*

"Do you really want me to go into details?" he asked.

"Yes," I replied, "with all due respect I'm not just going to take your word for it. Betzy and Raven were the romance of the decade for god's sake." By this point I was almost in tears, but I swallowed them back. I was determined to have my say. "And now here you are telling me, telling me what? If Raven's not my dad then...then...are you saying my mum cheated on him?" My thoughts were whirling.

The café was filling up with customers, there was an energetic buzz around us. My voice was loud and would probably blow his cover if I carried on like that. But, right then, that was the last thing I was bothered about. I could see Travis looking around, knowing someone would soon recognise him and ruin our moment.

"You've got a big bloody cheek coming in here, the big bloody pop star taking my dad away from me." My voice was breaking up. I was shaking.

"Cath, come on." Travis raised a hand. He looked round uneasily, ducking his head a little as he spoke. "I'm not trying to take anything away from you. All I know is, your mum and my dad had a very passionate, long term love affair. She meant a lot to him—and I really do mean a *lot.* He still had pictures of her in his flat, for God's sake! On the walls. Not much fun for his fiancée."

"Really?" Despite my anger, it was good to know he really cared about her.

"But they split up, Cath. For a very good reason."

"Which was?" I demanded, still trying not to cry.

"Because... Because your mum was carrying someone else's baby."

My mouth dropped open.

"I doubt your aunt actually knew, and your mum maybe didn't want to tell you when you were seven..." He shrugged. "Maybe your mum… sort of wished it was true. Maybe she didn't want you to know who your real dad was? I'm just guessing, I don't know, but maybe she wished you were Raven's daughter. Who wouldn't want a baby to come from the romance of the decade?"

"So whose baby was I then?" Tears started to seep from my eyes; there was no stopping them anymore. "Since you seem to know so much about it." I sniffed.

"I don't know, Cath. Honestly. I'd say if I did. I don't think Raven knew either."

"Oh hang on," I said sarcastically, "I don't suppose the small matter of Raven's will has anything to do with this?" I hated the bitterness in my voice, but I just couldn't stop it. "I didn't want a penny of Raven's money, that's not who I am, or why I'm here."

"That's not who I am either, Cath. I've got more money than I damn well need. I could buy this café right now, for cash. Besides, it's Sacha—Raven's fiancée—who gets his money."

I took a breath and reached in my bag for some tissues but, on top of everything else, I'd run out. Travis noticed and passed me a clean paper napkin, looking pained. He clearly hadn't anticipated my reaction but, then, he *was* just a man. I thanked him in a strained voice and wiped my eyes. I could only imagine what I looked like. My mascara was probably halfway down my face by now. I thought back to my shopping trip earlier: buying new clothes and dolling myself up to meet my superstar brother. And now. I was a wreck, crying into a café napkin.

"What I don't understand is," I said, "why tell me now?"

"I thought—well, Raven thought—that you deserved to know the truth."

"So how come it's only just come out that he's your father? The press are all over it this morning."

"You don't say? Yeah, I did notice. Social media has gone crazy. Sacha Tillens."

"His fiancée?" I asked.

"Yep, my would-be stepmom told his agent. The agent passed my details to the police and, next thing I know, it's out there."

"You don't think the police leaked it, do you?" I'd calmed down just enough to be as curious as I was angry.

"Who knows? It wouldn't be the first time." He looked at me with those blue eyes again. He really was a stunningly handsome man. But now that he wasn't my brother, what was I even doing there? It wasn't as if we'd be staying in touch. He was a rock star, and I was a drama teacher. Apart from our absent parents, we didn't exactly have much in common.

I dropped my crumpled napkin on my saucer and picked up my bag. "I suppose I'll get going, then. You've told me what you came to tell me. It was nice to meet you, Travis." I held out my hand.

But he ignored it. "Stay, Cath. Please. I didn't just ask you here to tell you Raven wasn't your dad. There was another reason I wanted to meet you."

"Which is?" I said cautiously.

"I think Raven was murdered. I'm convinced of it, in fact. And I've got a hunch it's connected somehow to what happened to your mum."

My heart started pounding again. "What makes you think that?"

"Because Raven told me."

"What… What do you mean?"

I saw Travis hesitate; perhaps I wasn't the only one being told not to trust anyone.

"I went to see Raven's attorney—his lawyer you'd say over here—I saw him yesterday. He called me. Said it was urgent."

"What was it?" I leaned in, almost forgetting the row we'd just had, but his blue eyes looked past me. I turned round to see two girls who looked as if they were on a lunchbreak come up to our table.

"Hi! You're the actual Travis Brennon!" squeaked one.

"Love your song *True Eyes*; it's lit," said the other.

"Lit?" I said.

"I think it means cool," said Trav, shaking his head. "Okay

girls. Sorry, I'm having a business meeting."

"Just a selfie; come on! What the actual fuck, you're Travis Brennon!" Trav posed with one, then the other, and then both girls as their phone clicked. One put her arm around him. The other blew him a kiss. Others noticed and soon there was a shuffling as more people wanted to muscle in on the feeding frenzy of fandom. The two girls were already on their phones updating their social media and sharing the selfies.

"Grab your bag, Cath: we have to go," Travis said quietly so only I could hear. He got up, and abandoning our table, I followed. "I've been here before; it gets worse. It's like a wasp finding you're eating jam; others will arrive like a swarm very soon. Believe me." The cacophony of dinging smart phones echoed in our ears as we left the café and ran.

5. The Park

After leaving ZZ's we darted into the crowd and disappeared. We weaved our way into Oxford Circus tube station and immediately out through another exit, coming up on the other side of the road. We reached Regent's Park and stopped at an outdoor café. A shady seat in the far corner of the grounds of the eatery gave us sanctuary.

"So, peace at last," I said, moving the detritus of an abandoned lunch, brushing the crumbs from a sandwich onto the ground. "So this is how stars live? This is what Mum experienced. Intrusion, hassle, listening ears and prying eyes."

"Sure. I have to be so careful. Girls, they ask for a picture, then a hug, a kiss, they just grab at me. It's not what I want," he said. As he took off his Ray-Bans I could see the anxiety in his eyes. Fame came at a price. It cost his dad his life and maybe my mum hers too. It was clearly taking its toll on Raven's son. I felt a little sorry for him: all that money, all those looks, all that talent and he couldn't even enjoy a cup of coffee and a row with girl in peace.

"So Travis," my thoughts went back to the last thing he mentioned before we fled the café. "What did Raven's lawyer want?"

"To give me a letter. My dad had been insistent that if anything happened to him I should be given the letter ASAP, before anyone had the chance to get it."

"Like who?"

"He didn't say."

"A letter to you and not Sacha?" I asked.

"Sacha gets his estate. I get a letter. I don't need his money."

"So what did it say? Can you tell me?"

"I can do better than that." He reached into his jacket pocket and, glancing around, he pulled out a brown envelope and handed it to me. I looked at him to make sure he was serious about me opening it.

"Well read it then, Cath. This is what today's all about." I pulled the white paper from the envelope. Travis scanned around us watching for any intrusion. I looked down at the letter.

"Travis, if you're given this it means I'm dead. I hope you're an old man before it happens but my guess is you won't be. I so regret letting you down, son. I should have been there for you. But you've turned out pretty well. I have another big regret. I loved your mother, but Betzy was my real love and I let her down too.

"I know her daughter, Catherine, has been told I'm her dad, but you know the truth about that. Please break it to her. She needs to know what happened to her mother. I'm working on a book right now that's going to blow the lid off the whole thing. It'll piss a lot of people off but I owe it to Betzy—and Catherine. Plus I can't wait to see the smiles wiped off their faces when the book comes out if I live that long. Look after Sacha for me, and my advice? Go find your own Betzy. True love comes in strange ways.

"Love, and rock and roll!

"Your dad, Raven."

I stared at the words and swallowed hard. Tears fell. I crept my hand forward and found his. He squeezed my fingers, and then gently let go.

"Thank you for letting me see that, and I'm glad we've met, even if it's just this once," I said. "I know Raven and Mum were a big showbiz romance, but that letter shows he really did love her. It wasn't just for show. You know she wrote *Raindance* for him."

"I know the song; who doesn't? I know your mum was a legend. It must have been awful for you when she vanished," he said, his hand hovering over mine. Not daring to touch. It occurred to me that Travis, the amazing star that he was, might just have been as anxious about this meeting as I was.

"I remember it vividly. Walking in from school to find my aunt sitting in our kitchen. She was as white as a sheet. Aunt Trish childminded me and picked me up from school sometimes, but Mum usually forewarned me.

"*'Where's Mum?'* I asked. I'll never forget her reply, or her face as she forced out the words.

"*'Catherine, she's gone, I'm not sure for how long, but she does love you.'* She held out her arms and hugged me. I waited every night before I fell asleep, waiting for the door handle to turn and for her to walk into my room with those magic words, *'Hello Catherine, I'm home,'* but she never did. I cried every night for months. I still do at times. I moved in with my aunt and my life changed forever."

"Do you have any idea what happened?" he asked.

"Oh Travis, I wish I did."

"Trav is fine, Cath. Call me Trav. We were almost bro and sis."

"Trav. Okay. I think… I think she's dead. She wouldn't have gone this long without getting in touch if she could." The words were hard to say, but if anyone could understand how I felt it should be Travis; he'd lost a parent himself. "To be honest, what's happened to Raven makes me even more convinced."

Trav looked at me. "You think I'm right, you think he was murdered?"

"Surely the police wouldn't be so interested if it were just a drugs death. They came to see me, you know."

"Really? Me too."

"They were asking about Raven's book. They thought I may have had it."

"Why would you have it?"

"Exactly," I said. "I'm not even related to him." Trav's face was a picture. I grinned to show I was joking, and both of us

burst out laughing, more out of relief than anything else. But as
started to laugh I began to cry again. My emotions were all over
the place but I knew I'd get through it eventually. What had I
actually lost? It wasn't as if Raven had been much of a dad to me,
now he wasn't a dad at all.

"Who *has* got the book, then?" I said, when I'd pulled myself
together again.

"Sacha, I think," Trav said.

"You've spoken to her?"

"Briefly, by text. She's gone into hiding."

"I think I would if I were her."

"The manuscript wasn't quite finished, from what she tells
me—but the juicy bits are all there. He'd been in talks with a
couple of publishers who were biting his hands off, but no one
had seen a copy yet."

"I'd like to see it myself," I said, "especially if it says what
happened to Mum."

"Sacha said it would bust the whole thing right open. Stories
of sex and drugs and rock and roll, and a whole lot more. She
said Raven wanted you to see it before it came out and, when
you read it, you'd understand why."

"Do you know where she is?" I asked.

"My guess is she's at Raven's house in France. He bought it as
a love nest for him and my mom back in the day. Sacha's parents
live in deepest Essex on the coast, but she's not there;

that's too obvious for anyone trying to find her. The house in
France is a pretty well-kept secret, though."

"Could you call her?" I said. "Tell her you're with me, and
how keen I am to see that book."

Trav shook his head. "She seems to have switched her phone
off and her emails are bouncing back. I'm in touch with Dad's
bass player; he and his wife are pretty close to Sacha. Maybe she's
got a second phone? I could ask them to give her your number,
or try to anyway."

"Thanks," I said.

Trav lowered his voice. "Sacha agrees with me that Raven was murdered. And she thinks she was meant to die too."

"Shit," I said. "No wonder she's hiding." I thought for a moment. "Listen, Trav, I'm not saying I disagree – I think you're right; I think Raven was murdered. But he did do a *lot* of drugs. Is it possible we're wrong and it was just a tragic accident?" I felt I had to ask, even if it offended him.

"But he hadn't—" Trav stopped, his voice briefly drowned out by the sirens of two passing police vans. He looked around. "He hadn't done drugs for years. He promised me all that was over. And Sacha backed it up: she said he'd been clean for two years. No, there's no way Raven did it himself. Someone gave him a massive overdose." His jaw clenched, making his toned face even sharper and firmer. He was obviously under a lot of strain. My outburst earlier probably hadn't helped.

"But promises can be broken Trav." I said gently.

"Of course they can," he replied, "the old Raven broke them all the time I'm sure. But he wasn't the old Raven anymore. Maybe meeting Sacha, maybe getting older, maybe accepting I was his son. He'd changed. I believed him."

"Did he doubt you were his son?"

"Deep down, I don't think so. He always kind of knew about me, but we didn't meet until I came over here to play, a couple of years ago. When I was growing up, he wasn't exactly the paternal type."

"Yes, I get that. Aunt Trish tried to get him to meet me," I said, trying not to sound – or feel – bitter. "He refused. She always said he was trying to get out of claiming responsibility, but I guess we know the real reason now."

"Well, he wanted a DNA test before he'd accept I was his child – even though Mom was with him when she got pregnant. That was kind of hard to swallow, but I guess, in a way, I don't really blame him. Rock stars tend to attract paternity claims, if you know what I mean."

I couldn't help wondering if Trav spoke from personal

experience as a rock star, as well as the child of one.

"When the test proved I was really his son, he went all in. Wanted to do the whole father and son thing. We decided we'd keep it all secret, though, just between us and my mom. With us both being public figures, we didn't need the extra pressure… not while we were getting to know each other. He said he could just imagine the headlines: *Travis Brennon and his drugged-up punk dad*."

"And I don't suppose it would have done your career much good if Raven had relapsed?"

"You know, I could have handled it, but he couldn't, he really cared. He was honestly a different guy after he dropped the drugs. He was really proud of himself for doing it too. It makes me sad to think of how the world will see him now – a failed junkie who just relapsed." He turned away clearly distressed, his hand touching his eye.

"It's okay Trav," I said gently touching his arm. I realised how much it meant to him. It was how I felt about Mum - the headlines, the gossip, the lecherous stories. It wasn't the woman I'd known, however briefly.

"He was trying to make a new life you know, with Sacha." Trav said, turning to me with his gorgeous blue eyes. "He'd even started to try to make up with mom."

"Was your mum in the music business too?" I asked.

"God no! Mom was very much *not* in the music business." He laughed.

"How did they meet?" I asked. The longer I spent with Trav the more I began to relax, and for a super star, he was pretty down to earth beneath the image, and now that the shock of Raven not being my dad was beginning to fade, I was enjoying his company.

"They met in Paris. She was a visiting lecturer at a university there. His band the Scented Slugs were playing a show. They hooked up afterwards in time-honoured fashion and things moved on from there. They spent time in London together, and sometimes he'd fly over in a private jet to see her in Paris. I was the result. Conceived in London, Paris or somewhere over the Channel in a Learjet. Don't overthink it!"

"I'd rather not." I laughed. "Sounds like a fun relationship. So, what went wrong?"

"Oh, the usual. I don't know the details, but I don't think it was pretty. Her time at the university ended, so Mom and I went to Boston, Massachusetts. That's where I grew up. She got tenure at Harvard."

"Impressive," I said. "What did she teach?"

"French literature."

"So, I guess you're more like your dad than your mum? You've gone into the music business."

"I suppose I am," he said thoughtfully. "Mom had always told me Raven was my father from an early age so I just accepted it. I formed a band at school but got nowhere. I went through college and did a few gigs… nothing took off. Then two years ago I heard that a band here in London wanted a singer—and they gave me a go. We hit the charts."

"I remember it was everywhere. It's one of my favourite songs. *Party Night Kisses,*" I said. "So you're now famous, more famous than Raven was back then."

Trav shrugged. "I've been lucky, I guess. Since I went solo a year ago, I've had success on both sides of the Pond. I now split my time between here and Boston. It's a lifestyle that suits me," he said, checking his phone.

"Sounds like a great life compared to mine," I smiled. "I'm a very boring teacher, in an even more boring school. Or I was. I've just been suspended, probably sacked because of my supposed father being murdered and my mum being Betzy Blac."

"Hey, that's unfair. It's nothing to do with how you do your job."

I shrugged. "Tell Miss Miles that."

"Okay, so I guess your career's not in the healthiest of places right now… but… otherwise, are you happy? Married with kids and all that?"

"Not exactly. One failed marriage and a few boyfriends is all I've managed so far."

"I haven't done much better myself, to be honest." He smiled.

I laughed. "You're kidding! You're dating Cinders O'Conner, aren't you? I think most blokes would consider that a success!" I'd seen photos of them together, splashed over the news. She was gorgeous, and a brilliant singer too. She'd won a talent competition called *Show Stoppers UK*.

"We broke up, actually. We had a few fun times together, but I'm back on my own again."

"I'm sure that won't last long!" I laughed.

"Maybe." Trav frowned. "It's not attracting women; it's keeping a relationship going that's the problem. Perhaps I just haven't found the right woman. I had a long relationship with an actress called Genevieve." I nodded but didn't say anything. I'd seen her picture too: she and Trav had been all over social media. She was equally as gorgeous as Cinders O'Conner.

"We thought we were *the ones,* you know. I wrote so many love songs for her… Now my next album's full of songs about our break-up." He gave a dry laugh. "Injunctions will fly before it comes out, you can bet. Her attorneys are bombarding me with emails right now. I'm not knocking her; I just want to tell our story. The story of a very hot love which went very, *very* cold. It's the gossip afterwards that always kills me. The kiss and tell. Search online and you'll see what I mean, not just about her but about all my exes. Problem is, people get paid for that sort of stuff; the grubbier the better as far as the press are concerned."

"That's hard," I said, and I meant it. I often wondered how Mum coped with that sort of thing. It was sad to realise what she'd gone through. We sat in silence for a few minutes. A pigeon flew down and pecked cheekily by our feet at the crumbs from the discarded sandwich.

"My mum and your dad found love."

"Well at least you can go on a dating site. Unlike me.

International millionaire singing star wants a girlfriend. Yeah, form a queue for the wrong reasons."

"I'm sorry it had a bad ending,' I said. 'You and Genevieve." He looked up and, as he smiled, I caught a glimpse of the man behind the image. On the surface he had a perfect life but the reality was obviously a lot more complicated. As Betzy's daughter, I, of all people should have known that.

"Sorry I got irate earlier; I was just in shock. I shouldn't have taken it out on you like that."

"No, it was my fault. I should have given you a heads-up before we met, but I was scared you wouldn't come."

"Most people would have just made a phone call. It was brave of you to break the news to me in person."

Trav's eyes narrowed. "Cath, we've got a bit off track but, as I said in the Café, I kind of have an ulterior motive for meeting you. I need your help."

"With what?" The idea of Travis Brennon needing my help with anything was flattering, if not a little confusing.

"Will you help me find that manuscript? It's the key to the whole damn thing, I'm sure of it." He turned the full force of those deep blue eyes on me, perhaps it was a tactic he used with all women or maybe he didn't realise the effect it had. "If Raven was killed—and I'm convinced he was—that's how we'll find the killer. And I think there's a very good chance we'll solve the mystery of what happened to your mother as well."

"Of course," I heard myself saying. "Of course I'll help." I imagined most women found it hard to say *no* to Travis Brennon. But this wasn't about pleasing Trav, this was about Mum. For the first time in thirty years, I'd have a shot at getting to the truth and finding out what happened to her.

"Are you sure, Cath? You need to be sure. I'm not going to lie to you—it could be risky, getting involved in all this."

"I don't doubt it," I said. "But I'm kind of involved already. I had a mysterious text from someone called DD saying I was in danger."

"Really? DD? Do you have any idea who that is?"

"Not a clue."

"It doesn't mean anything to me, either," Trav said. He seemed to be mulling something over. "We could ask Sarah? She'd know all the names from way back when."

"Sarah?" I said.

"You'll know her as Suzi Scums."

"Oh." Mum's former lead guitarist. "She sent me a card," I said, remembering. "And flowers. It was kind of her."

"She still hopes your mom will turn up one day. Not least because she's always dreamt of reforming Décolleté! I know she'd like to talk to you. I'll give you her number. The other band members might remember stuff as well."

"Good idea," I said. Was it wrong to feel a little excited? I'd just lost a dad and a brother, but I'd gained a partner in solving a mystery. "Is there anyone else I should be talking too?" I couldn't deny I was keen to meet names from Mum's past.

"Pete Benton, maybe. Remember him?"

I definitely did. He was a big-name DJ back in the day. I'd spent many hours listening to Pete Benton on Radio One and various TV music shows.

"He was a real friend of my dad's band," Trav said, "and your mum's. He used to introduce them on stage. I'll try sounding him out, see if he's got any information. And then there's Chris Latham…"

"Betzy's manager?" I said, remembering the name.

"And Raven's too. He's probably a good guy to get in touch with. He seems to know everyone."

"I met him years ago," I said. "He sent me flowers too. And his number. I'll give him a call."

"Thanks, Cath. It really means a lot to have your help."

"I'm not sure how much use I'll be, but I'm happy to try. I take it you don't trust the police to find the manuscript themselves?"

"It's not that I don't trust them," Trav said, "and I'm glad they're looking into it. But one thing I know about people in

43

the music business, a lot of them don't like talking to the cops. You and me, Cath, we're part of it: we're family to them. You're Betzy Blac's daughter! That's a pretty good backstage pass." He smiled with that Travis Brennon smile I'd seen in his videos, and I felt myself blushing. There'd been enough downsides over the years to being Betzy Blac's daughter; it was nice to know there were positives too.

"Okay, so let's swap notes and watch each other's backs if we can," I said.

He stood up, preparing to leave. My first coffee date with Travis Brennon was over, but it seemed there might be more to come.

"Whatever happens, Cath, we need to get that manuscript before it falls into the wrong hands." He fixed me with a serious look. "If they get it first, they'll destroy it, and then we'll never know."

*

Back home, it was 2am when my phone rang. I'd stupidly left it on. Trav and London seemed a long time ago. By the time I stumbled down the stairs to answer my mobile it had gone to voicemail. I listened to the message and heard the strained tones of panic from a very frightened woman.

"This is Sacha Tillens. I'm at Raven's house in France. Please come. We've never met but I need to give you his book. You should have it. It's about what happened to your mum."

6. Sacha Tillens

A few hours later, yawning through the dragging dawn in the early summer chill, I drove around the M25. I wished Trav could have come with me but there was no time. He'd not answered my text, but I couldn't wait—I had to get that manuscript. If Sacha wanted to meet me and hand it over, it was essential I saw her. If Mum had been murdered and the killer had struck again, then Trav could be right: he or I might be the next targets, and the only way to stop this madness was to expose the killer and find the truth. I decided a quick drive to the Channel Tunnel, an hour or two on the other side, and then I'd be on my way back: mission accomplished. I could hand it over to DCs Dennison and Patel and wait for the arrests. Once I'd read it, of course.

The smell of diesel exhaust seeped into my car from a clapped-out van in front, but my old VW couldn't find the speed to overtake it. I was en-route to Ebbsfleet station to board the Eurotunnel train to France. Sacha had texted me the address of the house where she was hiding: it was near Le Touquet, about an hour's drive from the Calais rail terminus. As the train pulled out and began its descent into the tunnel, I sent a text to Sacha: *"Hi, on way 2 meet u. Cath."*

*

As I emerged in the French sunshine, warm air wafted in through my open window. It smelt fresh after the train in the tunnel. My phone found a signal and Sacha's reply landed. *"I'm scared. Call me for where to meet. Sacha."*

I pulled over and called her number, I was worried.

"Sacha? Hi, it's Cath Edgley. I'm in France."

"Cath, hi. Thanks for coming."

"Have you got the book, Sacha?"

"Not over the phone. I'll tell you when I see you. You must get it before they do, Cath."

"Sacha, are you okay?"

"Trav must prove Raven didn't do drugs. Please help him. I've only told the police this, but someone broke into our room. We were drunk and I'd fallen asleep. I woke up and found Raven lifeless. I felt a sharp pain in my arm and realised I was being injected with something. I saw a shape; someone was there."

"What? That's really scary. Awful," I said.

"I struggled and screamed and the guy in the room next door came in and disturbed the attacker. He dropped the syringe so I escaped with a much smaller dose than poor Raven, but it all happened so quickly. The bastard pushed past the other hotel guest and legged it. The damn neighbour just took a photo before calling 999. I was in and out of consciousness, but they got me to A&E just in time. Raven wasn't so lucky."

"You told the police *all* of this?"

"Of course. But I decided to hide, and this is the best I could come up with. I'm on my way to the blockhouse at the end of the walk at St Cecile Plage where it meets the beach. Park at the nature reserve carpark and follow the footpath. I'll go into the open and wait for you there."

I was delayed leaving the terminal due to a broken-down lorry and a massive tail back. Was I being utterly reckless? Going to meet a stranger who might be being watched? I realised I was clenching my teeth and squeezing the wheel, sweat seeping from my palms to the soft plastic coating, gripped by my fingers. I headed south, pushing the car as hard as I could. Soon I dropped off the motorway and found the turning for the little resort of St Cecile Plage. The road to the town led me past new developments of holiday homes. Red roofed chalet bungalows soon gave way to taller, 1950s and '60s residences with neat gardens and painted shutters. Ahead was the centre and in it, according to the map, was the house that Raven Rain had bought as a hideaway to spend time with his then girlfriend Carly Brennon, Trav's mum. It was now a hideout for Sacha.

Behind the resort was woodland with winding footpaths leading to sand dunes backing onto a vast uninterrupted beach running along miles of coastline. I stopped the car in one of the parking bays by a low wooden barrier and was soon following a waymarked route to the old wartime blockhouse where Sacha had asked me to meet her.

My low, flat shoes were continually filling with sand; it wasn't a quick journey. I kept stopping to empty them out along with picking out pine needles and bits of marram grass poking into my feet. A few hundred metres along I came across a group of people who looked like refugees. Huddled behind dense shrubs, they watched me intently as I walked past. I turned to check I wasn't being followed; I was alone in an unknown environment with a language I didn't speak. Soon I could hear the sea and the path became a boardwalk as the dunes came into view. There were the remains of the Nazi blockhouse, its grey concrete roughened by waves, salt spray and wind.

I looked around. The vast beach stretched before me in both directions and across a hundred or more metres to the sea. There was no sign of Sacha. I called her name. I looked inside the remains of the blockhouse, tilted at an angle by years of shifting sand. I tried to call her, but her phone went to voicemail. A couple with a dog walked up behind me, smiling. The dog, a brown spaniel, tugged at the lead desperate to be let off. The owners laughed and shrugged their shoulders, saying something in French I couldn't understand about "*notre chien*" and its "*nez fort*". I smiled politely. The dog was freed and ran into the marron grass in the dune behind the blockhouse, barking and running round in circles. I walked towards it, calling Sacha's phone again. I heard a faint ringing, just as the owners of the dog shouted out, loudly, in panic.

I rushed up the dune, but its fine sand held me back, draining my muscles as I attempted the climb. Then I saw a pink phone case half submerged by sand. Its display lit up as a call came in. It was Sacha's. It was just going to answerphone from my call. I grabbed it and stuffed it into my bag as quickly as I could. The couple were calling the police. I feared the worst. I heard desperate voices from the man and woman with the dog; he was clearly talking to the cops, repeating key words, his voice in panic with staccato speech: *"Il y a une fille… Elle est morte, elle est morte!... Dans les dunes!"*

Creeping up behind them, I saw her. Sacha. I swallowed a scream and fell to the ground, my heart racing. I desperately wanted to pick her up, but I knew I couldn't leave my fingerprints on her. She couldn't die; she had answers, the knowledge I needed. She looked asleep. Her beauty was evident despite the greyness creeping over her flawless features. Beside her was a syringe. A small trickle of blood stained her arm where she'd been injected. It had only just congealed. Her nails were broken and dark blue bruises were forming on her wrists where she'd been held down. She couldn't have been dead for long, maybe just minutes. There was no dignity in her death. I looked away. There was no sign of her bag; she must have thrown her phone away in the last minutes before they attacked her, in the hope that I'd find it.

The couple were leaning over her body talking quickly on the phone to the police and to each other. I didn't want to hang around; there was nothing I could do, so I slipped away behind the blockhouse and ran along the beach towards the town. I took off my shoes, clutching them in my left hand, my bag in my right. Sacha's killers couldn't be far. Every step of the way I kept looking at the dunes forming the backbone of the beach to my left, looking in case they were coming after me, to kill me too, and get her phone. If they'd done their homework they'd have my photo, the one snatched from outside the school gates which appeared in several of the papers. I needed to get to safety; I needed people, but they were few and far between down that end of the beach.

As I neared the town the number of people increased. First, there were couples lying in the sand, then families with children and finally old people sitting near the paths to the resort's front, none of them aware of the murder in their midst. My pulse quickened and adrenalin helped my flight, although my chest hurt and my lungs felt like they were going to seize. I must have looked like a woman possessed. To me, I was.

Out of breath and after taking a wrong turn, I finally found Sacha's house down a side road off the High Street. I knocked on the blue painted wooden front door, its glass panel covered by an ornate metal frame. Nothing. I pushed the door with my bag so as not to leave fingerprints, and it creaked open. The keys were on the floor. Carefully, I went inside. I listened for movement, talking, any sounds, but there were none.

The sitting room had been trashed. Drawers opened and overturned. Chairs moved, cushions lifted out, pictures taken off the wall. The kitchen was the same: all the pretty painted, cornflower-blue cupboards were open, their contents emptied out on the floor. The smell of spilt herbs and spices offered a heady cocktail. Cups, glasses, plates smashed.

I knew the police would be there soon, so I couldn't touch anything and had to leave quickly. Besides, the intruders might come back at any time. Turning to the stairs, I rushed up and, as I neared the top, the dark menacing shape of a man appeared on the dim landing, holding a knife.

As my eyes accustomed to the light I saw his face, half hidden by a scarf. I went to turn but he ran to get past me down the stairs, slashing at me as he came. I kicked out and caught him but I fell backwards, banging the front of my temple as I tumbled.

Luckily, he was in a hurry and, holding the knife above me in his fingerless leather gloves, he kicked my leg, hard. I yelped and grabbed my aching calf. He ran past me as I rolled towards the door. Crawling into the daylight, my eyes met those of an old woman in the entrance of the house opposite. Emotionless, she shut the door. I watched the man jump onto the back of a motorbike which had just drawn up. It roared away.

7. La Femme Française

I knew I was too late to help Sacha, but was I too late to get the manuscript? The intruder wasn't carrying anything when he left, but if he couldn't find it then how could I?

Getting my breath back and ignoring the pain in my head and leg, I staggered up the stairs, careful not to hold the railings for fear of leaving fingerprints. I pushed a tissue to my head to stop any loss of blood; I didn't want my DNA left in the house, although I feared it was probably already too late. Reaching the landing I went into the front bedroom. There were boxes of papers and pictures pulled from the top of a wardrobe. Photographs had been roughly spread out on the carpet, including one of Raven and Mum, together, smiling. It was such a nice picture, a postcard to the future taken in Mum's past. At the time they probably thought they would be together forever. I grabbed it and pushed it into my bag. There was one of Carly Brennon too; she was a stunner and had clearly passed her looks on to her gorgeous son. I took it for Trav.

The mattress was pulled from the bed and had been slashed open with a knife, the jagged edges of the material peeling back like a gaping wound. The pillows were also ripped open and were now lying on the floor. Sacha's clothes were strewn across the room. Even the laundry basket had been upturned and searched. Books had been pulled from shelves and carpets torn up. Had they found the missing manuscript? I wasn't sure. There was no trace of it, but I couldn't search the whole house properly, there just wasn't time; I had to go. Sirens cut through the street noise outside. Glancing through the window I saw a police car turn into the road, its blue lights flashing. I held my bag tightly and limped down the stairs. I slipped out of the back door into a rear alleyway, getting out with seconds to spare before the Gendarmes arrived and thundered up the stairs.

Sunglasses on and map in hand, I played the innocent tourist as I tried to walk calmly back along the road out of town to find my car. There were an ambulance and two police cars in the car park. Police tape was being put across the footpath and I felt sorry for the hapless refugees who were being herded into a police van by armed cops. They were protesting their innocence, but the officers were in no mood to listen. The cops were photographing the number plates of the parked cars, including mine.

I drove to the next village, Camiers, and when I was sure that I wasn't being followed, I stopped outside a shop. Turning off my engine I pulled Sacha's phone out of my bag. It needed a password. Surely it couldn't be that simple, could it? I typed in *"Raven,"* and it worked. I couldn't believe how lax Sacha had been making her phone as accessible as that. It opened on an unsent message. It was a draft to me. *"Cath, I'm being watched. I've posted Raven's netbook with the manuscript on it to Brad…"* It ended there.

Poor Sacha, she must have been so frightened. What or who had stopped her from finishing and sending it? The memory of her lying dead in the sands would haunt me forever. But who was Brad? I switched off her phone and put it back in my bag. I didn't want to hang around, who knows where her killers were and how soon they'd be on my trail? I restarted my car and headed back towards the tunnel.

At the terminal they found me a space on the next train and I was waved into one of the lines waiting to board. I texted Trav.

"Sacha's dead. Someone's after the book but she got a message to me saying it was safe. Who is Brad? On my way home. Please meet me tonight. I'm scared. Cath x"

52

*

Tired and bruised, with my leg aching from the kick I'd been given by the thug at poor Sacha's hideaway, I drove through familiar streets heading for home, finally feeling safe. I'd arrived to meet Sacha minutes after she'd been murdered. If I'd worn sensible shoes I might have got there on time and could have saved her; or maybe I'd have been killed too? Would I have also been found lying there with drugs in my veins?

I was tired, cold, frightened, upset and in need of a long, hot bath. My neighbour Eileen watched me from her garden as I drove into the cul-de-sac. She nodded but didn't smile. Something wasn't right. Waiting outside my house was a car. Inside it were two detectives: DCs Patel and Dennison, who'd visited me earlier. I got out of my car as the two detectives decamped from theirs.

"Hello," I smiled. They didn't.

"Miss Edgley, we need to talk," said DC Dennison.

"Of course, come in. Cup of tea?" I offered as I went to open the front door, but DC Dennison stepped forwards.

"No time for tea I'm afraid Ms Edgley. We are taking you to the station."

"Why?" I asked, as DC Patel stood close beside me.

"Catherine Edgley, you're under arrest in connection with the murder of Sacha Tillens."

"Under arrest? Me? Why?" DC Patel's hand took my arm and led me towards their car. Eileen watched, open-mouthed, as he produced a pair of handcuffs.

"Hey, there's no need for that!" I protested as the metal rings clicked shut around my wrists. "I'm not a criminal!" My pleas were met with silence as the car door was closed and I was driven away. I heard a text arrive on my phone but had no way of reading it.

Across the channel, the French police would no doubt be

searching the dunes and the house, looking for clues and evidence of intruders, including me.

*

"This is an interview with Catherine Edgley. Present are DC Darsh Patel and DC Kate Dennison. So, Miss Edgley, do you speak French?"

"Not really, no."

"Pity. You might need to learn it."

"Why?"

"This," said DC Dennison, producing a document, "is a European Arrest Warrant. The French police want to interview you in connection with the murder of Miss Sacha Tillens and have requested we hold you under caution until they can see you."

I nodded blindly, after listening to them telling me I was to be held overnight in the cells pending further requests from the French police. I was offered a solicitor but I shook my head.

"I don't need a lawyer, I've done nothing wrong," I protested. "Look, I tried to save Sacha. Just read the texts on my phone!"

"We did ask you not to leave the area, Miss Edgley,' said DC Patel.

"And you went to France," said DC Dennison.

"To St Cecile Plage," said DC Patel.

"Where a woman was murdered," jumped in DC Dennison. It was as if they were finishing each other's sentences to confuse me, like some kind of double act.

"Sacha Tillens," continued DC Patel.

"A vital witness to the murder of Raven Rain."

"Please!" I said, interrupting their rapid-fire staccato phrases. My head was thumping, and the bright light was harsh against the pale green painted walls of the room. The red light on a tape recorder by the wall flashed on and off and a camera in the corner was capturing every moment. I looked at the dark glass behind my questioners and was sure someone would be watching from the other side. "Please slow down. Could I have a coffee? I haven't had a drink since the tunnel." The two officers swapped glances. DC Patel made notes as DC Dennison cleared her throat.

"We can arrange that, shortly. You were at a murder scene, Miss Edgley; we have witnesses. Your car was photographed at the car park. Your outing was a very quick day trip." DC Dennison looked at me. There was silence; they were waiting for me to respond. The red light on the recorder glowed. I was scared they'd twist my words, so I didn't reply.

"The murdered woman's bag is missing," said DC Patel, breaking the silence, "and someone broke into her house."

"A witness described someone looking very much like you leaving by the back door of the property," added DC Dennison. 'Shortly after an accomplice escaped on a motorbike."

"That man attacked me!" I said, raising my voice. I pointed to my head and stood up: frightened, angry and frustrated. Why didn't they believe me?

"Sit down please, Miss Edgley."

"I will, but you need to see the bruising on my leg where he hit me."

"There's no need for that, Miss Edgley. If you need medical attention we will arrange it," said DC Patel.

"Those injuries may have occurred earlier or later from any number of causes." DC Dennison narrowed her eyes and leaned in towards me. "Supposing I were a suspicious detective, I might think that Raven Rain's killer tried but failed to kill his fiancée when they killed him. So they wanted to make sure the job was done, especially if she knew where this missing manuscript was. Clearly for whatever reason they want to stop the book's publication."

"Well that suspicious detective would be wrong," I replied. "Utterly wrong. I went to meet her, to help her."

"What if, Miss Edgley,' said DC Dennison, 'you'd hired locals to kill her, and wanted to set her up, to entrap her, to ensure she was where you could get to her, a fairly isolated place at the end of a long beach?"

DC Patel smiled. "Now that's an interesting idea."

"Hired locals? What, who speak English? How would I find them in that time? I only had a text from Sacha last night. I'm being set up here."

"The French police are gathering their evidence, Miss Edgley. We'll see what they have in the morning. Meanwhile you'll be staying with us. Interview terminated at 19:55."

*

Fifteen minutes later, I was shown into a cell. My belongings had been seized and I was processed by the custody sergeant. My phone, bag, passport, everything. My liberty suspended. My fingerprints taken. I was offered food but I couldn't eat. I was sick with worry.

Being on the inside of a closing cell door was harsh, cold, frightening and claustrophobic. The four walls were broken only by a metal sink, metal toilet, thin mattress and barred window. I heard footsteps pass outside. The swearing shouts of a drunk being thrown into a nearby cell. His banging on the door echoed around the narrow corridor. His shouts and curses continued well into the night. I lay awake, unable to sleep. I could smell stale disinfectant which seemed to cling to the floor. I felt totally dejected. I was scared.

As I lay there in that dim, dark cell, a shaft of streetlight filtered through the barred window which separated me from freedom. This was where my mum's and Raven's killer should be. Not me. I'd gone from respected teacher and popstar's daughter to common prisoner, accused of murder and facing God-knows-what. I needed my own bed. I needed sleep. I needed Trav. Why had I refused a solicitor? It had all seemed so ridiculous at first, but the seriousness of the situation was dawning on me. I was actually in the frame for murder. Maybe the killer had set me up, maybe they were in league with the police? Were these two detectives bent? I decided to ask for a lawyer in the morning.

*

Minutes passed into hours. Hours leached into the approaching dawn. A chill spread through me. My limbs were heavy and, however I lay on that awful little bed, I couldn't get comfortable. What did I do for clean clothes? Washing? Where would I be held? A prison? What would the French police do with me? A headache started. My stomach churned. I felt I was being watched, although no eyes appeared at the spy hole in the door.

My mum had been arrested. Twice. Once for being naked and drunk in the Parisian fountain, the second for possession of cannabis. She was banged up in a cell for a night, too. They let her go after one of the roadies said the dope was theirs, because if she'd been convicted of possessing drugs, the tour of the States would have been in doubt. So that's what we had in common: we were both jail birds. I managed a sort of smile, but it didn't last long.

When I was little I had played Mum's records, listening to her voice. Later, when the internet came along, I watched videos of her performing on YouTube and other sites. Clips of concerts and gigs. I lay there in the cell singing her songs; it was comforting and gave me something to hold onto. The night dragged and the dawn seemed sluggish. Finally, I heard footsteps outside. The spyhole in the door was opened and then the lock clicked with a metallic sound which echoed around the cold harsh walls. It was eight o'clock. I waited for their words but when they came they were words I never expected to hear.

8. Karam Himsi

"You can go," said a young woman officer.

"What?" I said, unable to believe what I'd heard.

"You're no longer under arrest. DC Dennison would like a word though. Please come to the interview room. Can I get you a tea or coffee and some breakfast?"

"Just coffee please. What's happened?"

"DC Dennison will explain. Please follow me."

I walked into the interview room, where DC Kate Dennison was waiting. "Good morning, Catherine. Please take a seat."

"I'm hoping it will be," I said as I sat down.

"Miss Edgley, the French police have told us you are no longer a person of interest, and as such you are free to go. You are no longer under arrest."

"How come they've realised I'm innocent?"

"Witness statements."

"So it's okay to have arrested me, held me against my will, kept me in that cell for the night, is it?"

"Yes, it is, actually; the law allows for that. Had you been guilty we would have helped them solve a murder. Surely you must agree that we should find Ms Tillens' killer?"

"Of course. But you knew I wasn't capable of murder."

"We go on evidence, Catherine. Facts, not feelings. Did you see a group of refugees on your way to or from the beach where Sacha Tillens was killed?" she asked.

"Yes, yes I did. They were being herded into a police van

when I left."

"Well it's a good job for you that they were there. A refugee worker from a charity was visiting the group at the time. One Karam Himsi. The group heard Miss Tillens shout before her mouth was muffled. Assuming the refugees would be blamed for any crime committed anywhere near their illegal camp, Mr Himsi watched from the marram grass."

"Why didn't he help her? He could have prevented her murder," I said angrily.

"He may have been able to. But the sad truth is, that he and the other refugees are frightened. The two white assailants would have almost certainly beaten him up. The likelihood is that they would still have murdered Sacha, and then claimed they caught him or one of refugees in the act and were trying to rescue her. Who do you think the local court would believe? I'd hope they'd believe him, but the fact is, according to Mr Himsi, the refugees get blamed for every missing litre of milk and every stolen car."

"But the French police believed his statement?"

"They believed his mobile phone footage."

"What?"

"He filmed the two men committing the crime. He filmed them whilst lying down in the grass hiding from their view. It's not a full picture but it's enough to show them pushing her to the ground, and you can clearly see a syringe being held up by one of them."

"Horrible." My head dropped.

"Karam Himsi stopped filming after the couple with a dog and you turned up. Your reaction, and that of the couple, seems clear. The man and woman had been behind you on the footpath and saw you arrive in the carpark."

"Yes, I remember them."

"They told the police you were the only person at the scene, hence the police had you down as a suspect. And then you were seen in Ms Tillens' house in St Cecile Plage."

"That's where I got the cut on my head and the bruise on my

leg." The door opened. The young officer who'd opened the cell walked in with a cup of coffee.

"One thing," I said.

"Yes?" replied DC Dennison.

"Do you mind if I cry." And as soon as I said those words the tears started. Pent up emotion flooded out. "I can't believe all this has happened," I sobbed, "and I can't believe poor Sacha is dead." I laid my head on my folded hands. Kate Dennison offered me a box of tissues from beneath the desk. Her demeanour changed.

"Catherine, is there anything else you think might help us find Sacha Tillens' and Raven Rain's killer?"

"Only the name: Brad," I said. "The manuscript has apparently been given to him."

"We'll run it thought the system, but it's not much to go on. One other thing. We were called by a neighbour of yours to report a suspicious man loitering outside your house last night. We sent a patrol car and found it was one Travis Brennon."

"Shit, Trav! I asked him to come and see me."

"The officer explained you'd been detained but Mr Brennon insisted on coming here this morning to wait for you."

"He's here now? Trav's here?"

"Yes, would you like to see him?"

"Oh God, yes please." The officer who'd brought the coffee left and returned with Trav. I stood up and threw my arms around him.

"You've had a lucky escape, unlike poor Sacha," said Trav, as we sat next to each other on the grey plastic chairs.

"It was horrible, Trav. She was just lying there. Dead. I've never seen anyone dead."

"Tragic. She was really nice."

"Is it okay to ask you for another hug?" I said, holding back the tears.

"Sure. I think I need one too." He put his arms around me.

"I'll leave you for a few minutes,' said DC Dennison. 'And sorry again for the loss of your father Mr Brennon. Like you, he was quite a star. Catherine, your things are at the front desk and you're free to go."

I buried my head in Trav's chest and sobbed as he stroked my hair, listening to my mumbled recollection of the previous twenty-four hours.

*

Trav and I took a taxi back to my house. Eileen watched us arrive; she smiled and waved. I returned the gesture along with a short smile. Like mine, her life was suddenly more exciting that she could remember.

We walked into my calm, quiet kitchen. "Sorry, Trav. I'm not being a great host, but I need a shower and I need to sleep. I've been awake all night. I'm utterly shattered."

"I'm a bit wiped out too," he smiled.

"Were you at the police station very early?" I asked.

"No, I turned up just before eight to see if you were being charged. I'd lined up an attorney, well my PA had. Luckily you didn't need her." My phone rang.

"Sorry, Trav, I need to get this… Aunt Trish, nice to hear your voice…" Trav went into the hallway, making a call of his own. I sat down at the table and relived the last few days telling my stand-in mum all that had happened. "Aunt Trish, I'm getting texts from someone calling themselves DD, any ideas who that might be?" I asked.

"No, Catherine, I'm afraid I haven't. Are you all right with all this fuss about your mum again? It must be a dreadful strain," she said, the concern in her voice evident.

"For us both, Aunt Trish, no more heart scares I hope?"

"Well, I'm on so many tablets now Cath, I don't think my heart would dare to stop."

"Oh, please take care. I have to find out what happened to Mum after all this time, for your sake and mine. I know how important it is to you."

"Thank you, but please, be careful, darling. There are some nasty people out there."

"I will, and I know. I've already seen what they can do. Did you know Raven Rain wasn't my dad?"

"No. I honestly thought he was. Your mum was so in love with him. I asked him straight out and even when he denied it, I didn't believe him. I still can't believe he isn't."

"Well now I've met his actual child—Trav—and I know he isn't my dad. But I'd love to know who is."

"I wish I knew; your mum was pretty wild at the time. But don't think badly of her. Oh I'm so sorry you've had all this, Catherine." She sighed. "I wish I could be with you but I've still got Mary here, visiting me from Ireland. I'll be back in a day or so if you want to come home."

"Thanks Aunt Trish. Love you."

"And I love you, Catherine. Please be careful."

I ended the call, pleased she'd got back to me at last. Trav ended his call and came back in.

"All okay?" he asked.

"Yes, my aunt. She's okay, worried, but so am I."

"Would a hug help?" he asked, his warm smile and strong arms offering comfort and hope. He squeezed me tight. My head under his chin. His hands gently touching my shoulders and neck. I was feeling confused. Could we? Should we? We weren't related so it was okay, but would it ruin everything? Was I up to a relationship right now? And why would this superstar be interested in me?

"Cath, I need to get back to town, I've got a taxi due in a few minutes. Let's talk later, yes?"

"Sure. I wish you could stay but… thanks again for being there this morning," I said, trying to hide my disappointment.

"No worries. Keep the door locked and call if you need me, okay?" he said as left.

Exhaustion overcame me and I went up to my bedroom and lay on my pillow. I felt safe and warm in my dull but familiar room. The daylight flooding through the thin curtains was no barrier to my need to shut down and I was soon falling asleep. My brain was trying to absorb recent events. The nightmare of the cell was fading but the memory of seeing Sacha would never leave.

*

I woke at seven o'clock that evening. Someone was banging on the door. I went downstairs feeling dishevelled; my hair was a mess and I was wrapped in my old but comfortable dressing gown. I opened the door and was met by a man with a brown paper carrier bag. A taxi pulled away.

"Evening sleepyhead," Trav smiled, holding up a takeaway. "Vegetable biryani and a bottle of Pinot, okay?"

"Oh… Just a bit. Thanks Trav, you're wonderful."

*

Sitting at my Spartan and uninspiring kitchen table I felt underdressed in my very ordinary pyjama set, dressing gown tied tightly around my waist. What was I thinking? Here was a man who was used to people wearing the most expensive and exciting lingerie and nightgowns and here was I: exhausted, bruised and unsure, in everyday high street clothes. Mum watched over me from her photo on the wall. I'm sure she'd spent evenings with Raven in cheap, worn clothes. She'd just shrug with a take-me-as-I-am attitude. That's easier, I thought, when you're confident and beautiful. Right then I felt neither. I emptied the food onto plates from the silver trays it had arrived in.

"I hope it's hot enough, I could put it in the oven," I offered.

"It'll be fine," he replied. I told him about the text on Sacha's phone, now in an evidence bag in the police station, waiting to be sent to France.

"So who's done this, Trav?"

63

"Someone looking for Raven's book."

"Just that or are we missing something?"

"I can't think of any other motive. Raven didn't have enemies."

"This name: Brad? Is he a musician, or someone connected with music?"

"I don't know any Brad. It doesn't ring a bell with me. I'll ask around, but it's no one I know," said Trav. "Any more from your mysterious texter?"

"No. No more texts."

"Have you tried calling or texting them back?"

"Yes, it always just ends. Look, I'll try now." I pressed redial on the number. "There you go," I said, putting the phone onto speaker. "The phone's off. There's no voicemail set up. The calls are coming from a number in Holland."

"Holland? Weird."

"I wish I knew who it was. Another drink?" I asked.

"Yes please, another glass would be good."

"Trav… I'm being silly, but…"

"Go on."

"Please stay here tonight. I'm really scared."

"Sure. I don't have anything with me though."

It hit me. What had I started? There was a spare room but I couldn't offer him that: I had my sewing machine out on the table in there with half-finished changes to a dress I was taking up. There were piles of clothes laid out for sorting for charity, not the thing to expose to a pop star you're trying to impress.

"I've got a new spare toothbrush, and you can sleep in my bed, next to me, if you want." I emphasised the next to me, not with me.

He smiled and smirked, shaking his head.

"What's wrong?" I asked, frightened I said something wrong.

"Cath," he smiled across the table, those blue eyes and warm mouth pulling me in. "You're so English, so reserved and so sweet. Of course I'll lay next to you, I wasn't taking it as an invitation for anything else. Although…"

"Although?" I asked.

"Come on, sleepy head. Let's finish this wine and crash, before one of us says something stupid."

As I turned out the downstairs lights, Travis Brennon, international stunning superstar led me by the hand up my own stairs and into my bedroom.

Feeling utterly stupid embarrassed and unsure, I switched off the light. The streetlamp outside pushed a gentle glow into the room over the top of the ill-fitting curtains as Trav took off his clothes and stood there in his boxers. I slipped off my dressing gown and stood there with the bed between us in my red pyjama set, hoping he hadn't noticed the missing button halfway down the top.

"Cath, stop worrying. Just get into bed."

"Is that what you say to all the girls?" I laughed. The shape of his chest and arm muscles were picked out in the gloom.

"Night, Trav."

"Night, Cath. And just for the record, I'm glad you're not my surprise sister."

"Yeah, me too. Aunt Trish told me Raven had denied being my dad. She just didn't believe him."

"I do," said Trav.

"So do I now," I replied, rolling over. A light kiss brushed my shoulder. I didn't want it to stop, but I hoped it would. I knew if he touched me I'd be his, right there, right then. "Trav, sorry, but it's all too much right now."

"It's just a good night kiss Cath." We lay still and listened. Outside, a car drove by slowly, and then it turned at the end of the cul-de-sac and drove by again. It was probably a police car; they'd set up extra patrols. I was now a witness to a crime scene and the person who could lead them to a killer of at least two people, possibly three. I could still be a suspect in the murder of Raven Rain; I wasn't sure. I could also be being used by the police as bait to lure the killer.

Inside, Travis Brennon, one of the most eligible and sexy guys on the planet was in my bed. I could feel the strength of his arms and his soft warm breath on my neck as his arm held my shoulders, keeping me safe. It felt good.

"Trav," I said with a weak, anxious voice, reaching across the no man's land of the sheet space between us.

"Yeah?" He took my hand in his.

"I'm scared. Sacha died yesterday. She died trying to tell me something. She died asking for my help."

"It's okay. You're safe," he said, softly squeezing me.

But safe for how long?

9. Chris Latham

My phone rang at eight thirty the next morning. It was DC Dennison.

"Good morning Catherine. You might want to know that the post-mortem has been carried out on the body of Sacha Tillens in France. You'll read it when it's reported I'm sure but just to let you know, she died from a massive overdose of drugs, but defence wounds, bruises and angle of entry of the needle confirmed it was unlikely to have been administered by the victim, but we know that from the mobile phone footage. Skin samples found under nails were from an IC1 male. I'm also telling you because you may have been his next victim. You need to be vigilant."

"I keep thinking if I'd got there earlier…"

"But you might have been killed too."

"Did the name Brad throw up anything?" I asked, more in hope than expectation.

"Not yet. As I said earlier, it's not much to go on," she replied.

"And there's no sign of the missing manuscript?"

"None as yet."

"Okay, well, thanks for calling and letting me know. 'Bye."

I ended the call and relayed the information to Trav, who had just returned from picking up some fresh bread and milk at the local shop. Oh how tongues would wag if Eileen had seen him. Mind you, it was a bit of a coup having a megastar leave your house after staying the night. It would make my street cred rocket.

Somewhere in the post a package was on its way across the Channel, destined for Brad. I had to find him, and I had to get that book. There was another person who might have the answers I was looking for. I arranged to meet Chris Latham later that morning. I'd met him before, when I was eighteen; he'd handed me an award that Mum had been presented with. A newspaper's readership had voted her the perfect punk princess. She'd have been pleased. I think.

As her agent and manager, Chris Latham still controlled all the revenue from radio music plays and record sales: quite a big pile of pennies. He was almost retired now, but still seemed hungry to handle Mum's affairs. Judging by his stomach he must have been always hungry in other ways; he was in need of losing a few dozen kilos.

I'd driven there from Chestnut Close, waving reassuringly at my neighbour Eileen as I left. She was clutching a copy of a Sunday paper which had a big spread on the latest theories about my missing mum and Raven's murder. It did, of course, mention my being questioned over Sacha's death, something that I was sure wouldn't have escaped Miss Miles's attention. My quiet life was unravelling fast.

I'd never been able to let go of the hope that Mum might somehow still be out there somewhere; a glass of wine in her hand, laughing as the sun went down, sticking two fingers up to the world. But if she was, then why did she go, and why did she abandon me? That's why I believed she was dead; she could never have left me, surely? What mother could leave a seven-year-old child with no explanation?

I turned onto the M25 motorway and headed west; the traffic was building and people changing lanes, cutting in and out in front of me, demanded my attention.

Raven was the only guy Mum had ever really loved, or so Aunt Trish had told me. Mum's disappearance was weird. She'd gone to Scotland with her friend, Judy, to stay in a small croft on Applecross overlooking the island of Skye and she just didn't come home. Some say she boarded a yacht and headed across the Atlantic for a new life in America. Really? So why did she never say goodbye? Her passport, along with her most treasured possessions, her lyric book with all her songs in it, and her old microphone were left at the cottage where we lived. She'd used that mic at every gig and it never left her side, until that weekend. I found a note with it addressed to me saying I should always treasure it if she ever went away.

Why didn't she take me with her? What had I done? I was seven, for God's sake.

Aunt Trish always told me Mum had run away to America to work on a new album. She said she'd be back and would make me very proud when she was top of the charts again, where she belonged. It was comforting; like being told people go somewhere nice when they die. Comforting, so long as you don't peel back the thin veneer of fantasy.

As I grew up, every so often I'd hear one of her songs on the radio. I was sad, but also very proud of my mum. She was always kind to me; my overriding memory was of her stroking my hair when I was ill. She wasn't like her punk persona—that edgy, in your face, Boudica-type wild cat. It was just a show. Sure she was angry, sure she swore, and sure she could be a loose cannon, but with me she was my mum. A good mum. Until she disappeared.

When I moved in with Aunt Trish, I felt lost and alone. She was very kind and similar to Mum in many ways, but she lived a pretty normal life in a town in Hertfordshire. It was big and busy compared to the village life I'd known. The school I moved to was so urban. Aunt Trish had divorced the year before; it must be genetic, this failure to find a lasting love. She didn't have any children and she took to me straight away. I had a nice bedroom, lots of toys and a comfortable home. Aunt Trish was lovely, but she wasn't my mum. Only Betzy Blac was my mum.

After a year or so I started to wonder why Mum would never write or remember my birthday. Aunt Trish said it was the time zones and that she always remembered too late. The reality though soon dawned on me that she was gone, thanks to a brutal comment from a kid at school who'd heard his parents discuss the story in a newspaper. Stories Aunt Trish had protected me from. He told me she was dead, or hiding, or living a new life with lots of sex and drugs. I remember sitting in the Head Teacher's office, waiting for Aunt Trish to come and take me home. I'd hit him and broken his tooth. No one at school mentioned Mum again.

The traffic built and there were delays. I crawled slowly forwards. There was a dark blue Skoda Yeti two cars behind me; it had been there for the last few miles. Two men were in the front seats. My fingers gripped the wheel. Was this the killer? They must know what I looked like by now. Perhaps Trav was right: they were coming after me as well. After a few anxious miles, the Skoda turned off. I knew I couldn't sustain this level of anxiety for ever; I had to press on and resolve all this.

As I got older, I had nightmares. Imagining her in a shallow grave, or sinking beneath dark grey angry waves, calling my name as she slipped to oblivion. Horrible. I'd always put off getting a declaration of presumed death in the hope she was still out there, somewhere, living out her memories and living the dream. Aunt Trish had told me Mum wrote a will once. She had it, but refused to let anyone see it until, and unless, Mum was declared officially dead. But that time would soon come.

The satnav took me through a couple of villages where expensive cars and set-back houses indicated the upmarket areas I was entering. Inviting pubs and boutique shops replaced the usual High Street fair of betting shops and takeaways in the inner suburbs. I was soon on a quiet lane, and there was Chris Latham's house. I slowed down to check the name on the wall as the gate opened, before crawling into the drive, the gravel crunching beneath my wheels and parking next to a large black Audi. Locking my car, I saw him peering out from behind curtains. Just what would he tell me?

As I walked up a well-tended drive, my flat-soled shoes crunched the pebbles, newly washed by a shower which had recently passed. The weather-aged wooden front door opened and the smell of freshly cut flowers in a vase on a table greeted me, but all this would soon contrast with man himself. Chris Latham stood in his hallway with his hands in the pockets of a pair of well-worn, faded blue chinos, a baggy sweatshirt covering his expanding belly.

"Young Catherine." He smiled, offering me his hand. *Young?* "Come in, so nice to see you; you look so much like your mum."

"Thanks Chris," I said, taking his hand; it felt damp, clammy. It wasn't pleasant. I could smell crisps, salt and vinegar, on his breath. I leaned back in case he was going to lunge forward and kiss me. I could also smell the cheap aftershave.

"Thank you for your card and flowers," I said.

"The least I could do. Your mum and Raven were very special," he said, as he beckoned me to follow him along the hallway with its dark patterned wallpaper and thick carpeted floor. I heard a noise and was introduced to his partner, Syd, a Malaysian man in his late thirties. Syd offered to make us tea. We went through the kitchen and out into the comfortably quiet conservatory overlooking the patio and rear garden. There was the gentle hum of traffic in the distance, and above us the shape of planes from Gatwick and Heathrow heading for Europe and beyond. The song of a solitary blackbird brightened the patio, its yellow beak emitting a familiar shrill sound.

"Ah, the last one. There was another one in the garden but the cat got it, they always do, songbirds are so vulnerable. I found the nest; the babies were dead. They'd lost their mother. Do have a seat," he said, pointing to a wicker chair with a sun bleached yellow and white striped cushion.

"Chris," I interjected. "I needed to see you, to help me find out the truth."

"The truth?" he sat down opposite me.

"Was Mum murdered? Like Raven?"

"Wow. Straight in then. Murder's a strong word, Catherine. A very dangerous word, too. I'm a bit shocked, to be honest, hearing that from you."

"So, Chris, tell me about my mum and Raven."

Latham sighed. I watched him spoon two teaspoons of white sugar into his cup before stirring it slowly. *Trust no one* echoed around my head. Chris Latham drank his tea and toyed with a biscuit; he was like a small boy playing a game. After a pause he looked up; his unshaven chin and drained face told a story I couldn't quite read. He kept putting his left hand up to hide one of two scars. The scar above his right eye was, he told me, from a glassing one night when one of his bands went too far and incited locals at a pub gig with some badly timed jokes about them sharing the same father. Chris stepped in to protect his assets, namely the band's singer, but failed to protect his face. It had been headline news the next day: *Punk Show Punch Up Wasn't Funny, Says Manager Who Was Left In Stitches.* There was another scar, but that one he didn't offer to discuss.

I needed to push him about Raven's death.

10. Painted Flesh.

Clouds crossed the sky and dimmed the sun.

"Chris, the police interviewed me about Raven's death. Have they been here too?"

"Two of them, yeah. A man and a woman. Why would I want him dead? He earned me money. Lots of it in the past. Not a motive for murder, is it? Poor old Raven, but the ageing bad boy of punk went out the way he'd have wanted," Chris said. "Exit life stage left, before the end of his set, and with no encore. You know, Raven—or Nigel if you want to use his real name—he was quite nice underneath the exterior shell of rebellious, shocking punk."

"Well I doubt he wanted to exit quite yet."

"*'You know, Betz,'* Raven said to your mum in my office one afternoon when they'd finally crawled out of bed. *'Once we get the platinum albums we could run away. Leave it all, hide out on some Caribbean island; set up that recording studio, spend our days on the beach.'* He was a dreamer, our Raven. Good looking, but sadly not that bright. Great to spend time with, though; he was fun, energetic and, well, he and your mum were perfect as a couple—they even wrote a song together, a ballad. It never got released—far too soft and soppy, they said. Lovely track, though. There's a demo in my drawer, you can have it. They had their moments, she and him, when the press and the fans let them, of course."

"My granny, Betzy's mum, completely lost the plot once

Mum became famous, I was told. My Aunt said she disowned her: is that true? I know she was outrageous but…"

He smiled. "There's outrageous, Catherine, and there's outrageous in 1983. Your granny went into a tailspin when she first knew who your mum was in a relationship with. She burst into my office and demanded I split them up, as if I was some sort of youth club leader. I told her I was their manager, not their controller. Betzy went berserk. She stormed in, demanding your granny never ever come into my office again. They had a stand-up row in front of me, my secretary, and a bunch of lads I was trying to sign. I think those kids wrote a song about it, too.

"*'But darling, boys like Raven Rain only want one thing,'* she screamed, banging the table. *'Yep,'* Betzy told her. *'And it's the same thing that girls like me want.'* I don't think the old girl ever recovered."

"She died six months after Mum disappeared, you know. Granny. She never spoke to me."

"I hadn't heard. Sorry."

"No worries, Chris. I never knew her. So tell me the real story of Mum and those days. I won't be shocked. Really."

"Ha, you haven't heard it all, Catherine. Your mum and Raven had a very public affair, and they wore it on their sleeves. Thank God there were no mobile phones then, although one infamous polaroid picture was splashed across the papers. The one of them being arrested. It was bad. They were busted standing drunk and naked in a fountain in Paris, bottles in hand. It reappeared the other day."

"Yes, I've seen it."

"*'Oi Betz, looks like Inspector Clouseau's here!'* Raven said, according to the press. I can believe it too. The two of them had laughed as the embarrassed young gendarmes recognised them, and asked them to go with them to the police station.

"*'Madame, s'il vous plaît,'* one said, pointing to your mum's clothes discarded by the fountain's edge. They let them off with a warning, plus the promise from me of a few tickets on the door at the Paris venue the bands were both playing. Yup, they really were popular, although it didn't excuse the behaviour. It wasn't great seeing your mum's tits and his bare bum across the papers again."

"Not great for me either," I added.

"They did look good in those days, though. Your mum and Raven, that is, not her tits," he quickly added. "Mind you."

"Okay Chris, I'd prefer not to dwell on that one." I shuddered. I wasn't sure if he was playing for smutty laughs or not, but I was feeling uncomfortable. "Yes, I saw it, but it was Mum, that's what she did, and that's what she was."

"You're a teacher, right?" he asked.

"Yes, at a private girls' boarding school. It suits me. Well it did. I'm currently suspended."

"Oh? Been a naughty girl?"

"No. Because of all this."

"So they know who your mum was."

"They do now, and it's not a great career move having Betzy Blac as your mum and Raven Rain rumoured to be your dad. Did you know he wasn't my father, Chris?"

"I thought he was. But with Betzy… Well, no disrespect, but she was quite a girl and I'm not surprised about your school's reaction. The papers will love it: the daughter of a punk princess turned teacher in a posh girls' school."

"Actually, Chris, I think you're wrong. Betzy Blac was a good role model in many ways. She was a girl who grabbed the headlines, made her mark and made a million pounds as well. Big money in those days. She made you a fair bit too, I bet."

"Oh I earned it. It could have been worse you know. She and the band were offered soft porn shoots in so-called men's magazines, but they always refused and, contrary to popular belief, they never did any serious drugs. Well… A bit of dope, of course, but nothing with needles; unlike some of my bands, who had more track marks than Network Rail."

"Why were they so popular so quickly?"

"Good management, I could say, Catherine; but it was also the time, it was right for Décolleté. Back in 1979 when they started, the music industry was hungry for punks, and girl punks in particular were in high demand: the more shocking the better. This was pre-internet; they were among the first performers to flash on stage and talk dirty to the audience. They loved it. The crowd were mostly teenaged boys—that was their fan base—and a randy punk girl singer with a wet, braless, tight top on stage licking a vibrator and talking about sex sent them wild."

I shifted in my seat. This was my mum he was talking about. My mum who tucked me up in bed and read me stories about teddy bears. I wondered how much he encouraged her and the band to behave like this so he could exploit their sexuality to make money. I watched him pause to eat another biscuit, the crumbs dropping down his shirt.

"So it all made them a magnet for the red top tabloids and the Sundays. Those papers were desperate to snatch pictures of a drunk punk star slumped in a corner, nipples or knickers on show. We knew that, and we fed them. The band's drummer, Caroline, AKA Cassie Crack, was always ready to pose."

How ready, or how much did he push her to pose? I wondered. I had to move this on.

"So, Décolleté went on tour a few years after they formed, didn't they?"

"Yes. I found them at a university gig, where they were a support act. I got them signed to Trash Puke Records, a big label in those days. It was run then, and still is, by Robbi Rat Boy Romero."

"Who?" I asked, taken aback.

"Robbi Romero. The 'Rat Boy' bit comes from when he was a child actor in a TV series in the '70s. He played a boy who had a pet rat with superpowers that helped him solve crimes. His character was the Rat Boy, and it stuck. I think he likes it."

"And is he?" I asked. "A rat?"

"No. He's successful and… driven, I think is the word." He

smiled. "He could also recognise talent and gave them a record deal. The band charted twice in a month. Their second single, *Pink Bra Bust Up!*, went straight to number one. I've got the gold disc of it on the wall in my office; you should see it before you go. God, doing Top of the Pops on TV was a nightmare. I still remember it today. I was watching in the studio control gallery during the recording of the show; they filmed it in the afternoon, a few hours before it went to air. Well, Suzi Scums, the guitarist, and Cassie Crack the drummer—where did these names come from, hey?"

"I've often wondered that."

"Well, me actually! I made them up." I wasn't surprised at hearing that. "Well, Suzi and Cassie lifted their t-shirts to reveal pink bras. Except it wasn't their bras: it was their bare boobs painted pink."

"Clever," I said, wondering if it was their idea.

"Yes and no. The recording was stopped, and even though they were number one in the charts, the producer threatened to just play the track over the programme's end credits unless the girls behaved. Suzi and Cassie then posed pink and topless for the papers the next day; after of course, I made sure the story got out and arranged for the press to meet them. The group's reputation as bad girls just grew and grew. Sure, I stoked it up; sorry, but it was my job. It was great for the sales of records and gig tickets, it's how the biz worked."

Or how he wanted to work it. I smiled, trying to hide my growing uneasiness about what I was being told. Syd walked in carrying a tray of nibbles and a bottle of wine with two glasses.

"Ah, time for a glass. Fancy one?" said Chris. "It's rather nice," he grinned.

"Oh that's kind, but not for me. I've got to drive back, thanks."

"Well excuse me if I indulge, Catherine," he said, pouring a large glass and then taking two mouthfuls and a handful of Bombay mix before carrying on.

"Then came the infamous tour with the Scented Slugs, and so your mum's band were nicknamed the Scented Slags after a much-exaggerated story about a so-called orgy after the opening night. Well, no smoke without fire, and to be honest both bands were in the same room and…well… they were all out of their heads. The hotel staff asked me to go in with them to quieten it down. We were wide mouthed at what we saw when we opened the door. I don't remember that much, except they were all naked. I went back in the morning to find your mum cuddling Raven. The room stank of smoke, stale beer and stale bodies, it was pretty rancid. Someone really had thrown a TV set out of the window too, just like in the movies. I had to bribe the hotel manager with cash to keep that one quiet. Nudity was good publicity, but vandalism wasn't."

"Did you come up with the 'slags' line, Chris?

"Ha, busted! Well, it did sound good, and it did make all the tabloids, and they weren't exactly innocent."

"But you didn't find a derogatory name for the boys in the Slugs then?"

"That's how it works, Catherine; always has. The audience like a bad girl."

Did I really want this to carry on? I had to keep pushing. "So, the tour itself?"

"Oh yes. What a tour! It was a huge success, not least because of the publicity. Local moral crusaders tried to get the show banned in their towns, which of course led to extra nights being shoehorned into the schedule as more venues wanted to put the bands on. You see, the audience loves bad girls! It was a PR dream. We sold out everywhere, there were queues around the block and the records were high in the charts. No one would do live interviews with them in case they said something outrageous, which of course they always did, because they knew it would be reported, boosting the publicity even more.

"Betzy's mum was mortified. Her demure WI friends were all very shocked at what her nice little girl had become. The sad thing is, she could never get that it was just an act, and Betzy was still the nice little girl underneath the wild hair and black eyeliner spread across her face like war paint. She was playing at being a bad girl. The aggressive, angry voice and the continual sex talk were for show.

"But then, Betzy was no angel. Sorry, kid, your mum was no choirgirl. The tattoos were fake, as were the some of the rumours we deliberately spread about the band. They weren't bisexual; it was just a story put out by me to feed the constant innuendo and probing questions by desperate young male reporters. Betzy and the girls romping naked after a gig fuelled many a teen boy's fantasy, and some teen girls too. They just wanted to have fun and enjoy the limelight while they could, and make money of course, which they did, and they spent it as well. I said it wouldn't last and they needed to save as much as they could, but hiring rollers and bathing in champagne was just so rock and roll they couldn't resist it. Do you know your mum once chartered a private jet to go to Paris, just for lunch?"

"And I think twice about booking a taxi," I said as he paused to empty his glass.

"It didn't last. They were knackered. We toured as much as we could. She was trying to write new material but never had the energy or the time. The stage show exhausted her. It wasn't helped by the booze and the drugs of course. Artists today do exercise, they have personal trainers, they watch their diets, do gym. Not then. It was just all massive excess."

"But there must have been some trigger? Some reason for her to walk out at the end of the '84 tour?" I said, looking across the lawn to see a freshly killed blackbird lying on the grass, its song pointlessly silenced forever.

"Yes," he replied, hugging his glass. "There was."

11. Blackbird

Chris Latham paused and took a drink while staring out of the window. I could see his knuckles tighten on the arm of the chair as he shifted uncomfortably on the seat. He slowly turned back towards me but his eyes looked down. Outside a cat prowled passed.

"Your mum stopped being Betzy Blac and the band broke up. She walked away. It was after a gig, the end of an exhausting tour. I think she'd just had enough. She was totally burnt out. She left Betzy backstage."

"What do you mean?" I asked, puzzled.

"She binned the stage clothes in the dressing room, had the black dye taken out of her hair the next day, removed the piercings and changed her image entirely. Not even the other girls would have recognised her in the street."

"Why?" This seemed so unlike the Mum I remembered. Syd popped his head around the door and then went away.

"She said they'd had a good run. You could see it coming. She walked out on Raven; she dumped him after a major row and she wanted a new life. She'd had enough."

"Okay," I said thoughtfully, trying to take it all in. Aunt Trish had told me Mum had had a blazing row with Raven, and she'd just had enough. A similar story, but now even hearing it again, it just didn't ring true. Something inside me said *keep digging*. Latham was looking down, fiddling with the nail on his left index finger. He cleared his throat twice, then swallowed before carrying on.

"Two of the girls kept going and joined Raven and a couple of the Slugs to continue to tour and play her songs for a year, but the rest of the girls didn't want to go on without her. They got together a year or so ago and played in a punk revival show at a holiday camp. Sarah did the vocals: not very well but she tried. I went along as three of my old acts were performing there. Happy days, but it wasn't the same."

"What else exactly happened on that wild night, Chris?"

He went quiet and looked down. There was something he wouldn't say.

"I'm…not sure, Cath." But I knew he was. He knew exactly why Mum walked away. "It was the row with Raven; I think Raven may have hit her."

Really? But everything I'd seen and read about Raven Rain was that he was too stoned to swat a fly most of the time, especially after a gig. Hit Mum? It didn't make sense. I wasn't convinced.

"I'm going to try to meet Sarah from Mum's old band," I said.

"She's not the same woman as she was then," he said swiftly.

"What do you mean?" I asked.

"Well, she was a bit of a wild cat was Suzi Scums, our Sarah. I don't know how she is now or how she'll react. She's an old has-been. I'm not sure how much she'll want to—or be able to—help you." He paused, then steered the subject away from Sarah. "You know there's something of Betzy in you. Have you ever thought of going into the biz?"

"It's not going to happen," I smiled, taken aback by his compliment. "I studied drama at university, I even went to stage lessons at weekends as a kid. Of course I played at being a pop star in front of the mirror, lots of kids do, except I was playing at being my Mum."

"So do it!" he said, reaching for another biscuit.

"I don't have the confidence. Besides, it's too late now. I did a post grad teaching course to get a proper job, as Aunt Trish would say, and I now teach younger hopefuls to act, sing and dance." I smiled.

"It's never too late, Cath. Not with your heritage." Chris broke the biscuit in two and pushed a piece into his mouth, licking crumbs from his fat fingers.

"Chris," I said firmly. "Is my mother alive or dead?"

He paused but, before he could answer, Syd, brought some more tea and offered me lunch.

"Oh, no thanks," I smiled politely. "I have to get back," I lied. Realising time was almost up, I tried again. "So Chris, where is she? Where's Betzy Blac? Where's my Mum?"

"I don't where she is, Cath, or if she's dead or alive."

"What do you know about her disappearance?" I pushed.

"Not much. Oh, believe me, I wish I did. I've had the police, the tax office, her band, fans, journalists and others knocking on my door asking for answers too, almost every year since her disappearance. Your Aunt Trish was one of them, and so was Raven Rain."

"You must know something?"

"She went off to stay with a friend: Judy. She was her best friend at school. They stayed in a rented holiday let on Applecross, a place called… Tuaig I think. A handful of houses near to the beach and a good place to hide out. I'm not sure what happened but, out of the blue, I had a message from the record label. From Robbi. He told me Betzy had told him she was going to the States in search of stimulation for new material. She would go to America, to hideout and write a new album."

"Why so suddenly? Why did she go without her passport? How did she travel?" I asked, and wondered again: *Why didn't she take me with her?*

Chris picked up his cup and paused. "Cath, I don't know. Some say she flew from Glasgow, others that she boarded a yacht and sailed across the Atlantic. I never heard from her again. I hired a private detective in the States to track her down, but he turned up nothing. There was no sign of her going through immigration there. It's possible she crossed the Atlantic on that boat and landed in some small town on the east coast and slipped in, but there's been no trace of her since then."

"People must have looked for her," I said. I knew they had, but I often wondered why Aunt Trish had been so happy to just accept Mum was gone. I drank my tea in small sips.

"Sure, people have looked for her. There are two pretty dogged journalists who've done stories about her disappearance. One of them, Jez Deopham, was a pain in the arse when Betzy was around. He wrote for *Tomorrow's Hits Today!*: a music magazine that was big at the time. It's closed now. It did reviews of gigs and records, bands and people. He was a bit of a stalker of Betzy. Well, a big stalker in fact."

"Stalker?" I'd never known Mum had a stalker. Could he be her killer? Did he abduct her? I noticed Syd hovering around just outside. I felt uncomfortable.

"He did a few interviews with her and tried it on, you know. I saw him in action in my office in London. He would start asking her music stuff and then move on to intimate questions and getting really creepy. One night he wanted a dressing room chat at the start of a tour. Betzy agreed but he was all over her, tried to kiss her. Sarah and Caroline literally threw him out. He broke his wrist when he landed; well, they were pretty strong in those days. Caroline in particular, drummers usually are. So Jez wrote a really harsh review in the next edition, probably one-handed, serves him right. He was angry. It cost us a few tickets. He was obsessed with her; we had to get a restraining order banning him from approaching her. She was getting scared of him, a weirdo. Unpredictable."

"What was his take on Mum's disappearance?" I asked, looking at the biscuits but deciding against having one as I watched a large bluebottle land on the plate. The house was superficially clean; but look in the corners, look around the edges and it was grubby.

"Suicide. Pressure of the demands for a new single, new album, another tour, et cetera, plus the effects of drugs and drink."

"Suicide only works if there's a body or a note," I said.

"That part of Scotland is wild, Cath. The waters are fast moving, the tide range is big and the seas are deep. A body could vanish pretty quickly."

"So Mum could have been murdered?"

"It's a possibility, but I have no clues as to who would want to kill her. She may have been a punk wildcat, but she had no real enemies. No, there's nothing but speculation I'm afraid. It's a mystery and is likely to remain one, like the Marie Celeste."

No. I wasn't having this; I wasn't going to let it rest even if he was.

"Someone must know more. Who did security at those gigs?"

Chris Latham's face dropped, his eyes narrowed and his left had formed a fist. "Well, I doubt that's of any importance, but it was the Bleak Souls."

"The Bleak Souls?"

"Ummm. Don't say their name too loudly, they might hear." I could tell he was very wary of them, even now. "They're great if they're on your side, but shit if they're not."

"So who are they?"

"They're a breakaway group of bikers, all leather, studs and choppers. Linked with the Hell's Angels." Chris's gaze dropped again. "They did security in the early days at gigs, but sometimes they went for the fights, and they started them. Their leader was terrifying. Death Wish Danny: Daniel Fearon. He went to prison after killing two of his own members and maiming another. Maybe she ran off with one of them? Maybe they killed her? It's all guesswork and speculation, Cath."

"Why would they have harmed Mum?"

"You tell me. They were big fans of the Scented Slugs. If anyone upset Raven or the Slugs, then they upset them, and Betzy dumped Raven, so... He was upset. You work it out, but hey I'm not ever going to point a finger at what's left of The Bleak Souls. They may be about to get their pensions and could be as soft a quilted bog roll by now, but I'd hate to try find out, and I strongly advise you to keep well away from them as well. Seriously, they come with a very, very big health warning." Chris Latham seemed to shrink in his chair; even saying the name of this gang was enough to instil fear.

"Even these days? They must be much older now?"

"Even at any age."

"Okay, but what about this journalist? Can you spell his name for me please?"

"Jez Deopham. D, e, o, p, h, a, m."

"Where's he now?"

"You're serious, aren't you? You're going to try and talk to these people." Chris was worried.

"If Raven's dead, and Betzy hasn't come back or been in touch, then her body's either in America, Scotland, or maybe even somewhere in between. Who said she'd disappeared? Who was the last person to see her alive? I need to know, Chris, and I have to find out."

Chris Latham took a deep breath and put down his cup. "The holiday cottage owner turned up to clean, thinking they'd left but found the woman she'd been with: Judy, she was a complete wreck in some sort of trance from what I heard. All she said was Betzy had gone. This was before mobiles and the internet, Cath; it was easier to disappear and harder to trace people and calls in those days."

"Aunt Trish will have tried to find her," I said, searching for answers.

"Yes your aunt came to see me. She told me she'd called the police but they concluded she'd just gone AWOL. You are allowed to disappear, though, if you're an adult."

"Allowed to, yes, but unlikely to if you have a seven-year-old daughter without letting someone know you're safe." I couldn't help raising my voice, the frustration and sadness coming out. "Chris, does DD mean anything to you? Could it refer to this Death Wish Danny?"

"DD?" he repeated the letters.

"I had a mysterious text, just signed DD."

"DD? Nope. It's not Death Wish Danny, for sure. He'd never call himself 'Death Wish'; that was a name given to him by others. He hated it. Believe me, you'd never call him that to his face, not if you wanted to keep yours."

"So where can I find Death Wish Danny and Jez Deopham?"

"Don't," he said firmly, banging his mug down on the wooden table.

"I need to know," I repeated. "Believe me, you don't contact the Bleak Souls, they contact you. And if they do, then just run. As for Jez Deopham, I hear he does a spot on an online radio station: you know, no listeners but old guys playing the DJs they wish they'd been. If you're looking for Jez, that's where you'll find him, but I'd keep well away. There's no proof he was involved in your mother's disappearance."

"Thanks Chris."

"Cath…"

"Yes?"

"Please… Please, just don't go near the Bleak Souls."

I said goodbye and turned to leave. As I did he held my shoulder.

"Cath, don't delve too much into Betzy's disappearance. Leave your mother to hide or rest in peace wherever she is. And really, just don't go looking for the Bleak Souls."

"Well, I'm going to have to solve this mystery, even if it kills me."

"That's what worries me, Cath. It probably will."

12. SUZi SCUMS

I drove away with two theories in my head, theories I'd mused over for years. Murder and suicide. Murder seemed the most likely. Suicide was the ultimate in my being abandoned. Wasn't I enough to make Mum want to live?

It wasn't healthy for me to dwell on it. I pulled up outside a small café; I really needed a coffee and a sandwich after meeting Chris Latham. I sat down at a table near the back of the room away from the window. I reached into my bag and pulled out the two photos which I always carried of Mum. There she was, in her late teens and early twenties, her face full of confidence and dreams, dressed ready to go on stage. Black hair, heavy eye make-up, deep red lips, her trademark jacket and her dainty hands with black nail varnish. A sign of the times.

The other was the last one I had before she left. She was looking back at me while leaning over a barrier beside a river. She was wearing jeans and a dull cream cotton top, very plain in comparison with the Betzy she had been. She was smiling, but beyond the smile I could now detect a haunted look, a sense of regret, something I just couldn't make out, as if she was sending me a message from then to now.

I smiled at the girl behind the counter and asked for a refill. As I looked at Mum's face, frozen in time, one of her songs came on the radio. *Two Lovers in One Night*, an anthem for the sexually adventurous. It had charted in late 1982, and they were still playing it all these years later. Enduring I guess, like the mystery of where she was.

I stared at my cappuccino, the white aerated milk swirling slowly. My phone rang. It was Aunt Trish. The second conversation in a few days; that was unusual, we usually chatted no more than once a month. She asked if I was okay, and not being harassed by journalists. I said I was fine and could handle it; most of the interest had waned as I had little to say, but I knew it was all bubbling beneath the surface. Like me, people were digging for stories about the old days.

"Aunt Trish, are you sure you don't know anyone called DD?"

"No," she replied thoughtfully, adding, "just be careful."

"Careful of who?"

"Just be careful, Catherine. If Raven Rain was murdered, and that's what they're saying… Well, who knows who the killer is, or who she might go after next."

"She? Why she?"

"Oh, I meant he."

"Aunt Trish, I've just met Chris Latham." There was silence. "Hello?"

"Sorry. Yes, I've met him. Motivated by money, I seem to remember."

"He thinks Mum committed suicide."

"I know he does. A lot of people do. You know I'd have told you if I believed that. Truth is, Catherine, I really don't know. I just hope. Hope one day she'll just come home."

"Do you know anything about Jez Deopham or the Bleak Souls?"

"Oh him. I know that journalist is a pain in the backside. Your poor mum had to get a court order stopping him from hassling her. Damn pest."

"So I hear."

"As for those bikers, I don't like them. Rough lot, dirty too. Their leader went to jail, you know. Danny someone. Bad lot. Why do you ask?"

"Because they might know what happened to Mum."

"If they do, I doubt they'd tell you. Why would they? Look I know you want to know what happened to your mother, anyone would, but you can't bring her back and you could find yourself in trouble if you go around digging up the past."

"Everyone keeps telling me to back off and leave things be," I said, frustrated.

"For a good reason," she replied. "I didn't bring you up for you to disappear too."

"Thanks, Aunt Trish. I'll be careful. Love you." I said, ending the call. Despite her and Chris Latham's warnings about The Bleak Souls, I just had to find out if they could throw any light on that last night of the '84 tour when Mum walked out. Was Chris Latham's story true? Did Raven really hit her?

I typed *The Bleak Souls* into the internet search bar on my phone. I found references to old news stories about Death Wish Danny going to prison but no contact details. They seemed to have disappeared. I found a forum for motorbike enthusiasts with a few references to old rockers and Hell's Angels, so I posted a message saying I wanted to talk to them if anyone knew where they were. I hoped I'd get an email or a number, so I could at least make contact; I wasn't intending to actually meet them.

Someone I did want to meet was Sarah: Mum's guitarist also known as Suzi Scums who'd sent me flowers after Raven's death. I texted the number Trav had given me. It didn't take long to get a reply. As I got back in the car a text found my phone.

"Hi free tomorrow? Sarah x"

"Yes," I replied. *"Where are u? Cath."*

Her address came back straight away. She seemed keen. I wondered why.

*

The next day, I drove out of Chestnut Close as Eileen's curtains twitched, watching me leave. I headed to Lewes, just outside Brighton on the south coast. I was meeting Sarah James, AKA

Suzi Scums, the infamous lead guitarist with Décolleté.

Sarah lived in a cute Georgian terrace on a beautiful little crescent close to the centre of town. A watery sun poked through thin but gathering clouds as I rang the doorbell on the pastel painted door with trepidation. Who would be on the other side? A quiet, stay-at-home fifty-something year old woman, or a mad punk rocker? Was Chris Latham right? Could she be unstable? Unpredictable? Dangerous?

The brass button was stiff but relented as I pushed hard. A dull buzzer sounded from behind the door. A bolt was drawn across and the door opened. The woman who stood there wasn't the one I'd seen in photos, on posters or in videos; that woman was a real wild rock guitarist. The woman in front of me was more muted, although she was by no means your average fifty-something. She had grey hair streaked with red, an expensive top hanging carefully over a rough cheap t-shirt with torn jeans and bright red shoes. A guitar shaped broach was pinned to her top. Had she dressed like this for my benefit, or did she always wear this sort of stuff? She seemed pleased I'd come to see her. Her smile broadened as she shook her head and opened her arms.

"Shit! I've seen a ghost! Sorry; but oh wow, you're so like your mum."

"Hi, I'm Cath."

"I'm Sarah, but you can call me Suzi if it helps." She smiled. "Sorry, but Betz was very touchy feely and so am I." She reached out her arms towards me.

"I know there's a resemblance, but surely not that much?" I said, surprised. "Great to meet you too. I know you and Mum were close."

Sarah hugged me. "Cath, you're the nearest I've got to her in decades." She pulled back and just stared at me, holding my shoulders, squeezing them, rather too tightly for someone I'd just met.

I was suddenly aware of a large panting dog beside me, his fur brushing my legs. "Oh don't mind him, he's harmless," she said as the large, lumbering Alsatian sniffed my hand while wagging its long, hairy tail.

"Glad to hear it," I laughed nervously. "Thanks for seeing me. Trav Brennon gave me your number."

"No worries, Cath. I was going to contact you myself. You want to know more about your mum, hey? Don't we all. Miss the bitch… And I'm being nice by the way; that's how we talked to each other, bitch, slag, cow, slut, but they were all terms of endearment. It's okay, you can leave your shoes on."

"Are you sure?"

"Tiled floors so I mop them a lot, especially with the dog." From running her fingers rapidly up and down a fretboard on stage to mopping floors: how life had changed, I thought, looking at the woman who used to be Suzi Scums.

"It's a lovely house; nice area too," I said.

"When I moved here and people knew who I was, they were terrified. I even covered my tats up." She pulled down her top, revealing a shoulder sporting a large, not very well executed, tattoo of two crossed guitars. She pointed to the one on her wrist: a snake around a guitar neck. "Cool, hey? Well, it was back then. I wonder how I'll feel about in in another twenty years!" She laughed. "Come through," she beckoned. "All this— the town, the street, the house—it's as far away from punk as a black-tie Tory dinner. I've been here now for nearly fifteen years. Hey, come through to the kitchen and I'll make some coffee. Is that okay?"

"Sounds great, Sarah… or Suzi? What do I call you? Which do you prefer?"

"Both and either. Suzi morphed back into Sarah once the band stopped, but she's still there, waiting to get out."

"Coffee would be great, thanks," I smiled, still not knowing which name to address her by. I watched as she filled the kettle and made the drinks. Looking around the kitchen I was immediately drawn to a framed front page of a newspaper on the wall. A picture of Décolleté in full flow on stage, coloured smoke behind them, low light and Mum in front, hands grasping a mic, her left breast almost out of her vest top, her nipple visible and a pained look on her face as she pushed out the lyrics. The headline read: *Décolleté Dirt! Suzi Scums on Betzy's Blac's Boozy Binges!*

Sarah noticed me looking at it. "Oh, that. Totally fabricated, your mum didn't actually drink that much—well most of the time. That was another Chris Latham false news story; he was famed for them."

"Is there a Mr or Mrs Suzi here, too?" I asked tentatively, looking around for signs of a partner.

"No. I don't have a partner, but it's not for the lack of trying," Sarah said as she put a mug in front of me. "But as soon as men hear about Décolleté and that I used to be Suzi Scums, they change. Some of them are frightened off. It's sad, but somehow she's always there as far as they're concerned; and of course, some guys stay because it's Suzi they want to go to bed with, not Sarah. I may have performed songs with very explicit lyrics, but I don't necessarily want to act them out, thank you very much."

"When I was growing up, people treated me differently because of Mum's songs."

"Tell me about it. It's not just men who are scared off, either. I joined a book club a year or so back. One night we were discussing characters and I told them who I used to be. You could see them look at each other, eyebrows raised. It was as if I was about to spit on the floor, break out the drugs, rip my clothes off and shag their husbands. Now I'm Sarah. Why can't they let me be Sarah? I've had offers from women too, but... I'm not. You know what I mean. I was so shocked to hear Raven died," Sarah said, pouring boiling water into a cafetiere. "Nice guy underneath it all. He loved your mum you know. Worshipped her. I'm sure they would have married if she'd stayed with him."

I felt a pang of wishful thinking. If only they had, how different their and my life might have been.

"Yes, I was shocked too," I said.

"This new press interest after Raven's death has made me think about the old days again. I kind of think, if I can't throw off the ghost of Suzi Scums, then maybe I should be her again. I spoke to the others yesterday."

"The others? Décolleté?"

"Yes. Milk? I've got soya if you prefer?"

"Oh, either is okay, thanks," I smiled. Soya? Suzi Scums drinks soya milk? A bit different from the stuff she used to swill down in the old days. I looked around her kitchen and out into a leafy secluded rear garden beyond. There was a bronze statue of Jimi Hendrix on the lawn.

"Love your statue!" I said amazed.

"It's incredible what you spend money on when you suddenly have lots of it and you think it'll never stop coming. Jimi was a hero."

"It's quite a statement." I'd never seen a statue like it in a domestic garden.

"Someone tried to tempt me out of retirement only last year. They suggested I go back on stage for a tour, called *Remember the Punks and Power Pop!* They were offering to put together a session band, so a few dusty, ageing former frontmen and front-girls could go out and do their top five songs, to celebrate the magic of those days. It was after we did a holiday camp weekend."

A holiday camp weekend? How the mighty have fallen I thought. Back in Décolleté's heyday a holiday camp would have been the last place they'd have chosen to play.

"Yes, I read about that weekend," I said, smiling. "My Aunt Trish, Mum's sister, sent me a cutting she'd seen in a Sunday paper. It must have been fun."

"Yeah, maybe, but it wasn't the same without your mum. I sang—not very well, I have to say. Never could sing. Chris Latham's always asking us to re-form, but we'd never find anyone to replace Betzy."

"But if she came back? If my mum turned up alive?"

"That would be amazing. I'd certainly give it a lot of thought;

it would be hard to resist! I think I'd need a contract rider saying I had to be in bed by ten thirty, though, and I'd want fruit juice and green tea in my dressing room, not alcohol and dope like the old days! I couldn't put my body through all that again. Just playing my old red Fender would be enough. It sounds more appealing the more I talk about it. It's hard to get it out of your system, you know: once you've been there and you know the fans want you back."

"Try it," I suggested.

"Well if we had a decent Betzy lookalike." Sarah stopped and stared at me. A slow smile crept over her lips. "Hey… Cath, can you sing?"

"Me? Sing? Well, a bit I guess. Why?"

"You could pass for Betzy Blac, you know."

"Me? No." I laughed, embarrassed. "Me being Mum, on stage, in front of people? Don't be silly." She couldn't be serious.

"I'm not being silly. I'm serious," she replied.

"I studied and I teach drama," I said. "But I don't have the confidence to perform, myself."

"I bet you know all the songs off by heart, and you look very similar to your mum."

"I know them, yeah. It's a bit embarrassing to admit, but I spent my childhood pretending to be her."

"So you must be good at it."

"I doubt it. There's singing in front of a mirror with a hairbrush, and there's singing on stage. It's a bit different. People, like you, Mum and Raven were naturals. When did you last see Raven?" I asked, drinking my coffee.

"It was at that holiday camp gig. He turned up with Sacha to see some of the Scented Slugs. They were playing with Dead Reg—remember him? He supported us on a few tours. Burnt out really, but Reg somehow staggered through a set list, even though he had to have the lyrics in front of him on an iPad. No, you wouldn't know of him, you're far too young. Raven didn't perform, he just came backstage and said hello."

"I still can't believe he's dead. And Sacha," I said, putting down my mug.

"Yes. Sacha was nice. They were very much in love. She was a lot younger than him of course, but they made a great couple. She told me she'd been helping Raven write this book about those days. *Raven Rain Remembers—The Men Who Perverted Punk*. Well that was the working title. A bit long if you ask me."

"And what revelations does it have about my mum?"

"I don't know, Cath. I didn't discuss it with either of them."

"It must mention what happened that night she walked out of the band."

"Woah. You sound like a cop now, Cath."

"Not surprising; I've been interviewed by them, twice in a week. I was arrested for Sacha's murder. Released, though, otherwise I wouldn't be here."

"What? Arrested? That's grim. Bastards, you don't need that."

"I found Sacha's body, as I said, and… Well, it's a long story, but I was a prime suspect for twenty-four hours. Totally cleared now, though. Although I still think they might have me as a possible suspect for Raven's death."

"No. I saw your name in some of the reports, but you? A killer? Never. Even I can tell you're incapable of murder, and I've only just met you."

"Sarah, what happened on that night Mum walked out?"

There was silence. Sarah looked down and then looked up again, a hint of tears in her eyes. She shook her head slowly.

"I wish she hadn't walked away. I wish… Well, I wish a lot of things, Cath."

13. BOSS HOGG S

A gold disc of one of the many Décolleté hits was in a frame above the fridge. As Sarah got up to refill her coffee mug from a cafetière, I went for a closer look.

"That one's for *Tangled Sheets and Twisted Hearts*, one of the few Betzy and I wrote together. It was originally going to be the B-side for *Two Lovers in One Night*, but Robbie the Rat Boy at the record company put it out in its own right. Mind you, in those days, fans bought them sound unheard, just pre-ordered everything we released. Hard to believe it now. It helped pay for this, the house, and to be fair I haven't had to work for a living."

We sat down.

"You asked about the last night. Hey, you have to understand, my memories of that tour are faded and shrouded in a haze of dope, speed and booze. There are only really fragments of memory of that evening and the days before and after. It was the end of the band and I've tried to blank it out. We were at the top of our game, playing to tens of thousands, selling in the millions, then Betzy just pulled the plug." Her throat was getting red. It was either a hot flush or a nervous reaction like those that one or two of my pupils had: it came up when they were under stress. I plunked for the latter.

"Why did she just pull the plug?" I asked.

"Those bastards."

"Sarah, it's important to me. I think Mum was probably murdered. I think Raven was definitely murdered."

"Well. You're not the only one, Cath. Caroline—Cassie—has that theory too. She rang me the day after Raven died."

"Do you know anyone called Brad?"

"Nope, never heard of him. Why? Should I?"

"Just a lead, and DD?"

"DD? No, nothing. Look I'd like to help if I can," she said, leaning forwards, giving me a firm friendly smile. I found myself trusting her; Sarah could be quite soft, if Suzi let her be.

"I think Raven was killed because there's some inflammatory info in the book."

"You might be right, Cath. Unless Sacha thought it best to leave the past alone and destroyed it?"

"No. She told me as much. Also that book could have earned them a fortune. Besides, Sacha knew how important it was to Raven."

"But who would have been worried by what Raven could have written?" I asked.

"Lots of people have secrets from those days that they want to stay hidden. There's a guy who runs a successful chain of burger bars. He was the bass player in Stolen Ashtrays—they were a punk metal cross over, a bit heavy and violent, even for me. Not many people know that, and he's got a very grubby secret just waiting to be exposed."

I wondered what else was waiting to be exposed. Sarah was gripping her mug with both hands, her arms on the table. She lowered her voice almost to a whisper.

"Look, Cath, there are some seriously heavy bastards out there. You need to be careful if you start poking around."

"So Chris Latham said," I replied.

Sarah nodded. "I get together with the girls in a pub in Hoxton. You know, near Spitalfields in London?"

"Of course, yes."

"We meet once a month. Caroline, me, Rochelle—AKA Rocky—and Stephanie, better known to you as Stephy Stiffs. If you're able to join us one night, the girls would love to meet

you. We all loved your mum, Cath. We miss the bitch so much."
She smiled and reached across the table to take both my hands in
hers. I was holding the hands of a guitar legend, one of the few
female guitarists from that era to have won awards.

"I can believe that, Sarah." And I did.

"Hey, we may look mean and scratchy in those photos and
videos, but beneath the image we're all as soft as putty and
emotional wrecks. Punk and pop almost destroyed us. Maybe it
really did. It destroyed your mum"

"Or someone connected with it did. But you survived." I
smiled, pulling my hands free gently.

"At a price. I've taken sleeping pills for years. Better than the
nightmares, and better than what I used to take."

"If you help me find out what happened to Mum, then the
nightmares might stop. I think that would help both of us,
Sarah."

"Maybe it would. So how do you fancy meeting the girls?"
she asked. I looked up on the wall to see them all in their youth,
Mum beside them, guitars in hands, smiling to the camera. A
publicity picture to sell the Greatest Hits album released after
Mum walked out.

"I'd like that, yes," I replied. "It was good to meet Travis
Brennon. Raven's son"

"I wondered when that would come out," she said.

"You knew he was Raven's son?"

"There are lots of secrets in rock n roll, Cath."

"Like Raven not being my dad."

"I knew that, too. But before you ask: no, I don't know who
your dad is."

"Do you know the Bleak Souls?" I asked.

"Oh yes." Her eyes widened. I saw her hands form into fists.
"And if you see them just across the road, walk the other way.
Don't make eye contact. They're probably old and knackered
now, but they're seriously heavy and really bad news."

"That's what Chris Latham said."

"With good reason. They're okay if they're on your side, but fuck: God help you if they're not. Avoid them, really, Cath. Just keep away. They're called the Bleak Souls for a reason."

"Do you know them?"

"Not anymore. Look, at one time they were on our side, sort of guardian angels, doing security and stuff at gigs but… Well, when we needed them the most they'd buggered off, they let us down. Bad memories. I need to move on."

I knew I couldn't push her anymore.

"Did Mum stay in touch after she walked out of the band?" I asked.

"After she walked? No. No calls, no visits."

"I'm stuck, Sarah. Stuck wondering if she killed herself, if she was murdered, or if she could somehow still be out there."

"Yeah, you're not the only one. But the longer it goes on, the more likely it is she's dead." Sarah pursed her lips and looked down.

I stood up. She joined me and we hugged. It's what Mum would have done had she been there. As she opened the door to let me out, we agreed to meet in Hoxton with the remaining members of Décolleté in a couple of days.

"Thanks for the coffee and the chat," I said. It had been good to meet my mum's old friend, and I knew Suzi Scums was still there somewhere, hiding behind this quiet façade of normality in gentile suburbia.

"Pleasure's mine, Cath. You take care now, hey?"

"Of course. See you in Hoxton," I said as I got into the car. She waved goodbye and watched as I closed the door. As I set the satnav to home I saw her in the window, intently talking on the phone.

*

On the way home I stopped for petrol just before I turned onto the M25. I paid for the fuel and walked across the forecourt to my car. A text arrived. I stopped and pulled out my phone.

"Boss Hogg's Café, there's only one. Be alone. tomorrow. 7pm. The Bleak Souls. Ride to Live, Live to Die." As I stared at my phone it rang.

"Trav! Hi, how are you?" I asked.

"Pretty fine. Awesome shoot for my new album cover, they got me leaning over a bridge looking wistfully at a flowing river. The river's going to have names in it, you know, for the album title, and the single I'm releasing with it, *Names Flowing By*. How about you? Did you meet Sarah, or Suzi Scums?"

"Sarah, I guess. Although Suzi was in there waiting to come out. I've had a message from the bikers. You know the ones who provided security at gigs?"

"Woah, Cath. Now hold on, you need help with this one. I'll come too."

"No Trav. The text said come alone."

"You're not that naïve, Cath, surely." He sounded anxious.

"It's just a meeting in a café. There'll be people there, in public. Probably CCTV."

"But Cath—"

"It's in Kent, Trav; it's not the outback or deepest-wherever-you-can-think-of in the States. It's a café, and it's during the day. Sure I'm nervous, but I'll have my phone and it's just a meeting."

"Exactly who are you meeting?" he asked.

"I don't know, probably some seventy-year-old former biker, probably on a mobility scooter instead of a Harley these days. Look, I'd hardly go there if I wasn't sure."

"They have a reputation, Cath. At least text me the details, yeah?"

"Trav, I want to do this alone. If they turn up and you're there, they'll just leave again. I think they're probably more scared than I am."

Trav wasn't convinced and I had to admit, neither was I. I promised him I'd keep him updated.

*

Boss Hogg's café was on the old road to Eight Oaks, now bypassed by the motorway. According to the internet it was once a favourite haunt with bikers and was famous for punch-ups. I drove there with Sarah's warning playing on repeat in my head and DD's text still on my phone. Gingerly, I pulled into the near empty car park, its tarmac long since broken and cracked. Grass grew in odd patches and large oil stains discoloured the ground. There were two other cars there, so I felt safe. Almost.

The café was straight out of the seventies. As I walked in I was hit by the smell of grease and cooking burgers. It was sickly and unclean. The floor was old; cracked tiles that were as out of date as the food in the freezer. Their checked patterns felt sticky under my feet. There was brash red décor, faded washed out prints of unappetising meals, and a menu that comprised an assortment of dishes involving chips, eggs and meat. On the walls were faded pictures of bikers, repro ads for motorbikes, and a framed, signed cover of a Scented Slugs album.

Behind the bar stood a greasy-looking, fat, balding guy in his sixties. Long straggly bits of what was left of his hair caressed his wide shoulders. He wore a sleeveless t-shirt covered in marks. Long curly hairs crept up his neck and met his chin. His dirty nails and hands full of rings made me realise this was not somewhere that boasted a great hygiene rating. Soap here was clearly rarer than the steak.

"Yes? What can I get you, luv?" he asked, his eyes dropping down to survey my breasts and belly. A curl twisted his top lip as his stare hovered at my chest. Blackheads littered his spreading nose and there was a large, yellow tipped spot just begging to be burst on his grubby creased neck.

"Err, coffee please. Cappuccino?"

"No. We do instant," he replied. "With frothy milk."

As the milk was being whisked he picked up his mobile and turned his head as he spoke quietly. I strained to hear the conversation, but the noise of the coffee machine made it impossible to pick up anything more than mutterings.

Passing me the cup, he grinned and wiped his nose with his hand. I took the cup gingerly, wondering just what I was touching. A health inspector would have a field day in here, I thought. Carrying the cup, I sat by the window. There were dead flies on the ledge, the glass was smeared. The chair felt grimy. Solid, dried-up, dark red ketchup was caked around the top of the sauce dispenser on the table. The bottle of vinegar had things growing inside it. By my feet were dirty tissues. I was just glad I didn't need the loo. The whole place was disgusting.

The other four people in the café suddenly got up as one and walked out, leaving half-finished drinks and uneaten burgers. I felt uncomfortable. A little voice in my head said *leave*, and I stood up. I didn't want my drink. I just couldn't face the coffee, or even touch the chipped mug again, but as I reached for my bag I heard a noise. I watched through the murky, grease-streaked window as the other customers hurried to their cars. They drove away as motorbikes rode into the car park. First a big one, with tall 1960s easy rider type handlebars. It was followed by another, then four more joined them. Six large, helmeted figures in leathers dismounted as I watched from behind the glass. The bikers had parked around my car, blocking me in. A van drew up by the door to the café.

I pulled out my phone and called Trav. There was no service. Shit. I wrote him a text, but it wouldn't send. I looked around for a landline, but it was too late. Two figures walked in. Dark glasses, studded gloves and black jackets, the leather cracked and worn. On their backs were studs and cloth emblems reading '*The Bleak Souls.*'

I looked over to the counter to ask for help, but the café owner had disappeared. One of the bikers walked towards me and beckoned with his finger for me to follow him.

"Hi, I'm Cath." I tried to smile. They didn't respond. I picked up my bag and walked towards the door. They moved behind me. I left the café and went into the evening air, heavy with expectation and the smell of hot bikes. I tried to speak.

"Hi guys, I'm looki—"

But I didn't finish my sentence. A gloved hand smelling of stale oil and dirt was held over my mouth, its rough worn fingers pushing against my helpless lips. I was lifted up and carried towards the van, its doors held open. Not daring to struggle, I was pushed inside.

The van was empty but for a single mattress in the back. The door was shut and the lock engaged. I reached for my bag; it was gone. The warnings from Chris Latham and Sarah echoed through my head. What could I do? I couldn't fight them; I was one, they were six. This was a very, very bad mistake. Possibly my last.

I felt the vehicle start with a jolt, and the van shook as the tired diesel engine was revved hard before we sped off. I fell backwards with the force of the acceleration.

Was I going to be raped on this filthy mattress? Killed? Shown the bones of my mother? I was shaking. My pulse thumped in my head. I wanted logic and rational answers, but I could find none. I needed a plan, an escape, to fight, to plead, to bargain. The problem was, I had nothing, and what I did have they could take, anytime they wanted.

After what seemed like an hour but was probably only half that, the van started to bounce and I realised we'd left the tarmac road and were now on a dirt track. The sound of motor bikes echoed outside the cold tin space.

*

Ten minutes later, we stopped. The van doors were opened and cool fresh air rushed in. Six bikers stood there, shadows, silhouetted against the evening sun. I couldn't run, I couldn't fight, and I stupidly hadn't told anyone where I was going or who I was going to meet. They waved me out. I could barely walk; my legs were so weak. Two of them grabbed my shoulders. I was lifted and marched into a detached house; it was some sort of farm.

The door was pushed open. It smelt of damp and of ash from coal fires, even though it was June. It stank of stale cigarettes, beer and unwashed clothes. I was pushed into a large kitchen. A chipped and battered Rayburn cooker range hugged the wall, its paintwork faded and stained with smoke that had seeped from the ancient seals around its well-used doors. There was a rocking chair, it was empty I was pushed towards it.

"Sit!" I was ordered. I didn't move, so hands pushed me down into the chair. I had to be brave. I had nothing else. I had nowhere to run.

14. Death Wish Danny

"Drink," said the biker who'd carried me to the van. "No thanks, "I replied politely.

"It's not a question, it's an instruction, bitch. You will drink." There was no emotion in his voice. Two other bikers crowded around me. I began to shake.

"That's kind, but I really don't drink whiskey." I tried to stay composed.

"You do now, bitch," he said. "You'll do whatever we tell you to."

Two arms behind me pushed my shoulders down and his gang mate pushed the bottle into my mouth and tipped it up. I could smell the oil on his black gloves, cracked and torn. My hair was pulled and my head forcibly tilted backwards.

"Ouch!" I squealed but more of the liquid was poured in. "Please, don't…" I garbled, trying not to swallow or choke.

"Drink it!" he ordered, squeezing my cheeks. I swallowed two mouthfuls. It burnt my throat and tasted bad. I gagged.

"It burns," I said, trying to spit it out.

"It's rude not to drink with us; we always offer our guests a drink." I couldn't speak. I was shaking.

"Drink it!" he screamed. I did, swallowing mouthfuls of the hideously strong drink. "Why did you want to find us?" he asked.

"If you let me go, I'll tell you."

"You'll tell us, whether we let you go or not."

"Leave her!" barked a gravel-laden voice.

It was the leader of the Bleak Souls. Death Wish Danny himself had walked into the room. The bikers stood back. He was wearing black jeans and a leather jacket like the others. He had a scar across his cheek, a nose ring and three earrings. A dark beard and moustache hid much of his face. His hands were tattooed with the letters S-O-U-L-S across both sets of knuckles. The nails were long, chipped and dirty. His shirt was open and the tattoo of a knife was visible, its handle at the top pointing down to his heart. I breathed deeply as he stood in front of me. Was this my mother's killer?

"So. Talk," he said. I could see he was in his late sixties, like the rest of the gang.

"I'm Cath…"

"Tell us something new." His voice was raised.

"I'm trying to find out who killed my mother. She was Betzy Blac."

"We know that as well. So?"

"I thought you might know something about it, or could help," I said, my words slurring, the whiskey taking effect.

"You think we did it?" he roared, banging his fist on the table.

"No… No, I…"

"That would make me sad… Very sad, and very angry," he said, coming towards me, towering above me and narrowing his eyes. His words rolled into one and faded away as the room started to spin. My eyes felt heavy. I tried to stand but fell backwards, unable to speak. Arms held me and, as I fought to stay awake, the last thing I remembered was a single bare light bulb hanging from a fraying pendent on the ceiling. Dust and cobwebs clung to it and gently bounced in its radiant heat. The light faded as my eyes closed.

*

I woke to the sound of a boiling kettle. An old-fashioned whistle blowing like a loud bell in my ears. My head thumped. I daren't open my eyes. I was alive, but what had happened? I feared the worst. I ran my hands down my body. My clothes were intact. I opened my eyes and sat up. The thumping in my head began to increase. A woman with long, unkempt, hennaed hair was making a drink.

"No one's touched you love. Tea?" she asked, turning to look at me.

"Sorry?" I felt a breath on my neck. "Oh!" I jumped. Behind me, staring at me, his face just a metre above mine was Danny: menacing, unpredictable and dangerous. Leader of the Bleak Souls. Then a sense of relief descended on me; he seemed at peace, almost smiling. It was strange, like I was a new puppy or a vulnerable child.

"Sorry they made you drink," he said. "Not very respectful that. They're a bit wild."

So why was he, this man with a terrible reputation, being so caring? I was scared it was a trap; maybe he was a psycho who would suddenly turn nasty. No one knew where I was. My future lay in his hands.

I trod with caution. "Yes, thank you. Tea would be good," I replied. "What exactly happened last night?"

"You're okay. They're not bad boys, they're just wary. They wanted you drunk and unconscious, checked you for wires, you know, to make sure you weren't recording anything," she said, handing me an enamel mug with chipped edges.

"They searched me? Who are you?" I asked.

"I'm Shan. Pleased to meet you, Betzy's girl. I'm Danny's wife; well, the nearest thing to a wife."

"I just want to know what happened to my mum and to Raven Rain, and then I want to go home and leave you all in peace," I said quietly, more in hope than expectation. I held my head which was thumping harder. "My head really hurts."

"It'll pass," said Danny quietly.

"I feel like I've been drugged."

"No, you haven't." He stood up, clearly rattled by my accusation.

"Sorry, where's my bag?"

"It's safe," she said.

"Please, I need it." I was beginning to panic. "I need some headache pills."

"It's on the table, over there," she replied, pointing to the end of the kitchen. I tried to stand but unsteady feet and dizziness left me heading for the floor.

She caught me. "Woah, steady girl."

"Thanks. Oh, sorry, I'm not used to drinking like that. I'm just really dizzy." I was edgy too, not knowing if these two would just turn on me at any time.

Danny, who'd been watching me quietly, stared as I walked unsteadily over to the table, an old gate leg, dark wood remnant of the 1950s. There on the surface, the entire contents of my bag were spread out: phone, keys, tissues, tampons, make-up, pills and charger lead. It was embarrassing, but when I thought about what might have happened, it was nothing.

I pushed two headache pills from their plastic prison, the thin barrier snapping to free them. They fell out of the packet and bounced on the worn, dirt-engrained tabletop. I picked them up and swallowed them with the strong, milky tea. A few curdled lumps floated on the surface of the drink. Not sure what to do, I sat back down on the settee where I'd slept. Looking at it in the morning light it wasn't very inviting. Indistinguishable stains and marks covered the seat squabs. I wanted to go home and shower.

"Danny, I'm sorry if I upset you and your friends in any way," I offered.

"You didn't. If you had've, you'd have known about it. You might be waking up in a ditch beside the M25 minus your clothes. Or just not waking up at all."

I swallowed hard.

"We treat our guests with respect, so long as they respect us."

"I just want to know what happened to my mum."

"Breakfast?" said Shan, pulling a frying pan from a shelf above an old cooker.

"Err, toast. Maybe just toast, thanks." I smiled at her.

A feeling of relief spread over me as I realised they weren't going to harm me. I started to see a different side to this pair. There was something sad and pathetic about them and their tatty run-down home. I looked out of the window. Two rag-like curtains hung at its sides. Outside, through the dirty glass, two bikes glinted in the sun—highly polished and clearly loved—and there was my car. They'd moved it, brought it here in the night. It seemed undamaged, too. Everything this morning was a bonus. I reached for my phone but Danny picked it up.

"No. When you leave."

Shan made toast and we sat around the table, Danny looking like some ancient Viking warrior with his long greasy hair and bushy beard. The tattoos on his large hands flexed as his fingers moved to pick up his toast, the deep, dark, faded ink showing signs of age like the skin they stained. The tattoo of the dagger poked out from the gap in his shirt, its handle at the top with that frightening looking blade pointing straight to his heart.

"Back in the day," he began, "we were anarchists, outsiders, rebels." I could see the love in Shan's eyes as he told me his story. "We loved the punks. They were putting two fingers up to the state. We wanted to protect them. They looked tough at times, swore and cursed, but they were mostly middle-class kids playing a game. Right wingers and the skinheads hated them. So they needed protecting. This was before proper security with bouncers. Security at gigs was random. We stepped in. Sort of guardian angels for the music biz. We kept order."

"So you helped at Décolleté gigs."

"S'right."

"And the Scented Slugs, too?"

"Of course. Loved those guys."

"Did you know Betzy Blac?" I asked.

"Know her?" said Shan. "He slept with her."

I choked on my tea, spilling it down my sweaty top.

"Early days. Just the once or twice." Danny yawned, his mouth opening to reveal missing teeth.

"Err, she wanted that?" I asked, not believing Mum would willingly sleep with someone like him.

"I didn't fucking rape her!" He stood up, thumping the table. Shan held his wrist.

"Sorry," I gasped, my heart pounding. "I wasn't suggesting you did, I was just…"

"Shocked that a beautiful girl like Betzy would screw a monster like me?" he said, his face filled with anger.

"No…" I said, floundering, but of course that was exactly what I'd meant.

"In those days," said Shan with love in her eyes, "he was handsome. Look." She pulled a brown photo album from a drawer. The damage and distance almost forty years can put between youth and age is staggering. Here was a good looking, young Danny, dressed in leathers and looking tough but smiling, nice hair, all his teeth, no scar and no tattoos. He was standing in front of a Harley Davidson chopper, proud as punch. A pretty girl by his side.

'Is that… Mum?' I said, my mouth open in disbelief.

"That's her; they went on a weekend to Brighton together."

"It didn't work out," said Danny softly. "Musical differences. Isn't that what they say?"

I didn't push it further. Shan smirked and playfully pushed his shoulder. I shuddered.

"Do you know what happened on that last gig, the end of the tour in '84?" I asked. "The gig when Mum walked out and left it all behind?"

"Maybe."

"Will you tell me?" I asked.

"No."

"Why not?"

"I should have been there. I let her down."

"But..."

"Don't," said Shan, firmly, holding Danny's wrists. He clenched his fists and muttered.

"One day. I'll put it right," he snarled. "Believe me, I will put it right."

"I think we should arrange for you to go now," Shan said firmly. I knew I'd outstayed my welcome.

"Of course, thanks," I said. It didn't seem wise to disagree. Shan picked up her phone and spoke. "Put her back, boys." She hung up and looked at me. "They'll be here soon."

"They?" I asked.

"He's not a bad man, my Danny," said Shan. "He can be mental at times and he's done some pretty horrible things, but never to me. He treats me well." She smiled, stroking his arm as he stared at the table. "He's just haunted by some of the things that have happened. He would never have hurt Betzy. Not like some people."

With that, Danny put his hand over hers and looked at me. "Turn sideways," he demanded. I complied. "You look like her, your mother. Uncanny." He came closer and touched my hair. I froze and gulped.

"Who killed her? Where should I look?" I asked as I tried to move away.

"Look? I would look out for yourself. You can't undo what's been done," he replied.

"Is Jez Deopham responsible?"

"Deopham? He's scum. Live your own life. Go, leave the past where it belongs," he said and walked out of the room. Two bikers drew up outside.

"Your escort," Shan said, looking up at me.

"I don't need an escort."

"You will, with a blindfold on," replied Shan. "We like to keep our location a secret. Don't try to find us again."

"I won't. No I won't. I promise." I was certain of that.

The door opened and I felt hands around my face and a scarf pulled over my eyes. I was led to the door, my bag thrust in my hands.

"It's all there," said a biker, and someone gripped my arm. I walked forwards and realised I was outside. I heard the door of my car open.

"You sit in the passenger seat. I'm driving," I was told. I wasn't in a position to argue. My car engine fired up and I felt the wheels bump over the unmade track. Soon the surface was smoother, and I knew we were on a proper road. I could hear a bike behind us. After about fifteen minutes the car slowed and the handbrake clicked on. The motor was switched off.

"You will count to one hundred and then take off the blindfold. Understand?"

"Yes," I said. The car door opened and then slammed shut. I listened as a motorbike roared off with a skid as it left. I patiently counted to eighty-five and then pulled the scarf down, blinking as my eyes filled with sunlight. A large 'P' sign was on the left of the front of the car. I was in a layby. A lorry was in front of me. I slid across to the driving seat. Reaching for my bag I picked up my phone and switched it on.

There were three missed calls, all from Trav. A message landed: "*Couldn't raise u last nite. Really worried about u mtg bikers. Re Jez Deopham? Avoid! He's bad news x.*"

I called him.

"Hi, Cath?" he answered.

"Trav, I'm so glad to hear your voice. I'm fine. It's been a hell of a night, but I'm okay." I recounted the events of my meeting with the Bleak Souls. I could feel his tension and worry as he listened.

"Cath, you are totally and utterly bloody mad! That could have ended so very differently, and so very badly. Even *I've* heard of the Bleak Souls; they make some of the more notorious US chapters of the Hell's Angels look like choirboys."

"I'm sure. I think if they were all twenty years younger, it might have been different. But because I was Betzy's daughter, I was somehow okay; not sure why. Scary guys though, if not a little sad, clinging on to what once was."

"Sorry, but that was irresponsible and stupid, Cath. This isn't a game; there's a killer out there, and you may have just met him."

I started the engine and drove home. Trav was right; it could have ended so horribly. I'd have hated to have been on the wrong side of Danny back in the day or even now. And Mum sleeping with him? What? That wasn't something I wanted to dwell on. I checked my mirror for any signs of leather-clad bikers, but there were none. I was trying to absorb what I'd heard and looking forward to coffee and a shower.

15. Decollete

The morning started slowly. My body ached. I'd slept on the lumpy carcass of that settee at Danny's farmhouse the night before and my head was still suffering from the remains of a mega hangover. The long shower I'd taken when I finally got home helped, but my hips still felt like they'd been sleeping on rocks. I was exhausted. Adrenalin had pumped through me like there was no tomorrow during my visit to the Bleak Souls. That was two near misses, one in France and one in Kent. The next time I might not be so lucky. Was this really worth it?

Gazing across my bedroom, Mum's photo smiled down at me from my dressing table and gave me my answer. Yes, because she wouldn't have given up. Then I remembered. I was meeting Mum's old band later in London. What the hell was I going to wear?

I made breakfast and went through my wardrobe in my mind. True to the band's name, I'd have to wear something with a low cut, plunging neckline. After pushing my bowl to the side I picked up my favourite coffee cup, a large hand-painted mug and saucer from Portugal, and headed upstairs. I selected a thin white cotton top which perhaps revealed a bit too much, but I was meeting a bunch of women who'd been my mum's friends and bandmates, not parents or teaching girls in a stuffy classroom. I was also going to a pub in London where what I wore would be barely noticed among the bright young things and influencers.

Sitting in front of my little bedroom mirror on my chest of drawers, I looked at my minimal make-up spread out before me. I had to make a big effort. If the other three were like Sarah— confident and assertive—I needed to feel less inadequate than I did. The picture of Mum stared back at me from the frame. Blast. I just had to get my hair cut before I could do much more. I phoned round a few salons until I got a cancellation and headed out of the house.

*

The High Street salon did their best, but it was never going to be a replica of Mum. I had to describe it without showing them a picture; that would have been just too embarrassing. An untidy pageboy was the best I could come up with. So would it pass? It was close to hers but not quite as short or dark.

Back home, I stared at my reflection, imagining bright stage lights and the sound of guitars. I picked out a mid-thigh skirt, slightly daring for me, but it made a statement. I wanted to give the impression of confidence and self-assurance, even though it wasn't there. Before I changed, I put on the band's greatest hits album, loudly, to get into the mood. I drummed my fingers on my dressing table mocking Miss Miles and smiled. Okay, let's leave Miss Teacher behind and uncover Miss Rock Chick. So, darker eyes like Mum used to do, more foundation and dark lipstick. I never usually wore it, but I'd bought some specially; Mum always had dark red lips—or, at least, Betzy did. Finally, as *Wrecked Bed Regrets* blasted out, I looked at the finished article in the mirror. Yes, I could almost see Mum standing there and I felt she'd be pleased.

I set off: anxious but keen to finally meet Décolleté. They and Mum had been through so much together. I had to understand them to help me understand her. I still wasn't convinced by the skirt though, and regretted not wearing jeans all the way there.

I stepped out of Old Street underground station and made

my way past gleaming new buildings that merged with the remaining older structures. Late leaving stragglers vacated now empty offices giving way to cleaners. I soon left the well-trodden streets and walked into a trendy bar in Hoxton. Scanning the space, I saw the typical clientele you find in those places. Friends meeting after work. Loners reading the evening paper—maybe just not wanting to go home—and couples, perhaps lovers, meeting for furtive flirts and snatched moments.

And then I saw them. There they were, unmistakable, sitting at a table sharing bottles of wine. My mum's old band. Décolleté. Four legends who'd topped the charts, played capacity crowds in stadiums and at festivals, and four women who'd loved my mother. I could almost see her there with them, talking over old times, laughing and sharing memories. Sadly, a memory was all Mum was. I hesitated and then went over to their table.

"Hi Sarah, hello." I smiled weakly, interrupting their conversation.

"Cath! Great to see you, hey grab a seat, have a glass."

Four sets of eyes scanned me; smiles greeted me, but I could see them comparing me, assessing me, absorbing me. Sarah stood up, a broad smile breaking out across her face as she put both hands on my shoulders, pulling me forwards for a hug. My apprehension turned to relief. "Let me introduce you— Stephanie, Rochelle and Caroline, or as you would have known them—Stephy, Rocky and Cassie."

"Woah, it's almost as if Betz was back," Rochelle said, flopping back in her chair and shaking her head slowly.

"Striking resemblance," Caroline grinned. Stephanie nodded and got up to join what became a group hug. The smells of hair spray, make-up, perfume and a hint of patchouli sent my senses into overtime. I saw four sets of dark red nails, hands adorned by more rings than a jewellers, and faded questionable tattoos just visible under sleeve cuffs and necklines. Caroline was the one who'd changed the most from the early pictures—she was much bigger than she had been back in the day and the most conservatively dressed—but they were still Mum's band. They all had that air of experience that came from being performers, having tasted fame. Right in front of me, they were almost morphing back into character.

"Wow, the four of you, in person. So good to see you all.' I sat down, my legs unsteady; it was like I was seeing through Mum's eyes. I somehow felt I knew them. 'I know your music backwards of course. I've seen the pics and watched the TV appearances. I just wish Mum was here with you to make up the band."

Sarah pushed a glass my way and filled it with white wine. "House white, I'm afraid. But it's okay."

I nodded appreciatively and tried to hide my nerves. I didn't know what to say. I'd rehearsed a few lines but, now I was there, they just evaporated. As I looked from face to face I didn't just see middle aged women. Everywhere there were clues to their punk past. The few faded tattoos. Clothes that could have passed on stage today, and world-weary faces that had clearly lived life to the full. Gone, though, were the face piercings, outrageous make-up and exposed flesh.

"Are we what you were expecting, Cath?" asked Caroline.

"I'm not sure what I was expecting." I laughed and went red. "And I didn't know if you'd be wearing ripped tights and chains! You could be a social worker, Caroline."

"I am!" she grinned.

"And as for the ripped tights," broke in Stephanie, "are these okay?" She raised her skirt, revealing a large hole in her fishnets.

"Classic!" I said, shaking my head softly in appreciation. Was this just for my benefit, or did they dress like this all the time? I couldn't imagine dressing like them when I was their age, but I'd had a very different life to these women. They had a presence, they looked tough and determined, they were all big personalities and I quickly realised they were on a mission.

"Hey Cath, have to say you're looking a lot like your mum," said Rochelle.

"And the hair's been cut since I saw you. There was a

resemblance before, but now. Wow," added Sarah. "Oh don't look sad," she said kindly, noticing my face dropping.

"Thanks, I'm so confused about Mum. I still can't be sure if she's missing, or dead. If she is dead then did she kill herself, or did someone kill her?" I looked around at the four faces. The smiles had gone.

"She should be here with us now," said Caroline. "None of us are really sure what happened. Sometimes in the night I believe she's still with us, other times that she died years ago." She bent forwards, her long white fringe dusting her forehead, and touched my hand.

"Well if the bitch is out there, she owes us a lot of drinks," Stephanie grinned.

Rochelle laughed. "We meet every month and toast her health, so I reckon she owes us the contents of a Calais wine warehouse at least!"

"If she hadn't gone," said Sarah, "we'd still be banging out the hits, still be living the rock and roll dream and still being Décolleté."

"You get your washing machine fixed far quicker if you're a wild rock chick," laughed Rochelle. "Even a bloody old one!"

"And cabbies no longer say *I had that drummer from Décolleté in the back of me cab last week*. It's dull saying I used to be Cassie Crack, I still want to *be* Cassie Crack," she said.

"But come on Sarah," teased Stephanie. "I bet your fingers couldn't move fast enough for that riff in *Banging on the Beach* these days."

"Hey bitch! You don't know how fast my fingers can move… when I'm in the mood!" Sarah laughed and jokingly punched Stephanie's shoulder. "Give me half a chance. I do practise, you know, on the guitar too! Yeah I'm match fit even if you girls aren't," she teased.

"What?" said Rochelle. "My bass is regularly given an outing. Not so much fun on my own, though."

"Life is so dull, hanging on to the past is essential. A lost, wasted, but in many ways a perfect youth," said Caroline, picking up her glass and toasting. "Here's to the past, may it always stay alive," she said, emptying the wine into her mouth. The others followed.

"Problem is, not sure the bladder would take a two hour performance with all that jumping about these days!" giggled Stephanie as they all laughed.

"Not like that festival we did!" said an animated Rochelle. "We waited for so long until the band before us finished, they just wouldn't stop!"

"We were so fired up," said Sarah.

"And we'd been drinking lager all afternoon in the sun," added Stephanie.

"We were delayed so much and I was desperate for a pee," grinned Caroline.

"In the end you just ran from the back of the stage," laughed Rochelle.

"Yeah the nearest loos were full of road crew, no special ones for us, so I had to do what I could."

"Slipping under the stage if I remember!" giggled Stephanie.

"Yes, I still had my sticks with me though!" laughed Caroline. "A dead giveaway."

"Then you realised you weren't alone!" said Sarah with tears of laughter.

"Yeah when I was halfway through and heard a voice behind me saying *'Bloody hell that's Cassie Crack's bum crack!*'" They all dissolved into fits of laughter.

As the evening wore on we shared pizza, more memories and more wine, then switched to coffee. Clearly, time had tamed Décolleté, and although I wasn't expecting a riot, I wasn't expecting a Mumsnet discussion on menopause, grumpy husbands and constipation either. I kept trying to steer the conversation back to Mum and what could have happened, but every time I tried it quickly swung back to the mundane. If this was what our former punk rock heroes were reduced to, then there was little hope for the rest of us. I realised that if I wanted to delve into Mum's past and find out the truth I needed to get these women on board. Maybe they had secrets they weren't ready to share; not until I was one of them at least.

"Anyone think Death Wish Danny or Jez Deopham could have killed her? Or even Chris Latham?" The question was as welcome as a police raid at a wedding.

"If we knew, don't you think we'd have told the police?" said Sarah quietly, putting down her glass and leaning in to the table to face me. She seemed a little hurt that I might think they'd have kept that to themselves. "Catherine, we loved your mum. If we thought either of those three did kill her we'd do something about it, but we have no proof. They could all be innocent, or guilty. We don't know. Do you?"

"No," I replied. "But I want to find out, and I hope you do too."

"How?" asked Rochelle.

"The fans know stuff, I'm sure," said Caroline.

"Let's ask them," I suggested.

"There's no club or fan base on social media,' Stephanie said. 'Décolleté have been dormant for decades."

"Unless," Sarah said, "we went on stage and asked them."

"What do you mean?" I asked.

"We could do a comeback gig," Sarah said. "Make an appeal."

Caroline smiled at me. "Sorry Cath, Sarah's been asking the rest of us to get back on stage for years. She never gives up."

"But that might just work, you know," I said. The idea of Décolleté on stage without Mum was difficult to imagine, but anything was worth it if it uncovered the truth.

"We'd need a singer; we'd need a Betzy," Rochelle said. Slowly, they all looked at me.

"So you went to stage school, Cath?" asked Sarah.

"Well I studied drama at university," I said. "I learned to sing and dance but I became a teacher and… Wait a minute…" I suddenly realised what they were saying.

"So what if your mum's old band wanted a new singer, wanted to give it another go, wanted to do a tribute gig to Betzy Black?" asked Stephanie.

"To make an appeal to find out what people knew, to find out what had happened," said Sarah.

"What about singing a few of your mum's old songs, Cath? You look so much like her, and we can help you with the music," Rochelle said. The truth was I'd pretended to be Mum with a hairbrush microphone for years, ever since I could walk. Her songs were almost all I had left of her, and I knew the lyrics by heart. I'd spent hours growing up being Mum in front of the bathroom mirror. I wouldn't need many rehearsals. But what they were suggesting was a big step from dancing around a bedroom with a hairbrush.

"Phew, hang on!" I said, taken aback. But I couldn't deny they had a point. I did look like Betzy Blac and, if I worked on the hair and make-up, what could I achieve with a direct appeal to her old fans? It could bring out old memories, old guilt, old witnesses; and any shred of information would be gold dust. It could even reveal who Brad was, and DD. It was too good an opportunity to miss. I sat back and sipped slowly, knowing they were hanging on my reply, desperate for me to agree to this mad, bonkers idea. Perhaps Trav could help with publicity; he had like a zillion followers on social media. Maybe…

"Well," I started.

"Great, that's a yes then," smiled Sarah, and before I could open my mouth they all stood up and toasted Décolleté, the revival.

"We can rehearse at my place," said Rochelle.

"I'll only agree to do it in front of anyone if I'm believable," I insisted.

"Oh you will be," laughed Stephanie.

"Me being Mum? Being Betzy Blac? It's a tall order," I said.

"You'll be great," said Sarah, raising her glass to toast my new persona.

"Well just a little try out," I said. "No promises!"

"Of course," they chipped in one after the other, but the die was cast. The four of them stood up and hugged me, telling me I'd be great, and they'd be ready for it, and how I wasn't to worry, and it would be a blast and it could finally reveal what happened to Mum.

*

Travelling back to my car on the other side of London, I wondered just what I'd done and where it might lead. The rain began as I reached my car and started the engine to drive home. A text came through from Trav.

"Sarah says you're going to play Betzy! Go girl!"

What? They'd told Trav before I could? Shit, he was a *real* singer. Events were rushing ahead of me. I tested myself and I couldn't remember the second verse of *Raindance* let alone *Pink Bra Bust Up!* I put it down to nerves.

Back home, I closed my front door and picked up an envelope from the doormat. Inside was a card from two of my final year girls at school: Chloe and Emily, my stars.

"So sorry you won't be there for our performance, Miss. We'll miss you. Thank you for teaching us and for putting up with us. We'll do it for you, and make it special."

I was really touched, I put the card by the flowers which had arrived from them earlier. Wouldn't be there? I wouldn't miss it for the world. Fuck Miss Miles. Not long ago I was a simple English and drama teacher; now my own dramas had seen me accused of murder, being kidnapped, agreeing to perform live on stage with Décolleté, and having Travis Brennon sleeping in my bed.

As I went to bed, I kissed Mum's picture on my bedroom wall. I promised to do her proud. I could almost hear her wish me good luck and tell me to find the bastard who killed her and bring them to justice. I rolled over to switch off my phone as a text arrived. It was from Trav.

"Drawn a blank with Brad and DD. Good luck with the rehearsal!"

16. Ewling

Two days later, I walked into the village hall at Ewling. There on stage were four women, dressed like they'd just changed after the gym: baggy tops, jeans and flat shoes. Behind them a few tatty old amps, a set of drums, three guitars and a very lonely mic stand right in the middle. Nerves hit home, despite their warm embraces, encouraging words and welcoming smiles.

I knew I couldn't go back, after hearing them at the bar in Hoxton reminiscing and saying how dull their lives were now. It really meant so much to them, and finding Mum meant so much to me, but I still doubted the wisdom of my decision. My throat was dry, my head tense and my nerves as taut as the strings on Sarah's old red Fender.

"Okay: one, two, three!" counted in Sarah, and *crash!* the drums filled the stage in the empty, echoing hall, guitars fired up, and I looked at the handwritten set list taped to the mic stand. *Pink Bra Bust Up!* was the band's first number one chart topper, which had caused such a furore all those years ago. I went straight in—half me, half my mum, but Mum soon took over and I let it happen. I was soon recreating the moves I'd seen her make on old video tapes and singing in her style, angrily shouting some words and letting a softer voice wash over the chorus. The sound balance was pretty good, considering it was just a couple of practice amps, but they'd done this before of course. Maybe they'd even tried out other singers, but I was Betzy II, the nearest thing to Mum they had.

The door opened and a handful of people came in, found seats and watched. My nerves sent adrenalin surging through my veins. I wasn't expecting real people, an audience, however tiny. Sure, I sang in front of the girls in school to show them lines, and how to perform songs in musicals, but this was different.

During a break after the first five tracks, I noticed a few women were now hanging around after their earlier Pilates class as well as the caretaker and two walkers who'd been passing by; they all seemed to be enjoying our little performance.

Then I saw Trav: he'd snuck in and was standing in the corner, smiling. Shit, a real singer, a real star! How long had he been there? Watching me, a pretend singer. The next song ended with a crashing drum and a screeching riff on Sarah's guitar. Then the applause started. Sarah mouthed *"Go!"* and the girls started playing *Let's Get Fucked On Friday!*—one of the really tasteless tracks that had sealed the band's reputation. I knew the lyrics, of course, although I'd have preferred not to sing them; they were more explicit than I liked. But I was being Betzy, and I had to sing what Betzy had written. *Wedding Dress Disaster* followed. Décolleté were one again and unstoppable.

"Okay," Sarah grinned at us. 'Who fancies *Two Lovers in One Night!*'

"Chance would be pretty good!" laughed Caroline. We all cheered. *Hot Lips Cold Heart*, *Faded Flowers* and one of my favourite tracks, *Lost in Lust Again*, followed faultlessly, and then the emotionally-charged *Raindance*, written by Betzy for Raven. A song that always gets me teary, but singing it made me feel good, I really belted it out and got a huge applause from our attentive little audience.

We stopped, but the small crowd called for more. We shrugged, smiled and, encouraged by the surprisingly tight sound we were making, went straight into *Love Me More*, and then the fans' favourites: *Banging On The Beach* and *Wrecked Bed Regrets*. Hell, my mum had issues, no doubt. God only knows where she got the inspiration for those lyrics. I could guess, of course, but it was something I'd rather not think about. There can't be many daughters who have to sing about their mums having sex. Especially the sort of sex my mum sang about.

By the end of the set I was exhausted, exhilarated and emotional. I'd secretly dreamed of being Mum, and here I was. I ended the set feeling like only a performer can. Sweat made me realise I'd need a thinner outfit if I were going to do this, and I knew if I hid behind Mum I could be her. It wasn't Cath on stage. It was Betzy II, out there in front of the band she'd created. Travis Brennon, a real star, was smiling and holding out his arms. I climbed off the stage and wiped my forehead with a towel thrown to me by Stephanie. Trav walked towards me.

"Hey, Cath, you can sing! Go girl, go go go!" he said, putting his arm around me.

"I'm not sure, Trav, it's…"

"I am!" he interjected. "That was good, really good. For a first run-through, it was great. I've heard a lot of singers, and you can sing. You're a natural."

"She's good, hey?" Sarah jumped in, as the girls crowded around me, joining Trav. It made me realise how much fun it had been playing Mum.

"It was great fun, but I'm not convinced I can pull it off," I said. "I could maybe do backing vocals if…"

"Bollocks!" Stephanie shouted. "You were Betzy. With my eyes closed it could have been the bitch herself. Your voice is a dead ringer. With the right make-up and lighting it's totally believable."

"But it would be a tribute act," I said.

"Yes, except the real Décolleté with the real singer's daughter playing her part. Besides, how else will you find out what happened?" said Sarah. "That's why we're really doing this. To find your mum."

"She's right, Cath," said Trav. "Wake up and smell the coffee; this is a golden opportunity to find the truth. The killer is still my dad's killer, maybe your mum's too; that killer could even come and be there in the crowd."

"Well…" I hesitated. Cheers erupted.

"Knew you'd see sense," laughed Sarah.

"Hey, you need to do this. That performance for a first rehearsal was awesome. Really. You're all good and you deserve to be heard," said Trav.

I smiled and drank from a bottle of water just as two women from the WI came in and asked us to stop so they could use the hall. Mum would have laughed. The WI in the shape of her mum—my granny—had always asked her to stop. To stop being Betzy and to stop being an embarrassment, but she never did.

*

We unplugged our amps and moved our kit into the corner of the stage, promising to come and clear it out later. Leaving the Village Hall, we walked the short distance to Rochelle's house just off the main street. It was set back behind short iron railings with a neat cottage front garden. The building was rendered and painted cream. It used to be an old pub, she told us, and was now a comfortable home where she'd raised a family with her husband, a local vet.

I made my excuses and dived into a loo just inside the front door. As I walked into the toilet I passed a picture of Rochelle's kids, and then I saw one of Rochelle and Mum, arm in arm, smiling after a gig. Her smile and winning eyes bore into my head. As I closed the door I could almost hear her telling me to go out there and keep her name alive.

I walked into Rochelle's spacious kitchen to see the rest of the band sitting around her large statement table, and there in the corner, leaning against the wall, smiling, was Trav. I felt like I was the last candidate at an interview.

"We've decided Cath," said Sarah, passing me a mug of coffee.

"And there's no option to say no," added Rochelle.

"No backing out," said Stephanie.

"Absolutely not," reinforced Caroline. "If we're doing it, you're bloody well doing it!"

"We're booking the Strummers' Club for a trial gig," Travis said, grinning.

"What?" I mumbled, holding my hands to my mouth, not quite believing what he'd said.

"You'll be great, Cath. I can get my people to hire the PA, sort the publicity, the insurance, the crew, the ticketing and the whole thing. Don't worry."

"But it's costs," I said. "And if we bomb, who'll pick up the tab?"

"Cath, we've discussed it, the girls and I, and we're happy to risk it and pay if it fails," said Sarah.

"And I'll chuck in a bit too," said Trav. "But I know it's a safe investment. This will sell, believe me."

I was speechless. I listened to a rapid-fire conversation about stage positions, lighting rigs, sound systems, sound engineers, ticket prices and insurance. It was over my head. "Err, when?" I finally asked. "Sorry to interrupt but when are we doing this?"

"A week on Thursday," replied Trav.

"What? How come they have space?" I asked.

"We actually booked it the day you went to see Sarah. They had a cancellation."

"Sorry?" I said aghast.

"Yes," said Rochelle. "We knew you'd go for it, with a bit of persuasion."

"And if I'd refused?" I asked.

"Oh, we have ways," Stephanie laughed.

"We knew you wouldn't refuse, you're a natural," said Rochelle.

"So, rehearsals?" I asked nervously. "I need rehearsals. Lots of rehearsals."

"We've booked the village hall every day until then. Different times to fit around other bookings, but we've got space," said Stephanie. "Besides, after today, we know you don't need that many rehearsals: just learn when to start and end the songs and maybe build up your confidence. You'll be fine."

"And you're all sure? You're not just saying it?"

"No, we're sure," said Trav. We worked out a schedule and then Trav raised an event that would have to come first.

"Sadly," he said, "it's Raven's funeral tomorrow. You're all welcome, but Cath, it would be good if you could be there. For me?"

"Wouldn't miss it. After all, I thought he was my dad too, up to a few days ago," I replied.

The next rehearsal was after the funeral, but first I'd have to get through the morning, which I knew was going to be very busy and very sad. Especially for Trav. Raven was gone. There were plenty of ghosts to lay to rest and a lot of people would be there who I needed to see. Some might even have the answers I needed.

17. Robbi Rat Boy Romero

I drove through a bright cheery morning which was overshadowed by a feeling of sadness. Big puffy clouds blew across an otherwise blue sky as I pulled into the crematorium south of Raven's hometown in Oxfordshire. There were scores of mourners. It was an eclectic mix. Some were in traditional black and muted dark blues, others were in fan and gig gear. Punks, goths, metal fans and almost everything in between; I even caught a glimpse of a Bowie lookalike, two Debbie Harrys, a Prince and, of course, lots of Betzy Blacs and Raven Rains. There were some real stars from the '70s and '80s there, too. I wondered how many had shared moments in Raven's life. I drew up in an overspill car park and followed the crowd moving towards the uninspiring building ahead.

Over-run officials were totally taken aback by the turn out. They clearly had little idea how big Raven had been, or how many of his fans would want to be there to pay their last respects. They were trying to filter the crowd into two groups: relatives and then onlookers and fans. The latter were ushered to an area outside the main building with its chimney of no return where the service would be relayed on speakers. I passed two TV crews and an outside broadcast truck. The queue moved slowly, and I waited patiently to get to the gate.

"And you are?" asked a stern-looking man dressed in uninspiring black, like a doorman at a misogynistic men's club.

"Catherine Edgley; my mother was Betzy Blac."

"Not on my list. Sorry," he replied, checking a clipboard.

"She's on mine," said a voice beside me. Trav had turned up.

"And you are, sir?"

"Travis Brennon."

"And?"

"I'm Raven's son."

"Ah, of course, sir. You're that singer. There are a few photographers over there, I'm afraid."

"Be surprised if there weren't; it goes with the territory," muttered Trav, taking my hand and leading me through the gates.

"Thanks Trav. Sad day. How are you?" I squeezed his hand.

"I'm okay. Yeah, sad day."

"Oh," I said, pointing with a nod. "The police are here." There, in the corner, watching everyone go in, were DCs Patel and Dennison. I gave a short friendly wave; they acknowledged me and each raised a hand back, but there were no smiles, just piercing eyes, scanning the mourners.

"Who are all these people?" I asked. "There's so many of them."

"Not sure. That's Raven's mum, over there by the door. Do you see her?"

"Yes, in a black hat."

"That's her. His dad died years ago. Oh, look, there's Sacha's mum and dad. Mr and Mrs Tillens, the couple just going in now, both wearing grey. Can you see?"

"Yes, a sad day for them too," I replied. "Is your mum here?"

"I haven't seen her. I did ask her, but she didn't commit. Said she would if she could."

The reality was sinking in. Raven was gone. Sacha had been taken from us too. So young.

Trav scanned the crowd. "Over there, in the denim jackets and jeans, carrying guitars, that's two of Raven's old band. Looks like they're going to perform. Interesting. Baz and Sledge, I think. Yup, the very same. Ah, and that if I'm not mistaken is

Raven's sister welcoming people in. My Aunt, I guess. Oh and that guy over there, the tall one, wearing a hat, it's Pete Benton. I told you about him, a former celebrity DJ in the '80s. He was always seen with successful bands like Décolleté and the Scented Slugs."

"I know he was on the radio a lot," I said.

"He was a big name back in the day," replied Trav.

As we made our way through the mourners, some of them wanted to shake Trav's hand or just touch his arm. He wore a fixed smile and just kept going. A few people took our picture as we headed towards the building's entrance. As we went inside the sunshine was blocked out and the air was cool, almost stale. The place was just a functional funeral factory, built for burning bodies. I began to feel quite emotional and I could sense Trav was feeling the same. I found Sacha's parents sitting in a row halfway along. I smiled gently as I walked past them. The place was full and, before I sat down next to Trav, I looked behind me. Was DD or Brad here? Or maybe they were outside with the gathering crowd? I could hardly use the PA system to ask.

It was a strange atmosphere: part sad funeral and part gig. In the corner were a pair of guitars, a mic stand and a couple of amps, standing out proudly from the innocuous dull décor of the crematorium. I could tell the staff found it all very uncomfortable having such a huge crowd outside. Beside the kit stood two ageing punks, remnants of the infamous Scented Slugs. They were wearing black jeans and t-shirts adorned with Raven's picture.

The ceremony began with the coffin arriving to the sounds of *Trust the Truth*, one of the Scented Slugs' greatest hits. Walking in front of the coffin were Raven's sister, and Chris Latham in an ill-fitting suit. The leather-clad pallbearers were a surprise, and not a pleasant one: they were members of the Bleak Souls. I felt a brief panic, but I couldn't see Danny among them. It was strange to hear Raven's voice booming out inside the building and across the grounds to the crowds outside as his lifeless body was conveyed to the front. Muted cheers and applause filtered in through the open doors.

The bikers placed the coffin on the plinth, the studs on their jacket sleeves clanging as they made contact with the metal railings either side. As they walked out they were an ugly sight, adding a touch of menace to the proceedings. I caught a glance of the two detectives standing by the door watching them intently. I was sure the bikers had a reference or two on the police database and was glad to watch them leave. As they did I saw two women standing just inside the door at the back, both wearing hats and dark glasses. There was a hint of faded glamour; they were either deep in grief or trying not to be noticed. I made a note to ask Trav later if he knew who they were, but I was distracted by Chris Latham and Raven's sister, who took reserved seats on the other side of the aisle, whispering hello to us as they sat down.

The celebrant, a local humanist, started speaking. He welcomed us and we heard the story of Raven's life which included his time with Betzy. The eulogy was given by Chris Latham. His ill-fitting suit was embarrassingly too tight, clearly measured when his stomach was smaller. He had an air of confidence but his hands were shaking. Booze or nerves? I didn't know. You'd have thought from what he said that Raven Rain, AKA Nigel, was an angelic hero. Luckily he left out the more colourful references to Raven and Mum, including the Paris fountain incident. Then the celebrant introduced the two Slugs, Baz and Sledge, the lead and bass guitarists.

"This mic on?" asked Sledge, tapping it roughly. People nodded. "Okay, err hello," he said, donning his guitar and putting on a stronger accent to emphasise his punk past. "Our mate, the great Raven Rain, has been slain before his time by some bastard unknown."

"Yeah," continued Baz, picking up his guitar. "We'd like to play the quietest song he wrote. It was a single, did well in the charts, you might know it, it's called *Quietest Moments, Loudest Thoughts*. Made him a lot of money. We'd like to ask his son

Travis Brennon to sing it."

"Shit!" whispered Trav in my ear.

"Didn't you know?" I asked, surprised.

"No I didn't!" he whispered back. "Talk about surprise gigs."

"Are you going to do it?" I asked.

"I don't really have a choice, do I? I can't refuse to do something at my own dad's funeral."

"I suppose not."

"Wish me luck."

"Yes. Err, break a leg."

Trav stood up and walked to the mic. Suddenly he had become Travis Brennon, international star. His stage persona took over as he surveyed the audience and found a muted smile. There was a loud murmur inside the hall and a cheer from outside when he spoke.

"Hello, it's probably the first time ever that these two have played without being stoned or pissed. Sorry guys, no offence, but that's for springing this on me."

"You kidding? Baz had to ask what chords we started on," said Sledge, wiping his nose on the back of his hand. "He's out of it man."

"Ah, my mistake, they are stoned," Trav said. There was a ripple of laughter from inside and out.

"It would be an offence to Raven's memory if we weren't!" laughed Sledge.

"Cool it man!" said Baz. "The pigs are in." The laughter grew. Cheers and claps filtered in from the crowd outside and echoed around the miserable interior like rays of light. I watched Trav intently. He was a polished performer but this clearly wasn't easy. Changing the mood, he took control.

"Raven Rain was my dad. I'm proud of him, for all his talent and success, and despite his faults and failures. He lived life to the full. Look, guys, I haven't rehearsed this, or even been told about it before, and it would have been nice to have known this little surprise was bring planned," he said pointedly, looking at the two musicians who pretended to be checking their guitars. "But we'll give it a go. I'm sorry if it makes you cry, I can't guarantee I'll get through it myself either."

Sledge and Baz counted in and started the softly strummed song. G, C and D chords rang out as Travis hugged the microphone closed his eyes and sang his way through the track. He was brilliant. He didn't miss a word and the guys didn't miss a beat. The mourners even sang along with the chorus, joining in the wave of voices coming from outside. Some at the back of the crematorium were holding up their phones with lights on, waving them from side to side. Raven would have loved it.

I was fine until he ended and said, "That song was written for the other woman in his life; he loved Sacha Tillens as you all know. He and Sacha were going to get married. I didn't know my dad until a few years ago, I didn't know much about him, but I do know one thing – before Sacha there was my mum Carly, and before her Betzy Blac, and he wrote that song for her."

I lost it. Tears fell; I couldn't stop them. I wasn't alone; there were loud sobs coming from the back of the room. I looked round and the two women at the back were leaving, clutching tissues to their eyes. Others were crying too, Sacha's parents among them. My head bent and I felt Trav's arm around my shoulder as he returned to his seat. My tissue was soaked and I searched my bag for another but the packet was empty. Trav pulled a clean white ironed handkerchief from his top pocket and gave it to me. I muttered a muted "thank you" and tried to dry the tears. How different things would have been if Mum and Raven had married and both been alive. Even if he wasn't my dad, maybe I'd have grown up with them, probably in some massive house with a horse and a foreign holiday home. The daughter of two stars who were happy and in love.

As the mourners filed out, Raven's coffin disappeared behind the Curtain of No Return, while Baz and Sledge played an instrumental to send him off. The sound of electric guitars boomed out as the hall emptied, leaving the soulless void vacant for another set of mourners. I scanned every face, wondering who might be DD or Brad, but how would I know?

Outside it was sunny and the air was welcoming and fresh. I smiled and nodded to various people as I stood by Trav's side while he fended off questions and tried to be polite. I hoped my eyes weren't too red and my eye shadow too smudged. Mrs Tillens walked up to me.

"Hello, I'm Sacha's mum, I understand you tried to help her." I looked at this grieving mother, devastated by the loss of her daughter.

"Hi, yes, I'm Cath Edgley. I'm so sorry, I got to Sacha too late when I went to meet her. I'm really so very sorry." I'd replayed the events many times in my mind, but none of my endings turned out well. I was also worried how the Tillens would react to me. I had originally been arrested for their daughter's murder, after all.

"Thank you, Cath," whispered Mrs Tillens. Her husband was looking down, unable to respond. "We don't blame you," she said, raising her tear-stained face to meet me. I reached out and squeezed her hand. "We've got all this again for Sacha in a couple of weeks. Hopefully quieter and no press. It's so intrusive," she said. I smiled sympathetically. "We're going away as soon as it's over, to stay with our daughter in Canada."

"Where do you live?" I asked.

"Our home is at Bradwell-on-Sea. It's where Sacha grew up and it's too full of memories at the moment." She turned and, holding her husband's hand, walked away, both of them carrying their own grief and memories of a beautiful daughter they'd never see again.

I turned to re-join Trav, who was talking to the funeral celebrant as a man walked over to us and said hello.

"I'm Robbi. Robbi Romero. Known to most people as Robbi 'Rat Boy' Romero."

"Hi," I said, trying to smile. "You ran the record label?"

"Yes. I set up Trash Puke Records. It was a natural home for trashy, puking punks like your mum and Raven. No disrespect of course!" He laughed like he was telling a dirty joke in a bar. "That was their appeal: trashy punks, talented mind you, and a real looker your mum, quite the punk pin-up. You look like her too." He said, his eyes scanning my body, and I felt uncomfortable as he stared at my chest.

"Sad day," I said, trying to make conversation as the mourners filed passed. Robbie the Rat Boy, named after the character he'd played as an eight-year-old actor, would find it almost impossible to squeeze through even the widest of sewers today, even if a sewer was where he belonged.

"Yeah, it's tragic. Very sad. I thought he'd got it sussed, you know, given up the bad stuff."

"He had." Trav had seen the Rat Boy and, sensing my discomfort, he moved to my side and quickly came to his dad's defence. "Raven had stopped taking drugs," said Trav firmly.

"Not what I'd heard," retorted Romero. "He and Sacha were back on it. Big time."

"Really?" I said, unconvinced.

"That's the word," he nodded.

"You don't you think he was murdered then?" I asked.

"Who'd want to kill Raven? He was harmless; a relic, but harmless," said Romero.

"Hardly a relic," said Trav, clearly unhappy with Romero's description of his dad. "Retired but still respected and loved; just look at the numbers here today."

"A relic who was about to expose a few secrets and name some names," I said.

"Oh, everyone says that if they want to sell memoirs," laughed Robbie. "Hype, love, it's what we did to sell records and what people do to sell books. Secrets? He probably knew who was shagging who behind the scenes, but hardly earth shattering today. Spoiler alert—they all were! Especially your mother!" He laughed and turned to go. I bit my lip.

"Do you know a Brad or DD?" I asked as he left. He didn't

reply.

"Charming man," I said sarcastically.

"Yeah, the Rat Boy nickname stuck for a reason I guess," said Trav.

"Hmm, I wonder what he knows. Or what he did," I said.

18. UNWaNTed ATTeNTiON

Leaving the car park was like fighting through rush hour traffic and Christmas shopping all rolled into one. The overspill parking area was a field and some of the heavier cars were getting stuck, wheels spinning as they tried to escape. Some mourners were having to get passengers to push, their smart sombre clothes splattered with mud as wheels spun round spraying sodden earth.

Eventually I was in a slow-moving queue to the hotel where the wake was being held. I arrived to find a line of people waiting to talk to Raven's mother. I squeezed into a corner, grabbing a glass of sparkling water and a curling egg sandwich offered by a young lad in a badly-fitting shirt and trousers. He looked as uncomfortable as I felt. I scanned the room for the two women I'd seen at the back of the hall, but they were nowhere to be seen. Nor, thankfully, were the bikers who'd carried in the coffin. The roar of their bikes as they'd left earlier was a pleasant indicator they'd moved off, but I couldn't help worrying that they might be back, along with Death Wish Danny.

Trav was missing as well, but so many of the observers and fans had slipped in that I guessed he'd made his excuses and left. He could have told me. I looked around for someone to talk to, deciding that I'd abandon my uninspiring sandwich, drink the water and get out myself. A thin man in an old suit with even older glasses was looking at me, a bit too intently for my liking. I recognised him; he was the man who'd been watching me from the other side of the road when I first read the news of Raven's death. I turned my back on him and found myself face to face with Robbi Romero.

"Catherine. Hello again. Busy isn't it?" he said, drink in one hand, two sandwiches in the other.

"Hello. Sorry, I'm looking for someone," I replied, trying to give him the brush off.

"Popular man our Raven. Like your mother. Big personalities and big drug problems too."

I wasn't convinced. What did he want from me? I thought I'd try a bit of fishing. "So, do the initials DD mean anything to you?"

"Nope, should they?" he said pushing half a sandwich into his open mouth, crumbs and a flake of salmon dropping down his front.

"Death Wish Danny, perhaps?" It dawned on me that it could just be the old biker, but it didn't seem as if the warnings were from him. He'd surely be more forceful.

"Oh! I wouldn't call him Death Wish out loud; I'd be very careful."

"I've met him."

"At a distance, I hope."

"Not exactly. I stayed the night in his house."

Romero was clearly surprised. "And you're still walking? I find that very hard to believe." People jostled passed us. Robbie pushed the remains of the second sandwich into his cavernous mouth and looked into his glass; I could tell he was about to head off to the bar for a refill.

"DD?"

"Desperate Debs maybe? That was going to be the name of Décolleté. Debs was a school friend of Betzy, I think. When I signed them they were called Betzy and the Scums. I said that was crap, and they were looking at changing the name to Desperate Debs. Then I changed my mind."

"Why?"

"Betzy was wearing a very sexy low-cut top, she always looked hot. So I suggested naming them after that. Décolleté," he said, staring at my chest. "I see you've inherited some of her, shall we say, finer points." He smirked. I ignored it.

"What about Brad?" I pushed.

"Knew a Brad King, he was a sound engineer at Dub Station Studio. Very good sound engineer too. Why?"

"I'm trying to find out what happened to my mum."

"Leave it," he said firmly, swallowing the last bit of sandwich.

"I can't. What's your theory?"

"She buggered off and topped herself."

I was shocked and then annoyed by his brutal response; my mum wouldn't just bugger off. "Sorry, she would never have done that, not leave me at seven years old. Not if she had a choice." I was really riled, but trying to keep calm.

"She did a lot of drugs, Catherine."

I wanted to tell him to stop knocking my mum. I'd just about had enough.

"Not after leaving the band," I said.

"You sure about that?" he sneered. I wasn't, of course.

"Is she dead?" I asked him straight.

"I think she ran away to America then killed herself, if you want my honest opinion. I think she's dead, yes: suicide. She did threaten it a few times before, you know. Shame, she was a pretty girl, like you. I'd just get on with your own life and stop chasing dead ends and dead mothers. And as for a murder conspiracy, it's a far-fetched fantasy."

"I haven't mentioned a murder conspiracy," I said coldly.

"You don't have to, I know you're about to ask me. Truth is," he whispered, moving closer to me, his cigarette breath irritating my senses. "She contacted me, a month or so before she took her own life."

"Really?" I didn't believe him. "Why did she contact you?"

"She wanted her royalties paying into a different account."

"I thought Chris Latham handled that. He said they were

141

piling up in some bank account. One day they'd be mine and my Aunt Trish's, her sister's."

"But she thought Chris had, err… been siphoning money off. She wanted a different account setting up by me."

"And did you?"

"Only one for the receipts from the sales of Greatest Hits album we put out in 1990."

"Did it make much money?"

"Not much, no; huge costs, you know." I was suspicious. It had been a chart topper for two months at least. His fingers moved around the almost empty plastic beer glass, his nails long and dirty. There was a thick gold ring on his first finger and a Rolex on his wrist. He threw a handful of nuts into his mouth, exposing gold capped molars.

"Why did she kill herself?"

"Who knows. Drugs. Guilt at leaving you?" What a nasty thing to throw back at me, I thought. "Guilt or sadness at leaving Raven? Depression?"

"Where was she when she died?" I asked.

"Somewhere in Seattle was the last I heard."

I wasn't sure about any of this.

"So do you still look after mum's money?"

"Yes. It's still in that account; I just take a management fee but, until she turns up or you have her declared dead, it's stuck there."

I bet he took a management fee. A big one, too.

"Any idea where Raven's book manuscript is?" I asked.

"Yep. Still in the fantasy world of whoever suggested it. Was it real or just another rumour? Not sure his doped-up brain was capable of writing a shopping list, to be honest. If he did, it would only have one thing on it—more drugs!"

"It was real; it was called *Raven Rain Remembers: The Men Who Perverted Punk*."

"He'd have problems writing Raven Rain remembers to tie his shoelaces."

"Travis Brennon doesn't think he was still doing drugs."

"Oh, being off drugs was an act: one of his best. I don't think there was any murder. It was an overdose. Seen it before; a real shame. He was a nice guy, but it was always going to end one way."

"Sacha Tillens told me there was someone in the room and that they were drugged in the bar."

"They were always drugged! They were drugged before they got to the bar, drugged by themselves."

"Sacha was murdered. I saw her body."

"Possibly. I don't know, but there are some strange dudes about. It could happen anywhere. A stalker, probably, followed her to the blockhouse; she was a pretty girl. Models usually are."

"How do you know she was attacked near the old blockhouse? I didn't think the police released that information to the press?" I said.

"Oh, that depends on who you ask. I have pals in the cops, you know. We belong to the same men's club, as it were." He grinned. I fumed. My anger was spilling over.

"What the fuck happened on the last night of that tour in October 1984 when my mum walked out of the band? You seem to know everything, so tell me."

"Calm down love, you'll get your knickers in a twist. No one told you yet?"

"I want to know what you know," I replied, looking daggers at him.

"Oooh, well. She had a big bust up with Raven over drugs. Out of character I know, but he hit her, he was so stoned. Out of his box. She told him she was leaving and he demanded one last romp on the bed, sort of separation sex. Can't blame him. She refused. He hit her, then took what he thought he was owed."

I was stunned. No, that wasn't right. It didn't ring true. Was Raven really that double-edged and two-faced? He loved Mum, he'd never force her. I'd just been told at the funeral how tender and caring he was. Not the traits of a rapist. I looked around, a few people were eavesdropping. It was almost unbelievable: here was Robbi Romero alleging Raven was a rapist at his funeral.

"Sorry, I don't believe you. So you were there?"

"It was a long time ago and I was pissed. Drinking champagne, celebrating the end of a very successful tour. I fell into a taxi as soon as the encore was over."

"So who was Raven going to name in the book?"

"Dunno. Someone other than himself I guess. Members of Décolleté?"

"You?" I asked accusingly.

"Me? Ha! I doubt it. I championed him, and her. I made them into stars. Don't forget there were other bands on the circuit with secrets. Crooked accountants, dodgy venues with unsafe kit and fire trap dressing rooms. Maybe he had a handle on all of that. I doubt it was about the Scented Slugs and Décolleté. So what's this about rehearsals, are you a singer yourself? You'd look good on stage, need to show yourself off a bit though, you've got a nice body under all those clothes. Make the most of your assets, love. Show them off."

"I think you'd better go," I said scowling. I'd had enough of this creep.

"You might need me one day. Nice to meet you too. I need one or two of those sausage rolls before they all go." He needed a slap in the face rather than a sausage roll. As he turned, the thin man in the old suit and old glasses took my picture before pushing through the crowd and slipping away.

"Who was that?" I asked a one of the Slugs who'd played at the service.

"That," he said, "was Jez Deopham."

19. Faces iN The Mirror

It was the night before the first gig. I was dreaming of walking out onto the stage. As I embraced the applause my name was chanted, and then I froze. I couldn't speak, I couldn't sing.

A few hours later, I stood in front of the full-length mirror in my bedroom, trying to see myself as a singer. The top I'd chosen was tight. I was agonising over letting go, letting go of Miss Edgley, demure drama teacher at Beckthorn School for Girls, and embracing the spirit of Betzy Blac and the punk pantheon that went with her. The skirt I'd bought fitted, at a push; it made my bum look bigger than Mum's, but it would do. Looking at a close-up picture of my mother, I realised I was failing to truly look like her; I was older now than she was then. As I sighed there was a knock on the door. It was Aunt Trish.

"It's Betzy's microphone," she said, standing on my doorstep. "You should have it: a talisman. I've got her original lyrics book here too, all her songs written in longhand."

"Oh Aunt Trish, thank you. Come in, so nice to see you," I said as I hugged her, surprised by her unexpected visit. We went through to the kitchen and I took the nylon case and unzipped it. There was the familiar mic as seen in numerous photographs, posters, newspapers and magazines. Betzy's original mic. I'd have loved to be using that for sure, but today's music systems were digital and this was a relic of the analogue age. I ran my fingers over its shiny black surface. I kissed it and smelt it. She was gone, but my fingers held it as hers had done all those years before, and it felt good.

"Aunt Trish that's so sweet of you," I said, placing the treasured relic of Mum's career on the table. "I'll put the kettle on."

"Well, if you're not too busy, go on then, but just a small cup. I don't want to be looking for a loo at some petrol station on the way back."

"Busy? I'm nervous more like."

"You'll be fine, and your mum would be proud," said my aunt, pulling a chair back and sitting down, her ancient, torn brown leather handbag by her feet.

"I'm beginning to regret agreeing to this; it's all a bit much. Aunt Trish, this might be a weird question," I said as I filled the kettle, "but do you know where Mum's old school friend Debs is?"

"Oh, Catherine, that is going back. No, I never really knew her."

"And Mum's friend Judy? The woman she went to Scotland with before she disappeared?"

"I didn't know her very well either. Why do you ask?"

"I'd like to talk to them. I'm trying to track down all of the people who were in Mum's life during that last tour," I said, putting tea bags into the pot. "Are you coming to the show in London?"

"Oh, I don't like being out late," she replied. "Not now, not with my health. But I hope it goes well Catherine."

So did I.

*

I went by cab to the venue, but instead of feeling like an embryonic star I was feeling sick and anxious. I was as nervous as hell as we got closer and closer. I should have been excited—this was a chance to perform on stage, to be my Mum—but I was scared. Had I been too confident, too enthusiastic? Why did I allow myself to be talked into it? It was too late to back out now.

I walked through the door with my clothes, my make-up, and Mum's mic as a talisman. The band were there, setting up with a couple of music tech kids from the local college, who were desperate to help and gain experience. While they tuned the guitars, set up the drums and moved the amps, the sound engineer set up the mixing desk. I watched like a stranger observing from a distance; it seemed so unreal, despite the rehearsals. They were a bunch of friends playing music; I was a nervous newbie full of doubt and panic. This was real, this was a performance with an actual paying audience. I momentarily flashed back to my nightmare and shuddered.

Sarah could see I was nervous and we sat down together to run through the set list. The past days had seen us rehearse the gig three or four times a day at the village hall and in Rochelle's sitting room, her kids complaining about the bloody noise. I'd practised my moves, written a few things to say between tracks and worked out the little cues and signs we'd give each other to come in, start and stop the songs. The girls had played them so often they knew it all by heart, and as I knew the words it was an easy fit. The gig wasn't just a chance to play at being Mum, it was a chance to illicit new information, to help me find DD and Brad, and maybe even catch Raven's murderer. He could be there, the killer, in the crowd.

Trav told us to just treat it like a rehearsal, as it would be a friendly audience. Despite my fears that we'd hardly sell any tickets he said we should just enjoy it.

Then came the sound check and, dressed in normal clothes, we ran through three songs so the sound engineer and the music tech kids could check sound levels, positions and lighting. We did the opener, a mid-set song and the encore. It was difficult in the afternoon to produce any form of atmosphere, and we were dressed like we were going to pub. It was a big empty room, but the posters on the walls of the famous people who'd played there inspired me. Then it hit home. I realised this place used to be the infamous Dirty Dog House Music Cellar where Décolleté played their pre-tour warm ups. There was an original poster too, just below a group of them on the left, near the door to the ladies. Shit. My mum had actually stepped out on to this very stage.

I looked up. The lighting rig hung from the black ceiling like it was defying gravity. The thin, blacked out, long narrow windows at the top of the walls allowed a bit of grey light to seep in from the street above where pedestrians hurried by, unaware of the preparations below their feet. At the top of the pillars were fans and an aircon unit humming to itself. The bar was at one end and the staff were stacking bottles in glass shelves, writing the night's specials on the chalkboard and unloading plastic glasses from boxes. I knew there would be various friends and relatives of the band in the audience, and Jane and Kate from school. They were unaware I was performing, they just fancied a free night out and found it fun to be on the guest list of a band so I'd invited them along. Kate, who taught biology, was the same age as the group; she told me she'd loved Décolleté when she was at Uni. I was due to meet them by the bar at 7:45. They knew Betzy was my mum, but not that I was about to play her role.

Trav walked in, smiled, came straight over and gave me a knowing hug. There was real tenderness in his eyes.

"So how's it going, star?" he asked softly, his gleaming white teeth cutting through the house light gloom.

"Oh, you know, apart from a total lack of confidence, nausea, violent diarrhoea and a feeling that my period's about to start irritatingly early, I'm a gibbering wreck but, I'm, just fine," I replied, going red at what I'd just said. He smiled and took my hands, his floppy fringe falling forward as he learned toward me.

"Well, I can't help with the rest but, as for confidence, you'll get it when the lights come on. Focus on one imaginary face mid-way through the crowd. Just own the stage."

"The crowd? You sound as if we've sold some tickets."

"Just a few."

"How many?"

"All of them! Capacity crowd, eight-hundred-and-fifty!"

"No! Oh I wish you hadn't said that, Trav!" He hugged me closer. I buried my face in his chest, and felt warm and protected. He smelt comforting and safe, but I knew a man like Trav wasn't for a girl like me.

"Oh," he said. "I've got a TV crew coming, two leading music bloggers, a newspaper reviewer and a promoter who's looking at putting a tour together."

"You bastard!" I managed to laugh, but I was shaking with nerves. Sarah and Caroline sidled up.

"Better not fuck it up then, Cath!" Sarah grinned, and gave a mock punch to my chin. "It's all on you, girl. So, no pressure, hey!"

I swallowed hard and fled to the loo.

*

Time evaporated. Only an hour and a half to go. The girls were always ready. They'd never really stopped being Décolleté.

I peeked outside at the queue waiting in the street on that fume-filled summer evening. Many were clearly of an age that'd seen the band in its heyday. Some were younger, and others just curious. Were Brad or DD here? In this line? Would Raven's killer turn up? Sacha's too? I saw a guy from TV and an actress from a soap, but as the crowd built I couldn't watch anymore. I was beginning to get seriously scared about what was to come. Someone grabbed my arm. It was Sarah, pulling me back inside.

"Dressing room. Now!" she ordered. I didn't dare refuse. "Your mum had nerves too you know, Cath."

"Really? I thought she was totally cool."

Sarah laughed. "No, Betzy threw up before some gigs. She'd walk around chanting the lyrics, she was so paranoid she'd forget them and end up frozen in the spotlight unable to sing. You just reminded me of her."

We made our way back to the dressing room. Sarah put a reassuring hand on my shoulder and squeezed it tight.

"Cath when you walk out as Betzy, you *are* Betzy. Whatever happens, you carry on, even if there's a riot. It's a low stage so I don't think anyone will grab you, but if they do, take control, sing down to them and push them away. Make big theatrical gestures and, if it gets tough, nod to Johnny at the side: he's security, he'll sort it. Got it?" I nodded blankly. "Now, do you want food? Most of us eat afterwards but there's stuff here."

"No, no thanks. I'm okay."

"One alcoholic drink is all we're allowed. Otherwise we risk blowing it. You can get arse-holed afterwards, but not before."

"No. I need a clear head, but thanks."

"Right, time to get ready," said Sarah.

"Okay. I just need to check if someone's here yet." I smiled.

"But no running off!" Sarah said holding my shoulders as if she thought I just might.

*

I'd been holding off getting changed until I'd met Kate and Jane. It was a quarter to eight, so I slipped out to find them by the bar. The crowd was growing like the pace of my pounding heart. I quickly spotted them looking a bit overwhelmed in the bustle.

"Hi guys, you got here!" I hugged them both.

"Yes, thanks, it's amazing," giggled Kate, her hair freshly cut. "We just gave our names on the door and they let us in! Magic! It's so nice to see you, we miss you at school and so do the girls."

"Thanks, I miss you all too."

"I haven't been to a live show like this for years," said Jane, emptying her glass of cheap white wine in its plastic beaker. They looked different, wearing make-up and new clothes. I wondered what they'd think of mine when I walked out onto the stage.

"Brings back such great memories, Cath," Kate smiled at me. "But it's not the same without Betzy Blac. I wonder who's

150

singing tonight? It just says special guest vocalist on the posters."

"Someone in the queue reckons it'll be that girl who won that TV talent show," said Jane. "But I think it's someone from the same era, another woman singer from an old band. I wonder who?"

"Not sure," I grinned.

"Well, it'll be great," said Jane. "There's a hell of a buzz in the queue outside. Someone said some of the old Scented Slugs were here as well!"

"Oh wow!" I said, taken aback. I hadn't known that. Hopefully the Bleak Souls wouldn't be turning up too. Trav pushed through the melee.

"Hi Cath, shouldn't you… be somewhere?" he said meaningfully.

"Oh, hi, yes. Let me just introduce you. This is Jane and Kate, we work together. Girls, this is, err, a friend of mine who's helping with backstage stuff."

"Hi guys," said Trav, smiling, the half-light protecting his identity. "I'd better get back. I think you're needed too, Cath."

I gave them a nervous smile.

"I'm sure I know him from somewhere," remarked Jane.

"Wow, it's that your new boyfriend Cath? You're a dark horse, any more like that in your back pocket?" said Kate.

"No, just, just a friend," I said, as Trav beckoned me to follow him through the crowd.

"He looks very familiar."

"Really Kate?" I replied. "Maybe. I've got to go, girls. See you soon; I'll be near the front."

"Thanks for getting us in for free, Cath. It was kind of your mum's old band."

"No worries. Hope you enjoy it!" I said and pushed ahead, weaving my way through the crowd. Flashing my Access All Areas pass to the security guy like a rock star, I returned to the dressing room.

"Cath!" Caroline greeted me. "Thought you'd done a runner!"

I went to speak, but I couldn't. There before me was 1984 writ large. I was back in time, facing four music legends. No longer the fifty-odd-year-old women I'd jumped on stage with in that village hall. Here were the icons that were Stephy Stiff, Rocky Rump, Suzie Scums and Cassie Crack. How they'd let their manager pick those names was beyond me, but I was awestruck. Their make-up and costumes were unbelievable. Four heroes, here to help me turn my nightmare into a dream-come-true.

"There's something here for you, Cath." Steph handed me an envelope. "It was left at the box office. By a well-wisher, I think. Johnny from security's just brought it through."

I looked at the brown manila envelope and cautiously opened it, pulling out a handwritten note.

"Catherine, I was your mum's friend. I need to tell you something important. I will see you backstage at the end of the performance. Judy."

20. Pete Benton

"Cath, get dressed. Need some help?" asked Sarah, now dressed as Suzi Scums.

"Err…" My legs wobbled. I felt so weak, I started to slip backwards. Four sets of arms held me up, and I stood there in a daze.

"I've got my clothes in that bag," I said, nodding towards a holdall in the corner under my coat.

"No. Whatever you've brought along to wear, you're not going to wear it."

"What?" I gasped.

"We have your stage clothes here," said Suzi.

"But—"

"But nothing, Cath. When Betzy walked out after that last gig," Cassie said, "she left her stage clothes in the dressing room. She left Betzy behind."

"But we didn't," smiled Suzi Scums. "We kept them. We hoped she'd come back one day and be Betzy again. So far she hasn't…"

"But you have," added Cassie Crack.

"Just let us do this Cath," said Suzi firmly. It was an offer I couldn't refuse.

*

They took down my jeans and tugged them over my ankles. They pulled on designer torn, fishnet tights. I saw Mum's old short black leather skirt, which featured in so many photographs, pulled from a bag and tugged over my thighs. It hugged my waist as they did it up.

"Stay with us, Cath," smiled Suzi as they lifted my arms and, as if I were a child, they took off my top.

"Sorry, Cath, forgive us but you can't wear this. It's not Betzy at all." I was pushed forward and a hand went to the clip of my new bra.

"Woah, hang on!" I protested, but I was held firm.

"Really sorry, Cath. But we've got to make you Betzy and she didn't wear bras on stage. It's got to go."

I shrugged and let them slip it off. Mum's very low cut, loose stage top was shaken out and pulled over me. I went scarlet as I felt my nipples harden with the chill and the material brushing against me, but my embarrassment soon faded as their professional make-over turned Miss Edgley the quiet teacher into a stage-hungry singer ready to face the fans.

"I've brought make-up," I said.

"So have we: Betzy's make-up. Well as close as we could get." replied Cassie. "We want you looking as much like the real thing as possible." She said as they twisted the chair away from the mirror. I obeyed their instructions:

"Purse your lips…"

"Close your eyes…"

"Head back…"

"Nails out…"

"Blink…"

"Open your mouth…"

"Who's drawing the fake tattoo?" Suzi asked. "Okay, I will. Chest out. Keep bloody still, girl!"

I closed my eyes as a damp sponge with liquid foundation was gently smeared and massaged into my face. My hair was pulled back and, as the foundation dried, powder went on top. The patting around my nose and eyes tickled and I wanted to sneeze.

"It has to be thick, Cath: stage lights don't take prisoners." Stephy layered on eyeliner and turned my lips a dark blood red. I felt my skin go taut as the make-up hardened.

"My hair?" I asked with trepidation.

"It'll pass," said Suzi. "Take a look." I stared into the mirror and was amazed at the level of detail they'd gone to, to turn me into Betzy Blac. It was good. Mum would have approved. Then, while waiting for my black nail varnish to dry, the chair was swung round. The legends had made their own punk princess from a kit of parts, using Betzy's daughter and Betzy's clothes and make-up. They handed me Mum's ripped and faded denim jacket and the image was complete.

I stood up, turned around and felt my smile turn to sadness. The girls were welling up too.

"Wow, fuck. You look so much like her, it's uncanny," said Rocky. "It's like the bitch is back with us. I'm sorry." She started to sob.

"She always was with us," said Stephy, almost in tears too. "It's just now we can see her. The resemblance is incredible." Tears flowed, filling every face.

"I knew it would be a bit emotional, but not like this," sobbed Cassie. "But hey girls: stop the tears or the make-up's ruined."

"We loved her, your mum, she was something else. She wrote the songs, made the image, led the band. She was a star. A fucking legend," said Cassie, squeezing my shoulder. We hugged, for the first time I felt like part of the band. I'd been co-opted into Décolleté, and it was time to earn my keep and repay their faith in me.

There was a knock at the door. "Is it, err… safe to come in?" It was Trav.

"Safe? I'm not sure," Stephy laughed through her tears. "There are four punk panthers in here, four captive cougars."

"Wow! Cath!" said Trav.

"No, not Cath." Suzi threw her arm around me. "Now we're

155

in costume, we're in character. You get that, Betzy, you're an actor. Okay?"

"Sure, Suzi, I get it, and thanks for the make-up, girls. It's absolutely stunning."

"Five minutes to stage," said Trav. "I've got someone special to introduce you to."

"Really?" I said.

"Pete Benton. He's offered to introduce you tonight."

"We know him well," Suzi said. "He used to introduce quite a few of our gigs, especially on that last tour. He used to bring his brother Rupert along, and he always had a bunch of friends he wanted on the guest list. They did a lot to promote our gigs but were, well, hangers on I guess." I saw Cassie throw Suzi a look, and detected the girls didn't seem too enthusiastic, but he was well-known and he might trigger memories from the audience which, after all, was what we were really there for: information about Mum. I thought of the note I'd received from Judy and wondered again what she wanted, but there was no time to think about that now. The sound of the mic check ending leaked into the room.

"Hear that?" asked Suzi. "That's our cue to get on stage, girls. Let's go, come on, let's get going, wake up! This is it! We've waited decades for this. Let's go, rock and fucking roll, bitches! Yeooow!"

"Good luck girls," said Trav. "And Betzy, please, own the stage. It's a golden chance to find out what happened to your mum, grab it and use it." He smiled, squeezing my arms.

"You look so much like her, they'll believe she's back," said Stephy. "It's sure to bring back memories."

As I headed to the wings, I tried to reassure myself. I'd spoken at speech days, sung before the girls and so I'd thought I'd be fine, until I saw the crowd. They may have been parents, daughters and sons themselves, but this was no sodding speech day. My past and my present were colliding in front of eight-hundred-and-fifty eager fans. The background music stopped. The crowd surged forward in a temporary silence broken only by the hum of the amps: expecting, wanting, demanding.

"I'm not sure I can do this," I stuttered, frozen. Suzi Scums shook my shoulder as we stood in the shadows at the side of the stage. She wasn't taking prisoners and I didn't dare argue.

"Just do it, bitch. Do it for Betz. And remember, we're all in character!"

"Okay. Sorry Suzi. Okay, I'm… I'm ready," I whispered. But I wasn't.

I saw Trav nudge DJ Pete, who walked up to the mic. He looked every bit the faded frontman, the presenter of popular music shows and live radio broadcasts. He looked well-to-do and part of the music scene establishment. It was good to have him there introducing us: it made it seem genuine.

"Hello! I'm Pete Benton, are you having a good time?" Like a true DJ he waited for a response. "I remember this band back in the early '80s, when music really was music! Raw and full of emotion." Cheers erupted from the floor. "I used to introduce them on stage and I never thought we'd see them again. I loved Betzy. Didn't you?"

"YESSSS…. Betzy… Betzy…" chanted the crowd.

"Betzy was a legend," continued Pete. "Tonight we're so-ooooo lucky. Tonight we have the original line-up. It really is Suzi Scums, Rocky Rump, Stephy Stiff and Cassie Crack! Plus…" He was interrupted by cheers, stamping and clapping, "Plus, we haven't just got a stand in, we've got Betzy royalty, Betzy DNA—we have the *actual daughter of Betzy Blac*! She's the nearest thing to Betzy on the planet, apart from the Princess herself, wherever she is, bless her." More cheers, more stamping and more applause.

"Tonight, welcome back one of the best bands of our time. London, tonight you are watching, you are making—no, you are living—history. They're back! It's the one and only DECOLLETE!"

The responding roar amazed and scared me, but above all it

inspired me. Somewhere a small voice crept through the chaos, and I remembered my mum on my first day at school: "Time for a new era, Catherine."

Huge cheers washed over me and, as tears trickled down my cheeks, I was shoved out onto the almost darkened stage by Suzi and Rocky. Suzi screamed. Cassie stuck her fingers up and the crowd loved it. The pantomime had begun; Décolleté were alive. It was as if Mum was too, and I'd been taken over by her.

I turned my back on the audience, sidled up to the mic and moved as the lights hit their maximum brightness and we were engulfed like a starburst. The crowd went wild as I pulled the mic from its stand. I saw open mouths and jaws dropping when they saw me, the image I was presenting. Some believed Betzy had returned, others just clapped and cheered, delighted I was living up to the legend. I knew I couldn't disappoint them.

"Hello London!" I began. "We're Décolleté. Do you remember this number one? It's *Pink Bra Bust Up!*"

"YESSSSSS!" replied a throng of voices as one, and Cassie hit the drums, Suzi's fingers flew up her fretboard and Rocky's bass pounded through the floor. Stephy's guitar churned out the riffs and the words left my lips like a train from a tunnel. I focused, as Trav said, on a faceless person in the middle distance. The last chords of *Pink Bra* faded and the applause was overwhelming. I didn't want it to end. It gave me confidence. Trav was right: I took ownership of the stage.

"Thank you!" I screamed back at them. "Here's another one you might remember, *Wrecked Bed Regrets!*" Track after track ran into the next, as sweat poured from every centimetre of skin.

We paused after the fourth song and I took off Mum's jacket. I was about to say something banal and pithy, but Kate and Jane in the front row were almost wetting themselves with delight.

"Cath! Cath, it's you!" I heard them scream, just metres from my legs. I spun round and there was a roar. I was drunk on punk, high on the night; in love with being Betzy, and doing it for Mum. My lovely mum. If I died right there, died right then, I'd have achieved so much, bringing her back to life, even for one short night. Exploding like a firework brightening an empty sky.

I watched Trav watching me, and for a second I allowed myself to dream. I just wanted to fall into his arms and wake up in another world where my mum and his dad were alive. Then Cassie hit the drums and we ran into *Let's Get Fucked On Friday*. The girls were total professionals. Queens of the night. Together we tried to feed the hunger and quench the thirst of the audience, but the more we gave, the more they took. I was a woman possessed. Sweat and adrenalin drove me on. Everything ached but I didn't care. The crowd were like needy new lovers in a first-time frenzied fuck. Breathing as one, savouring the scent, waiting for the moment. But this was no climax, not just yet. The big "Oh!" was still to come.

We'd played for forty-five minutes and I announced we'd be taking a break, until Suzi rushed forward and asked the audience, "Unless you want us to carry on?"

The crowd gave us their answer: "Yes!" Eight-hundred-and-fifty yes's. We weren't allowed off stage. A TV camera was in the wings getting close ups as phone cameras clicked and excited fans smiled, danced and drank. Kate and Jane were jumping up and down and I caught a glimpse of security pulling one guy off the floor for being too excited and crashing into the people by his side. Then I saw them, in the centre of the crowd: Chloe and Emily, the girls from school. They waved and cheered. They should have been doing homework or resting in their dorm. What the hell would they tell the others? I was beyond caring.

"Let's go! Décolleté lives!" I shouted at the top of my voice. Gulping from a bottle of water I heard Cassie Crack start revving up for *Two Lovers in One Night*, and there out of the corner of my eye I saw two guys I recognised from Raven's funeral, original members of the Scented Slugs. As we ended *Two Lovers*. I turned to Suzi and said: "Just go with me, please?"

"Sure, Betzy, you lead and we'll follow. We always did." She smiled, tears in her eyes. I nodded to Rocky, Stephy and Cassie and they all grinned.

"Enjoying it?" I asked the crowd, who positively screamed with delight. "There are two guys out there I want to invite on stage. This is unrehearsed and may go horribly wrong. But it's Baz and Sledge from the Scented Slugs!" More roars and the two ageing punks climbed on the stage and gave me a hug. The girls hugged them too; there were genuine tears in their eyes. I'd recaptured a moment, rekindled a dream.

"I don't suppose," I said to the crowd. "I don't suppose these guys still remember the Slugs' biggest hit, *Sexplosion Ocean*?" I remembered the funeral performance and hoped I wasn't setting up a disaster. If these guys were stoned it could ruin our show, but it was too late.

Baz and Sledge whispered to the girls and they borrowed Rocky's bass and Suzi's Fender and looked at me. "Well, I know the words!" I said and shouted, "This is for Raven Rain's son, Travis Brennon... Yes, he's here tonight!" The crowd were beside themselves as Baz and Sledge kicked off with Cassie playing along. I hit the cue and fumbled my way through one of Raven Rain's most popular songs as the audience sang along delighted with a bonus from the past.

"So," I said, as the two Slugs left the stage. "That was written by Raven Rain, now here's one my mum, Betzy Blac, wrote about her love for him. A bit slower, a bit more sensual but a very beautiful song. Can you help me remember the title?" I asked and the words "*Raindance*" came thundering back. Suzi played the intro then Rocky's bass started as the lights changed to subtle reds and we cut through the applause to perform.

"He took me to a rain dance, in a wild and special place. I undid the buckle, he undid the lace. We jumped naked in the river, his hair fell on my face." I closed my eyes and sang the song which I knew had meant a lot to Mum, tears pouring down my already wet cheeks. My voice began to crack as emotion overcame me. Trav rushed onto the stage seeing me start to fall apart; he held me close, and leaned into the mic. He helped

160

by singing the words with me until the final chords died away. The crowd recognised him and seemed to think it had all been planned as a duet as they swayed, their arms held high.

"Wow, a bit of emotion and a lot of post punk history on this stage tonight," I said wiping my eyes. "I don't want to ruin the mood but before we carry on, a quick thank you to Travis Brennon!" More applause and cheers came up to greet us. "Hey, my mum, the real Betzy Blac disappeared after this band's last gig in October 1984. Her former lover, Travis Brennon's dad, Raven Rain was found dead a few weeks ago and his fiancée Sacha was murdered a few days after that. Both Travis and I think these events are linked. We need to find what happened to Betzy Blac and who killed Raven and Sacha." I paused, hoping I hadn't ruined the whole event. "There's a phone number and an email address at the entrance of the club. Please call us, anonymously if you want, but any information could help us solve the crimes and find my mum."

A ripple of applause became a torrent banishing my fears about the appeal falling flat. I was about to speak again when Suzi waved her hands, leaned over to the mic and started chanting Mum's name. The audience took over and the noise level began to rise.

"Betzy, Betzy, Décolleté, Décolleté" was chanted, increasingly loudly. Suzi tapped me on the shoulder and nodded to Cassie, holding her sticks above the drums. It was time to rock.

"This one's called *No More Tears, No More Fears!*" More cheers and we ploughed on. Soon we got to the end of the set. We had two possible encores left and we still hadn't played the band's biggest hit: *Banging On The Beach*. My body began to complain; I had little left to give. I knew we had to wind it up as the girls would be shattered too.

"You've been a great audience! They are Décolleté, and I've been Betzy Blac, thank you. We've got just one more tonight, one you'll know. It's about…. *Banging…*" and the audience replied as one, "*On The Beach!*" I looked round at the band and it was 1984 again.

21. Sir Rupert

We left the stage, the last drum sounds still echoing in our ears before finally fading as the applause took over, drowning everything else out. We took our bows and waved as we left the stage, hand in hand under the dimming lights. House music slowly faded up and the lights came on to show the crowd it was time to go home.

"You fucking nailed it! Well done, Cath," said Suzie, now back to being Sarah, hugging me. She was crying like the rest of us: a mix of sheer relief, happiness, memories, and the pain of missing Mum. We collapsed around the dressing room as we listened to the background noise. It was a scene repeated a thousand times backstage after a gig. Only a performer can know how we felt. The crowd were leaving, but the applause would echo through my head forever. I'd split a nail, lost an earring, and ached like I'd been dragged through a jungle and survived a fever—but it felt absolutely amazing. My body was shaking and pulsating. I'd never experienced anything like it. The exhilaration and the love I felt out there that night would stay with me forever. We were absolutely wired and totally absorbed in the moment. My ears were ringing and every limb was like lead. Johnny, the security guy, came in with a list of people wanting to see us. We ticked off the ones we knew. Kate and Jane were the first, squealing like teenagers.

"Ohhhh!" they bleated running up to me. I was half-sitting, half-lying on the settee, water bottle in my hand, a towel around my neck. My make-up was smeared, sweat was drenching me, and my feet were hot and tight in my shoes. The fake tattoo was now just a smudge on my chest bone.

"Cath, that was stunning, we had no idea!" Jane said.

"The girls at school will be absolutely amazed!" added Kate.

"Yeah," I grinned proudly. "Two of them were here in the audience." Just then Chloe and Emily walked in, looking very grown up and clearly excited by the performance they'd seen.

"Miss!" they shouted together. "That was awesome!"

"Chloe, Emily, nice to see you, but…"

"We are eighteen. Just," laughed Emily.

"School think we're tucked up in bed," Chloe said. "We sneaked out and got a taxi."

"Bad girls!" I laughed. "Well, I'm glad you all enjoyed it," I croaked. "Sorry; my voice is going."

"Your mum would have loved it," said Kate.

"Yes, she really would have done."

"Well, you've got to do this again now," said Jane. "You're brilliant. A natural."

"Thanks," I replied. "We'll see." They all hugged a very sweaty Miss Edgley and left.

For a few minutes we were on our own.

"Shit, I feel old!" said Caroline, shaking her arms. "I think my hands are going to drop off. I haven't drummed like that for so long."

"Yeah I feel about eighty," laughed Stephanie. "That guitar feels far heavier than it used to!"

"What do we expect, hey? We were kids back then, we're old women now," said Rochelle. "I'll order some walking sticks for the next gig!"

"Chris Latham's outside," said Sarah.

"And Robbi 'Rat Boy' Romero," added Stephanie. Neither seemed that happy to see them, and none of us could remember saying they could come backstage, but they wandered in like they owned the place.

"Hi Cath, or rather Betz. Good to see you again," Robbi said.

"Hello" I said, unimpressed.

"Could be worth us looking at a digitally remastered greatest hits album on DVD and digital," he said. I could almost see the pound signs in his eyes. "Or a re-record with your vocals."

"Lots to discuss," cut in Sarah, coming out of the shower, back in civvies.

Caroline went to take her place. "Excuse me, but I need to shower and change. My kids will want their mum back; they're a bit embarrassed by her on-stage persona."

"Happy to help!" offered Robbi, looking Caroline up and down, her sweaty t-shirt clinging to her braless chest.

"Fuck off," said Sarah, unimpressed.

"Oh dear. Sorry, I thought it was the '80s again and that was allowed! Great show girls, and think about that re-release." Robbi left.

"That was brilliant Cath," said Chris. "I can see your mum in you. So good. It was like we were back in the early days. Did you catch up with the Bleak Souls?"

"They caught up with me, thanks," I replied.

"And you're okay? Did they say anything?"

"No. Not much," I replied.

"And have you learned anything of value tonight?" he asked.

"No sign of Brad or DD, but my mum's old friend Judy has asked to see me."

"I don't know her. But look, if I can help, I'm still your mum's agent."

"Thanks Chris."

"I'll leave you to it. Keep in touch and keep me updated." As he left, DJ Pete walked in with a guy I didn't recognise.

"That was the best comeback gig I've ever seen!" said the ageing DJ. He was wearing a faded bomber jacket. Stephanie and Rochelle were sitting opposite me quietly drinking water and watching.

"Very impressive. It could have been Betzy herself on that

stage," said the man with him. "You really were very good."

"Oh, this is my brother Rupert Benton. Or rather, Sir Rupert," said Pete. "Don't worry, he only got the knighthood for some boring industrial thing." He laughed, punching his brother's shoulder jokingly.

"Oh?" I asked, looking at Sir Rupert, a tall thin man with a narrow, well-trimmed moustache and an almost convincing hairpiece. He looked like he was trying to keep up with his brother, a man who had the sort of hair that never seemed to thin. Pete's jacket was still carrying the logo of his old radio station in those square 1980's letters which look so dated now. I wondered how often it actually came out of the closet.

Rupert was inconspicuous in comparison, wearing black chinos and an expensive, more formal jacket. The only hint of an interest in music came from the extremely faded, black Décolleté tour t-shirt with the infamous 1984 dates just legible under a picture of the band. Mum's face distorted by years of wear. A true fan who was clearly someone who liked Betzy Blac.

"So pleased to meet you. I'm the dull brother." He smiled. "I run Benton's Pharmaceuticals. You were brilliant out there; it could almost have been the '80s again. You're so like your mother; she was such a lovely person."

How refreshing, I thought, to hear someone describe her a lovely person rather than go on about her sexuality or looks.

"She certainly was," added Pete. "And sadly, I don't get recognised much these days more's the pity. Seriously, that was good. Bit of a strange break in the middle, that appeal though. It kind of interrupted the flow."

"But that's why I did it: to try and find information."

"I think you're chasing a dead end, if you want my opinion. The conspiracy theorists have got to you, Catherine. I'm afraid I tend to go with Robbi's theory about a sad suicide," said Pete Benton.

Had he and Robbie discussed it recently I wondered? Rupert was staring at me. I looked straight at him.

"Sorry, I didn't mean to stare, but you look so much like your mother you know," he said. "The clothes were so evocative. She had a real presence on stage, and you got close to that tonight."

"Thank you, well, they're her clothes, the ones she wore in '84."

"That's incredible. It was a special tour and a special last night," he replied. "May I touch the jacket?"

I was taken aback by his strange request but I nodded. He picked it up and then sniffed it like a dog would, making me feel uncomfortable.

"We must go," interrupted Pete, noticing my reaction.

"I've been told it was a horrible night, for Mum. That last show," I pushed.

"Oh, I think she enjoyed herself underneath it all," replied Rupert.

"A row with her boyfriend can't have been nice though," added Pete, swiftly.

"Do either of you know DD or Brad?" I asked. They shook their heads. Pete threw a firm glance at his brother and they left.

Sarah was trying to attract my attention. A TV crew wanted an interview with Stephy and me, as we were still in costume. I quickly clean my face, slipped Mum's jacket back on to cover the sweat and we set up on the empty stage.

"Where do you want us?" I asked the reporter.

"Just in front of the amps and those guitars will be great. It's nicely lit by the stage lights they've put back up for us; but not too bright, don't worry. Just look at me, ignore the camera and if you can give me short answers it will help." He turned to the camera. "So this is an interview with Cath Edgley and Stephy Stiffs. Okay. Firstly, Cath, it must have been strange playing your mum, the great Betzy Blac?"

"Of course, but it was an honour, and it was great to sing with these girls, such talented performers," I replied, smiling.

"Stephy Stiffs, is this just the start? Is this a Décolleté revival?"

"I think the band would love that. It's up to Cath here, but the idea is to find what happened to our friend and her mother: Betzy."

"How was it having Cath Edgley playing her mum Betzy Blac?" he asked Stephy.

"She was wonderful," she replied. "We've lost a sister, but we've gained a daughter."

I made an appeal which they sadly edited out, but I knew any publicity would help. They grabbed a quick interview with Trav and DJ Pete Benton, who both lavished praise on the performance. I was embarrassed but proud. I hoped Mum would have been too. It was as if we'd started a whole post-punk, power pop revival.

*

When I got back into the dressing room, Trav was drinking coffee. Now there was a real star. He looked so gorgeous surrounded by the detritus of the dressing room, stage clothes hung over holdalls on chairs, damp towels in a laundry basket, empty mugs, glasses and bottles and paper plates with sandwich crusts and a half-eaten pizza. He passed me a cup of coffee.

"You need to get changed, Cath, you'll get cold," he said, gently putting his jacket around my shoulders as I slipped Mum's off. His hand brushed my neck. I felt weak and tired. I wanted him to come back with me, but I know I'd end up being hurt. Why would a man like Trav want a needy nerd like me?

"Thanks, Trav. The shower's empty now Caroline's out."

"You did it, girl. You owned it; you were Betzy." He smiled at me.

"Thanks for helping out with *Raindance*. Always a tough one for me, that love song." Especially when my mum wrote it for his dad about the pair of them having sex.

"Pleasure. Great duet. The audience loved it."

"I did like it, Trav, playing Mum out there on stage. Maybe too much."

"Good. You need to carry on, see where this leads. Has anyone owned up to being DD or Brad yet?"

"No, but I didn't tell you. Mum had a mate at school and they were going to name the band after her: she was known as Desperate Debs. No idea where she is now though."

"If it really is her sending the texts… It could also be a member of the band, or someone connected with the band who knew the original name."

"But who? The girls? Chris Latham? Robbi? Pete the DJ? Jez Deopham? Even Danny from the Bleak Souls…" I mused. "Hey thanks so much for your help. This wouldn't have happened without you."

"No worries. And hey, we turned a profit!"

"I hope Mum liked it," I said, getting teary. "Sorry. I'm getting overwhelmed here. Give me a hug and excuse the sweat," I whimpered, pushing my face into his chest.

"Hey, come on. Teary sometimes goes with the territory. And as for sweat, you should see me coming off stage!" We hugged, closely. I wanted more.

Trav left as I headed into the shower, while the rest of the girls packed their things to go. I was waiting for Judy, and was surprised she hadn't shown up by now.

Alone in the dressing room and wrapped in a towel, I looked in the mirror, amazed at the transformation back to little me. As I did a shape appeared behind me. Someone slipped through the door.

"Who's there?" I asked, turning. But I immediately knew who it was: Jez Deopham, Mum's stalker.

22. JUDY

"Please leave," I said, my breathing increasing. I was alone, in nothing but a towel, and here was a man my mum had had to get a court order to stop him pestering her. I pulled the towel tighter and prepared to scream.

"I'm not here to hurt you. I need to talk to you, about Betzy," he pleaded.

"Keep away from me! Mum had to get a court order against you."

He grinned. I was scared.

"You looked stunning out there dressed as your mum, just the same as she did. Beautiful. And now, in that towel, wow."

"OUT!" I shouted, unable to move my arms for fear of dropping the towel.

"You see this?" He raised his shirt.

"Don't want to see any more of you than I can now. SECURITY!" I shouted, hoping to hell they were still here.

"I'm not making advances. Please." He raised his shirt a little further to reveal a large scar across his stomach.

"Shit," I said, genuinely shocked.

"Your mum had friends. They warned me off."

Who did he mean? The girls in the band? They wouldn't do that to him surely? Raven? No, he was too soft, wasn't he? The Bleak Souls? Maybe.

"Who did that? The Bleak Souls."

Jez Deopham looked away and pulled his shirt back down.

"I'm not saying."

"She was scared of you, but it doesn't justify that."

"She didn't know about it."

"Really? Look, why are you here?"

"Because I believe she's still alive, and together you and I can find her."

"If you have information then tell me, or tell the police. I'm doing nothing with you."

"Okay. I have evidence. I loved her—Betzy—I want to find her too," he said, moving forwards.

"That's far enough. SECURITY!" I shouted again. "What evidence? Why do you think she's alive?"

"I think I know what happened in '84."

"What? Tell me," I demanded.

"Not here, not like this. I still love her. If she's alive and I help you find her, she will realise I'm not who she thought I was."

"Mum didn't want you, nor do I. SECURITY!" I screamed, getting desperate for help. Johnny from security didn't show up. Luckily, Trav did; he'd been waiting for me outside. My expression told him all he needed to know.

"YOU—OUT!" he shouted, grabbing Deopham's arms.

"For fuck's sake, Catherine," Deopham shouted, lunging towards me. "Betzy Blac is still alive and I want to find her; it's the music story of the decade. It's my life's work and she's the love of my life."

"Ms Edgley wants you to leave," said Trav, pulling Deopham out of the room, twisting his arm behind his back.

"Johnny, customer for you!" shouted Trav as he dragged Deopham down the corridor. I heard the gruff voice of the security guy as he threw him out.

I sat down in the chair, shaking. What if Trav hadn't come in? What would Deopham have done? Did he know anything or was he just fishing, trying to get to me? If he really knew where Mum was, surely he'd be there, trying to see her?

Trav came back. "He's gone. Creep or what? You okay, Cath?"

he said, moving towards me but stopping short of touching me, my bare shoulders inches from his arms.

"Trav, hug me for fuck's sake. The guy scares me." Trav squeezed me tightly, the towel being the only thing between my naked body and his arms.

*

The sharp lights of London flashed across the black cab's windows as I made the journey out of the city and back to Chestnut Close. When I arrived there was a big bunch of flowers waiting in the porch. The card read: *"To our new Betz, you were stunning. Your mum would have been proud of you, we were. Your band. Xx"*

*

The next thing I knew I was waking up with a headache. The bedside light was still on; there was a dead moth beside it. I was dehydrated. My face felt scrubbed and sore from applying and removing the heavy make-up. My legs throbbed like I'd walked a marathon. My ears were humming and my throat felt swollen, I could barely speak. Not exactly the Hollywood image of a post-gig pop star, even a pretend one.

As I lay in bed a car drew up outside. Doors opened. There was a knock. I staggered down pulling my old thick dressing gown around me and let in the world.

"Sorry to call so early, Catherine. We need to speak."

It was DC Dennison and DC Patel.

"You're not here to arrest me again are you?" I asked, beginning to panic.

"No. Can we come in please?"

"Of course. But please excuse me, I've just woken up." I invited them through to the sitting room.

"Do you know a Judy Spencer?"

"Yes—or, well, I know of her. I've never met her; she was

once Mum's best friend. Why?"

"Did you meet her last night?"

"No. She sent a note—I've still got it, I think—saying she wanted to see me after the show. But she didn't turn up."

"If you have it, we'd like to see it. Just for the record, can you formally confirm where you were between ten and eleven o'clock last night?" asked DC Patel.

"Err, standing on a stage in front of eight-hundred-and-fifty people, pretending to be Betzy Blac."

"That's the time we believed Judy Spencer died," said DC Kate Dennison.

"Died?"

"Yes," said DC Patel. "She was hit by a tube train; we believe on her way to see you. Witnesses say she jumped."

I fell back into the chair. Another death? "No. That's so sad. She was going to tell me something she felt was important. That's awful, poor woman. Are you sure she wasn't pushed?"

"We've been through the CCTV," said DC Patel, "and it looks like she did jump. No hesitation either. It was just after nine o'clock. We've traced her movements to the venue you performed at. She went in to the ticket office at seven-thirty and then left, presumably to leave you that note."

"But why…? That's just terrible," I said, unable to comprehend the news.

"We're not suggesting you had anything to do with her death, Catherine, we just wondered if you had any idea why she might have taken her life?"

"None. Unless… Unless it was guilt?"

"Guilt?" repeated the male detective.

"Yes, somehow connected with whatever happened to my mother."

"Sorry to have had to bring you sad news, Catherine. Are you okay?"

"Yes, I will be. Just a bit shocked by this, and pretty shattered from last night."

She smiled at me, like she was on my side, like she understood me. "We'll show ourselves out," said DC Dennison.

I called Sarah.

"Sarah. Hi."

"Hello star, how are you?"

"Shocked. The police have just left."

"What did they want?"

"It's about Mum's friend, Judy. She was found dead last night during the gig."

"Fuck, how, where?" Sarah asked, trying to take in the news. "I never knew her, but what? Is it connected with us? Raven? Sacha?"

"I'm not sure. They say it was suicide but she was going to meet me. She said she wanted to tell me something."

"Guilt? Guilt over something she knew or should have done, or something she did?" said Sarah. "I know she went to Scotland with Betzy the weekend of her disappearance. Judy came back alone. I know Jez Deopham went to talk to her once; he wrote an article about the mystery of Betzy Blac. It was all speculation because Judy told him very little: well, she was barely quoted in the piece he wrote. She was in a psychiatric unit at the time, I think. Betzy's disappearance badly affected her."

"I need to go there, to Scotland, to retrace Mum's steps. Just in case it triggers something. Aunt Trish knows where Mum stayed."

"Be careful, Cath. How are you physically after the gig?" she asked.

I sat down. "I'm pretty exhausted; you must be too."

"What, because I'm old?! But, you're right, yes. I'm wiped out. It's the post-gig crash, it's what happens, it's how we all feel. You rocket through to the stars on the adrenaline and the applause and then crash down back to earth when the lights have gone cold and the amps are switched off. The adrenalin stops when you're no longer on show. Then, in my case, you get home to find the neighbour's sodding cat has crapped in your planter by the door again and there's a mass of junk mail through your letterbox. Hey, it'll all seem worth it when you see the papers."

"Really? Why?"

"The reviews are brilliant. I'll text you some links. You were stunning, Cath, utterly great. We must go on tour, but according to the TV report we already are! Apparently you said so. So that's fixed then."

"But—"

"No buts."

"Oh, by the way after you'd left Jez Deopham turned up."

"What the eff? He's bad news, Cath."

"Trav and security threw him out."

"Sex pest. Dangerous. Avoid. Did he make a grab for you?"

"I thought he was about to, but he said he had information for me. I felt really uncomfortable, I was only wearing a towel. Guys like that… just horrible."

"I wouldn't trust him. I think the police missed a trick not holding him after your mum disappeared. I'm not convinced he's just an innocent old perv."

"You think he might have killed her?"

"I'm not saying that, but there's something deeply unsavoury about Jez Deopham. Was he working with someone else? Robbie the Rat Boy, maybe? Who knows, but hey we might find out with this tour."

"That's the hope and the plan. Thanks Sarah." I ended the call and turned on my PC. I sipped a tea while I waited for it to load, then I searched for my name and Décolleté, and there it was in the online editions.

Décolleté delights—surprise reunion gig with Betzy's daughter Cath Edgley in stunning tribute to her mum.

So much for my hiding under all that make-up! An online music blog read: *Stunning display - what a star - Betzy Blac is back in the guise of her daughter. Tour to follow? A must-see sell-out for sure!*

Then there was the TV piece on a news channel. Wow, that

was me on stage with the girls, but it looked and sounded like Mum out there. Then I saw a video clip on social media of the moment when Trav joined me for *Raindance*, and it felt good watching us performing Mum's classic song together.

My landline was ringing. I tore myself away from watching the clip. My mood changed when I found out who was on the phone, and I wished they weren't.

"Miss Edgley? It's the Head's secretary here. Miss Miles urgently needs to see you."

"Sure. Err… when? Midday would be good."

"No, now!"

"Is that an order?" I asked, taken aback.

"What do you think?"

*

An hour later I was waiting outside the Head's office. I felt like a naughty schoolgirl. What a costume change from last night! My feet were in the tight, dull boring flats that I only wore for work, tucked neatly under the chair. My make-up was so subtle it was almost unnoticeable. I was wearing the dark blue suit I put on for work evenings, and a rather strained and worried look on my tired face. My hands were folded demurely across my lap, held firm to keep my fidgeting fingers still as the old school clock on the wall above me ticked relentlessly on.

Behind the door she'd have read the papers and maybe even seen the clips online, if she knew how to do that. That made me smile: the thought of her watching me singing on stage. What part of my contract could that have broken? I couldn't recall a clause about performing in public; I was a drama teacher after all. I didn't want to be sacked; It was nice work, and I needed the money. I really did enjoy it—the job, the girls and the people— but with this all over the headlines? It would be such a shame if I had to leave; I'd done nothing wrong. I'd never advocated bad behaviour, drugs or anything immoral. I'd been a perfect professional, as I was described by my head of department only the year before. It would be pretty unfair if I were judged on a persona my mum had in the past, rather than the person I portrayed last night as a tribute to her.

As the clock struck the hour, the Head's door opened. Right on cue.

"Would you come in, Miss Edgley. Or is it Miss Blac?" she said sarcastically.

"No!" I surprised myself as it fell out of my mouth. Then I took aim and fired. "I'm Cath, Betzy was my mum." I struggled not to lose it completely, I had a thumping headache, my limbs felt like lead and I had cramps in my belly. In spite of all this I was still infected with the previous night's punk persona and Mum's music, echoing in my mind. I was rapidly stepping out of Miss Edgley, demure drama teacher, and into Betzy Blac the sequel.

"I've tried to be understanding, Catherine, I really have. Last time we spoke I kindly offered you paid leave to help you come to terms with this business, but you've only dug yourself further into it. I'm told that last night you made a complete spectacle of yourself, pretending to be your mother, some awful punk woman. I hear you swore! You sang about all sorts of inappropriate things and quite frankly were an embarrassment to yourself and this school."

"I was being my mum as a tribute to her, a tribute for one very important reason: to find out what happened to her, and to help the police find the killer of Raven Rain. I'd have thought trying to solving murders would have been applauded by Beckthorn School for Girls."

"Your mother was an outrageous embarrassment."

"My mother was a star. Loved by millions." Her shock, accompanied by a sharp intake of breath, was palpable. I carried on. "My mother achieved hundreds of thousands of record sales, made a name for herself and earned more than a million. I'll bet some of the parents and grandparents of the girls I teach here have even bought her records."

"Your mother's music was tat, rubbish, pop."

"My mother's music was, and is, the soundtrack to people's lives. Her lyrics were about love and dreams and waking up with strangers. You need to be a passionate, warm-blooded and human to appreciate that, Miss Miles." I surprised myself, and her.

"Really, Miss Edgley! I will not be spoken to like that. I'll expect your resignation letter on my desk tonight."

"No. If you sack me I'm going to the press. Don't forget I do know about various incidents here over the years which will make for interesting reading. I can see the headlines now: *Punk Star Spills Beans On Snob School Secrets*. Remember Mr Snell and Miss Jameson? The girl who walked in on them remembers. She told me about it." She went silent. I offered to leave with a year's salary and a glowing reference.

"Get out!" she stormed, banging the table with her fists.

"I wouldn't threaten me, Miss Miles; you might regret it. I'm no longer the quiet little drama teacher who's been hiding in these dusty corridors and classrooms. I've woken up. I'm glad we have an agreement."

I walked into my classroom and emptied my desk. I took one last look around and wrote one last thing on the whiteboard.

"Carpe Diem! Seize the day! Rock and roll, good luck! Cath Edgley."

I'd miss the smiling faces and seeing the talent develop in my girls. It was time to move on. I had a killer to catch.

23. SCOTLAND

The sun was high as I drove north to Scotland. I had a few days before full time rehearsals, and I needed to see where Mum had been when she vanished. My research had led me to a small hamlet on Applecross called Tuaig. Aunt Trish had found the details in an old diary. I'd found it was still available as a holiday let, albeit with new owners, so I'd booked three nights. It was a long way to go for such a short stay, but I just felt the need to go and see it before rehearsals started in earnest.

I wished I'd met Judy. She was clearly a tortured soul and held clues to Mum's disappearance. Clues she took with her to the grave.

After many hours of motorway, stops at services and coffee to keep me awake, I crossed the border and eventually passed Loch Lomond. I was nearly too tired to carry on and was regretting not having broken the journey with a hotel stop en-route, but I finally climbed upwards to the Applecross peninsula. The road across the mountains to the coast was utterly beautiful and very dramatic. Soon I could see the sea and across to the Isle of Raasay. I joined the coast road heading north, finding the small collection of three simple, squat crofts I was heading for. Each had fences to keep the deer out of their gardens.

I didn't think I could have driven another mile. It wasn't a journey for a single driver. My back and buttocks were aching and my arms sore from gripping the wheel. Relieved the journey was over, I parked and switched off the engine. Getting out to stretch my legs, the fresh peat-scented air welcomed me. Was this where Mum took her last breath? For a moment I just stood and held on to the open car door, my body trying to remember what upright felt like.

I stared at the small white painted croft where I was staying, the place where Mum had been all those years ago. Two small windows sat in the roof above two bigger ones below on the ground floor. A growing sense of gloom crept over me and I was beginning to wonder just why I'd come all that way. Then the door opened and a woman in her seventies walked towards me, smiling.

"Hello, you must be Catherine. I'm Megan, I sent you the confirmation email. I own the house. So you're staying for three nights."

"Yes, thank you. It looks lovely," I said.

"Oh, I'm sure you'll enjoy your stay, the house is quite comfortable," Megan said, looking at the building. "There's a few groceries in the kitchen as we're a wee way from the shops."

"How long have you owned the house, Megan?"

"Oh six years now. We moved here from Edinburgh." I was disappointed. For a moment I thought she may have met Mum.

"Do you know the previous owners?"

"The old owner, Mrs McLaren? No, she died before we bought it. Why do you ask?"

"My mum stayed here thirty years ago."

"Och, that's a lifetime ago. We're all newcomers in the hamlet now," she said. "Well, I live in the one across the track up there. The sand coloured one with the grey windows, you see?"

"Yes, very nice."

"It's very quiet here; nothing ever happens. That's why we like it."

"Looks lovely. Is the other house inhabited?"

"The one on the side of the hill there? No, it's empty, been empty for decades I'm told. No one goes there; the roof's too dodgy, bits keep falling off."

"Why doesn't the owner restore it?"

"Och, too expensive, and besides there are so many others nearby to be restored or rebuilt. The barn in the grounds of this one for a start," she said, nodding towards the building beside the croft, her straggly grey hair tied up at the back. "The roof half fell in years ago. Keep out as it's all a bit flaky for sure. Anyway, here's the key," she said, taking a Yale key on a tartan leather fob from her pocket. "You'll find everything you need, there are two double bedrooms so take whichever you want. They're both made up. There's a bathroom downstairs with a small sitting room and kitchen. I know it's June, but I've had the heating on—it's not as warm up here as it is where you've come from down south. Have a good stay and call me if you need anything. We're going out now but we'll be back later tonight. You won't be disturbed, there's no one else around for half a mile."

"Thanks, I'll be fine," I said, taking the key. Was this the same one Mum used when she was here, I wondered.

I took my bags inside and closed the door. There was a faint smell of damp, warmed by the rising heat from the radiators, but it smelt clean, if not a little uninviting. The kitchen was spacious and well equipped. A photograph of a stag on a hillside was in a frame hanging on the far wall. The room was an extension to the original property and had larger windows and straight walls. The rest of the house reflected the environment it was built in, and built for. The windows were tiny to minimise the heat loss in winter, and the walls were thick to do the same. It was all painted white, with simple furnishings and rugs over cheap looking fitted cord carpet.

I climbed the stairs and picked the room I instinctively felt Mum had slept in, although I no way of telling, of course. I lay my bag on the bed and went into the kitchen. Opening the fridge, I found some of the groceries Megan had mentioned, including a delicious-looking pizza. I switched on the large oven and waited for it to heat up, setting the timer on my phone. While the pizza cooked, I went to the window and looked at the darkening hills beyond. Was Mum somewhere out there? Or was she over to the west, below or beyond the waves?

As I took the pizza out of the oven and found a plate, I heard a car. It cut through the quiet of the evening and drew up outside. My heart raced. I was alone. I looked towards the owner's croft along the track. Her car was gone. I looked at my phone, but there was no signal. Outside, a car door was opening. A burst of panic spread through me. I grabbed a large carving knife from beside the sink and shrank back behind the wall by the door, hidden from view. There was a firm knock.

"There are two of us in here," I shouted.

"I damn well hope not," came the reply. The door opened and in walked a familiar figure. "Hi, Cath. Thought you could use some company. Sarah told me where you were; why didn't you tell me? I was really worried."

"Trav! Oh, it's so good to see you."

"Great greeting!" He grinned as I dropped the knife, the jagged blade hitting the floor tiles with a clang.

"Sorry. I was a bit spooked hearing a car draw up. So how did you get here?"

"I flew to Aberdeen and got a taxi. It's bloody miles!"

"Yeah, a bit out of the way."

"So why didn't you tell me?"

"Because I didn't want you to think you had to come with me. You've got your album to finish, and why would you want to be bogged down by me? You've done so much already. The last thing you need is a needy, mad woman on a crazy mission to drag you down."

"Cath," he said, holding my shoulders, his beautiful face close to mine. "I came because I care about you. If there's a killer out there, it's a bit gung-ho to put yourself at risk. You should have told me. I called round to your house and your neighbour Eileen said you'd gone away for a few days. I thought it was something I'd done, so I called Sarah and asked where you were."

I started to cry. I'd never had someone care for me like this apart from Aunt Trish. This guy really was wonderful, but what did this super handsome megastar possibly see in me?

"Hey, what's this? I don't usually have that effect on people," he said.

"You're just so lovely, coming all this way to look after me. I'm so stupid I should have told you, asked you."

"Hey, I'm here now. Look, I've got a bottle of wine and some food in the car," he said.

"That sounds good, but you're just in time for pizza."

"Sounds perfect, I love pizza. Let's eat it, crack the wine and then get some sleep. We have to work out what happened the night Betzy disappeared."

I knew I wanted him to share my bed that night. I just didn't know whether it should be as a friend, or a lover.

*

"Trav," I said as I stood in a t-shirt and pants, looking as unsexy as I probably could. "I had no idea you were coming; if I did I'd have brought something more appropriate."

"Hey. Cath, you look terrific," he replied in his designer boxers and top, his firm chest and shoulders offering comfort and security.

"I can't risk falling in love Trav, and if we…"

"Cath, it's okay. I came here to be with you, not to seduce you." We hugged. His fingers rubbing my shoulders, my breasts firm against his chest, separated by two thin strips of cotton. His warmth spreading to mine. We lay on the bed hand in hand and I looked out of the window, the curtain still open.

A cloud moved and moonlight brightened the sky. I imagined Mum sleeping in this room, maybe in the same bed the night before she disappeared.

"Goodnight Trav, thanks for coming."

"Couldn't let you face this alone, Cath. Besides, Sarah and the girls would kill me if I let anything happen to you. By the way, a promoter I put Sarah in touch with is planning a Décolleté tour: venues are being booked and publicity put out. They're picking up dates."

"Picking up dates?"

"Another band has cancelled a tour which was ready to go. They've split up."

"Sounds drastic."

"Yes. So's the singer's wife running off with the drummer."

"Ah."

"Yep, The Stolen Horses are no more, so you're going to need to start serious rehearsals soon."

"I was expecting to."

"Yes, as soon as we're back. It'll be pretty much full on. We've taken their tour, we're using their road crew, sound and light system, transport everything, just shoehorned into their itinerary. It'll be great."

"Can we sell tickets?"

"I'm convinced we can and I'll bankroll it if not."

"Seriously?"

"Seriously."

"Wow. Sounds good. I've lost my teaching job,"

"Really?"

"Yeah, my Head didn't think me strutting my stuff on stage being Mum went too well with the image of her school. But it's a stage show, a piece of theatre. I'll bet my final year drama class would have approved." I rolled over to face him.

"I certainly enjoyed it, and so did the audience as you know," he said, his hand brushing the hair from my cheek.

"Is the band still tied in to Chris Latham as manager and agent?" I asked.

"Don't you like Chris?" He looked at me quizzically.

"Not hugely. His heart seems to be in the right place but I'm not sure," I replied.

"I agree. Sarah doesn't seem to think the band are tied to him but Décolleté 2 has been set up as a business name and the girls have signed with a new agent: mine. You can add your signature when you get back," he said, his hand touching my neck.

"For someone who's not come all this way to seduce me you're doing a good job of it," I smiled, my pulse rising.

"But that's not what you want, and I'm not doing anything to risk our friendship or your sanity. Besides, if I hurt you, I'm sure Suzi, Rocky, Cassie and Stephy would ensure I was unable to make love to anyone else, ever again!" He laughed, making a frightened face.

"You're so sweet. What if I decided I'm a big girl now and I wanted you?"

"Let's solve our mysteries first hey. I can get hurt too, you know."

I kissed him.

"Goodnight Trav, and thanks."

"Next time, though, let me know and I'll hire somewhere maybe a bit more suitable. I know this is where your mum stayed but it's probably gone downhill a bit since then. Don't look too hard, but isn't that mould up there on the ceiling?"

I sniggered and pulled up the sheet, the faint smell of damp musty walls creeping around me. The recent paintwork was already beginning to peel.

"You must have stayed in some amazing places?" I suggested.

"Sure have: Cali beach houses, Parisian penthouses, Caribbean hideaways. But some hideously trashy dives too." He laughed.

*

It was about 4am when I was woken up by Trav standing above me holding my shoulders. I was sweating, trying to sit up and panting.

"Cath, Cath it's okay. I'm here, you're having a nightmare."

"NO!" I screamed, then fell back on the pillow. Trav turned on the light. The weak, dirty sixty-watt bulb throwing its pale light on the room. "Sorry."

"It's okay. What was it?" he asked.

"Mum. Her face. She was calling to me, trying to say something but her face kept breaking up into pieces like a shattered mirror."

"Hey, come on. It's okay, it's just a bad dream. Do you want some tea or something?

"What time is it?"

"4am," said Trav. "You've missed a fabulous moon, but it's clouded over now."

"The wind's got up and the rain's started," I noticed, looking out of the window.

We sat together in the kitchen drinking tea, the rain hitting the black windows, the curtains still open. I looked at Trav, who was deep in thought.

"So this nightmare," said Trav. "Where was your mum in your dream?"

"In a grave, a makeshift grave," I replied. "I think there's a body out there, somewhere."

24. The Hotel

Morning would be with us before long. Dawn was early in June, but it would be a dull, damp start. The rain had continued. Dark clouds had rolled in from the west, covering the horizon in a carpet of gloom. It showed me why the small house had massive thick walls and small windows. The winds rattled the glass, the door shook and the roof took a pounding as thick raindrops hurtled down. Trav came back from getting dressed. He walked back into the kitchen in a pair of faded jeans and an old Betzy Blac t-shirt.

"I like your top," I smiled, knowing he'd worn it for me.

"Your dream, Cath," he said, sitting down at the table opposite me.

"It was just so real…"

"Tell me about it."

"I just had an image of myself looking through the curtains on a night like this one, rainy and windy. Someone was pulling Mum along the ground. Pulling her into that small barn outside, the one with the collapsing roof. I dreamed I floated out of the window and into the barn and then…." I started to shake. Trav got up and put his arm around me.

"And what?"

"And Mum turned to me… she looked so scared… her face shattered into pieces, then I screamed and, the next thing I knew, you were looking at me."

"You know it was just a dream," Trav said. "But let's go and look, just to prove to you she's not there. The police would have checked that barn when they searched for her. But let's put your mind at rest. As soon as it's sun up let's go and check it out."

We watched as black turned to dark grey, and dark grey to light, but the cloud blocked out the sun and the rain continued its downward journey. Eventually I couldn't wait any longer and, deciding it was just light enough to see, I stood up.

"There's a big umbrella by the door, let's go," I said.

Trav and I walked close together under the umbrella. The rain was harsh and persistent as we ventured out of the door; it was almost as if it didn't want us to see what was in the barn. The path was slippery and the ground heavy and solid. Puddles formed and ripples spread out as large drops of water landed. The barn looked less and less inviting as we approached it, the broken-down door hanging at an angle, rusted hinges twisted, weakened by the devouring rust. As we went inside, the rain was funnelled by the bent and broken corrugated iron roof, hanging down at the far end. The noise of the rain on the rusting roof sounded like a snare drum being repeatedly struck by a deranged drummer.

"But the police will have searched in here, surely?" said Trav, raising his voice above the noise.

"They looked, but according to Aunt Trish they assumed she'd been thrown over the cliff or jumped, or run away on a yacht to America."

"How did they know about a yacht?"

"Apparently a US-registered sailing boat had left the nearby marina the day she went missing."

We looked around. The remains of a lawnmower and some old garden tools were at one end and some pieces of wood lay against the back wall. Rain ran down the moss-covered bricks, glistening in the low light.

"Well, there's nothing here," said Trav.

"Nothing visible," I replied. "But is there something under the floor?"

"Under these flagstones?" Trav kicked one with his heel.

"There's only one way we'll find out," I said.

Trav nodded and picked up an old spade. He started to lever the biggest stone up. It wasn't keen to move.

"It's the peaty soil underneath; it's like glue, very boggy. It's trying to suck the slab down again when I start to lift it."

"Let me put the fork under it too." I grabbed another old tool and pushed it under the edge of the slab of stone.

We worked the tools further and further under the stone slab as the rain thundered down. It finally gave way and we were able to lift it. Once it rose, we laid it upright against the side of the barn and tackled the adjacent slab and, between us, began to make it move. Slowly but surely the second slab rose to deliver its secrets. Gradually we inched it clear, and there, there under the peat, in the dim light and cool air, was a human jaw with scraps of skin attached, almost mummified and black. I stared in disbelief.

The bone was part submerged, and mostly decomposed, but the teeth told us it was human. We worked on the next slab along and, as it rose, we were greeted with the sight of the rest of the body. Lying on its side. There was skin showing through the muddy peat, black and shrivelled. Pieces of material which had once been clothing were clinging to bone.

"Mum?" I gasped and looked away, beginning to cry.

"Shit. Let's get some air. Come on." Trav put his arm around me and led me outside. "This rain. Come on, back in the house." We'd left the umbrella in the barn and the rain soaked us before we reached the back door, but we staggered inside, shutting out the downpour and the horror. I sat by the cooker in the small armchair, unable to speak. I was shaking; what I'd just seen was haunting me. Trav put the kettle on before going upstairs to fetch me a blanket.

"You're in shock, Cath. Put this on." He picked up his phone. "I've got two bars; I hope it's enough. I'm calling the cops."

Two hours later, a tent had been erected in front of the barn. White-suited forensics officers brought out the remains of the body. After Trav and I gave statements, we were told we could leave the house. I'd told them of my dealings with DCs Dennison and Patel down south. They promised to liaise with them. I just wanted to leave. To get home, go and see Aunt Trish, tell her I'd found Mum. After all this time was this really her? Had I found her, at last? My poor mum, buried in this desolate barn? It was horrible. Megan the house owner watched the police car drive away. She walked over as we put our bags into my car.

"You'll not be wanting to stay on then," she said. "There's no refunds I'm afraid."

"We're heading back south in a few minutes," said Trav.

"Ay, well, safe journey."

*

We barely spoke. It was a long, painful ride. Exhausted, drained and with my mind working overtime mulling over my dream and what we'd found. We gave up and stopped at a hotel, unable to carry on. It was an uninspiring, rain-beaten roadside motel.

"You ought to eat, Cath," Trav said, looking at the paltry menu on the table in our room.

"Sorry. I can't. You get something though. I'll be fine."

"This is the best I could do; they only had a double room."

"Like that matters?" I smiled. He opened his arms and I hugged him. My poor mum, unloved and alone, lying in that shallow grave. It was too horrible to think about. "I'm glad you're here. I can't sleep alone tonight. My mum was there in that barn, for all those years," I sobbed. "Judy betrayed her, her best friend."

I sat on the bed, Trav stroking my head. He was so sweet. I felt myself weaken. I needed him. I needed love. I edged closer to see if he'd react. He touched my cheek. I looked up at him, my tear-filled eyes pleading for more, but what was I doing? What if he rejected me? I moved my face closer, my mouth facing his. I so wanted him to kiss me, but he hesitated. Oh God, I was setting myself up for such a fall. He was going to say no, but then his lips touched mine, softly. He pulled back and looked at me.

"Cath, is this really what you want?" he asked, his face so close, his lips so inviting.

"I've lost my mum. I've lost my job. I fear I could lose you. Please," I said, desperately grabbing his head and pulling him towards me. We kissed, we really kissed. I opened my mouth and felt his tongue. There was no going back.

I pulled off his top as he removed mine. "Turn off the light," I whispered. I was self-conscious; I wasn't a model. His skin was soft, he smelt nice, he was warm. In the dark of that ordinary room his gentle but strong arms and soft meaningful kisses wrapped me in a purposeful embrace as we lay down. It felt wonderful to be wanted and not rejected. Was this what it was like to be truly loved? We had a special moment and a special night. If it were going to be a one-off it would be a lifetime memory. It would linger not as the night I slept with a mega star, but the night I slept with a beautiful man.

*

The noise of traffic woke me, four hours later. The hum of the fan from the small bathroom drilled into my ears. I opened my eyes to see Trav walk out of the shower. I watched as he dropped the towel and stood with his back towards me to pull on his underwear and jeans. Taut, firm muscles spread from his shoulders to his bum. The backs of his legs were firm and strong. He slipped on a shirt and turned round, showing his flat stomach.

"Hi," I murmured.

191

"Morning, beautiful. Coffee? Well, sort of coffee, in this sachet I think."

"Sounds perfect." I yawned, not wanting to get out of bed.

"Breakfast?"

"What, the all-day breakfast that's been there for at least a day?" I half smiled, sitting up, my t-shirt bunched around my tummy. "About last night," I ventured.

"I won't tell if you don't. Cath, it was lovely. You're lovely," he said tenderly, touching my cheek. I knew it was probably a one-off. I told myself I had to be old enough to face the truth. It was what I needed then, at that moment, and I wouldn't let myself have regrets, no matter what happened next. Even so, as I looked into his beautiful face I started to break down again. Why was I crying? Was it the news about Mum or the possibility he might still reject me?

"Hey, don't cry. Isn't what happened what you wanted?" he said, sitting beside me and holding me tight.

"Yes!" I insisted. "Sorry, it's me, I just can't let myself believe we could ever work, or ever last, we're different people from different worlds. Let's find my mum and your dad's killer and then…"

"And then? We're not so different, Cath."

"Yes, we are—you're a megastar, you've had models and actors and why would you even give me a second look? What am I? A failed teacher, a dull ordinary girl obsessed with her missing mother? Why would you want me?" I pushed my face into his chest and sobbed. He just hugged me and squeezed my hand. No one had even been so sweet, but however nice he was, I feared this memory would hurt me a lot in years to come.

*

We drew up outside Aunt Trish's house that afternoon. Had I really found the truth and ended my dream that Mum was somehow still alive? That body in the mud was her, wasn't it? It had to be; who else could it be? I had to go on tour now; it was even more important to find Mum and Raven's killer. Someone out there knew who it was; someone would talk, eventually, I was sure. We walked down the side passage, the ever-present weeds growing between the cracks on the slabs. I knocked on the familiar green door to the kitchen, the paint peeling. As it opened, Aunt Trish looked somehow smaller and weaker than when I'd last seen her. Her eyes were drawn and her face was pale.

"Catherine! You needn't knock, darling. How lovely to see you. And this must be Travis. My, you're even more handsome in real life than you are on the telly." She gave me a knowing look.

"Nice to meet you." He smiled and offered his hand. Aunt Trish led him inside with me in tow. She closed the door. The familiar smell of her kitchen greeted me: newly baked bread, fresh cut flowers from the garden in a vase on the table. It felt homely, warm and safe, like it always had.

"Cath's told me a lot about you and how good to her you were when she was a girl. You've done a brilliant job," said Trav, immediately earning brownie points with Aunt Trish.

She reached for the ageing light brown electric kettle. "I think so, but sadly she doesn't seem to think so herself; lacks confidence her teachers always said, but perhaps this newfound singing career will sort that out." It was good to hear Aunt Trish and Trav getting on, but I had to break the news about Mum.

"Thanks Aunt Trish. I have some sad news."

25. Old Haunts

Aunt Trish walked to the sink, kettle in her hand.

"Oh? What's that, dear?" she asked, turning on the tap. I got up and stood behind her, putting my arm around her shoulder.

"Trav and I have been to Scotland, to Applecross where Mum was last seen."

"Why ever did you do that? It would only upset you," she said, shaking her head. Turning round she sat down at the table.

"I needed to see if I could find anything out about Mum's disappearance and, well, the truth is… We found a body. In an outbuilding, buried under a stone slab. I think it's her." My aunt's face drained. She looked up in horror.

"What? Really? A body? In Scotland? Are, are you sure? But after all these years it would have decayed."

"The peat, Aunt. Peat preserves bodies."

"But… Do the police know?" She wouldn't look at me. Her eyes staring down.

"Yes, Trav called them straight away. They're doing checks. Forensics."

"But," she said, looking puzzled, "I'm sure the police checked at the time."

"They did, but not in that old barn it seems. Well, not under the floor," I replied, hugging her tightly.

"I was sure she was in America…" She put her hands over her face.

"I'll sort it out Auntie, please don't worry." I could tell she wasn't convinced.

"Why don't you show Travis your old room, it's much as it was when you left it. I need to…"

"Yes of course, come on Trav."

We climbed the stairs. My room was a time warp: just as I had left it when I went off to university. I sat on my old bed. The pink and white horizontally stripped duvet cover and pillow slips were still there, as was the square radio alarm clock by the bed, its green digital display still proudly working. The wallpaper with its pink and grey pattern and matching curtains brought back so many memories of my sitting at the little desk doing homework, struggling to get the A level grades I needed.

A few old clothes, ill-fitting favourites, sat in the dark recesses smelling of mothballs with small bags of long dead lavender. This was where I would sit, in front of the mirror playing at being Mum, singing her songs while listening to an old greatest hits CD or some early cassette tapes. The hairbrush I used as a microphone and the Décolleté tour t-shirt I always wore were still there, the dates and venues displayed on the back over a picture of the band on stage. Mum's face with mic held high on the front, and the words Décolleté, *The '84 Road Rage Tour!* printed underneath. The last date on the back was etched on my brain. London, October 12th.

"That's what I used as a mic to pretend to be Mum." I offered the hairbrush to Trav, who smiled.

"Yeah, guilty, I've done that too. When I was a kid, but you can now play at being your mum properly, with a real mic," he said softly.

"I spent so much time up here, on my own. Sometimes my friend Anne would come round, or I'd go to hers, but it was a lonely childhood, you know. This wasn't the first house I lived in with Aunt Trish after Mum went. We had to move so I could change schools. I was pretty traumatised… I got teased at my old school when they knew who Mum was. I'd have boys rushing up, singing lines from her songs in the playground, tormenting me, laughing that she'd run away to get away from me. Kids can be so cruel."

"That sounds rough, Cath."

"When I changed school no one knew who Mum was. It was fine, normal. As far as people knew my mum had died and I was an orphan." My phone rang.

"Hello, Cath Edgley," I answered.

"Miss Edgley, it's DC Patel here. I have some information for you about the body at Tuiag."

"Yes?"

"We've identified it." I grabbed Trav's hand, my lip started to quiver, my pulse increased.

"Oh, right. Sorry, I'm a bit upset." I squeezed Trav's hand and looked at Mum's picture smiling back at me from the wall.

"Yes, we used dental records as the body was too decomposed for a visual ID."

"Oh God." I felt Trav's arm around me as I waited for the awful news. I put the phone on speaker, unable to bear hearing it alone.

"Catherine. It's not your mother."

"Sorry?" I couldn't believe what he said.

"The body."

"What do you mean it's not my mother?"

"The body, it's not Elizabeth Black."

"Are you sure?" I looked at Trav who raised his eyebrows, his mouth opened, as surprised as I was.

"Certain. It's male."

"Male?" I repeated, unable to take it in. "So who is it? Who was under the barn?"

"Catherine. Wherever your mother is, she isn't in that barn. Let us know if you find anything. Betzy Blac is still a missing person."

"I'm going to appeal to her old fans. I'm singing with her band and we're doing a tour."

"We can't advise you doing anything that would put you at risk, Catherine."

"I don't think I'm at risk with the girls in Décolleté by my side."

"We need to keep in touch, and if any threats are made towards you, directly or indirectly, please tell us."

"Of course. Can you give me a number people can ring if they can help? Like they do on those TV crime shows?"

"Yes certainly. I'll get back to you. Thank you, Catherine, and please keep us informed." I put the phone down on the bed and looked up at Trav. It sank in and a huge dark gloom lifted.

"YES!" I squealed. "The body in the barn, it isn't my mother!" Let's go and tell Aunt Trish. Oh I can't believe it." I kissed Mum's picture on my wall.

"It's great news," said Trav, "but it doesn't prove she's still alive."

"But it proves she's not there in that barn, and after that dream, I was sure she was. But if it isn't Mum, who's body is it? And who killed them?"

"Who knows? But at least you're smiling for the first time in days." Said Trav.

"Of course!" I replied. "The body isn't my mum, and last night I got to sleep with Travis Brennon." I grinned and then started to go red realising what I'd said.

"And I got to sleep with Cath Edgley," he replied, kissing my cheek. He knew how to make me feel special. Even if I didn't think I was.

*

That night, I drove back through the gates of Beckthorn School for Girls. After what I'd been through in the previous few days—the highs and lows of finding a body and thinking it was Mum, and actually sleeping with Trav—I wasn't sure I was up to the stress of my former workplace and a possible confrontation with

Miss Miles, but I couldn't let my girls down.

There was a party atmosphere as I walked into school. The Head's office was empty, the light was off and the secretary, her Rottweiler-like gatekeeper, was nowhere to be seen. On the door were two of my final year girls. I joined a queue of parents waiting to go in to see their little girls, all grown-up, playing adults on stage. When I got to the front of the line the girls on the door shrieked with delight.

"Miss! So glad you're here."

"Fantastic! You've come to watch. They'll be so pleased."

"I wouldn't have missed it for anything." I smiled at the parents and saw Jane, talking to my dull looking stand-in.

"Cath!" she called out, rushing over. "Lovely to see you. How's things" She was clearly as pleased to see me as I was her. After a brief chat, I slipped backstage and into the dressing area.

"Miss!" came an excited and unified response when the girls saw me walk in. They stood there, my best performers, half made-up and half in costumes, transforming themselves from school leavers to the cast of West Side Story.

"Good luck everyone! Sorry I haven't been here, but I've been thinking about you all."

"Miss!" said Chloe.

"Chloe, you look terrific," I smiled.

"Thank you, Miss. We got into trouble yesterday during the matinee."

"Really?"

"Miss Miles was very unhappy."

"Why?"

"Well Miss," added Emily, another top of her class student destined for big things, "the two of us did a duet in the interval. Chloe played the piano and I sang."

"Why should Miss Miles be upset?"

"We sang a song for you," said Emily.

"Now we know who your mum is," added Chloe.

"We sang *Raindance*," Emily grinned.

"I don't think Miss Miles likes the lyrics."

"I'm not surprised!" I said, shocked. "Did you change them?"

"No!" giggled both girls.

"We left them in, even the line: *'Taking each other's clothes off and rolling together in the reluctant rain'.*"

"Yes, I can see why that wouldn't go down too well," I laughed.

"Well, we're leaving at the end of the week, so she can't do much now," said Chloe. "Since we saw you play we've been listening to Decollete's music—I've been playing all the tracks on my bass guitar, Emily's been singing. We love them, Miss, we know them all now," she said, an excited look in her heavily made-up eyes, ready for the school stage lights.

Emily shuffled from foot to foot as her nerves built up.

"We want to try and find a band to play in over the summer, to earn some money to help with my fees at uni," said Chloe. I gave her my number and promised her a reference if she ever needed one.

"Any tips about nerves, Miss?" asked Emily, biting her nail.

"Yes. Believe in your own talent; you both have a great presence, girls, you needn't be nervous," I said, trying to instil confidence, knowing how fragile it could be.

Emily was still biting her nails, something I'd watched her do in class during exams. "Were you nervous at the Club the other night, Miss?" she asked.

"Scared witless!" We all laughed. "But I was being a raunchy rock chick in front of a big crowd. You'll have these eager mums and dads eating out of your hands. Now get out there and enjoy it!"

*

Sitting in the back row, I watched the show unfold. The kids were great and the parents loved it, clapping enthusiastically. Then came the interval and Emily and Chloe appeared on stage.

"We have a little song. I've been banned from singing it," said

Emily, "but the others haven't." The entire cast and the rest of the class came out from behind the curtain. The piano started.

"This," said Emily, "is for Miss Edgley and her mum Betzy Blac. It's *Raindance*."

The girls started singing as one. At first I was seized by panic—I knew I'd be blamed for this—then I realised the audience were singing along, too. Some of the parents obviously knew and loved the song. I laughed as I saw Miss Miles looking like thunder by the door. When the song ended I stood up, along with a few of the parents, and applauded. Miss Miles shook her head and walked off. She didn't return for the second half, which went well. Emily and Chloe were both brilliant but then I knew they would be. After the final curtain, I went backstage to congratulate the cast. Chloe and Emily rushed out and hugged me. As I left the building Miss Miles watched with narrowed eyes, muttering darkly, and I knew I'd never be welcome in the school again.

26. AN OCEAN BETWEEN

The next day, I walked into a rehearsal room on the edge of London. The band were there along with our new promoter, a tour manager, a choreographer, and a lighting director. We'd be putting on our stage clothes and running through the set while they compared notes, made plans and moulded us into a dynamic stage show.

While we were getting dressed, I told the girls what had happened.

"…but when we lifted that slab I was convinced it was Mum. I was dreading telling Aunt Trish, and you guys too, and then when the police told me it was someone else, a man. I was so relieved, although as Trav says, it doesn't prove Mum's not buried somewhere else."

"I'll bet Betz kicked the shit out of him and buried him herself," said Stephanie, zipping up her skirt. They all started talking at once.

"She did go to the States then?" Caroline asked, pulling on her t-shirt.

"Unless she went over that cliff?" suggested Sarah, looking in the mirror.

"No," said Rochelle. "I think someone rescued her. So, anything happen? You know, you and Trav?" She grinned at me, and gently pushed my shoulder. "Come on, confess."

"Why do you ask?" I said, unpacking Mum's stage clothes and pulling off my top.

"Really? We really need to spell it out?" said Sarah, looking at me through her Suzi Scums made-up face. "Come on, we know he went with you, and we know you were upset."

"How?" I asked, slipping on Mum's jacket.

"I texted him while you were at that travel stop hotel. We were worried, about our Cath."

"He told you?" I asked, shocked.

"He just said you'd had a rough time and needed looking after," said Sarah. "And just now you walked in here like a self-satisfied smug woman who's just bagged a pop star. I'll bet you slept together."

"Well…" I was going red and coyly laughing, proud of having slept with Trav. It's not every day you sleep with a megastar.

"KNEW IT! You lucky bitch!" said Rochelle. "If I were thirty years younger…"

"And single!" Stephanie reminded her.

"Yeah, well, you know what I mean. Hey, well done Cath. But it may not be forever yes?" said Sarah, in a mother-like moment.

"I'm not unrealistic," I replied. "I know it's about as likely as my being on stage at Wembley, so I'm keeping the brakes on and bracing myself for being dumped."

"Can we have you guys in the stage area please," called Steve, the tour manager.

"Chorus line and openers," I laughed.

*

The rehearsals continued as we honed our positions and the tech guys tried out various light moves. The people putting the show together suggested some costume changes but I wouldn't swap Mum's stage gear for anyone. We finalised the set list and worked on alternate encores, then posed for publicity shots. It was hard work and, after the previous forty-eight hours, my concentration was lacking but the enthusiasm of the others carried me through.

We'd just changed and were saying our goodbyes when we

were interrupted.

"That was great." Robbi Romero had crept in unnoticed. "You're a dead ringer for Betzy, Catherine."

"Thanks, but these are closed rehearsals." I smiled politely, wanting him to leave.

"To the public, yes, but I'm management—well, I was, and I want to be again. There's a lot of interest in this tour. Trash Puke Records would like to put out a live album—all you have to do is to sign to us; the rest of the band's contract is still in force as it's never been changed. I've brought the contract with me." He smiled, his gold-capped teeth glinting in his cavernous mouth. The others crowded around.

"We need to discuss this together," said Sarah coldly.

"But it's only Catherine who needs to sign," he said. "Then it's all done and dusted. It's a great opportunity, Catherine. Don't throw it away."

"I'm sorry, Mr Romero." I wasn't going to be pushed around. "I'm not signing anything yet—maybe not at all. You say the old contract is still in force? That might be a something we need legal advice on." His expression changed.

"You'll regret that attitude, young lady," he said with a hint of menace in his voice. "You might need my help, if you don't want to end up like your mother."

"I think you'd better leave." I spoke firmly, feeling the others bristling beside me. If he was picking a fight he sure was going to lose.

"Get out, now," said Sarah firmly. The Rat Boy muttered and walked away, calling me the C word under his breath, slamming the door as he left.

"Was the use of that word plural or singular?" asked Caroline.

"Prick. And that's singular, to describe him," said Sarah. The door opened and Trav walked in. I opened my arms and hugged him; he responded.

"He doesn't seem happy," he said, having just passed Romero leaving. "Hi Cath, hi girls, oh, why's everyone looking at me like that?" he asked.

"Sorry, I was just pleased. And happy," I replied.

"I'm sorry I missed this morning," he said, rubbing my arm gently, "but I've got to go back to the States for a week or so. It wasn't planned and I really don't want to, but I have meetings with accountants and attorneys. Hey," he said, turning to face me, "remember I said there'd be legal stuff re the new album and a former girlfriend? Well, yeah there is. So I need to sort it, meet her and her lawyers and sign stuff, but then I'll be back."

We hugged outside in the street. It was awful watching him close the taxi door and as his cab drove off my heart sank. Sarah came out and put her arm around me.

"He'll be back. It's okay. Whatever happens, Cath, we've got you." I hugged her, watching as his taxi turned the corner at the end of the street. However hard I tried not to, I was falling in love with Travis Brennon.

*

The next two weeks were continuous rehearsals and run-throughs. The opening night was approaching, and it had to be good; it would determine ticket sales for the whole tour. We met our stage crew and the roadies who would be looking after and setting up the kit—a far cry from the old days, the girls told me. The demands of modern digital quality audiences required a much higher standard, although we wanted to retain the raw sound of Décolleté live. We managed both, thanks to our brilliant crew.

I missed Trav. I wanted to enjoy long nights and late mornings wrapped together under the sheets, but we had to complete our mission. Somehow love was an illusive prize for the end. I'd never wanted anyone as much as this and I couldn't bear the idea of not being us.

The tour bus arrived outside the rehearsal rooms for us to approve. I'd never seen one before and neither had the girls.

In the band's heyday they had roamed the roads in old vans. When I saw the dates and venues I realised why we needed it. It would be our home for the fifteen-night tour. We were travelling the length and breadth of the country. I looked inside. It was cleverly laid out. There was a seating or lounge area first, and then a bathroom and a small kitchen opposite. Behind that were six beds in person-length pods either side of the bus, each with a curtain across them. This was followed by a changing area with racks for clothes at the back. It seemed so extravagant. I just hoped we could fill the venues; someone had to pay for all of this.

Ticket sales were taking off and we'd sold out a third of the venues just a week after the tickets went on sale. Press interest was rising, and someone had leaked the story of *'The Body in the Barn,'* meaning that the question *'Where is Betzy Blac?'* had become big news again. It was filling pages of print and megabytes online. A press call was arranged and we let selected reporters and cameras into the rehearsal room. We posed on stage and gave them one song before answering questions. Inevitably they all wanted to know if Mum was alive and if we had any idea who'd murdered Raven. It gave me the chance to appeal for information and give out the number the police had supplied.

My confidence should have been steadily increasing; instead it was becoming more fragile by the minute. Trav kept me on track and sane with regular calls and texts from the States. I was just scared he would find someone else to love while he was away and I'd lose him forever.

When I fell into bed that night, my ears were humming from the assault of the day's rehearsals. As I agonised over whether I'd be ready for the tour, I heard a text land on my phone. I'd taken to keeping it by my bed, partly to ensure I didn't miss anything, and also so I could dial 999 if I felt threatened. I switched on my bedside light and picked it up. What I saw wasn't conducive to a good night's sleep.

Betzy didn't kill the man in the barn. DD.

*

The bus drove through the concrete campus and down the slope to park outside the square grey building that housed the students' union. The Lower Common Room at the University of East Anglia was the first night of the tour. Reg, our driver, opened the door and smiled.

"Sorry we're late, but here we are: first stop on the magical mystery tour, Norwich! Have a good evening."

Reg was cute. Late fifties, a former coach driver between London and the airports, he was friendly, jovial, a bit of a comic. We got off, carrying our stage clothes in an eclectic collection of covers and cases, mine the dullest of the lot. Parked next to our coach was a minibus and van with our road crew and hired PA system. It also carried our precious kit: guitars, drums and mics.

I was frightened by the cost of it all, even though tickets had almost sold out everywhere. It was an amazing feat considering the tour had been so hastily organised, and shoehorned into what was going to be another band's dates. I hoped good reviews from our first gig would push sales to the top.

The band used to extend their tours when they sold out back in the day, and I wondered if we'd ever reach those dizzy heights again. Trav had worked really hard to help promote us, using his enormous social media following to plug the tour, but I had to make sure it didn't bomb. I hesitated before going in through the small door at the side of the building leading to the dressing rooms. It was a bit like going into a giant bunker, and I knew once inside I wouldn't emerge again until the last notes faded, and the stage lights went dark.

27. Opening Night

"Nerves, Cath?" asked Rochelle as I missed my footing and tripped. I almost dropped my outfit as I reached out to steady myself against the wall.

"Yup, sorry. Just a last-minute panic. I keep thinking my throat is tightening up and I won't be able to sing."

"Goes with the territory. I always think my fingers won't move. I'll try to make a chord and they'll just freeze and refuse to budge. You'll be fine. Pretend it's a rehearsal."

"A rehearsal with a capacity crowd who've just spent £30 each to see us."

"Really, you'll be fine." She smiled, touching my arm.

"I have to be, I can't let everyone down. Imagine the nightmare of bad reviews and demands for refunds," I said. It was something I'd worried about in the early hours of a few nights.

"You will. European tour next and then, who knows… Well, the States look inviting!"

"Rochelle. Woah slow down, Norwich is hard enough. They might not like us."

"Oh, I think they'll be on our side. Here we are: the dressing room."

I put my clothes down. A text came through on my phone.

"Give 'em hell Cath, you can smash it! Trav x"

I kissed the phone and smiled. Leaving my clothes and make-up on the table, I walked to the box office where the staff were setting up. The first people were already queuing outside.

"Is it really sold out?" I asked, showing my Access All Areas pass to a young student, one of the entertainments committee.

"Hi, yes, it is,' she said, with a smile. 'Capacity crowd, fifteen-hundred-and-fifty! That's really good, no support act either." I didn't know if that made me feel better or worse.

I walked through to look at the auditorium and the waiting stage. The road crew had been busy setting up the amps and speaker stacks. The light show was still being tested and the sound desk fired up; various noises filled the space, one merging into the other as the techies struck chords on guitars and spoke into microphones.

Behind the bar, staff in black t-shirts unpacked plastic glasses and turned on the tills. I looked around; I'd only ever been in venues like this as part of an audience. I was feeling like a rabbit in the headlights until the light show changed, and there was a massive picture of my mum's face, filling the screen behind the stage. She was smiling and looking down at me. I smiled back.

"Okay Mum, I get it. I'm ready," I said out-loud, to the amusement of the sound engineer beside me, busily taping the set list to his desk behind a small metal enclosure.

"You'll be fine, Cath!" he laughed confidently.

The girls came on to the stage for a sound check. We should have done this three hours ago, but an overturned truck on the motorway had caused a massive delay. I jumped up to join them. We only had time to run through one song completely, so we picked *Hot Lips, Cold Heart* after I said I'd forgotten the words, which I hadn't of course: it was just nerves. My voice was faltering: dressed as Cath Edgley it was hard to get in the mood. The sound guys and the music techs tweaked amps and faders and moved mics. When they gave us the thumbs up, we rushed into two verses of *Pink Bra Bust Up!* and the opening of *Banging On The Beach!* to make them happy, and then we left the stage to get ready—all except Caroline. The guys were concerned about the sound of the cymbals and wanted even more tweaking and checks. In the old days Caroline would just hit the skins with the sticks, but now someone was measuring the height of her arms, the seat and the high hat. She was getting grumpy and impatient.

At the entrance, the doors were about to open. The bar staff were ready and the crowd were keen to get inside. Excitement and expectation were building. I could feel tension in the dressing room as I walked back in.

I jumped into a chair and opened my make-up box. I slowly morphed from being Cath Edgley, teacher, to Betzy Blac, singer. Outside, through the high slit vents of the stage door, I could hear the crowd moving forwards, chatting loudly. The clothes went on and I'd nearly become my mum. Finally, with the jacket, the transformation was complete. I turned round to the others, who were all ready and sipping coffee, looking at me approvingly. Sarah—now full-on Suzi—gave me a thumbs up, then stuck her finger up and burst out laughing. They were picking over a biscuit, cheese and sandwich buffet. A bin liner for discarded wrappers sat next to the table. Bottles of wine and a corkscrew were waiting for after the show. The girls were confident and cool, ready to unleash Décolleté onto the waiting world. It was as if they'd never stopped. I drank some water, knowing I'd dehydrate fairly fast on that stage.

"Looks good, Betz!" Sarah, now Suzi, grinned at me. "How are we feeling? Good, yes?" she asked the room.

"Terrific!" laughed Rochelle, now Rocky Rump.

"Do you think he or she might be out there?" I asked. "The killer, in the crowd?"

"Who knows," said Stephy, "but we've got your back."

The girls looked pretty good. Make-up thick enough to scrape off with a putty knife, and clothes their grannies would have hated. Cassie had amended her outfit; the years hadn't been so kind to her weight-wise and she was feeling a little uncomfortable, comparing herself to the others, but as she said it was easy to hide behind the drums. She was wearing dark jeans and a baggy Sex Pistols album cover t-shirt, her hair dyed pink for the tour.

I wanted to hug them all for getting me this far, and I knew I couldn't let them down, despite feeling a little lost without Trav, my talisman and biggest fan. I knew he would have been there if he could. Well-wishers had sent messages, as had our new management, but they just flowed over me. I was concentrating on getting it right. I had one go, one throw of the dice: it was now or never. I had to be as good, if not better, than I'd been at the try-out gig in London, and this was the start of a tour, the opening night. It had to be a success.

The crowd was piling in and the house music was playing. The bar queues were growing and I sneaked a look around the curtain in the wings. A security guy checked me out and then nodded as I craned my neck to see the people who'd actually paid to see me. They were a wide range from old fans to students whose parents might have been Décolleté fans themselves. There were even some families, couples with teenaged children. I took a deep breath and went back into the dressing room, my confidence slipping.

The hour before we went on felt like an age. I kept going over the set list in my mind and wishing we'd had even more rehearsals, but it was like sitting an exam: there could always have been more time spent revising. I was testing myself—what was the second verse of *Two Lovers in One Night*? No, I couldn't remember, but I kept telling myself it would all come back.

Steve Hewitt, the tour manager, looked in and smiled. He'd seen it before. "You'll be fine. Believe it! Okay, stage time. Have fun, girls. Give them a taste of heaven."

He muttered something into a mic on a headset and motioned to us to go on.

We moved silently into the wings and waited, unseen by the expectant crowd. Suzi patted me on the back and whispered: "Go Cath: be Betzy!"

I gave her a smile; for all her bravado, I could tell she was nervous too. I was here, in Mum's place, about to lead her band through the set list of singles she'd taken to the top more than thirty years before—the outrageous, pioneering, punk princess rock chick that was Betzy Blac. She'd been praised by one generation and despised by another, even including her own mother. Her screaming sensuality had demanded to be heard, and demanded a place in music history. Now she was a legend reborn, alive in me: the daughter she never saw grow up.

It was time. The house music stopped and the lights went out. The expectation came to boiling point, the crowd started to clap and chant. It became a torrent and then a roar. As I walked forward my make-up hardened in the almost instant heat as the lights burst on and flooded the stage. I was feeling almost naked before this image-hungry crowd, hundreds of eyes on me as phone cameras flashed and I fed the online frenzy.

To the sound of rapturous shrieks and applause I tilted my head back and waited for the follow spot to close in on my face, the rest of the stage going dark until I screamed the magic words: "Oi scumbags! The bitches are back! We're Décolleté and this, this is for you!"

Suzi and the band took their cue, just as they had with Mum all those years ago. Décolleté were alive, and full of fire: their fingers less nimble, their bodies less taut, but their passion still as strong. There was a split second of silence before Suzi shrieked and jumped into the air, her hands hitting the strings of her red Fender guitar. The assault on the ears of those in front of us began. Speakers flexed in cabinets, spewing airborne emotion at the speed of sound. The opening power chords screamed out. Cassie's desperate drums demanded to be heard. Heads shook and waved in front of me, people jumped and cheered. The lights burst on and off like a supernova as I scanned the heaving crowd and wondered if DD or Brad were out there.

Colours changed, from deep reds and cool blues to brilliant white and everything in between, darting in and out of the smoke billowing on to the stage. The stage crew followed the script to the letter. Fans were raising their hands, cheering and calling my mother's name, wanting me to be her, reborn, to glimpse what once was. And all the time I wondered: was the killer out there? Watching, waiting, wanting to end the show once and for all?

While I played Betzy Blac on stage, Mum was somehow still beside me, somehow cheating death. There were tears in my eyes and pain in my throat, but I sang, screamed and thrust my way through her raw, uncompromising, love-hungry lyrics.

Song rolled into song and the lighting and stage moves worked well. I hadn't realised how much I'd absorbed during those intense rehearsals in London. The crowd were loving it and when I took a moment to appeal for information, as I'd done at our first gig, Mum's face appeared behind me with the number the police had provided. The crowd clapped as I asked them to help me find my mum and Raven's killer, then the lights dropped, leaving just a follow spot on Mum's face and the number.

Suzi played an elongated intro into *Raindance* and the crowd erupted as the lights came back up. As I sang this international best-selling love song, I thought of Trav still in the States as I sang the last line: "*So the storm tried to wash our love away, but we swayed together throughout the pain, and you and I'll dance forever, in the falling rain.*"

The audience joined in and carried on after I'd finished, wanting to reprise the chorus, but it was time to press on.

"Okay, let's turn it up. Remember this one? *Hot Lips, Cold Heart!*" I shrieked, and the band took their cue. Adrenalin surged as we performed the set list. The encores were welcomed as Mum's hits were blasted out while camera phones flashed and arms waved.

We came off stage after the second encore with the crowd still banging their feet on the floor and clapping loudly, chanting "*Décolleté!*" over and over again. But we'd had enough, we were exhausted. As I walked back to the dressing room a warm glow spread through me. Yes! I'd got through it. I hadn't frozen, forgotten the lyrics or faltered. I'd managed to play my mum with her band to her audience and they'd loved it. I couldn't stop smiling. The girls gave me and each other big sweaty hugs. Wet faces, smeared make-up, sweat and a few tears ran together. Steve the tour manager came in.

"You were brilliant," he said, throwing a towel around my shoulders. "But, hey, save your voice—after that performance your throat needs to relax or you'll regret it later. You've got another performance the day after tomorrow, then three in a row. Great show tonight, though; if they're all this good you've really cracked it."

"My throat's tight already," I said, wondering how Mum had coped.

"Shhh, rest it," he smiled.

"Keep away from booze, Cath," said Sarah, pulling off her soaking wet t-shirt and black bra top, heading for the shower. "Drink lots or the dehydration headache tomorrow will be a stunner. I've seen it and felt it so often."

"Can you guys handle the guest list?" I asked, knowing there'd be a few journalists, friends and hangers-on wanting to talk.

"Did you see Jez Deopham?" asked Stephanie, towelling her hair. "He was in the front row."

"No," I said anxiously.

"I thought I did," said Rochelle. "I wasn't sure, but that was your side of the stage, Steph."

"Well, if he wants to come backstage, it's a no," I said firmly.

"He knows that," said Sarah. "I don't think he'll try to bother you tonight."

But I wasn't so sure.

28. Reg

I was soon on the coach, drinking fruit tea and sucking cough sweets. My throat was hurting and my limbs ached. None of us spoke as we reflected on the night. It was actually happening; the tour had started. I just hoped someone in the audience would contact the police after my appeal, to pass on any scrap of information that could help.

The coach headed for Leicester, the next stop on the tour. We were due to spend a couple of nights in Oakham at a hotel for a rest the next day and to de-brief on the first night and check the reviews, maybe tweak the set list. It was after midnight and the roads were almost empty. We'd all gone quiet. Stephanie was asleep in her seat, Sarah was reading, Caroline was texting her kids and Rochelle was in the small bathroom. As we hit the bypass at East Dereham there was a rustle from the back of the coach. Someone was in one of the bunks behind a curtain. Stephanie looked at Sarah and then got up to investigate. She pulled back the material.

"Fuck! Intruder!" she screamed.

"Sorry, sorry!" A man's voice came from the bunk. "There's something I have to tell you!"

Sarah jumped up. She reached into the bunk and grabbed him by the hair. He squealed. I got up and stood behind the girls.

"Jez Deopham!" she said. "What the hell are you doing here?"

"I can handle this twat!" Stephanie grabbed him round the

neck with both hands and pulled him off the bunk.

"No!" he tried to say, as he stumbled, and struggled to stand up, his vocal chords constricted by Stephanie's grip. "I'm—I'm here to—to help!"

"Like fuck," said Sarah angrily. "More like to assault Cath. Look, her mum wasn't interested in you and neither is she, you fucking perv!"

"No. I—I know stuff, I've—found things out."

"What stuff?" demanded Stephanie, relaxing her grip just a little so Jez could talk.

"I know who Cath's real father is," he spluttered. "And someone is trying to stop your tour!"

"Who's my father?" I asked, but Sarah spoke over me.

"Who's trying to stop us?"

Jez swallowed. "I'll tell you if you promise not to savage me."

"Savage you?" Sarah said, furious. "You're lucky to still have both balls. Now fucking talk!"

Reg, the driver, shouted from the cab. "All okay back there?"

"Nothing we can't handle, Reg," said Sarah. Stephanie let go of the beleaguered Jez Deopham who looked frightened and unsure.

"Looks like a diversion ahead, late night roadworks," said Reg and turned the coach down a small lane.

"No!" shouted Jez. "That might be them!"

"Them?" I asked. "Who are they?" Before Jez could answer, Reg shouted as the coach turned a tight corner.

"Shit! The road's blocked; there's a sodding tree across it! Hold on we're going to…"

As Reg spoke I saw a tree lying half across the narrow road ahead. We fell forwards as the coach braked hard and, despite Reg's best efforts, we hit the tree. I grabbed Sarah to brace myself. She put both hands on the side of a seat back as the coach jolted to the left. I looked behind and could see headlights approaching us then, bang, something hit us. My head was thrown forwards and back as we were rammed in the rear by a large van. I felt the coach twist and roll and, as if in slow motion, it passed the centre of its gravity, reaching the point of no return. I tried to hold on and wedge myself between seats as the vehicle rolled over to rest at a forty-five-degree angle on some trees and shrubs. There was a moment of silence then a jolt as it slipped further, followed by the sharp crack of breaking branches as we fell sideways, disorientated.

"Shit!" cried Caroline. "My leg's stuck."

"You'll be okay," said Stephanie, pulling Caroline up from Jez Deopham who she'd fallen onto. Rochelle was rubbing her head which she'd banged against the bathroom door. I was leaning on Sarah, who was clinging to one of the bunks. Jez groaned and stood up.

"I was trying to tell you!" he pleaded.

"Get out quick!" shouted Sarah. "Grab what you can." I pulled down the holdall with my stage gear and make–up inside—there was no way I could leave Mum's clothes—and hurried to the front. Reg was slumped in his driving seat, blood spreading across his white shirt. Part of a tree branch had come through the side window. It had pierced his shirt and his skin. Like a lance it was buried in his chest. Reg was silent.

"No!" I screamed. "I think Reg is dead!" I stared at the lifeless shape of our driver.

I tried to get out. The others were behind me, waiting for me to open the door. It was facing the dark sky, its weight too much for me to push. I tried the emergency door switch, but there was just a tiny weak *whurr*.

"Let's have a go," said Sarah taking my place and, joined by Caroline, they both pushed. But the door wouldn't budge.

"Is that fuel I can smell?" asked Stephanie.

"It's okay," said Rochelle. "Diesel doesn't go up that easily."

"No," said Jez in a panic. "But petrol does." He pointed through the front window to a man in a hoodie who was emptying a can of petrol over the coach's front wheels, half lit by the headlights. "Those tyres will go up like a rocket. Quick—the back window—it's an emergency exit." We fought our way to the back, fumbling over bedding, food and other stuff which had tumbled out in the crash. The coach creaked as it sank further into the foliage with our combined moving weight. It slipped another few degrees.

There was a bang, smoke billowed, and the front windows of the coach cracked across their entire length and then splintered, making a grinding noise before giving way and breaking up, bursting inwards as they broke in the intense heat. Flames spread around the cab; the petrol had gone up and thick, acrid smoke billowed from the tyres. The trees holding the stricken coach gave way and the vehicle rolled completely onto its side, sending us tumbling onto each other by the back window, now vertical to the ground.

Sarah found a small emergency hammer in a cradle and quickly broke the glass to free the handle. "Okay, I think I can get it open," she said, pushing hard, but as she pushed out, someone on the outside was pushing in, pressing his foot against the window to stop it opening. He was wearing a scarf over his face and fingerless leather gloves. Was it him? Was it the man who'd attacked me at Sacha's house in France? In all the chaos I couldn't be sure. Stephanie was pressing 999 on her phone while Sarah and Jez pushed against the emergency exit window.

"Police! Help." said Stephanie.

A small drawer filled with cutlery had fallen open next to me and I grabbed a paring knife as Sarah smashed a bigger hole in the glass.

"Move!" I shouted and pushed her to the side, thrusting the knife through the glass into the leg of the man who was trying to trap us inside.

"*Putain*!" he cursed in French as he cried out in pain. I stuck the knife into him again and he backed off, holding his leg. His accomplice in the hoodie was less keen to leave. He ran, screaming, towards the back of the coach, swinging a baseball bat.

Rochelle shouldered the remaining window glass and at last it broke. She squeezed through as the man swung his bat and brought it down on her shoulder. She cried out and fell back, crawling into the corner of the wrecked bus, clasping her arm in agony.

"Stay and die, you bastards," shouted the man with the bat.

Jez pushed past us and climbed out.

"I know who's told you to do this. Stop, it's madness!" he pleaded, but his words were met with a crack on his head from the baseball bat. Jez Deopham slumped to the ground as the man brought the bat down on his skull again.

Stephanie and I scrambled out; it was a choice between burning to death or fighting. I thrust the knife towards the two men, screaming as loudly as I could. Sarah joined me, along with Caroline, who was wielding a fire extinguisher. The man with the bat ran towards us as Caroline pulled the tag, directing the spurting foam at our attacker's eyes. He turned away, rubbing his face, as sirens approached ahead of us. His friend shouted to him and, clutching his leg, they ran back to their van and drove off without lights, doors swinging open as they left. I turned to see Sarah pulling herself out of the wrecked bus, dragging holdalls and bags behind her before helping Rochelle to get out too. She lay in the road, clutching her shoulder in pain and cursing. The fire roared and we stood back watching the tour bus burn.

Jez Deopham was lifeless, blood spilling from his head to form a thick, crimson puddle on the dark, damp tarmac of the country lane.

"He really was trying to warn us," said Sarah.

"He may have been a stalker," I said, "but he tried to save our lives. He was so close to telling me something important too. Are we sure he's dead?" I went over to him. I held his wrist and tried in vain to find a pulse.

"He's gone, Cath," said Stephanie beside me as I held his hand. It was limp and cold. His mouth was silent and his eyes open, rolled back in their sockets. I was grateful for the darkness hiding the true horror of the scene. Sirens got louder as they approached. Blue lights getting brighter as they flashed around the darkened trees. Soon paramedics and the police were all over the scene. A fire crew played hoses on the burning coach. A police officer bagged the petrol can and the abandoned baseball bat. The ambulance crew looked at Jez Deopham and shook their heads.

Rochelle was sitting down, clutching her shoulder.

"Hospital for you, I'm afraid," said a young woman in a green uniform feeling Rochelle's shoulder. Silhouetted by the dying flames of the ruined coach, she shook her head, the blue lights from police cars reflecting her uniform. "I'm guessing it's a broken collar bone, but we need an x-ray."

"Fuck," Rochelle said softly. "Please can I have some decent drugs? This bloody hurts."

"Try to keep still. The good news is," said the paramedic, "if it is a collar bone it can mend. The bad news it, it will take six to eight weeks."

"Tell me this isn't real," said Rochelle, bursting into tears.

I kissed her head. "I'm so sorry Rochelle, it's all my fault."

"No, it's not," said Sarah. "It's the fault of the people we're trying to catch. It's just so awful."

"We could all be dead right now in that coach, like Reg," said Stephanie, sounding almost hysterical.

"Hey," said Caroline, grabbing Stephanie's shoulders, hugging her. "We're not dead. We're out, we're here, and we're all alive."

"Who did Jez think was responsible, I wonder?" asked Sarah.

"Someone who doesn't want me appealing for information," I said. "The same person responsible for Raven and Sacha's murders, and for Mum's disappearance all those years ago."

The senior paramedic injected Rochelle. "Okay. This should help. We're going to move you inside the ambulance now," he said, packing away his equipment. "We need you all to come back to Norwich, to the hospital, and I think the police will want to take statements too."

"Looks like the bad guys have succeeded," said Caroline as Rochelle was helped up, calling out in pain.

The four of us stood there surveying the wrecked bus. Jez Deopham's body was being put into a black van. Poor Reg was still in the smouldering coach, dead in his seat.

"We can't carry on now," said Caroline. "Rochelle's out, and I'm not sure I want to take this sort of risk anymore. I've got kids."

"I agree," said Stephanie. "Sorry, Cath, but it's over. They've won."

29. Chloe

The next morning I was sitting alone at breakfast in a private dining room the hotel had set aside for us. I called Trav.

"Cath? Good to hear you, but you know what time it is here?"

"I think so: about 5am? Sorry but I had to call."

"What's happened?" he asked, yawning.

"Our coach was rammed. The driver's dead. Rochelle's in hospital with a broken shoulder and Jez Deopham's dead too."

There was silence.

"Cath, you'll have to run this past me again, slowly. Are you okay?"

"Shaken but fine. The rest of the girls are okay too." I explained the sequence of events as Trav listened. The others started arriving and sat down near me, no one spoke.

"So I'll let you know what happens." I said.

"So frightening. Awful. Hey, one good thing, I'm scrolling through some reviews online, the gig was brilliant by all accounts."

"Might be a tour for one night only," I said. "We have no bassist, and not much appetite for carrying on. I'll call you back. The girls are here. Be careful. Miss you."

"Hey Cath, it's you who needs to be careful. Call when you can."

I ended the call.

"Morning Cath," said Caroline, sitting beside me. We all sat together picking at croissants and cereals.

"How's Rochelle? Anyone heard?" I asked.

"I called her earlier," Stephanie replied. "She's back home, and comfortable. She's angry over the attack, but relieved she didn't end up like Jez Deopham."

"I think we all are," said Sarah, pouring coffee from the large jug into her cup. "We've got company." She said as our tour manager, Steve, walked into the room. It was a relief to see him.

"So glad you're all safe. I should have been with you, on the bus."

"Don't be silly," said Stephanie. "You might be dead too."

"We're trying to find you a stand-in bass player," said Steve.

"Forget it." Caroline folded her arms. "We can't do it, Steve. Not without Rochelle. She's a big part of us, and I don't want to end up dead like Deopham either."

"No, we can't do it with fucking maniacs trying to kill us. Bastards," said Sarah.

"Come on guys," said Steve, keen for us to continue. "You owe it to Reg and Jez to carry on."

"Jez Deopham may have stepped up at the end," Stephanie said. "But he was still a sex pest. He was obsessed with Betzy. Cath looking so much like her must have set him off again; that's probably why he was on the bus."

"I'm not so sure," I said. "He said he knew who my dad was, and what happened to Mum," I replied.

"If you believe him…" Caroline shrugged. She turned to Steve again. "Even without having targets pinned to our backs, how could we find a bass player who knows our stuff and can play a whole tour, starting tomorrow night?"

"And they have to be female," Sarah added.

"I don't want my husband to be a widower," Caroline said, "or my daughters to be orphans."

"I can keep the loonies out," said Steve. "I've booked twenty-four-hour security for the tour. Look outside, they're here now." He pointed out of the window. Sarah stood up followed by the rest of us, peering through the window. A black Range Rover was outside. Two men sat in the front seat, handheld radios on the dashboard.

"That's Celeb Secure," said Steve. "They're former diplomatic protection officers from the Met Police. They're trained in anti-kidnap, riot and assault procedure. They, or their colleagues, will be with you in three rolling shifts a day until the tour is over. We'll look again after that."

"Shit, that must be costing a fortune," I said, beginning to panic. "The ticket sales will never cover it."

"Err, well I wouldn't be sure. This morning's reviews are stunning. Look." Steve pulled out a pile of newspapers from a tote bag he was carrying and we scanned the headlines. *Delightful Décolleté… The Girls Are Back In Town!... Betzy Lives Again!... Great Gig! Go Girls Go!... Sensational Showstoppers!... An Era Reborn!*

Steve opened his netbook to show us the online reviews, including clips of the gig from fans' phones. Of course the burning bus was trending on social media and in the rolling headlines, along with lurid reports of Jez Deopham's murder, but every single review and social media posting referred to either a 'fantastic' or 'amazing' or 'brilliant' opening night. I couldn't help feeling pleased in spite of everything. I'd done it. I didn't freeze, forget the words or fail to perform. I didn't let anyone down, especially the girls.

"Does this mean tickets are selling?" Sarah asked.

"Tickets have sold out everywhere," Steve said. "Last night's events were awful, but, for good or bad, publicity works. I got a call from the promoter on my way here."

"And?" asked Stephanie.

"He was offered three more nights in big venues, including a last night at…." He paused for effect.

"Where?" I said, not enjoying the suspense.

Steve grinned. "Don't panic, but it's a small venue called Wembley."

"Fuck, you are kidding?" said Sarah. My heart raced.

"We'll never fill Wembley," I said, shaking my head.

"And I thought I was mad," Sarah said.

Caroline shook her head. "So what are you saying? We go on tomorrow night, in Leicester, without a bass player?"

Steve craned his neck as a large coach drove into the hotel car park, almost blocking it

"Here's your new tour bus arriving," he said. It was bigger than the last one, longer.

"It's huge," said Caroline.

"Yes, because we need room for a celeb secure guard inside too. Female, don't worry."

"The bass player?" Sarah pressed him.

"Well," Steve shrugged. "Leicester says we can rehearse all day as the Hall is empty."

"Great. But who with? We can't just buy one online." Caroline rolled her eyes.

"Maybe the local garden centre has a grow-your-own bass player bulb?" Sarah's voice was laced with sarcasm.

I heard my phone ringing. "I better get this," I said, and everyone fell quiet, mulling over our situation.

"Hello, Miss," said a quiet voice.

"Chloe?" I recognised her. One of my favourite pupils and the star of West Side Story.

"Sorry for ringing, Miss. But it's all over social media and on WizzNews and the TV and radio. It's everywhere. The attack on the tour bus last night." She was talking so quickly I could hardly keep up with her.

"It's kind of you to call," I said quietly. "There's no need to worry. We're all fine, apart from poor Rochelle but she'll get better soon. Sorry, hold on a moment, Chloe, Sarah wants me." Sarah was tugging my arm and pointing to the TV screen in the corner of the room. Stephanie turned up the sound. Rochelle was giving an interview outside her house, her arm in plaster. A strapline was running underneath the pictures read: ....*Décolleté undefeated, tour goes ahead despite attack...*

"The show will go on," said Rochelle, onscreen. "The girls are determined. Décolleté lives! My collar bone is bust, so I can't play. But I'll still be there, cheering them on." She turned to look into the camera. "Whoever you are—whoever did this—I want you to know we will track you down. We will find you, and we will find Betzy Blac. And, to everyone watching today, if you have any information please call Crimestoppers or your local police station. Thank you!"

"Wow," said Sarah. "Well, I guess we have to carry on now. If it's what Rocky wants."

I'd been so focused on the interview, I'd almost forgotten Chloe. "Are you still there?" I said into the phone.

"Yes, Miss."

"Sorry, Chloe. Look, I'd better go, we have to find a new bass player."

"That's why I'm calling. I could do it, Miss."

'What are you talking about?"

"Remember our chat at West Side Story? I told you I want to be in a band, Miss. Remember? You said, if I ever needed a reference, to call you. Well, I've heard there's a band called Décolleté that needs a stand-in bass player… Double bass is my instrument and I can play electric bass, no problem." Before I could speak, she continued, "I know all the songs. I can be there tonight! Emily's mum will drive me."

"Emily's mum?" I said, confused.

"Emily wants to come with me. Is that okay? I've spoken to my mum and dad, and, well, they're a little bit worried—you know what parents are like—but I've told them I know you'll look after us. And we are eighteen."

"I don't know, Chloe." It was such a surprise I couldn't think how to answer. "What about school?"

"I've finished school now, remember?"

"Okay, but… I'd have to ask the rest of the band…"

"Go on, Miss. Ask them." I covered the phone with my hand and turned to the girls. They'd been waiting in silence. "Don't get excited, because I'm not sure it's a good idea. But I might have found a bass player…"

Sarah's eyes lit up. Stephanie whooped. I told them a little bit more about Chloe, including her starring role in West Side Story and her place to read music at Cambridge. They weren't keen without an audition, but we had few other options: it was use Chloe or pull the gig. They had to trust me and gave a reserved, but unanimous yes, on the proviso we'd put her through her paces when she arrived.

I spoke into the phone again. "Sounds like you're in, Chloe. I'll get Steve, our tour manager to sort you a contract. You'll be properly paid."

Chloe screamed down the phone. "Thank you so much, Miss!"

"You'd better drop the Miss if you're going to be joining our band. We're both adults now, and we're not at that bloody school anymore! I'm Cath off stage and Betzy when we're playing, okay?"

"Of course… Cath!" She giggled.

"I'll get Steve to take your details and send you directions. Give him Emily's mum's car registration and he'll ensure you get through security. It's been tightened up—make sure your parents know that, okay? And Emily's too. She can sleep on the bus as well to keep you company."

"Wow, Miss—sorry, Cath—thank you. She'll be overjoyed. It's a dream come true."

"We've got to rehearse, so be there by three if you can." For a moment I almost sounded like Miss Edgley, the drama teacher. "We can set up and run through as many times as you need, and again tomorrow."

"That's weird," said Sarah smirking, "we've never had anyone in the band who can actually read music and is a proper musician before!"

*

Décolleté drove into Leicester: the coach, the road crew's minibus and the kit van, escorted by a black Range Rover. TV cameras and fans were already waiting for us at the venue. We presented a united, smiling front, publicly unphased by the attack on our bus and the death of two people; we were now determined to carry on.

Every chance I had, every time I found a camera or a reporter, I'd say, "If you know anything about Betzy Blac's whereabouts or who killed Raven Rain, Sacha Tillens, Reg Wiley or Jez Deopham, please tell the police or call Crimestoppers now!"

Emily and Chloe arrived shortly after us. They had changed from quiet, demure schoolgirls to adults with skinny jeans, tight tops, flawlessly made-up faces and beautifully cut hair. I'd seen them draw up and went out to meet them, one of the Celeb Secure guys by my side; no one was taking any chances.

"Hey girls, give me a hug," I turned to Emily's mum. "Hello again Mrs Rogers. We last spoke at the parents' meeting. Thank you for bringing the girls. I can assure you they'll be well looked after."

"I've no doubt, and thank you, it's such an amazing opportunity for them both," she replied and, with that, the three of us transformed from teacher and pupils to bandmates and friends.

"Look, about the girls… By 'the girls' I mean Décolleté. I know they're old enough to be your mums, if not grandmums I guess, but they can be a bit rough around the edges, okay? They swear, and they talk about sex, and they even take their clothes off at random times—"

"Just like our school dorm, then!" laughed Emily. Her mum rolled her eyes.

"What I'm trying to say is, they might be rough sometimes but they're decent on the inside." I turned to Emily's mum. "They'll behave in front of the girls I'm sure," I said, knowing they wouldn't.

She gave me a knowing look and raised her eyebrows. "I think these two can hold their own. Be good girls; I'm off." And with a brief hug for her daughter she drove away, leaving Emily and Chloe with two big holdalls stuffed with clothes and make-up. I led them inside to meet the band.

"Hey girls, meet our new stand in bass player. This is Chloe, and Emily."

Everybody clapped and cheered. Chloe offered to shake hands.

"We don't really do handshakes round here," said Sarah, "give me a hug."

The girls went round, warmly welcomed by the band and Steve.

"First rule," said Sarah sternly. "Nothing that happens off stage gets leaked to the outside world without my say-so. No secret pics, stories or gossip. I mean that. No comments on social media either. Okay?"

"We understand," said Emily. Chloe nodded in agreement. For the first time since arriving, they looked a bit timid. Sarah could have that effect on people.

"Okay, shall we have coffee first?" I offered.

"I'd rather get going," said Chloe. "Back in a mo, where are the loos?" The two of them scurried off, deep in conversation. I hoped they hadn't been put off and were now regretting their offer to join us.

"Good to see your protégé's so keen." Sarah winked at me. "Okay, ladies. Positions please."

"You've never called us ladies before, Sarah," Caroline smiled as she headed to her drum stool "And what position would you like me in, love?" She smirked and stuck out her bum.

"Be polite, there are young ladies present," said Stephanie in her usual quiet, understated way.

"Are you kidding?" Chloe said walking back and hearing the conversation. "We're no different to you—except forty years younger!"

There was a moment's stunned silence—then Sarah burst out laughing, and the others followed. I caught Chloe's eye and gave her a smile. She looked like she couldn't believe what she'd said.

"Chloe," Sarah said, when she'd finished laughing. "I think you're going to fit in just fine. Okay, bitches!" Her voice rose into a scream: Sarah was becoming Suzi. "Let's rock and roll! We'll try Chloe out on *Pink Bra Bust Up!*"

I beckoned to Emily. "Can you sing the vocals, Emily? I need to rest my voice. You know the words, don't you?"

"Every single one. Thanks, Cath, this is brilliant. Count me in."

The rehearsals went like a dream. Chloe played every note and every number perfectly. The rest of the band were reassured we had the right stand in. What she couldn't remember, her musical aptitude and ability meant she could pick it up; she could follow the chord sequences just by watching Stephanie's rhythm guitar moves. Emily made a good hash of singing too. They both had a future in music.

"Emily," I said during a break, watching the sweat pouring from her neck and soaking her t-shirt. "You can really sing, you know."

"Thanks, Cath. I want to do it professionally. I've written a few songs, too—I was wondering if I could sing them to you? Chloe accompanies me on keys."

"Of course." There was a keyboard in the truck and, as we took a break, Emily and Chloe performed three songs of Emily's, one of Chloe's and a couple of brilliant covers of classics.

"Cath," Stephanie called, as they came to the end of their impromptu set. "Your phone is ringing."

I went over to my bag to answer it. I didn't recognise the number.

"Hello, is that Catherine Edgley?" asked a calm voice on the other end.

"Yes it is. Who's this?"

"It's the John Radcliffe Hospital in Oxford. I'm afraid to

229

tell you that your aunt, Patricia Black, had a heart attack this morning."

"Oh no, is she okay?"

"I'm sorry to have to inform you," the voice said, "that she died a few minutes ago."

I sat down on the floor; it felt as if my legs were giving way. In a moment everything had changed.

"I'm sorry, can you repeat that please?" I said, trying to take in the news.

"She came in unconscious an hour ago," the voice continued, in the same calm tone. It seemed unreal. Behind me, while he talked, I could hear the girls' laughter, Emily and Chloe chattering excitedly. "She collapsed on a trip to Oxford with friends." He paused. "I'm very sorry for your loss."

"Oh that's awful." I let out a sob. Sarah must have noticed that something was wrong. She came over, stroking my shoulder. I gave her a grateful look. "Do you need me to identify her or anything like that?"

"No need. Her friend was with her when she died. She had her driving licence with her and other identification too. Are you close by?"

"Leicester."

"I'm afraid that's probably too far for you to come and see her here; we'll have to move her shortly. If you would like to talk to our relatives' office which deals with bereavements, they can discuss the details with you."

"Of course. Did she…" I felt strange asking, but I wanted to know. "Did she say anything before she died?" Sarah squeezed my shoulder.

"She didn't regain consciousness, I'm afraid, so she didn't know anything about it probably. Did she have a religion?"

"No." At least she was largely unaware and wasn't in pain, I thought. He gave me a number to call to arrange to collect her stuff. I explained it would be a few days before I could get there.

"If you wish the bereavements office to appoint an undertaker, please let them know as soon as you can."

"Thank you. I will. Thank you for telling me." I hung up the phone.

"Bad news?" Stephanie asked, she'd also noticed that something was wrong and came to join me.

"Yes. Just give me a moment." I pulled tissues from my bag and rubbed my eyes. "My Aunt Trish, who brought me up—Mum's stand in. She's dead."

"Oh Cath, I'm so sorry. How?" Sarah asked, as the others gathered round. The laughter and chatter had stopped.

"A heart attack."

"Oh, Cath." Sarah squatted down next to me. "Here, let's hug. It's okay to cry." Caroline crouched at my other side, and they each put an arm around me and hugged me.

"I'm going to miss her like hell. She looked after me, loved me, cared for me. She was a mum to me as much as she could be."

"It's tragic," Sarah said.

"I'll hold it together," I told her. "There'll be time to grieve later, but right now I have to focus if I'm going to keep this tour together."

"Hey, Cath, no one would blame you if you couldn't." I glanced up to see Steve had come over. Chloe and Emily were standing behind him, looking worried.

"I'd blame me," I said. "I'd never forgive myself. I have to carry on, I can't stop now. We must find Mum; Aunt Trish would want that. But listen, I need to make a few calls and start making plans. There's the undertaker to arrange, and I need to let her friends know… Can you manage without me just for now?" All I wanted was to find a quiet corner and a coffee; and to be alone with my thoughts for a while.

"Okay." Sarah took control. In that moment I understood why Mum had loved her so much. "Come on, let's see how the new girl copes with *Hot Lips, Cold Heart!* It's our hardest track, thanks to that awkward key change, so do your best, Chloe."

They left me and went back on stage.

Cassie's drums rang out and Chloe found the bass line. She was perfect. So were Emily's vocals. The next gig was heading towards us like an unstoppable train. We'd have to find Chloe some stage gear, I realised as I headed off to get a coffee and break the awful news about Aunt Trish.

I was already dreading her funeral, having to say goodbye. I couldn't believe I'd never see her concerned and caring face again, but at least I'd always remember her wishing me good luck for my new role, playing her sister—my mother—on stage. I just had to make it happen and, even more importantly, make sure I found the truth about what happened to Mum.

30. Mandy

Rochelle arrived mid-afternoon, just in time for the sound check for the gig that night. We'd slept in the tour bus after going out for a group curry. She walked in, arm in plaster like a conquering hero. Cheers and applause rang out loudly.

"Rochelle, how's the shoulder?" asked Sarah anxiously when we'd all calmed down.

"Still cracked unfortunately."

"Not surprising after that bastard hit it with a baseball bat," Stephanie said.

"He could have hit your skull," added Caroline. "Like poor Jez Deopham."

"Don't even go there," I said. The four of us linked arms and gave her a very gentle hug.

"This," said Sarah, beckoning Chloe over, "is our temporary Rocky, except we need a stage name for her."

"Hi Chloe, thanks for depping for me." Rochelle smiled, genuinely pleased to see her young understudy.

"Thanks for letting me use your lovely Fender bass, it's beautiful." Our apprentice was enjoying every moment.

"Pleasure. So what can we call you?"

"What about Cheri Smoulder?" offered Emily.

"Happy with that!" said Chloe. "Mysterious and silly at the same time."

"Okay, Cheri it is," said Sarah. "We'll put it on our social media with a picture: special guest appearance on bass by Cheri

Smoulder."

"Can I see what you can do, Chloe?" asked Rochelle, and we mounted the stage. I took the mic and we performed *Two Lovers in One Night!* and *Raindance* for the stage crew and sound guys. Rochelle's broad smile and thumbs up to Chloe signalled her approval.

An hour before we were due to go on, it hit me. As I watched Chloe get ready with her new stage gear, as excited as a puppy on its first walk, I realised my stand-in Mum was dead. I'd never see Aunt Trish again, never hear her soft caring voice, never feel her warm hugs and never watch her opening the front door to welcome me in. I was suddenly frozen in the cold grip of grief. Sarah noticed. Not much passed her by, she was more sensitive and aware most people realised.

"Cath," she said softly, putting her arm around me. "It must be so hard. Are you okay to go on?"

"I have to," I replied, biting back the tears, clamping my bottom lip between my teeth.

"No, you don't," said Emily. "I can sing, you know that. I can stand in for you, borrow your clothes. We're not that different in size." Sarah looked at Caroline and Stephanie, and I could see there was a growing consensus for Emily to play Betzy. It was a safe option: you couldn't have a singer, a front woman full of despair and doom. "I really can wear the jacket tonight. I really do know all the words and I've watched the moves."

"No, I'm fine; the last thing Aunt Trish would have wanted was to crash the show. I'm fine, honestly. Let's fucking rock and roll!" I forced a grin, fixed a firm, fake smile and went to take a peek through the curtain at the side of the stage to watch the audience assemble.

*

Forty-five minutes later I saw the sound engineer, at his desk opposite the stage, pick up the hand-held radio and tell the tour manager he was ready. The TM nodded and the house lights went out. You could taste the anticipation. The crowd started chanting *"Décolleté, Décolleté, Décolleté, and then Betzy Blac, Betzy Blac, Betzy Blac."* The stage was in darkness as we took our positions, guided by the thin LED torch lights of the tour manager and music tech guys. I could hear Sarah's breathing as she morphed into Suzi Scums.

I paused, counted three and then went into action.

"Hello. Jeez, what an ugly audience!" I shrieked as the spotlight found my face. "We're Décolleté and it's our job to rock your frigging world!" Loud cheers and applause erupted; the whole of the front row were banging the stage with their fists. I could see the excited faces, once again there was a wide range of fans from students who'd just discovered our sound to older people re discovering their youth.

"Who's ready for a Pink Bra Bust Up!" I yelled. The response was astounding. They all were.

After the first two songs I apologised. "There's a slight change to our line-up tonight as someone has broken our bass player. Some bastard with a hammer has smashed Rocky Rump's shoulder, but she's come along tonight to be part of the show— we couldn't be without her even if she's unable to play." Rocky walked on in costume to a huge cheer.

"How are you, Rocky?" I asked.

"Surviving and hoping to get better soon." The sling carrying her busted shoulder was on show, emphasised by a torn t-shirt. "But as you've just heard," she continued, "we have a brilliant stand in on my guitar—hey, don't bust it, bitch!" She gestured to Chloe. "Please make her feel at home—tonight on bass it's Cheri Smoulder!" More applause followed.

I took back control. "Cheri Smoulder is the mysterious daughter of circumstance sent by the music gods to keep you, our fabulous fans, fed on brilliant bass lines. Shall we see what she can do? Come on, bitches, let's rock and roll! Décolleté will never be silenced!"

Chloe performed to perfection and Rochelle took a bow with the rest of us after the final encore. When I did my mid-show appeal for information, a woman in the second row held up an A4 piece of paper with "Please See Me!" written on it. She was clearly an original fan, but now dressed in everyday clothes, not glammed up for a tribute gig like this. When we came off between encores, I asked a security guy to find her and bring her backstage as soon as the show was over.

"Hi, I'm Cath," I said as the security guy let her in to the dressing room. She looked nervous. "Thanks for attracting my attention."

"Thank you for seeing me," she said. "You were brilliant." I looked at this woman in her early fifties. She had nicely cut hair with natural curls. A t-shirt lay under a thin jersey top. Her tight jeans emphasised her slender body. "The last time I saw Décolleté and met the band it was very… different," she said, stopping and looking down. I could see she had more to say, but she seemed so uncomfortable I didn't want to push her.

"Can I offer you a drink?" I said. "We've got some wine? Water? Coffee? Excuse my sweaty state, by the way. I haven't had a chance to change or shower yet."

"No, thanks. I just… wanted to give you some information."

"Shall we go somewhere quieter?" I said. The girls were being their usual chatty selves and I could see she felt intimidated.

"Yes, please," she replied. I led her to a small unused dressing room along the corridor. It was cold and starkly lit with unflattering bright lights, and had just one chair by a table with a make-up mirror. I stayed standing and offered her the seat.

"So, you said you had information?"

"Yes. About the last time I came to see Décolleté."

"Can I ask your name?"

"Mandy," she said. "Amanda Morrison. I was at the last gig your mum performed at, the end of the 1984 tour with the Scented Slugs."

"Go on," I said.

She hesitated; I could see it was a painful memory.

"I… I was offered drugs, by security. They told me if I bought some I might be invited backstage afterwards, to party with the bands. I was told I'd get a fluorescent stamp on my wrist. It all seemed so exciting—I was only fifteen at the time."

"That doesn't sound good." Surely Mum didn't know about any of this? I thought.

"My friends and I wanted to meet Raven Rain. He was our hero. We didn't do drugs, we weren't like that. But they told us it was a new sort of drug… they said it was wonderful. We just thought we'd try… just that once."

"Who gave you the drugs?"

"A biker; he was part of the security on the door. He was a member of..." She hesitated. "The Bleak Souls, I think. It was written on his jacket."

"What happened, Mandy?" I prompted.

"We took the tablets. Nothing happened at first, and then twenty, thirty minutes later… we started to feel lightheaded and our pulses were racing. It felt sort of good, for a little while. But then it turned scary. My friends couldn't catch their breath properly. They had chest pains… one of them collapsed."

"Do you know what the drugs were?"

"No."

"What happened to your friend? The one who collapsed."

"She went outside to get some air. We found her later."

"And she was okay?" I asked.

"No. She was dead."

"Shit. That's terrible," I gasped.

"I still have nightmares about it. We were told someone else died that night, and others were taken to hospital. We read later that some of them had had strokes. Those drugs were everywhere at that gig. I wasn't thinking straight, my mind was everywhere. I went backstage afterwards, encouraged by the biker, I showed my wrist stamp and got in. I can't remember what happened, but I can tell you I didn't get to meet Raven Rain. It all went blank. I woke up on the grass outside the hall at dawn and…" Her voice dropped to a whisper. "I'd had sex."

"You were raped."

"I couldn't remember anything about it, but I hadn't consented, so… Yes."

"Did you tell the police?"

She nodded.

"And?"

"They took details, launched an investigation. But no one was charged."

"Shit. I'm so sorry. You poor thing. I can't believe my mother would have known or condoned that. No way. Did the rest of my band know?"

"They weren't there, not in that dressing room."

"But if two people died that night, it must have made the news?" I said, surprised I hadn't this before.

"That's the thing. It was the 12th of October, that was the day the IRA blew up the hotel in Brighton, where the Prime Minister Margaret Thatcher and her Cabinet were staying. It was all over the news for days afterwards. There wasn't space for much else."

"That's awful," I said. I could see how much it still upset her, even after all these years. I could hear a trace of bitterness in her voice, and I didn't blame her.

"I do remember one thing," she said, looking straight at me. "As I lost consciousness I heard Betzy Blac—I'd have known her voice anywhere. She was shouting and screaming at someone."

"Do you know who?"

"Sorry, no. I went blank. That's literally all I remember."

"Thanks so much for coming to see me," I said. "I know how difficult it must have been. Would you mind if I take your details?"

"Of course. I want those bastards caught as much as anyone."

"So do I, Mandy."

She wrote down her contact details, and I thanked her again for coming to see me. As she stood up to leave, she took me aback by asking for my autograph. I was only a pretend star, standing in for a real one. I scrawled my name on a flyer advertising the gig. As I returned Amanda Morrison to the main dressing room so she could be shown out by security, a familiar face walked in, arms open and a big cheesy DJ smile, such a contrast to Amanda's expressions of a few minutes ago.

"Great show, girls!" It was Pete Benton, who'd introduced us at our very first gig. "Your mum would have been proud, Catherine. You were brilliant."

"Thanks Pete. I didn't know you were coming."

"I turned up late but caught the last few songs. Just fabulous, and your new stand-in bass player—wow, she has a future!"

Chloe overheard and laughed coyly as Amanda left with security.

"Sorry, I'm Pete Benton." He shook Chloe's hand. "I was a DJ back in the day." She was too young to have heard of him. "I used to introduce the band on stage. I was Décolleté's biggest fan—well, second, really. The biggest was my brother Rupert who was totally bonkers about them; still is."

"Is Rupert here tonight?" I said.

"Oh, he's so sad he missed it. No, he's stuck in a hotel in London tying up some big deal with a bunch of Russians. You know, he's a shaker and mover these days! If he had come he's unlikely to have shown his face though, he's far too polite these days to barge in backstage. Unlike me!" He laughed.

"Pete, can I ask you a question?" I said, waiting until Chloe headed off to the shower. "Do you know if there were dodgy drugs being sold at Decollete's gigs? Back in the day."

"Oh, Catherine, sadly there were drugs sold at every gig, with every band." He looked sad, shaking his head. "I don't think it's headline news that there was lots of pill popping back then. Problem was the kids mixed them and overdoses were easy. Real shame. Didn't do drugs myself, I saw what they did to people."

"Okay, guys, thanks for coming," said Steve the tour manager. "But can we have all visitors out now please, the girls need to rest." He looked straight at Pete as the two guests said their goodbyes.

"Sure, yes, hey Cath, I'm sorry to hear what happened with your tour bus. Who the fuck would do that?"

"Someone who doesn't want us to play," I said. "Or for me to appeal for information about my mum."

"They haven't caught them yet, I take it?"

"Unfortunately not."

"Well, just be careful, hey? Not that I'd recommend the Bleak Souls for security but it would never have happened back in their day. They'd have sorted those bastards out!" He grinned and then turned and looked at Chloe, who was coming back into the room dressed in just a short towel. I could sense Chloe beginning to feel uncomfortable.

"Keep your ears out for anyone mentioning those drugs, Pete. Thanks: goodnight."

"Sure thing Catherine," he said as he left the room. I stared into the mirror as I picked up a cotton pad and cleanser. So why was Mum shouting? Had she uncovered the truth about the drugs and the rapes? Or was she having that fight with Raven? I wiped the last of the lipstick from my aching mouth.

31. Maz Laski

The following morning I called DC Dennison on the number she'd given me.

"Hi. It's Cath Edgley, are you free to talk?" I asked the detective.

"Miss Edgley. Catherine. Hello. We're very keen to talk to you; we have information coming in from your appeals—quite a lot of it, in fact."

"That's good, so have I. It's very frightening and shocking, too."

"I'd be keen to hear what you've been told."

"I have a contact for you. She's happy to give a statement, I think." I passed on Amanda Morrison's number and address.

"Thank you, I'll give her a call. We've been put under a DCI who has knowledge in this area; she's keen to meet you. When's convenient?"

"Well, as you know we're on the road. We're in Sheffield tonight."

"We'll be there this afternoon. Where exactly are you going to be?"

*

Six hours later, I recognised DC Dennison drive into the grounds of the hotel in an unmarked police car. I was watching through the window of a conference room they'd allocated us. I sat back in one of the wide high-backed, so-called comfy chairs in the tall ceilinged room, the smell of cleaning sprays and cheap potpourri was all pervading. The hotel porter opened the door and two women walked in. Kate Dennison I knew. The other was striking. Cropped bleached blonde hair with darker roots, two statement earrings, no make-up and a brown old style flying jacket. Straight jeans and black boots completed the look.

"Hello, Catherine. Thank you for seeing us," she said. "I'm DCI Maz Laski. You already know DC Kate Dennison, of course."

"Where's DC Patel?" I asked.

"Now acting Detective Sergeant and working on a local murder case," smiled DC Kate Dennison.

I was quite shocked at Detective Chief Inspector Maz Laski's appearance, an unlikely looking police officer. Her outfit was quite a contrast to the smart office look worn by Kate Dennison. "Not what you expected for a DCI?" she said. "Years in drugs and vice; well that's my excuse." She smiled. She had muscles too. I was glad she was on my side.

"Hi, yes, sorry, good to meet you, and thanks for travelling so far to see me. I hope it's of use. Can I get you some coffee? Tea?" I offered.

"Thanks, Catherine. Two coffees would be good, but I can get them," said Kate Dennison, heading towards a filter jug on the side table laid out for us with an array of biscuits and croissants. What a difference. It didn't seem that long since she was questioning me on a murder charge. The two women sat down and surveyed the room.

"Are the others here too?" Maz Laski asked.

"Yes, they're in their rooms I think, or maybe the hotel pool. So, did you get a chance to speak to Amanda Morrison? She came to see me after the last show."

"Yes we have," said Kate Dennison, "but can you tell what she told you first please?" She pulled a notepad from her bag.

"Sure. She said she was fifteen at the event on October 12th,

1984, the last show my mother performed. She was sold some very dodgy drugs and almost certainly raped. She says a friend of hers and someone else actually died as a result of the drugs sold to fans that night."

"It was three actually," said DCI Laski. "Another girl died three days later in hospital."

"That's terrible." These girls had been younger than some of my students. It was tragic to think of their lives ending under any circumstances—but to think it had happened at one of Mum's gigs. I shuddered. "Do we know what it was?" I asked. "The drug?"

"We have a fair idea," said the DCI. "Back in 1984, Ecstasy was just beginning to find its way into music venues and parties. It really took off a few years later, but then people started experimenting with it. We think MDMA was the main ingredient in the drug the girls took, but it seems to have been mixed with speed, and also an anaesthetic called Ketamine." She hesitated. "It seems there may have been Rohypnol, too."

"The date rape drug," I said.

Kate Dennison finished her coffee and checked her phone.

"Yes," the DCI continued. "That combination could have fatal results, especially if the doses were high, and in this case they were very high. The effects on those who died were cardiac failure or strokes. Some people basically overheated, and the strain on their veins and arteries was too much, even for young healthy kids."

"That's so awful." I was shocked by what I was being told.

"Whoever made it would have known the likely effects it would have," said Maz Laski.

"Hell," I said. "Good job that batch didn't go any further then."

"But it did," said DC Dennison. "We've checked the records and there were fatalities on other nights during that tour with Décolleté and the Scented Slugs. We've checked the post-mortem results and are fairly sure it was the same drugs being peddled at those events. Sadly, it was before reports were digitised of course, and allegations of rape are hard to collate over the whole tour. But there are reports coming in of quite a few."

"Why wasn't it investigated further at the time?" I asked.

"Different police force areas and a major terrorist alert meant officers had other concerns," said Kate Dennison. "Even drug squad officers were reassigned. The IRA activities on the mainland proved the biggest internal threat the country had seen; don't forget they almost killed the Prime Minister and her cabinet."

"That's not an excuse though," the DCI jumped in. "I hope there'll be an inquiry into all this later."

"So, the band, their management, security? Who was involved?" I asked.

Stephanie opened the door and looked in. She was towelling her hair.

"Hi, I'm with the band. Are you okay, Cath?" she asked.

"I'm fine, thanks. This is DCI Laski and DC Dennison, they're being really helpful," I replied.

"Okay, so long as you're all right." She nodded to the others and closed the door.

"We don't know who was involved," said DCI Laski, "but we do want to find those responsible—the makers, suppliers and sellers. The rape allegations are all credible but unfortunately there are no witnesses; the victims had all blacked out. Forensics were only being developed in the mid-'80s and not used at the time. These girls knew they'd had sex but didn't know who with and certainly didn't consent from what we can gather."

"You can use Amanda Morrison's statement, though? That's a start, isn't it?"

"I'm afraid not," DC Dennison said. "When I called her, she told me she was withdrawing the allegations."

"What?" I said.

DC Dennison cleared her throat. "To be honest, she sounded frightened. It wouldn't be out of the question to assume that someone has threatened her."

"What? But who knew? Do you think he was there tonight? The killer in the crowd?" My heart raced. Someone had threatened Amanda, already?

"Why do you say that?" asked the DC, frowning.

"Just a feeling," I said. "When I'm out there on stage, I always wonder if the killer is in the audience. Watching."

"That we don't know. But we do know that someone has spooked our witness. Amanda won't talk," she replied. But who'd scared her into silence? I knew it couldn't be one of the girls, and I was quick to defend them.

"I know the girls in the band well enough to know they'd never get involved in selling drugs, and certainly not rape, for god's sake. They took drugs at times—I think all bands did back then—but they wouldn't sell them, I'm sure. I'd stake everything on that. I'd trust them with my life. I already have."

"We're not suggesting they were involved. It's unlikely they'd go back on stage now if they'd been involved back then; why would they appeal for witnesses to a crime they committed? But they may know who was involved," said the DCI. "They may be protecting someone, or they might be under threat themselves."

"Do you want to interview them?" I asked.

"Not yet," said DCI Laski. "But there's a possible link with the drugs and your mother's disappearance—"

"My mum wouldn't have had anything to do with bad drugs."

"We're not saying she did, Catherine," said DCI Laski. "But we can't rule anything, or anyone, out at the moment. Of course, you knew your mum and can't believe she would be capable of anything like this. But you wouldn't be the first daughter not to accept her parent could be a criminal."

As she said this, an awful thought hit me. Could Mum have run to avoid detection or arrest? Surely not. No, it was too horrible to consider.

"Of course, there's always the chance that she may have discovered what was happening and walked out as a result," suggested DC Dennison, almost as if she could read my thoughts. "She might even have been a victim of the drug herself."

"We've had seven women call us as a result of your appeal," said DCI Laski. "They're all saying they had bad experiences with drugs at those gigs. And one witness heard your mother screaming at Raven Rain, after the show on the 12th of October. They report later hearing more shouting and what seemed like a fight, followed by screams which they assumed were coming from a dressing room."

It was almost too much to take in. If Raven was the person Mum was screaming at, did that mean he was involved somehow? "Was that person on the drug too?" I asked. "The witness, I mean."

"No, it's someone who bought the drug but didn't take it. They were frightened and just pretended they had. They are a very credible witness. We believe your Amanda Morrison may have been there at that moment too. We will get to the bottom of this, Catherine." DCI Laski said firmly. She stood up and walked to the window. Turning, she said, "Someone knows, to speak frankly, who made that bloody crap and who sold it. We don't want the foot soldiers who handed it over for a few quid, we want the main supplier and the people who allowed it to happen and profited from it. And, of course, we want the rapist or rapists. Those drugs were only sold to women, young women: we think they were being selected as potential targets for sexual assault."

"Music is supposed to be about having a good time and sharing lovely sounds, not this filth," I said angrily. "If the appeals are working, I'll keep making them and I'll add the call for information about the drugs too." I couldn't believe what I'd been hearing. People hijacking mum's gigs for these horrendous acts. "I'll ask the girls, when it's the right time. I need some water," I said, getting up and walking to the side table to open a bottle of sparkling water. "Any news on the tour bus attack?"

"Not much, I'm afraid," Maz Laski said. "We've seen pictures

246

of the wreckage and the location. Someone may be very keen to stop your appeals."

"We now have a private security firm guarding us," I said.

"We met them on the way in," the DCI smiled. "You're in good hands—one of them was in the Met with me—but do be careful, Catherine. Whoever's behind this doesn't play nicely. Perhaps someone wanted your mother dead or out of the way because she had information, or because she was about to expose those responsible."

"So Raven Rain's book really could point the finger?" I said quietly.

"It may well do," said Kate Dennison. "Unfortunately, we don't have any good leads on the manuscript. If you hear anything, you'll let us know straightaway? It's even more important now. I believe it names the key players, and that's why Raven Rain was murdered."

Frustration swept over me. If only I'd got to Sacha before the killer did—not only to save her life, but to get hold of that manuscript. "Have you found out anything more about the name—Brad—I mentioned earlier?"

"We've run that through the data base but drawn a blank," DC Dennison said. "It may be an alias."

"We'd like to be at the next few gigs," said DCI Laski. "So if your appeal gets any responses we can take their details there and then, straight away, before anyone can persuade them to change their minds. I had no idea of the scale of the assaults until now."

*

After Sheffield we were on the tour bus en-route to Manchester. Sheffield had been a struggle, wondering if any other witnesses were being intimidated. I was happier knowing Maz Laski and Kate Dennison were there to meet anyone with information.

I told the girls about my chat with the DCI and the DC. They listened intently and exchanged glances when the row between Betzy and Raven was mentioned. They were all shocked at the extend of the assaults but they didn't seem that surprised. It kept me awake and was going round and round in my head. My phone rang. It was Chris Latham.

"Catherine! Chris here. How's the tour? Great reviews! Hey, I've been talking to Robbie the Rat Boy, and he and I thought it was time to put out a remastered greatest hits DVD. Whaddya think, star?"

"Sorry, Chris. Robbie knows I'm not keen on this; I don't think the girls are either. I'm not signing to Trash Puke Records. We've been too tied up trying to tour, avoid being killed, and trying solve a few crimes to discuss new releases yet." I couldn't help being sarcastic, it was a bit much of him to be pushing me into a record deal with all this going on. "I think Steve's having the output of the sound desk recorded—and I know we've had some video done so we can look at it later, but not yet. We're also with new management now, you know that."

"Catherine, an agent's an agent. Don't forget that we made Décolleté, Robbi and I. Without us your mum might be working in a burger bar. I came up with the name, the girls' names, the lot—so don't write us off. I've looked after your mum's money and I still do. When she is declared dead you will need me to hand it over. I could make things difficult."

Was he threatening me?

"Chris, is this a threat? To stop me getting Mum's money?"

"I don't make threats, Catherine. I'm just saying you will need my help and my signature. If I had yours on a new deal it would make things run a lot more smoothly."

"I know what you did for Mum and the band in the old days—but you did it to make money after all. It's not a charity, and we are allowed to move on after more than thirty years. Legally, I will be entitled to Mum's money if there's a will leaving it to me. You know that."

Sarah, who was sitting next to me, looked at me. "Trouble?" she asked, hearing the tone of my voice. I shook my head and raised my eyebrows.

"When the tour's over and when I know what happened to Mum, I'll talk it over with the girls."

"Catherine, I'd advise you not to dig too deeply into your mother's past. I've said it before and I will say it again: there are some dangerous people out there, and don't underestimate Robbie either."

"I'm well aware of that. I was on a burning bus, remember? Were these people dangerous enough to sell dodgy drugs at Mum's gigs?"

"We knew nothing about that. Try your motorbike pals. Take care, Catherine."

I ended the call. Who the hell did he think he was? Demanding we signed to him for a new record deal. He had no interest in finding Mum or helping me all these years so why now just because we might be marketable again. And what did he really know? Was he afraid of Robbie Romero? The Bleak Souls?

Sarah knew I was fuming. "Are you okay, Cath?" she asked, putting her hand on mine.

"Angry and frustrated," I replied. "That twat Latham, pushing and pushing for us to sign to him and Romero again. He knows things, he really does, I'm sure. Who's he protecting?" I spent the rest of the journey in a bad mood, earbuds in listening to *Chilled Ibiza*, trying to imagine relaxing on a hot beach in the sun, away from conspiracies, criminals and having to perform again that night.

*

We drew up in Manchester in good time for the sound check. The road crew were running in and out like ants carrying the kit and the rig. As I picked up my stage clothes ready to take to the dressing room, fresh from the dry cleaners I heard a text land on my phone. Putting down my clothes I read it.: "*Still trust no one! DD.*"

249

32. Dreamy Donna

The rest of the dates went well and there was a four day break between the last night of the tour and the grand finale at Wembley. The girls were having a rest, and I was having a funeral: Aunt Trish's.

It was the first one of the day and the crematorium was almost empty; such a contrast to Raven Rain's funeral. She had a few friends and neighbours there but no relatives, except me. Her cousin in Dublin couldn't make it. It was a sad end to a fairly sad life.

I'd had one big surprise that morning. As I prepared to leave the house there was a knock at the door. Opening it revealed a wonderful sight.

"TRAV!" I hugged him, his arms squeezed me tightly. "You didn't say you were coming back!"

"I had to try, you'd said it was your aunt's funeral, and I didn't think you should face that alone."

"Oh that's so thoughtful," I said. "It's so nice to hold you again." But how long could I keep this man? Had I already lost him and this was a final act of sympathy or guilt that he was about to dump me and move on, back to the show biz celebrity girls. "Sorry there's no time to offer you coffee; I need to leave."

"Cath, that's not a problem. Let's go. I can drive if you want."

"That's a kind offer, and it's a much nicer car than mine, but no: I need the distraction and I know the way. But I'm so pleased you're here. How did the meeting with your ex go?"

"Oh you know, cordial. But hey, we've today to concentrate on," he said.

It was so nice to have him with me, helping me to cope with the loss of my lovely aunt. Her neighbour and friend, Linda, came over when we arrived and gave me a big hug, saying how much she'd miss their daily coffee together. It was Linda who'd been with Trish when she collapsed and stayed with her until she died. Another friend of Aunt Trish's was distraught and crying loudly. I tried to hold it together. Was I now the last of the line? I was the only family member there. Mum would have been devastated at losing her sister. At least the weather was kind, it was a bright sunny day, white fluffy clouds drifted slowly across the blue sky.

Aunt Trish had been fantastic to me; without her I'd have been adopted or fostered. I stood up and gave a short eulogy, praising her parenting skills, her kindness and her love, and then I started to read her favourite poem and an extract from her favourite book. As I did, I looked up. Two figures had entered at the back of the room: women, wearing sunglasses and hats. They looked just like the ones who had stood at the back of Raven's funeral. I would catch them this time. I finished reading the extract and nodded to the undertaker, the signal for my aunt's final journey.

I watched her coffin disappear forever, but when I turned back, the two women had gone. In their place was a large bouquet of flowers left by the door. As the mourners filed out, the service over, I looked at the card. It just read: *"So sorry xx."* I hurried out and caught a glimpse of a taxi pulling away from the entrance with the two mystery mourners inside.

I called to Trav, who'd been talking to Aunt Trish's friend. "Did you see those two women?" I asked him. "They were the two at Raven's funeral, I'm sure. They left this bunch of flowers but the card doesn't say who they're from. Any idea?"

"It's your aunt's funeral, I'm not sure I know anyone who'd come. But you think they were at Raven's too? That's unlikely.

Mourners in dark colours and big hats can look the same."

After sandwiches for half a dozen people at the local pub, we went back to her house. Trav nipped in to the local corner shop to grab some milk while I went inside. I sat on my old bed, always kept made up for me since the day I'd moved out. I'd been there recently with Trav but it felt like I'd never been away.

I made us both some instant coffee with Aunt Trish's electric kettle. The rust seemed to have spread even further since I last saw it; the water seeped from below the spout and trickled onto the brown worktop.

"It's a bit of a time warp this place," said Trav, walking through the back door with the milk. "I got some cookies too. Thought we could use them."

"Thanks. Let's go through to the sitting room," I said, putting milk in the mugs and carrying them through the small hallway.

"Wow, that TV set is almost a museum piece," said Trav, spying my aunt's television in the corner.

"It is, but she liked it because she could work it. No fancy smart stuff, just on and off."

I looked at a photograph of her on the mantelpiece.

"She was well meaning and kind, as you said in the service. You'll miss her," said Trav touching my shoulder.

"I know I will. I was thinking, I ought to go through her papers and files. Just to see if there's anything related to Mum that's important."

"Sure, lead the way. I'll help."

"Before we do, come here," I said opening my arms. "Just hug me, it's difficult being here in this house without her."

Upstairs in Aunt Trish's bedroom was an old wooden sea chest, which I knew contained all her important papers. It was locked. I searched for the key without success.

"Did she have a favourite ornament, Cath?" Trav narrowed his eyes in concentration.

"I don't know… She always loved that ginger spice jar, on the unit in the sitting room. Mum gave it to her. Why?"

Trav smiled and went downstairs, returning a few minutes later with a key. "This was inside it."

"You'd make a good burglar, Trav."

"Well, if the music sales stop, I'll need a plan B," he replied. I smiled weakly. He handed me the key and I unlocked the chest. Inside were files marked *'House Deeds'* and *'Bank Accounts.'* Beneath these was an A4 envelope with *'Will Details'* proudly displayed in italics. Under that was a biscuit tin, its bent and scratched lid showing a thatched cottage in an idyllic setting with the words *'Rother's Glorious Biscuits'* in a Victorian script. Opening it, I found a letter wrapped up in a cloth held together with an elastic band. It was from Mum. It was signed Betzy. I sat down on the floor, my heart raced and my mouth fell open.

"Trav, look… fuck… just look."

"Here, let me see." He leaned over my shoulder as I read it out loud.

May 2nd 1991

Hi Sis,

It's been shit leaving you and especially my little Cath. To be honest I can't barely cope. I cry every night, but by leaving her, I know, or I hope, she and you are safe from those bastards. Knowing what I do, means I am a dead woman walking. The guys I got a lift with were very sweet, although crossing the Atlantic by small boat was utter crap. The sea sickness was the pits.

"So she did leave by yacht," I said to Trav.

"Without a visa? Passport? I know it was a while ago but they were still pretty strict about getting into the country even then."

I appointed an accountant here in the States to handle my US royalties and receipts and, as far as I know, I can trust them. They didn't mind my false passport I was using. They are drip-feeding me some money from the account in various creative ways so no one will notice. I've found a kindred spirit who's offered to let me stay for a

253

while. I can't say where and I won't be in touch. It's for your and Cath's safety.

"So she's alive? Living under an alias?" I thought out loud.

"At the time she wrote this, yes, but after that?" replied Trav. "No computers then so passports were just a visual check and much easier to forge in those days."

I read on.

Please destroy this letter. Please love Catherine for me. Be the mother I can't be. One day she'll understand, I had a choice—stay and see her and me both killed, or run and hope they'd think I was dead. I know she'll never understand or forgive me, but I've done this for her.

I started to cry. I couldn't read on. Trav cuddled me and took over as I listened, a tissue held to my eyes.

I have been planning this for a couple of months. I had to escape quicker than I thought I would. I had no chance to tell you in person, I had no choice. Someone was sent to kill me, luckily someone else killed them first and helped me escape.

"So that's the body under the barn?" I said. "But who killed him?"

Trav read on:

You have my will, one day have me declared 'presumed dead' and give it to Catherine. She will be rich when Chris Latham frees the UK funds. You will find a large sum of money in my cottage, behind the bookshelf. It will cover Catherine's and your costs, but please use it as cash so no one sees a large deposit in your bank account and asks questions. If my body is found floating in the Hudson River or left beside the Highway, or if you have me 'presumed dead,' please give Catherine my old doll. If she undoes the dress she'll find a ring taped to the doll's tummy. It's the diamond engagement ring Raven gave me but which we never announced. It's worth a lot. Emotionally and financially.

Don't trust anyone, however much they say they want to help me. I know they'll be trying to track me down. I miss the girls, I miss you and I so miss my little girl.

Betzy xxxx

Trav and I sat for a long time in the kitchen, drinking coffee, staring at the faded ink on the airmail paper lying on the melamine tabletop in front of us. After a long pause I spoke. "So she did get to America. By boat."

"There's an airmail mark on this envelope. Looks like it was posted in Little Compton. It's a small town on Rhode Island, Massachusetts. There are a lot of boats there; it's close to various harbours. I wonder if she's still in that area?" he mused.

"Or still alive," I said, mournfully. "I need to read Aunt Trish's will." I opened the envelope and found a note: *'My Will is with Rogerson, Brant and Stent Solicitors on the High Street. Trish.'*

I pulled out my phone and made an appointment to see them. By chance they had a cancellation later that afternoon. A bit of good luck, for once. To kill time, we left the house and went to a café for something to eat whilst waiting for the revelations in the will.

Sitting at a small table in the corner, Trav was facing the wall, keeping his back to the majority of people hoping no one would recognise him. He was wearing a baseball cap and dark glasses. It was the only light moment of the day.

"You look more like a member of an American indie band than a chart-topping singer," I sniggered quietly.

"Don't remind me. But sometimes it works," he said, shaking his head. "Fame doesn't come cheap." We waited for our lunch, two paninis, but I was too anxious to eat. I sipped my coffee and watched the clock, urging it on to get to our appointment at the lawyers.

*

Sitting in the dull waiting room, overseen by an even duller receptionist, we were eventually welcomed by a young man who introduced himself as one of the staff. We walked through a maze of small offices along a creaking dim corridor. The building was a former eighteenth-century merchant's house and the floors creaked. It was as if the place was groaning with the weight of files tied with ribbon, stacked floor to ceiling and old gunmetal grey filing cabinets overfilled with paperwork. We went into an office and there, behind a solid imposing old desk, sat a solid imposing old solicitor. His measured tones and slow movements didn't help my stress, and I became even more tense waiting to hear the contents of the will.

"So Miss Edgley," he said, as Trav and I sat in two old brown leather chairs in front of his desk. "Your aunt, Patricia Susan Black, has left everything to you, except for a few items of furniture and a couple of paintings she wanted her neighbour and friend Mrs Linda Cummings to have. There's also some jewellery for her cousin Mary Jameson in County Antrim. She has left her house and the income from Elizabeth Black's cottage to you. Miss Edgley, I would recommend we have your mother presumed dead so you can have access to her will, which is also lodged with us. There are considerable sums of money involved, as well as her cottage, your former childhood home."

"Perhaps soon, but not yet," I replied calmly.

"The last thing your aunt says, is you should have your mother's favourite doll from her childhood. It's been deposited with us for safe keeping. I took it out when I was preparing the papers for you. Here it is," he said lifting an old cardboard box from behind his desk. "It's a 1960's doll, it's in a shoebox lying on a bed of material, it's labelled in what was presumably your mother's handwriting when she was a little girl. The box says *'Dreamy Donna's bed'*.

"Fuck!" I shouted, causing the solicitor to reel backwards in alarm.

"I beg your pardon?"

"Don't you see, Trav? Fuck."

"Sorry Cath, you've lost me…" Trav said.

"Dreamy Donna, that's DD! Is it Mum who's sending me those texts?"

"Woah, hold on Cath. Don't raise your hopes—"

"But Trav, it's not Desperate Debs, it's Dreamy Donna!"

"It might be, Cath, it might be. But it's a big 'might be'. Don't get your hopes up too high."

"Sorry, but can we return to the matter in hand?" asked the solicitor, clearly surprised by my outburst. I could hardly focus; thoughts were rushing around my head. Could DD really be Mum? Alive and sending me texts?

33. Brad

Back at Trish's house, I took Dreamy Donna from her shoebox bed to wake her from her lengthy slumbers. Holding her to me I could smell something familiar. It was a long-lost scent. A faint hint of my mum. Trav could see the wave of emotion washing over me and hugged me close as I held the doll between us and howled like a child, remembering both Mum and Aunt Trish. Faint flashes of Mum taking me for walks, playing in the garden, sleeping in a tent, brushing my hair, cuddling me when I felt ill.

Carefully, through the sniffing tears, I took off Donna's dress, and there was a ring taped to the doll's bright pink plastic belly.

"Wow, this is a big diamond!" I said, holding the ring to the light. Trav squeezed my shoulder, his arm curling around me.

"One day, Cath, you'll need a ring like this. Or even have this ring put on your finger." I looked at him and my mouth went dry. No, I couldn't even allow myself such thoughts, I didn't want to be hurt any more than I was already expecting I would be when Trav went.

I locked up Aunt Trish's house and drove back home. Thinking of the morning's funeral, my mind drifted back to Raven's, and to Sacha's parents. I realised how sensible they were, going away to help recover from their daughter's death. Perhaps after the tour I'd have a quiet holiday somewhere. At least I could afford it now. I wondered if the Tillens were still in Canada, where they'd said they were heading to escape after burying their daughter.

Then it hit me as I pulled into Chestnut Close and home. I stopped the car outside my house, switched off the engine and thumped the wheel.

Trav gave me a quizzical look. "Cath, I get that you're excited to be home, but—"

"I've got it. Trav, I know where the manuscript is. It's so bloody obvious!"

*

Trav opened some wine while I heated a pre-cooked spaghetti bolognaise I'd made first thing that morning. We filled two glasses of wine to toast Aunt Trish and Dreamy Donna, the doll soon to be sitting beside my bed on a chair.

"So," he said. "The eureka moment in the car. The missing manuscript of Raven's book: you think you know where it might be?"

"Yes. I've been searching for a man called Brad."

"I know. So have I."

"Okay, but here's the thing. You know how I spoke to Sacha's parents at Raven's funeral?"

"Uh-huh."

"Brad isn't a person. It's a place. It's where they live, where Sacha grew up—Bradwell-on-Sea in Essex! It said Brad in the unsent text, but she'd been disturbed and couldn't finish it. I think she sent the manuscript to her parents' house."

"Genius, Miss Marple! Well done. Of course, I knew her folks lived somewhere in Essex on the coast, but I didn't know exactly where. It all makes sense. Will they let you in?"

"They were going to stay with Sacha's sister in Canada."

"Well, you'll have to break in then," he laughed.

"If I have to I will," I said, getting parmesan from the fridge.

"Hey, hold on, that's madness, get the cops to go in for you—that way you can't be arrested for burglary. That could be a seriously bad career move, Cath!"

"But then the police would seize it. I might not see it for years if there's a long trial. That manuscript has it all, Trav—people, places, crimes. It must do, or people wouldn't kill for it."

"Those people might come to the same conclusion as you about where the manuscript is."

"That's why I must get there first. Don't you see, Trav? If it says awful things about Mum I can take those bits out. No one will ever know; I can protect her."

"Shall I get the Celeb Secure guys to go with you?"

"They know DCI Laski, they might feel they have to tell her. I probably would if I were them, and the text from DD said trust no one." Trav's phone rang.

"Sorry Cath, a rare call, it's my mom, I need to get this." I smiled and watched as he walked to the hallway talking on his phone. I put our plate into a warm oven to keep them warm. He was soon back in the kitchen.

"Everything okay?" I asked him, getting up to get our food.

"Yes, sure. Mom was interested in this new woman I'm supposed to be dating."

"Oh?" I asked surprised.

"Yes, Betzy Blac's daughter apparently. She and I have been seen together coming out of a motel room." He grinned.

"It was only time I suppose." I said, happy to be romantically linked to Travis Brennon.

"She also asked me about the hunt for Raven's killer and the book he was writing. I guess she's concerned what he says about her as well."

"What did you tell her?" I asked picking up my wine.

"I said you thought you'd tracked down the manuscript to Sacha's parents' house and were going there as soon as you could. Maybe tomorrow. She seemed relieved. Hoping, I think that it will all soon be over."

"I hope so too."

"Cath, I'm really worried. This is crazy. I've got one final singing track to lay down tomorrow morning, I can't cancel, everything's booked, I have to finish it. Just hold off until later and I'll come with you."

"No, really, I can do this. I'm going alone."

"Cath the bad guys might already have got there first. They might already have it."

"They might, but they might not. I can't risk not getting there first. I can do this alone Trav."

"Like you could do the meeting with Sacha? You could have died! You were arrested! Like you could do the meeting with the Bleak Souls? You were kidnapped! You could have been gang raped, murdered!" He was getting animated and clearly worried.

"But I wasn't," I said, getting angry. Why was he trying to stop me when I was so close?

"Cath, you're overwrought, you've lost your aunt, you've been under tremendous pressure in the last few months. You've turned yourself from a teacher to a rock singer and a detective. You're now pretty convinced DD is your missing mum, who's texting you from Holland, and yet she hasn't called or written or got a message to you via Sarah or the others, or the cops? I know you want her to be alive. I get that, but please don't get your hopes up and don't risk your life again, Cath, the odds really are stacked against you."

"Like they're stacked against us?" I said.

"What?"

"I thought you were going to dump me by text from the States."

"Where did that come from?" he asked, clearly surprised and hurt.

"I know you will dump me one day. Maybe go back to your beautiful ex."

"Cath!"

"It's only a matter of time, Trav, before someone with perfect tits and a Hollywood smile takes you away."

"Oh, fuck. I can't take this. I flew in overnight; I got an early flight just to see you. I'm exhausted, I'm trying to help, and I'm worried you're going to get yourself killed."

"Oh just go."

"Really? You want me out?"

"Trav, no, but I know it's only time before you tire of me. You can't possibly want someone like me when you've got your pick of popstars, models and beautiful fans. If I do it now, then I can't be hurt later."

"Cath," he said, moving towards me, opening his arms.

"No, don't make it worse. Just go," I said, my throat tight and my pulse high. Trav stood there, shaking his head, and without saying another word he picked up his phone and walked out of my house, closing the door quietly behind him.

I sat there, staring at two uneaten plates of food, tears trickling down my cheeks. I was in shock. I'd just split with Travis Brennon. I'd driven him away. Told him to go. I'd been so worried he was going to dump me that I'd dumped him. What had I done?

The phone rang and I leapt to answer. "Trav, I'm so sorry, plea..."

"Cath, it's Sarah. What's happened?"

"Oh, I'm so stupid, I've just sent him away. Trav. I told him to go."

"What? Why?"

"My old insecurity. I can't believe he'll really want me, not for long. He'll find someone else for sure," I said. I felt embarrassed. Like a mixed-up teenager.

"Has he?"

"What?"

"Cheated? Got a reputation for two-timing?"

"No. Oh, Sarah what have I done?" I picked up the wine glass he'd drunk from and kissed where his lips had been.

"He'll be back if he's serious."

"Not now," I sobbed.

"Wait and see. So how was today?" she asked softly.

"Oh, you know. Not easy. But I found a clue to who might

be sending me texts."

"Really?"

"Yes. I think it's Mum." I heard Sarah hesitate. I could hear her breathing, considering the enormity of what I'd said.

"Cath. We all want her to be alive, especially me, but, I think you might be very disappointed and very hurt if you keep believing she's going to come back one day."

"I know, but… I found a letter from Mum to my aunt when we were going through her stuff after the funeral. In it, Mum says: '*Knowing what I do, means I am a dead woman walking.*' And that's why she had to leave. So I'm hoping beyond hope that she's still out there."

"Cath… maybe you should consider grief counselling?"

"Maybe."

"Look, some good news," Sarah said, obviously trying to change the subject. "Live versions of *Pink Bra Bust Up!* and *Raindance* have been viewed hundreds of thousands of times online. Are you happy for us to release them properly? We won't be using Trash Puke Records."

"Of course, count me in."

"We've had requests for a Stateside tour and Australia and the rest of Europe too. Cath, you're a star in your own right now, and Chloe's been offered a job by two bands already."

"Woah, slow down, I'm not sure about touring again. Can we see how Wembley goes first?" I was taken aback by developments. "How are ticket sales?" I asked.

"Sixty-eight thousand tickets sold with two days to go," she replied.

"Shit, how can I walk out in front of a crowd as big as that?!" I replied. "Look I'm taking tomorrow off, I have something to do. I'm going to Bradwell-on-Sea in Essex, to Sacha's parents' house. I think Raven's missing manuscript is there. I was just about to email the girls and Steve to say I won't be in rehearsals. I'm sure you can use Emily to stand in. Thanks."

I ended the call and went to bed. Sadness weighed me down

as I hugged the pillow he'd slept on. It was soon wet with my tears.

*

At seven-thirty the next morning the traffic was surprisingly light as I drove east around the M25 heading for deepest Essex. Bradwell-on-Sea is at the end of the Dengie peninsula in a quiet part of the coast. Queuing to go under the Dartford Tunnel beneath the River Thames, my phone rang. It was Steve. I got through the traffic, pulled over and called him back.

"Morning Steve, I missed your call. It's a bit early for you isn't it?" I said, teasing him. "Sorry, I was driving."

"Hi Cath, a bit odd: the police called me, said they couldn't raise you and needed to talk to you urgently. They asked where you'd be today."

"Really? My phone's on. Who was it, Maz Laski?" I said, surprised.

"They didn't say. A male voice, quite gruff."

"Hmm, the two officers I'm dealing with are both women. Strange. I'll call one of them later, I need to press on, Thanks Steve." I ended the call. I couldn't think why they'd want to talk to me unless they had a new lead, but then they had my number.

I drove as quickly as I could to Bradwell-on-Sea. It was a slow twisting road. I passed a local postman getting out of his van. I stopped and asked if he knew where the Tillens lived. I said I was an old friend of their daughter, and I wanted to see how they were. He told me they'd gone away, but after telling him I just wanted to leave a note, having come from London, he gave me the address. It was a small house standing on its own, just outside the village on a road leading to a farm track.

I left the car and walked around the outside of the property. It looked empty and unloved. The curtains were drawn in the upstairs rooms and there were leaves inside the front porch where the wind had blown in garden debris since the Tillens had gone to Canada. I looked around the back. There was a row of brightly painted ceramic plant pots. Was this where they'd hide a spare key, I wondered? I lifted each one, but nothing. Then I spied a concrete moulding of a cat asleep under a tree. I instinctively walked over to it and lifted it. There, in a plastic bag, was a key. It fitted the back door. As I stepped inside, there was no sign of a burglar alarm. It seemed safe enough to look around the house.

There was a pile of post on an old washstand in the hall. Letters, cards and bills but nothing like a manuscript or a memory stick containing one. I walked upstairs and found Sacha's bedroom. On the bed was a pile of clothes, bags, cases, pictures and then, bingo, a large padded envelope with a French postmark she'd addressed to herself. It was heavy. I sat on her bed and opened it. I pulled out what I'd been searching for. Raven's missing netbook and on it, I hoped, the manuscript.

34 Friends and Foes

It was finally in my hands: the would-be book that Raven and Sacha had died for. I opened the lid, turned it on and waited. There was no password. But there, on the desktop, was an icon marked *'Book.'* I opened it and stared at the front page. The title read:

Raven Rain Remembers
The men who perverted punk.
This book will shatter illusions and bring the guilty to justice.
In memory of Betzy Blac, my first real love.

My pulse raced. I sat down with the manuscript. I'd found the missing words, but would they help find my missing mum? I swallowed hard and scrolled through to chapter fourteen, which Sacha had told me to read. As I looked at the words my mouth fell open—but the revelations were soon interrupted. The front door I'd locked was opened with a bang and the sound of splintering wood. There were footsteps on the stairs. I was no longer alone. Shock hit me as two familiar figures walked in.

"Hello, Catherine," said the first.

"Hand it over," added the second.

"Surely not you two?" I was staggered.

"Who were you expecting?"

"Robbie Romero? Maybe Death Wish Danny? But you?"

Chris Latham and Pete Benton came closer.

"Catherine," said Chris, looking pained. "I tried to warn you to stop this stupid quest and to leave well alone. You're as irritating as your bloody mother."

"You're not getting this," I said, pushing the little laptop under my legs. "Others know where I am; they'll be here soon."

"Oh, Catherine you're so naïve," Pete Benton smirked. "Did you think we'd come alone?" Two burly men moved in behind them. Tight t-shirts highlighted flexing muscles and shaven heads. Thin pursed lips and neck tattoos framed unmoving expressions.

"So this reveals you were dealing drugs. You're banged to rights when this gets out, which it will," I said defiantly, playing for time.

"Okay Catherine," said Chris. I could see he was finding it difficult. "So you guessed we were selling drugs as a side-line."

"A very profitable side-line," added Pete.

"Those drugs were killing kids!" I shouted. The two thugs moved forwards in front of Chris and Pete. "You're pathetic, the pair of you, you need minders to protect you from a single woman?"

"You're not just a woman, Catherine: you're Betzy Blac's daughter," said Chris Latham. "And that's just what your meddling mother said: the drugs are killing the kids. She was going to ruin it all. She was going to call the police."

"Weren't the millions from the tours and the record sales enough?" I asked. I was feeling sick inside; what had these men done to my mum?

"It's never enough, Catherine," retorted Chris Latham. "But I only thought we were going to sell a bit of dope and speed, I didn't know what Pete and Rupert had in mind."

"So it wasn't just for money, was it, Pete?" I said accusingly. "You were raping these kids."

"Perks of the job," said the ageing DJ, emotionless.

"You disgust me!" I shouted, leaping up from the bed, my nails aiming for his neck. Two hefty hands pushed my shoulders back down as the four men towered above me.

"That was my brother's idea. I shouldn't take the credit. Rupert made the drugs. He's a brilliant chemist, but he needed financial backing to set up his company."

"Benton Pharmaceuticals? I know them. They're big. Is that why they're big? Because you got investment from perverts in exchange for supplying them with doped up teenage victims?" I was held firm, unable to attack this apology for a man.

"Yes. That's how he got the funding to make it big. So what?" shrugged Pete. "He brought guests to the gigs. Rich men. He arranged girls for them, knocked out by the drugs. They invested in his business. Look, those kids would have probably had sex those nights anyway, so did it matter who with?"

"You sick bastard." I snarled at him and bared my teeth in the most animal display of hatred and disgust I could muster. So Mum finally worked it out and was going to pull the plug on you all, on that night, October 12th, 1984.

"Mind if I sit on the bed?" asked Chris quietly.

"I can hardly stop you," I said. "Neither could those poor girls. I'm disgusted by you, Chris. Mum trusted you; you were her manager, her agent, for god's sake."

He sat down anyway, uncomfortably close to me, the scar on his face almost glowing as he started to sweat. "Betzy was going to ruin everything. Rupert had promised his backers and he needed their money. We had to stop her. Besides, I couldn't stop them."

"Who actually sold the drugs to the fans?" I felt sick just talking to them, but I had to know. "Who handed them over and took the cash?" Chris Latham didn't want to answer so the old DJ took over, he seemed to be enjoying my shock and revulsion.

"The security," said Pete.

"The Bleak Souls?" I asked.

"Four of them," he replied.

"And that's why Mum walked away from the tour?"

"She had a massive row with Raven, too; the atmosphere was

shit."

"That's enough Pete. She needn't know any more," said Chris.

"Oh no, this is fun," Pete Benton replied, looking at me.

Chris Latham inched back onto the mattress. He looked worried. He seemed to shrink on the bed, almost apologetic and looking for forgiveness. He fiddled anxiously with his fingers while looking at Benton, who clearly frightened him.

"Betzy said she was going to the police and we couldn't let that happen. Two of the Bleak Souls came into the dressing room with Latham here," said Pete. Sweat was beading on Chris Latham's forehead. "Latham, you're up to your neck in it just as much as me," said the DJ.

"Not quite as much as you, Benton. That's enough. Please, stop now," Chris pleaded.

"Why? Why stop? What's he going to tell me?" I asked, again trying to stand but the thugs wouldn't release their grip. Latham wiped his forehead with a grubby-looking checked handkerchief. He looked down as Pete spoke.

"I forced Betzy to take the drug she was so very cross about. Poetic really." He laughed. "My brother and I held her mouth open and pushed the pills into her."

"She might have died!" I said angrily, struggling against my assailants.

"That was the hope," said Pete, sneering. He folded his arms in defiance. "That was the plan, that way there'd be no police and a big push for record sales. A win-win situation for us. *The legendary Betzy Blac will be sadly missed, but her music lives on in this specially packaged memorial album*."

"How could you?" I shook my head in disbelief.

"Easily!" he sneered. "Unfortunately for Raven he walked in and saw it. The two bikers beat him up until he collapsed. They would have killed him but I said no. That's when Rupert took control. It was his operation really. I was the front-of-stage smiley face. The affable bloke at the party, everyone's friendly DJ. No one suspected anything."

"So what happened?" I demanded. "Are you too scared to tell me?" I taunted.

"I might even show you, you stupid meddling little bitch," said Benton, leaning forwards and squeezing my cheeks together, trying to open my mouth. I shook myself free and tried to bite his hand.

"Rupert raped Betzy," said Chris softly.

"And you bastards didn't stop him?" I kicked out and hit Benton's leg.

He yelped. "You stupid bitch, you're going to regret that," he snarled, holding his shin. "I bet Latham doesn't have the bottle nowadays: see that scar of his. The real reason he got it was your mother, she was a real hellcat. She also did his two front teeth, the bitch. Raven was unable to do anything to help her, he was unconscious thanks to the Souls. It was fun, well for me and Rupert at least. I don't think your mum enjoyed herself."

I screamed at Pete. "I thought the Bleak Souls were their friends? You sick bastards."

"Some were," Chris said. "That's why it came to a head in the early hours with a massive fight at Boss Hoggs Café."

I noticed Chris Latham backing away from me, he was sweating profusely, clearly regretting his actions all those years ago.

"So where is she? My mother?"

"Oh, your mother was given an ultimatum. Kill herself or watch her sister and daughter die. No one has heard from her since. She was a good girl and did what we asked."

"But she didn't!" I shouted. "She escaped to America."

"Where she probably carried out our wishes and ended her life," grinned Pete Benton.

"Chris, no!" I said shaking. My arms went weak, my legs felt unable to move. Adrenalin pumped through me but I was panicking.

"Pete, surely…" said Chris Latham, turning his head away.

"You won't feel anything," said Pete. He took a bottle from

his pocket and opened it, tipping a pile of pills into his left hand. Latham was rocking back and forwards on the bed. "You'll take these and then you just won't wake up."

"Pete, isn't there another way?" pleaded Chris Latham, standing up.

"It's too late. She's got to die. Open her mouth, boys." They grabbed my head. I twisted, clenched my jaw and struggled as Pete uncurled his hand. "Take your medicine and be a good girl," he grinned. I tried to scream but as I opened my mouth, dirty fingers tried to push the pills between my lips—just as Caroline, Sarah, Rochelle and Stephanie burst through the door.

"CATH!"

"You've gotta be joking!" laughed one of the thugs.

"You old tarts had better go back and take some hormone replacement pills before you get hurt big time," said the other. The pills dropped to the bed. I bit a finger as it left my mouth.

"Don't worry." Pete was hiding behind the two thugs. "We've got enough pills for all of them."

"For fuck's sake, Pete, you're crazy!" I could see Chris was panicking. "Killing Cath was never part of the plan—you can't kill four women as well!"

"And two girls," said Chloe, walking in followed by Emily who immediately kicked one of the thugs in the shins. He let go of me and turned to face the girls. I struggled free and threw my hands around his neck. I was bursting with adrenalin and a newfound strength.

The other thug shielded Benton, who pushed passed my rescuers and made for the stairs. "All yours Latham, I'm off," Benton shouted.

Emily threw herself around the neck of the other thug as he pulled a knife. Sarah and Caroline jumped on top and pulled him down. Rochelle pulled a hockey stick from the top of Sacha Tillens' wardrobe and smacked in on the head of the first thug. Stephanie grabbed it and hit the other one with it. The first jumped up but hit his head on the side of the bed. Sarah grabbed a vase of dried flowers and broke it over the second man's head. Chris Latham stood in the corner, hands over his face, shaking. Our combined weight was holding the thugs on the floor, but it was pretty much a stalemate and we wouldn't keep them down for long. For fifteen minutes we wrestled, tussled and struggled to hold them, but they were strong and we were tiring.

35. Dad

There was a loud crack; the sound of a motorbike chain hitting the wall stopped everyone dead. A leather clad arm was holding it. Death Wish Danny had arrived.

"Shut up. Sit down. ALL OF YOU!" he shouted. The menace in his voice filled the room. His fingers wrapped the greasy chain around his tattooed fist. The shock broke the stalemate and Sarah and the girls stood back. The thugs jumped up. The girls surrounded me and no one dared speak. Through the window the roar of motorbikes echoed outside and five bikers soon crowded the landing, blocking the door. The Bleak Souls had arrived. My heart sank.

"Just listen. All of you!" roared Danny, taking off his sunglasses. The girls recoiled at the sight of his scars.

"Danny," Chris edged towards him gingerly. "You want to avoid prison, don't you? So help us sort this out. Maybe just rough them up? Please." Danny grabbed Chris with one hand and threw him to the floor. Chris Latham groaned and curled up, trying in vain to squeeze his big body under the low bed. The thugs stood back raising their hands, the fight in them gone.

"If you're going to kill Cath you've got to kill us all," Emily said.

"Calm down girl. No one's killing anyone. Not here." Danny pushed past Chloe and put his tattooed hand on my shoulders. I looked into his tired eyes. His voice faltered. Then he shocked me. "Hug me," he said. Playing for time, I hesitantly put my arms around his cracked, black leather jacket waiting for his next move. It smelt bad: stale sweat mixed with old oil.

"Catherine, I'm so sorry. I let Betzy down." He released me from the hug and I saw a tear run down his cheek. "I should have been there to protect her. I loved her. I knew about the drugs but not the rest of that shit. I told Rupert Benton we were out. He laughed and said half of my crew were still in. They weren't in it just for the money either. They got girls as well. I told those guys they were out of the Souls but they wouldn't accept it. We had a fight. A mother of all fights. The Souls imploded that night."

"So I heard," I said.

"What you don't know is I killed two of them. They were boasting about assaulting Betzy, so I stabbed them through their hearts because they'd broken mine. That's why I went to prison. I never told anyone why I'd killed them—it would have shamed Betzy—but they'd violated the girl I loved. The judge blamed it on gang rivalry. Only those who were there that night knew the truth, and they'd never tell."

"So the Bentons got away with it," I said, looking at Latham, half under the bed.

"When I got out of jail seven years later, I told that pair of bastards I was coming for them. They told me Betzy would die if I did. And so would you, Catherine. They'd have killed you too. That's why Betzy went on the run when you were seven years old. She was the only one who could testify against them. With her dead you'd be safe. She did it for you. So you could have a normal life."

It was a lot to take in. "The Bentons hired someone to kill her?"

"Yes. Judy had told them she would be in Scotland and they wanted to make sure she was no longer a problem."

"And all these years later, when the Bentons heard about Raven's book, they ordered his and Sacha's deaths as well?" I was piecing it together.

"Yes," said Danny. "I didn't dare get involved in case they

killed you too."

"But who killed the man in the barn in Scotland?"

After a moment, Danny said, "I did. Betzy had gone up with her friend Judy, or Judas as she should have been called. The Bentons had paid her to drug Betzy so that man—Mickey Bawdsey, his name was—could kill her without a struggle. That way there'd be no blood. Judy would say she'd run away so the police wouldn't look for a body. Betzy got suspicious so she called me. I'd only been out of clink a few weeks. I rode up there, all day and half the sodding night. I got there just as Bawdsey was dragging her outside the croft, drugged up to the eyeballs. He was going to bury her alive, the bastard. Judas Judy was unconscious inside, drugged up too. He was probably going to kill her as well—destroy the evidence. When I saw what was happening, I lost it and smacked the fucker on the head with a spanner. Bust his skull open."

Chris Latham whimpered by the bed, his hands covering his head. Danny spat on him.

"I buried him in the barn where he was going to put Betzy. I took her to Oban on my bike, and we found an American yacht. We paid the guys on it to get her out of the country. She'd planned to make a run for it knowing they were closing in, and I'd arranged a fake passport from a geezer in the East End for her. But after they sent that bastard to kill her she had to bring her plan forward." Chris Latham raised his hands to protect his head.

"I'm not surprised you're worried, Latham," sneered Danny. "Your mates, the Benton bastards, set me up with a convenient gang fight a few months later. I got another twelve years to keep me off the streets."

"Wait," I said, my mind racing. "That last gig. Please tell me my father's not one of those bastards who raped her."

"I didn't touch her, Catherine. But Pete did," pleaded Chris Latham, shaking.

"God no, not him." I was devastated at the thought of Pete

Benton being my dad.

"No. It was none of them," said Danny.

"How do you know?" I asked.

"Because, Catherine, I'm your father."

"What?" I couldn't hide my shock.

"If you weren't my daughter, our meeting the other week wouldn't have been so nice."

"How are you so sure you're her father?" asked Sarah.

"Raven was caught playing away in the States. There were pictures in the papers. Betzy chucked him just before the tour. We went out for a drink, me and Betzy, and just rode off into the sunset. We ended up in Brighton for a weekend. That's when you happened." Danny's voice was thin and emotional. "But I was just a rebound squeeze. She loved Raven, always did, always will. Raven begged her to take him back, but she wouldn't. Because she was eight weeks pregnant with my kid."

"Is this for real?" I asked.

"I never bullshit. I'm your dad, Catherine."

I froze, my mouth open, unable to take in what I'd heard. Sirens from far away became louder and louder until they echoed around the house. Emily looked out of the window.

"Wow, the police are here in force," she said. The thugs backed away and stood against the wall.

"Police! You're going down too, Danny," said Chris Latham.

"Who cares, so long as I sink you bastards first. I can't live with this any longer, Catherine. I let Betzy down. I let you down, too."

"How did you know where I'd be, Danny?" I asked.

Danny looked at me. He held my shoulders. "A friend told me I needed to look after you. Asked me to come here this morning."

"Who's the friend?" I asked. But he just smiled briefly before the angry scowl returned. We hit the hogs. I got Shan to call the cops when I was on the way, to give me long enough to get here before they did. I wanted to catch the Bentons. I'm handing you over to the law, Latham." He grabbed Chris and dragged him down the stairs.

Clutching the netbook, I went out into the sunlight. There was DCI Laski and DC Dennison. Five other officers decamped from a van and stood around us, poised. I hoped the Bleak Souls and the two thugs would play nicely.

"Cath, are you okay?" said the DCI. "I hear we just missed Pete Benton."

I nodded.

"I know where they've gone," said Chris, as he was pushed into a police car. "There's a Benton's pharmaceuticals plant ten miles away. They'll be leaving from there. You'll have to be quick though. Catherine, I really am so sorry." I ignored him.

"We have to be bloody fast." Danny jumped on his bike and revved the engine. "You can bang me up later, but I have to finish this." He raced away as we piled into a police car to follow him.

"Shouldn't we arrest him?" asked DC Dennison.

"You could try! You'd have to catch him first." said the DCI. "Besides, arrest him for what? Saving Cath's life and leading us to the masterminds? Follow him, if you can."

The bikers roared away, my newfound dad at their head, the ancient Bleak Souls emblem on his faded jacket, followed by his ageing gang members on their well-worn bikes. The sun glinted on the side of his old, chipped helmet as he rode off. I was pushed back into the seat by the acceleration as the car sped up. The sirens screamed as we raced along the road. My phone rang.

"Cath, it's Trav."

"Trav!" I was amazed to hear his voice. "Oh, about the other night."

"Not now Cath. Is that a siren?"

"I'm in a police car, following my dad, at eighty miles an hour!"

"What? Your dad?"

"Yes. It's complicated, where are you? London?"

"Closer. I've just arrived at the Tillens' house. The girls from the band are here talking to the police."

"We need to talk… Sorry, I'm being thrown around here, and feeling sick to be honest. I have to go. Fuck we're overtaking blind, shit, I can't look."

"Cath."

"No, really. Talk later. Ugh." I ended the call, dropped my phone and was thrown against the side window of the car. I gripped the seat as we went over bumps taking a short cut on a back road. I could just see the bikes ahead. Two walkers stood back, mouths open as we tore past. My knees pushed together as I braced myself.

"I think we're there," said Kate Dennison from the driving seat.

"We're you a traffic cop in a former life?" I asked her.

"Nope, never done the advanced driving course either," she replied.

"Decamp!" Maz Laski shouted, opening the door as the vehicle came to a screaming halt, the sirens blaring and blue lights flashing. We'd arrived at an industrial estate on a leafy site in the Essex countryside. "Call for back up," said the DCI as Kate Dennison pulled out the radio handset, but Danny and the Souls were in no mood to wait. Danny turned his bike and drew up alongside us.

"See that helicopter on the pad over there? That'll be the Benton brothers doing a runner. The fuckers ain't getting away with it this time," shouted Danny, revving his bike.

"You'd better leave this to us, Mr Fearon," said DC Dennison.

"Fuck that!" Death Wish Danny revved his faithful hog. "I loved your mum, Catherine. Make sure you find her. Live to ride, ride to die!" He smiled, reciting the Bleak Souls motto.

Two of the Souls rammed the perimeter fence, flattening it as their bikes fell sideways. Danny raced over the broken wire and headed straight at the helicopter, increasing his speed as he turned the throttle flat out. The copter's rotor blades began to

278

turn. Danny's engine sounded as it if would seize. The blades speeded up. He lent back, lifting the front wheel off the ground, and then chopper met chopper at more than a hundred miles an hour.

There was a split second of silence followed by a blinding flash and a hideous noise.

"DOWN!" shouted DCI Laski, her voice almost drowned out by the explosion and roar. I threw myself to the ground, lifting my head up just enough to see the aircraft and bike disappear in a fireball. Black smoke billowed skywards. Danny had done the right thing and two of the two nastiest bastards on the planet were dead, but so was the dad I'd never known.

*

We spent the afternoon giving statements at the police station. While I was there, Chris Latham asked to see me. He'd promised a full confession if I agreed to meet him. He was waiting in a stark cool interview room. A young, uniformed officer stood by the door.

"Catherine," Chris Latham said, as I sat down in front of him. "I cannot say how sorry I am. Danny did the right thing; I'm not so brave. I let myself be led on by the Benton brothers. Believe me, they would have killed you a long time ago if I hadn't begged them not to."

"Words fail me, Chris. My mum trusted you. You let those animals rape her."

"I couldn't stop them." He put his hands over his bowed head and began to cry.

*

It was dusk when I drove home, exhausted. My head was spinning, reliving the last few hours. As I got out of my car a familiar figure walked from around the side of my house.

"Trav, oh it's so good to see you, I'm so sorry for what I said." I blubbed as he hugged me.

"Hey, Cath. Can we go in? It's beginning to rain. You hungry? I can do the takeaway bit again."

"I think I'm too tired to eat," I replied, opening the front door and showing him in. As I turned to close it, I saw Eileen in the street waving.

"What's happened to the manuscript?" he asked, taking off his jacket and putting on the back of a kitchen chair.

"The police promised to give it to the interested publisher once they've made a copy. Now Latham's confessed, and Danny and the Benton brothers are dead, it's not so important. There won't be a trial. Latham will go for sentencing but he's pleading guilty, so the book can be published. There'll be no trial jury to influence with its contents, unless the French guy is caught and prosecuted, but I doubt they'll find him. He was just a hitman. I really thought Robbie Romero was the main man."

"Never judge criminals, or lovers, by their covers. Oh, I forgot to tell you, rehearsals at ten-thirty tomorrow, on stage at Wembley."

"Oh, what! I almost forgot I'm playing Wembley. That's going to be bloody tough."

"Yes, it will be. But even tougher to cancel. Cath, eighty thousand people are coming."

"Wh… I thought we'd only got to sixty-odd thousand tops." I swallowed hard.

"Well, you'd got to sixty-six thousand, and then some idiot said they'd be a support act."

"You?"

"Yep."

"*We* should be supporting *you*!"

"No, and Cath, I'm going to be your support act. I kind of like supporting you. Oh, and it's an early morning too, we're on the sofa of breakfast TV at eight-thirty. Live. You, Sarah and me."

"Oh what! I'll look awful. Do you know how little sleep I've had recently?"

"That's rock and roll baby. Stars like you don't sleep, they just rock on!"

I laughed. "Right now I'd better rock off to sleep."

"I'll leave you in peace."

"Oh no. You don't get away that easily," I said. "The last time you left here was awful. I sent you away. I'm so sorry. I want a nice ending this time. I don't want you to go."

"Oh if you want a date, I'll get my people to talk to your people and..."

I grabbed his shoulders and kissed him, trapping the words in his mouth.

"I need a shower. You'd better come with me so you can't escape." I smiled, pulling him towards the stairs and the bathroom. Like giggling teenagers, we tore each other's clothes off and dived under the shower. The hot water and steam enveloped us as his wet arms spread around my back. I felt our thighs touch and ran my hands down his strong back, the sound of the shower like a waterfall around us.

"This is a bit like *Raindance*," I said.

"Cath, it's actually raining outside."

"Is it?" I replied staring into his beautiful eyes. "Well, you know there's only one thing for it then."

"What, do it in the rain? Like your mum and Raven did in the song?" He was grinning.

"Don't we owe it to them?" I asked.

"You romantic lunatic." He kissed me. We grabbed towels and left a trail of wet footprints across the floor, down the stairs and through the hall. We crept outside into the back garden as I put my finger to my lips

"Shhhhh!" I whispered. "What would Eileen say if she came round!"

"Good job it's summer," he said.

"I never thought I'd be so keen to see big dark rainclouds,"

I said, pulling him to the ground. "At least the grass is long!" I laughed.

"Hey, I think I love you, Catherine Edgley."

"Think?" I said.

"I mean know." Travis kissed me. The fears, worries and pain were washed away by the warm embrace of love as we lay in the gently falling rain under a cloud filled sky, biting our lips to keep our joy to a whisper. This was one performance we didn't want an audience to see.

36. Carly Brennon

"Good morning! It's eight-thirty and you're watching *The Day Starts Here* with me, Carrie Forshaw."

"And me, Scott Turner. Tonight, a sold-out Wembley Stadium will see an amazing show."

"Yes," said Carrie, as Trav, Sarah and I sat on the sofa on the set of the nationwide breakfast TV show. I watched as the presenter continued reading the autocue into a clip of a recent gig. "Décolleté were massive in the early '80s until their iconic singer, the great Betzy Blac, walked into the shadows. She disappeared completely seven years later, leaving her young daughter in the dark as to where she'd gone. That daughter has led a quest to find out what really happened, and tonight completes a nationwide tour fronting her mum's old band and appealing for information."

"Yes," said Scott. "And that appeal led to an amazing trail of events which resulted in the deaths or arrests of a number of people wanted in connection with serious crimes."

"But," jumped in Carrie, "everyone is now looking for Betzy Blac herself. Cath Edgley, aka Betzy Two, and Sarah James, also known as Suzi Scums, are with us now. Sarah, don't you look different off stage! Here's a picture of you in full costume. Wow, the difference!" The presenter grinned, as a full frame picture of Suzi Scums filled the screen. "Plus, a man who needs no introduction, except to remind you he's the son of the late Raven Rain. Welcome to an international singing star—it's only Travis

Brennon!

"Hi, hello, good morning," we said in unison.

"So," asked Scott, "Cath, is Betzy Blac dead or alive?" Everyone was looking at me, the big dark camera lens behind the autocue was focused on my face. I was trying to hold it together. I caught a glimpse of myself in the monitor.

"I wish I knew." I felt my lip quiver but Sarah sitting beside me squeezed my hand, Trav on the other side squeezed the other. "I was convinced she was dead, then I thought she might be alive. Now? I'm not so sure," I said.

"If she were alive, and watching this," asked Carrie, "what would you say to her? Can you ever forgive her for leaving you?"

"If Mum was watching now? What would I say to her?" I turned and looked straight into the camera. "Mum, I love you— there have been times when I've hated you for leaving me. But now I know you were trying to protect me." I turned back to the presenters. "I'd like to give her a massive cuddle. She is my mum and I miss her to bits."

"So, Sarah, what can we expect at Wembley tonight?" said Carrie.

"A lot of love, a lot of great music and a lot of emotion. It's been a dream to have Décolleté back on the road. The girls and I have worked so hard to help Cath complete her quest and, along the way, we've found new life and a new purpose. Décolleté will continue whatever happens and, we hope, with Cath here singing."

"Well," said Carrie, "let's remind ourselves of what the fuss is all about. This is a clip of Décolleté on stage a week ago when they played Glasgow. This song is called…? Anyone?"

"*Raindance*," Sarah answered as the video played. It was faded after a minute and the presenters looked to camera.

"Great stuff!" said Scott.

"One thing," said Trav. "The profits from tonight's show are going somewhere special, aren't they, Cath?"

"Yes," I said. "Because of the crimes I've uncovered, the

girls and Trav and I have agreed we're donating the money to a number of rape charities."

"Wow!" said Carrie. "What a great idea. And a reminder that that show is being broadcast live, and I guess the fee for that is also going to these charities?"

"Yes, all the profits are," I said. "Décolleté lives and Décolleté will make a difference."

*

We left the studio and headed to Wembley in a taxi. We walked on to the stage to see where we'd be later that night. Scores of staff were in the stadium preparing for a sell-out crowd. I walked into the backstage area and found the girls. We hugged, cried and laughed, but I had to ask them a difficult question.

"Girls. Did you know my mum was raped?" There was silence. None of them wanted to answer, they looked at each other. Stephanie broke the silence.

"No. We thought she'd had a mega row with Raven. We also thought she'd maybe had a fling with Pete Benton."

"That night," said Caroline, "we were locked in our dressing room. They said it was for our own safety as some yobs had got through and were taking on the Bleak Souls in a fight. We were told Betzy and Raven were locked in with the Bentons."

"We heard some screams and shouts," said Rochelle, "and eventually Caroline shouldered the door of our locked dressing room."

"Betzy had gone. She'd left her stage clothes in a pile and just gone," added Sarah.

"We thought that the touring, the drugs and the bust up with Raven was all too much for her so she'd walked away," said Stephanie.

"She told us earlier that night she was convinced someone was selling bad drugs to the fans, but she didn't say who," added Rochelle.

"We didn't know the full extent of the drugs operation or why they were selling them, Cath; we had no idea what was going on. Pete had very cleverly concealed it. His brother was always there with guests, we thought some were record execs or promotors, you know how elated and tired you are after coming off stage, we just wanted time on our own to get changed and then chill away from anyone. We didn't ask questions, we didn't feel we needed to, we were surrounded by people we thought we could trust. Sorry Cath, we all let Betzy down. If we'd have known what was happening, well we'd have died for her," said Sarah.

I nodded and got up.

"You okay, Cath?" asked Stephanie.

"No. But I will be, in time." I smiled and walked off, and leant against a speaker cabinet to reflect on what they'd said. The girls sat quietly together until Chloe and Emily turned up and broke the spell. I walked back to join them slowly.

"Okay, so we have rehearsals for the biggest show of our lives," said Sarah. "What are we going to do about you Rochelle? How's the shoulder?"

"I'm okay. Well enough to play a part in the encores. But Chloe needs to be on standby in case the painkillers fail."

"Is this against medical advice?" I asked.

"I haven't asked for any, so therefore they haven't said no." She grinned.

"You okay with that, Chloe?" I asked our young stand-in.

"Of course! playing with you guys is a dream."

"Except it's real. Eighty thousand people in front of us, and millions around the world on live TV," said Caroline.

"No pressure then, girls," said Sarah.

"And I thought that first gig in that cellar was tough enough," I smiled.

Steve Hewitt came in. "Hi guys, the TV went well this morning. We've had a few requests for the guest list."

"Who?" I asked.

"A couple of women who say they're former colleagues of

yours: Kate and Jane? Plus twenty young women who were your drama group?"

"Ha! Of course." I grinned. "No Miss Miles then?" Chloe, Emily and I laughed.

*

The rehearsals were weak and worrying. We had so little energy and such little presence that I felt a fraud. Trav was watching and came over when we were finished.

"Cath, it will gel, believe me. Once you're in costume and there's an audience."

"I hope you're right, Trav,"

We sat back and watched Trav's rehearsals. It was weird watching the man I'd spent the night with, and made love to, singing in front of a band. The sound was full, beautiful and moving. It was obvious why he was a global star. And this guy was supporting us? We would have been proud to have been the support act for him.

The day went on and we went through the set again. I worked out a final thank you speech for the point in the show when I usually did the appeal. I would make a last call for help to find Mum. Surely after all this publicity, if she was still alive she'd have come out of hiding by now? I sat in the wings and watched the rehearsals of our support act. If I hadn't been on stage I'd have wanted to be in the audience for tonight's show.

"You okay Cath?" asked Sarah, touching my shoulder. "I've been looking for you. We're all worried if you're all right."

"Thanks Sarah, you're so sweet. Underneath that punk bitch façade." I smiled.

"Oi—watch it bitch or I'll have you!" She laughed.

"Yes thanks I'm just coming to terms with it all. It's so hard to take it all in, but I'll be okay."

*

Trav and his band did a sound check and then we went out and ran through some of our songs. The TV guys wanted to work out positions for the handheld camera operators who'd be on the stage or at the front and to get the feel for the music as it would be done live. After getting the thumbs up from the sound guys and the TV producer, we drifted off to find a bit of solitude, each picking a chair, a corner of a dressing room or quiet area where we could be alone with our thoughts to rest and prepare.

I'd fallen asleep and only woke when I heard Chloe walking past; she was on the phone to her mum, explaining how the guest list worked and, yes, she really would be let in without a ticket and, yes, she would be given a backstage pass to come and see everyone after the show. I pulled myself into wakefulness and realised just how tired and stiff I was. Then adrenalin took over. We were on stage in a few hours. Minutes were precious and slipping away.

I went into the dressing room and opened my case. My stage clothes were in plastic bags delivered from the dry cleaners. My make-up seemed to be calling me from its box as if Mum herself wanted me to take on her persona again, urging me to slap it on, thick and fast. I was about to start when a woman popped her head around the door.

"Hi, that's my job tonight."

"Sorry?"

"I'm Abbie. I've been drafted in to help with make-up, if that's okay," she said, carrying a large make-up case and aprons.

"Sounds great, but why?"

"For the TV," she said, putting the case on the tabletop and opening it. "There'll be close ups, big close ups, and you want to look your best, hey?"

"Look my best after the weeks I've had? Tough job!" I laughed. "I think after tonight I'm in need of time out. Alone."

"Alone?" she queried. "Word is you and Travis Brennon are an item, who wouldn't want to spend a few weeks alone with Travis

Brennon? I'd be there like a shot, along with loads of others. Oh sorry!" She blushed. "I shouldn't talk about your guy like that!"

"No worries," I smiled. "Anyway. I'm not sure I believe in happy endings anymore."

"So you'll be glad I'm here, because," Abbie said, tactfully changing the subject, "even if the camera doesn't lie, it can't see through make-up, so we can make you look a bit fresher and less sleepy!"

"Thank you, that would be lovely." I sat back to let her do her work. It felt good. After a cleanser, the foundation went on first, then the powder and blusher. Then she worked on my eyes and lips. I almost drifted away as her hands worked their magic.

"Cath, can I just put a quick dab on your neck please… great… oh, the fake tattoo, hang on I have a photo, yes… and… we're finished!" She gestured towards the mirror.

"Wow! That's the closest to Betzy I've ever looked. Well done!"

"It's my job, I've been studying your mum's pictures. Pleased you like it. Okay, I've got Stephanie next, then Chloe. See you soon."

"Thanks, Abbie," I said. As she left, Trav walked in. She looked at me, then raised her eyes and blew me a kiss

"You okay, Cath? You seem a bit distant. You're not regretting last night?"

"No, not at all. You?"

"It was beautiful."

"Yeah." I smiled. I looked lovingly at him but I couldn't believe it was real and we actually had a future.

"Cath," he said, squatting down to face me as I sat in the chair. He took my hands in his. "I want us to have something, but you don't seem so sure."

"I think we could have something. What happened last night or in that awful hotel will never leave me. But I can't believe you really want me."

"Cath, what do I have to do…?" he was interrupted by a loud knock on the door. It opened and DCI Maz Laski came in.

"Oh, sorry." She stood in the doorway.

"It's okay, I'm just leaving." Trav walked out, squeezing my hand as he stood, then closing the door. My eyes hovered on the handle.

"Chris Latham confessed to more than we imagined," Maz Laski said, drawing my attention.

"Really?" I asked.

"Yes. There were other tours too with the Benton brothers selling their drugs. Other girls who were their victims, boys too."

"Nothing to pin on Romero?" I couldn't believe he was innocent.

"Nothing. He's clean, as far as we can tell. There's something else." She hesitated. "I wanted you to hear it from me first."

"Oh?" My stomach tightened. What now?

"I'm sorry to have to tell you that Chris Latham won't be going to prison."

"What?" I was aghast. "Why not?"

"He walked out from the police station after giving his statement. He was allowed out on bail as we didn't think he'd abscond, and he'd signed a confession. He told us he wanted to go to his solicitor's and sign some papers relating to your mum's accounts which would favour you, if she was proved to be dead. He was due to report later for a Magistrates' Court appearance. But I had no idea."

"You had no idea of what?" I asked.

"No idea of what he would do next. As far as we can see from CCTV cameras and a witness..."

"Yes?"

"It seems, just as Danny Fearon did, Chris Latham also wanted to put things right. After leaving his lawyer's office he walked to the nearest railway line, climbed a fence and plugged earbuds into his phone. Putting on his favourite song he walked onto the track. The last thing he heard was Betzy Blac singing *Raindance* as a freight train ended his life. It was still playing when they took it off him; it was on repeat."

"SHIT!" shouted Sarah as she put her head around the door. "Have you guys seriously seen the size of the crowd out there? It's unreal!" She saw the DCI and frowned. "Oh, sorry, is this a bad time?"

"No, I was just leaving," DCI Laski said. I was trying to imagine Chris Latham's last moments. My mum's voice in his head. I nodded as DCI Laski left. Did I feel sorry for Chris Latham? Yes and no. It meant all of those who'd assaulted Mum, or been in the room while it happened, were now dead.

I told Sarah the news as I put Mum's jacket on and went to look out from the stage to see the build-up for myself. More fans were coming in, filling the seats, some rushing to the front. The lighting rig was being run through its programme again and the background house music was echoing around the unfilled rows of seats. Unfilled, but not for long; they just kept coming, thousands of people now flooding through the entrances, crowding in to see us, to see me. It was terrifying.

"You know who's here tonight, Cath?" Sarah asked as we surveyed the crowds.

"Oh don't frighten me, who?" I replied.

"Genevieve Rogers."

"Trav's ex? Flawless skin. Impossibly beautiful."

"That's her. She's on his guest list too."

"Bastard," I said harshly. Trav had invited his ex? I felt my heart sink. So maybe I was right all along. Last night had been a glimpse of someone else's future, but not mine.

*

The lights were getting brighter as the evening approached. The sound of the massing crowd filtered through backstage. Trav came into my little dressing room.

"Hello," I said flatly. "Your jacket's a bit smart. You're usually more casual."

"Well tonight is very special, Cath. You seem subdued."

"Well it was a very special night for me," I said. "It's the last time I play my mum."

"So why aren't you enjoying it?" he asked, touching my shoulders.

"I haven't got my exes on the guest list, like some people."

"Oh, for ff… Cath, Genevieve asked for a ticket, it's courtesy. I've had a lot of legal hassles and got an agreement with her lawyers over some lyrics. I just want to keep things amicable. Besides, she'll know I only have eyes for you."

"Do you?" I asked.

"Cath, look, we'll do this later. Right now there's someone I want you to meet." Trav beckoned me to follow him. "She's in the green room with the girls."

"If it's Genevieve, she can…"

"You think I'm that insensitive?" I wanted to carry on talking about Genevieve but we walked out and crossed the corridor into the green room. Inside, there was a strikingly beautiful woman in her fifties. Age hadn't dimmed her looks. She was sharing a joke with Stephanie and Chloe, who were all dressed up and ready to play.

"Cath, meet Carly Brennon, my mum."

She smiled and gave me a brief hug. "Cath, hey, wow, you look the spit of Betzy. Good to meet you, I'm Carly."

"Hi, Carly, good to meet you too. I can see where your son gets his stunning looks. Are you just here for the gig?"

"Wouldn't miss it! I've been in Amsterdam for the past couple of weeks with a friend from home."

"Great. Well, I hope you enjoy the show."

"I'm sure we will. I brought my friend along; she's really looking forward to the show."

"It's a bit in your face at times," I said, "but I hope she enjoys it."

Mrs Brennon smiled. "Oh, I think she knows the band's reputation."

"We do a pretty emotional version of *Raindance*, which…"

"Which your mother wrote to express her love for my ex-lover Raven," said Carly, interrupting.

"Yes," I said softly.

"Don't worry. I'm fine about it. I left Raven, after all."

"Tragic. His death," I said glancing at Trav who was standing quietly nursing a glass of sparkling water.

"Raven did love your mum, Cath. No one could take her place. I hear you and my son are pretty close now."

"We're good friends, yes," I replied.

"Just friends?" she asked.

I smiled.

"Oh sorry, I mustn't pry." She smiled. "Have a great show, Cath."

"Thanks, Carly, enjoy it. And, please, do bring your friend to meet me afterwards if you'd like to."

"Oh, I might just do that," she said, turning to go.

37. Encores

I walked out to check the stage once more and to try and steady my brewing nerves. I glanced around the army of techies who seemed to be constantly checking the drum sound and adjusting the symbols. The lighting was now dim after running through tens of pre-programmed moves with varying intensities of brightness. I was lost in the moment, my heart in turmoil, and my nerves building to explosion. Just how fast could my pulse rate rise before something popped?

"Cath!" called Sarah. "I've been looking for you. Thought you'd done a runner!"

"I still might," I muttered.

"No time for that." She grabbed my hand. "Come on, girl, it's going to be starting soon. The producer's just told me we're going on air; let's get back to the green room and watch the TV."

Moments later, I stood in the crowded room with Trav, his band and the girls, all watching the opening of the live transmission. There were shots of us, shots of Trav, and archive photos of Mum, followed by live pictures of the excited crowd. Images of Raven and Sacha flashed across the screen. The presenter, DJ Lisa Fulham, appeared on the stage, where we were about to perform.

"Good evening! Hello Wembley, are you all right?" A resounding *YES!* echoed around the stadium. "Wow! What an amazing few months for an amazing young woman. Not long ago, Cath Edgley was a teacher in a boarding school. Since then she's survived attempts on her life, she's persuaded the police to reopen the case of her missing mother, and she's worked tirelessly to bring a bunch of alleged criminals to justice.

"She's helped re-form one of this country's—no, the world's—most popular punk, power-pop bands. Her journey has led her here tonight, to the stage of Wembley stadium.

"This evening, we have a very special performance. Not only have we got amazing Travis Brennon playing his first gig in six months, we have Décolleté, the essence of an era, led by the indefatigable Cath Edgley." The crowd clapped and erupted in a massive cheer.

"I have some breaking news - police have confirmed the deaths of four people wanted in connection with investigations into the murders of Raven Rain and Sacha Tillens. One of them was my former colleague, DJ Pete Benton. He was a respected performer who, it seems, had a very dark secret. Perhaps the truth will come out with the forthcoming book by the late great Raven Rain. Let's hear it for Raven!" The DJ stopped talking as applause and cheers rose up from the crowd.

"Okay! The profits from tonight's show are going to charities which support rape victims. That's at the insistence of Décolleté with the full support of Travis Brennon. Yes! That deserves one hell of a cheer!" She paused again. "There's just one missing piece of this amazing jigsaw: what did happen to Betzy Blac? Will we ever know? Let's remind ourselves of the music we're about to hear!" A montage of video clips, old and new, followed.

*

The stage manager walked in to find us. "Travis Brennon and band, you're on. Lots of good wishes coming backstage for you including one from Genevieve Rogers." I looked daggers as Trav shrugged. "Go!" said the stage manager, urging Trav to take the stage.

"Good luck," I offered.

"Thanks, Cath. You okay?" he asked, trying to hug me, but I shrugged him off and looked away. Truth was, no, I wasn't all right. I wanted him but I daren't dream. I'd seen the way girls looked at him, Chloe and Emily seemed to swoon when they were near him, and there were thousands of Chloes and Emilys out there as well as the unbelievably beautiful Genevieve-sodding-Rogers with her flawless looks, so why would he want me?

The TV pictures cut back to the stage where the presenter, Lisa Fulham was standing in the centre interviewing a fellow DJ. Then she turned to camera. "So, it's time. I hear movement behind me. Tonight, Wembley, London, and the rest of the world, which I believe has just joined us! Yes, this is a global transmission so welcome wherever you are! Planet Earth, are you ready for the utterly wonderful Travis Brennon?" A huge roar erupted. Lisa Fulham joined in the applause, before walking off stage left.

The house lights dimmed and a gentle drumming started with keys and guitar filtering in. Trav's rich warm voice filled the stadium as he started one of his best-known songs, *Party Night Kisses*. The light flooded the stage and he went into superstar mode. Track after track brought applause and the crowd were loving watching the man I'd slept with the night before. I'd never lose those memories and I hoped he'd always keep a bit of me somewhere in his thoughts.

"Cath, sorry to drag you away, but we need to have a pre-gig hug, and you look like you need one too," said Caroline, obviously sensing my sadness. "Are you okay? What's happening with you and Trav?"

"I don't know. I think I've just done it again and driven away someone I'm in love with."

"We're with you, Cath," she replied, hugging me.

*

While Trav and his band were onstage we allowed ourselves a small glass of wine in the dressing room to toast the end of the tour and the final gig. I had to force myself to perform in one last show. However sad I felt, I couldn't let the girls or the fans down. I had to act the part again. I tried to make a speech. It helped.

"Whatever happens tonight, girls, even if I fall off stage and fail you, we made Wembley, we made money for rape charities, we have a new record deal for the live recordings of the tour and, more importantly, we've brought a lot of bad guys to justice." I smiled and raised my wine glass. "Thank you." The girls raised their glasses too.

"It was you who made it happen, Cath," said Sarah.

"But you persuaded me. I couldn't have done it alone."

"I just wish you'd found the answer to your quest, Cath," Rochelle said. "I wish we'd found Betzy."

So did I, but I couldn't let it show. I turned to Chloe.

"Happy to play a crowd this big?" I asked her.

"Of course. You taught me well, thank you." Looking at the TV set in the corner we could see Trav was finishing his set.

"Thank you, you've been a great audience!" he shouted, wiping the sweat from his forehead with a towel which he threw to the crowd. I watched them fighting over it like baying dogs, girls screaming to touch his sweat. As the final chords of his last song finally faded he said, "I'll be back to do a very special duet later!"

A wave of clapping and cheers followed him and his musicians off stage. The lights went down and his band's kit was swiftly removed, revealing ours behind. We hurried through and prepared to go on. The presenter came back, lit by a follow spot.

"Travis Brennon! What a performer! Now, I think the time is about right, I think the stage is ready, yes, I see a flashing light to the side telling me it's time—it's time for the women already voted band of the year by our listeners, the band that's made the headlines for the past few weeks and taken the music world by storm. Please welcome Cath Edgley as Betzy Blac, and tonight's top billing. Yes! They're here. It's… Déc-o-lleté!"

The crowd rose, chanting the band's name, clapping and shrieking, and we hadn't even played a note. We rushed on under the cover of near darkness and took our positions, breathing fast but controlled, sweat beginning, fingers on guitars and drumsticks, tension rising, concentration at its peak. I nodded to the stage manager, who spoke into the handheld radio. The spot burst on and lit my face. My pupils narrowed to cope with the intensity. I counted to three and then I spoke.

"Hello, London, this is for those who thought they never make it, those who had overwhelming odds against them; for the victims, for the underdogs, and yes, even for you scumbag punks as well!" A huge cheer and laughter filled my ears. I paused then carried on.

"Hello planet! We've a world-wide audience tonight I hear. Yay! You are all amazing, and we are here to rock the effing globe! Now, a bunch of very bad men tried to crash us, they tried to burn us, they tried to kill us, but we're the band they couldn't stop! If you're a bad man, don't ever underestimate what five women with guitars, drums and mics can do. In fact, don't ever underestimate what any woman can do! We are…. Décolleté! Let's have a *Pink Bra Bust Up!*"

We threw ourselves into action, the words firing from my mouth as this punk classic was thrown to the hungry audience, who devoured every note. I could see people dancing; I could see my drama group girls in the VIP enclosure, along with Maz Laski and her colleagues and friends. They may have been detectives, but they were dressed for a rock gig. There in the wings were Trav and his mum, Carly Brennon. Trav gave me a thumbs up when he caught my glance.

We ran though the opening numbers. Chloe was coping well, flawlessly plucking Rochelle's bass. Song after song followed, the girls enjoying every second. *Wrecked Bed Regrets* and *Wedding Dress Disaster* saw brilliant solos on lead, bass and drums. We'd dropped *Let's Get Fucked On Friday* at the request of a number of TV stations, but the rest of the repertoire stayed in the set.

Towards the end it was time for the final appeal to find Mum. I'd held off until we got to *Raindance*, where Trav was going to join me for a duet. We'd then planned a two track encore. I began the appeal as the stage went into darkness apart from the follow spot lighting me.

"A great song, written, like the others, by a great woman, Betzy Blac. That's her picture behind me," I said, knowing the screens beside the stage would show a close-up of Mum's face. There was a buzz behind me and Rochelle came on and took her bass from Chloe, grinning widely.

"Oh yes!" I was pleased she felt able to come on. "Can we have a big round for our stand-in bassist, Cheri Smoulders!" I said. "She's helped out brilliantly whilst Rocky Rump has been coping with a bust collarbone, thanks to some bastard with a baseball bat who tried to stop us. Rocky, though, is a tough cookie, she's here and she's going to play the last few tracks with us."

"Wouldn't miss it for the world!" she shouted, leaning in to my mic.

"Okay, so I have made this appeal at every gig we've played, asking for help to find my mum, the great, possibly late, Betzy Blac. But something keeps driving me on. If anyone knows where she is, please let us or the police know. Someone must know what happened to her." I paused and bit my lip, just hoping for some final answer, a remaining piece of the jigsaw. I took a breath and forced an excited smile. "Joining me for this track is Travis Brennon!" Huge applause erupted as Trav walked on as the lights came up giving the stage a red sunset hue.

Sarah started the intro slowly. I was puzzled; we hadn't rehearsed this. Trav was smiling. Sarah then repeated the intro, rather than going into the chord sequence. Trav grinned and addressed the audience.

"Hey, guys, you having a good time?" The roar that came back was reassuring.

"You know sometimes you try and tell people things and they don't get the message? So I want this little lady here to understand something and maybe you can help me?"

"Yessss!" came a mass reply.

I didn't know what was happening; I looked behind me and Sarah just put her thumb up. Chloe and Emily were giggling in the wings. Caroline winked at me.

"Okay audience, repeat after me. Cath Edgley." The audience bounced my name back. Trav smiled and spoke to them again.

"Now repeat, Cath Edgley, I love you!" I was stunned, as eighty thousand voices echoed back: *"Cath Edgley he loves you!"*

He whispered in my ear. "Now do you believe me?"

"Yes!" I stumbled, my voice faltering.

"You said I was a star and you were an ordinary girl. Huh, some ordinary girl—you're a star yourself!" he smiled. "Okay, Suzi Scums, hit the track!" Suzi went into the chord sequence and, hand in hand, Trav and I sang Raindance. I just wished Mum could have seen it.

As it ended, he kissed me. I hugged him. He lifted me up. The crowd loved it, but the applause died away very quickly. Unexpectedly, the lights came up fully and Chloe walked on with a woman.

I looked at Sarah; her mouth was open and her hands reached for her cheeks. She was shaking her head and mouthing expletives.

Trav spoke. "Err, before these guys play the encore—and, guess what, they'll do two!" The crowd screamed their approval. "I have to tell you, my mom's here tonight. She's had a friend living near her for the past twenty-five years, in Boston, Massachusetts. She stayed very much in the shadows, I never met her, and I certainly never knew who she was. But she's brought her along tonight, because her friend is quite important to this gig. This friend wants to see someone, she wants to see her daughter, a daughter she was forced to abandon three decades ago. Yes. We finally know where Betzy Blac is—she's damn well HERE!"

Everyone went silent as the woman walked across the stage, quickly found by a follow spot. The cameras zoomed in and her face hit the screen. There were gasps, applause and screams as she came up to me and opened her arms. I couldn't believe what was happening.

"Mum?"

"Catherine."

"What…" I could hardly believe what I saw.

"I love you more than you'll know. Girls, my lovely band. For what you've done in exposing those bastards, thank you. Catherine, Suzi, Rocky, Stephy and Cassie, you're all my heroes."

I was dumb and in shock.

Mum whispered in my ear, "I know you must be so angry, Cath, but please, I'll tell you later, I promise. Just keep going, Catherine. The show can't stop."

I was caught in the spotlights, cameras on my face, the whole world watching my tears falling.

"I have no words," I told the audience. "I'm trying to hold this together, guys, please help me." I started to collapse, falling backwards, Sarah grabbed me, her guitar pushing into my back. Massive applause and cheers came from the crowd and hugs came from the girls. I handed Mum the mic and backed away. I was too broken up to sing.

"Hi, world, I'm Betzy Blac. I've been away too long. Nice to see my little girl and Raven's son have got it together. They just sang *Raindance*, which I wrote for Raven—well, here's another I wrote for him. Let's see if I can still do this. Let's all go *Banging On The Beach*! Suzi, Rocky, Cassie, Stephy, stop effing staring and bloody well earn your keep! LET'S ROCK AND ROLL, BITCHES. HIT IT!"

The band pulled themselves out of their stunned silence and started playing the first encore. The crowd were ecstatic seeing Mum at the front of the stage for the first time since October 12th, 1984. She smiled at Sarah and turned to the crowd. My mum's voice was older, but still as strong. I couldn't believe her precious singing was filling the arena. We were transfixed. When the song ended, the band clapped Mum and cheered her, along with the adoring audience. Mum beckoned me over and kissed my cheek.

"Here's the mic; it's your show." She grinned as the applause ran on and on. I was frozen, unable to react. Trav took control; a true pro, he grabbed the mic.

"Let's give these two a minute, hey let's have a singalong. This is appropriate, Paul Simon's *Mother and Child Reunion*, sing it with me!" And, like a campfire singsong the crowd joined him, the girls picking up and playing along as Mum and I hugged, and cried, and hugged some more.

"Why didn't you tell me, Mum?" I said in her ear, clutching her hand.

"While the Bentons were alive, you and I were in danger. If they had the slightest inkling I'd show up they'd have killed you, believing I'd have told you what happened. They killed poor Raven when they got wind of his book. Raven thought I was dead. Everyone did. I've been in hell not seeing you grow up." I was speechless. "I've been following events from Amsterdam, sending you texts: yes I am DD. I finally broke cover when I contacted Danny and begged him to help you. Once Trav told his mum you were going to Bradwell-on-Sea to get the manuscript I was sure the Bentons would be on to you, to end it once and for all. I knew if you'd seen that book they'd kill you. Danny died to ensure they could never hurt either of us again. It's now finally over."

"Danny—Dad—did us proud, Mum."

"I knew he would Catherine." I regained what composure I could and, wiping my eyes, I took the mic.

"Wow," I said to the audience. "We… Sorry, this is amazing. I'm just as blown away as you." I took off Mum's jacket. "This belongs to the real Betzy Blac. It's her show now," I said, putting the jacket on Mum's shoulders as she mouthed: *"Love you, Catherine,"* then she addressed the audience.

302

"This one you'll know. But I want to share the vocals with my beautiful, talented daughter." She pulled me across to her as we stood together in front of the mic. "It's *Two Lovers in One Night!*" she screamed. More cheers, more music and more love flowed from, and to, the stage. As the track ended, Mum spoke again. "Okay, one last offering, and somehow appropriate! It's *No More Tears No More Fears!* she shouted, and the band fired up. The last encore ended and we all went to the front of the stage for a bow and a massive group hug. There were tears from every eye, on stage and off. The screens by the stage were running a crawler caption reading: Breaking News…Betzy Blac is alive!

The sound would fade but the echoes would last forever. I'd caught the killer in the crowd, I'd got one of the most wonderful men in music, and I'd finally found my very special Mum.

The End

Epilogue

Dear Kate and Jane, Sorry I haven't been in touch since the Wembley show but I've been having some time with Mum here in Menorca. We've had a very emotional few days but when I heard what she'd been through to make the decision to go, I knew she really did love me, and I know we'll get there in time.

Trav? Well, a bit of secret this but I'm wearing a rather nice engagement ring which his dad once gave to my mum. We don't want the press finding out, but we're getting married at a secret location next year, so don't tell! You're both invited of course. I have to dash, Trav's just flown in from the States, his new album's topped the Billboard 100. It was delayed because he dropped three of the tracks and wrote three new ones about some dull English drama teacher who fell in love with a megastar. He's trying to persuade me to form my own band with my bridesmaids Emily and Chloe, and hey, you know… I just might.

Rock and Roll, Bitches!

Love Cath xxx

Did YOU ENjOY ThIS BOOk?

If so, you can make a HUGE difference.

For any author, the single most important way we have of getting our books noticed is a really simple one—and one which you can help with.

Yes, you.

Us indie authors and publishers don't have the financial muscle of the big guys to take out full-page ads in the newspaper or put posters on the subway.

But we do have something much more powerful and effective than that, and it's something that those big publishers would kill to get their hands on.

A committed and loyal bunch of readers.

Honest reviews of our books help bring them to the attention of other readers.

If you've enjoyed this book I would be really grateful if you could spend just a couple of minutes leaving a review (it can be as short as you like) on this book's page on your favourite store and website.

About the Author

Phil's career in TV and radio saw him doing everything from tracking down criminals in Spain and going on high-octane police chases, to interviewing pop stars, politicians and celebrities. He's met the rich and powerful and the most needy and humble, and his writing reflects this. As he told us: "I love fast moving action thrillers which offer escapism, entertainment and excitement. My stories are for rainy days and lonely nights, sunny beaches and poolside bars. They're for anyone who enjoys great locations and gripping tales, with jeopardy, tension and a fight for justice, love, hopes and dreams."

After leaving University Phil joined the BBC and enjoyed various roles from presenting a local radio breakfast show to being a TV Newsreader, Reporter and Producer for both BBC East and ITV Anglia. He also worked on BBC Breakfast Time in London, and wrote scripts for a BBC TV comedy show. He even found himself playing football against Radio 1 in a premier league stadium! Phil produced and presented documentaries and feature programmes, as well as being the face and voice of Crimestoppers in the eastern region for many years. He also created the successful TV series: "999 Frontline".

Phil wrote The Little Blue Boat children's books set on the Norfolk Broads, which were produced as a play. He lives near Norwich with his wife Fi, a former nurse turned silversmith, and has three grown up children. Phil loves music, travelling, walking, and sailing, which he's written about for numerous magazines; but his passion is writing, and bringing exciting new characters with amazing stories to the page.

AC*k*NOW*L*edgement*s*

With thanks:
To Pete and Simon at Burning Chair for their enthusiasm and support.

To my writing friends for their endless encouragement – Andrew McDonnell, Sally Harris, Jonathan Blunkell, Catherine O'Hanlon, Bridget Kinsella, Arun Debnath and Sarah Louise Dean to name just a few.

To Paul Boswell for technical advice.

Grateful thanks to my brilliant editor, Lynsey White.

And to Fi, for everything.

This book is dedicated to the songwriters, singers and bands who help us make the good times, get us through the bad times, and give us the soundtrack of our lives.

This story is inspired by my time on a student Entertainments Committee at Leicester University, and from meeting some outstanding performers, stars and musicians as a radio and TV reporter and producer.

AbOUT BUrNiNG ChaiR

Burning Chair is an independent publishing company based in the UK, but covering readers and authors around the globe. We are passionate about both writing and reading books and, at our core, we just want to get great books out to the world.

Our aim is to offer something exciting; something innovative; something that puts the author and their book first. From first class editing to cutting edge marketing and promotion, we provide the care and attention that makes sure every book fulfils its potential.

We are:

Different

Passionate

Nimble and cutting edge

Invested in our authors' success

If you're an author and would like to know more about our submissions requirements and receive our free guide to book publishing, visit:

www.burningchairpublishing.com

If you're a reader and are interested in hearing more about our books, being the first to hear about our new releases or great offers, or becoming a beta reader for us, again please visit:

www.burningchairpublishing.com

Other Books by Burning Chair Publishing

The Retribution, by Mike Wardle

Push Back, by James Marx

Shadow of the Knife, by Richard Ayre

A Life Eternal, by Richard Ayre

Point of Contact, by Richard Ayre

The Fall of the House of Thomas Weir, by Andrew Neil Macleod

The Curse of Becton Manor, by Patricia Ayling

The Brodick Cold War Series, by John Fullerton
Spy Game
Spy Dragon

Near Death, by Richard Wall

Blue Bird, by Trish Finnegan

The Tom Novak series, by Neil Lancaster

Going Dark
Going Rogue
Going Back

10:59, by N R Baker

Love Is Dead(ly), by Gene Kendall

Haven Wakes, by Fi Phillips

Beyond, by Georgia Springate

Burning, An Anthology of Short Thrillers, edited by Simon Finnie and Peter Oxley

The Infernal Aether series, by Peter Oxley
The Infernal Aether
A Christmas Aether
The Demon Inside
Beyond the Aether
The Old Lady of the Skies: 1: Plague

The Wedding Speech Manual: The Complete Guide to Preparing, Writing and Performing Your Wedding Speech, by Peter Oxley

www.burningchairpublishing.com

P N JOHNSON

Killer in the Crowd

313

Milton Keynes UK
Ingram Content Group UK Ltd.
UKHW041620291124
3202UKWH00001B/9